Praise for *Single Wife*

"Slyly intelligent, witty, an entertaining look at modern life in NYC—*Single Wife* will appeal to anyone who's single, married, and/or both!" —Tama Janowitz, author of *A Certain Age*

"A strong debut. . . . What sets this one apart . . . [is] its spirit of playful inventiveness, at times reminiscent of Iris Murdoch."

—*Kirkus Reviews*

"Full of insightful characterizations and sharp, incisive language . . . Gripping and dreamy, this tale will please fans of Margaret Atwood and Alice Hoffman, and win Solomon her own legion of readers."

—*Publishers Weekly*

"Employing a seemingly effortless, breezy style, first-time novelist Solomon speaks with panache to the issue of commitment. . . . A witty, accomplished debut." —*Booklist*

"A profoundly entertaining romantic mystery, a meditation on loss and self-deception shot through with humor and grace, Nina Solomon's quirky *Single Wife* is definitely a keeper."

—Gary Shteyngart, author of *The Russian Debutante's Handbook*

Single Wife

A NOVEL BY NINA SOLOMON

NEW AMERICAN LIBRARY

New American Library
Published by New American Library, a division of
Penguin Group (USA) Inc., 375 Hudson Street, New York, New York 10014, U.S.A.
Penguin Books Ltd, 80 Strand, London WC2R 0RL, England
Penguin Books Australia Ltd, 250 Camberwell Road,
Camberwell, Victoria 3124, Australia
Penguin Books Canada Ltd, 10 Alcorn Avenue, Toronto, Ontario, Canada M4V 3B2
Penguin Books (N.Z.) Ltd, Cnr Rosedale and Airborne Roads,
Albany, Auckland 1310, New Zealand

Penguin Books Ltd, Registered Offices: 80 Strand, London WC2R 0RL, England

Published by New American Library, a division of Penguin Group (USA) Inc. Previously published by Algonquin Books of Chapel Hill, a division of Workman Publishing. For information contact Workman Publishing, 708 Broadway, New York, NY 10003.

First New American Library Printing, June 2004
10 9 8 7 6 5 4 3 2 1

LIBRARY OF CONGRESS CATALOGING-IN-PUBLICATION DATA:

Solomon, Nina, 1961–
Single wife / Nina Solomon.
p. cm.
ISBN 0-451-21211-8 (trade pbk.)
1. Married women—Fiction. 2. Runaway husbands—Fiction. 3. Missing persons—Fiction. 4. New York (N.Y.)—Fiction. 5. Deception—Fiction. I. Title.
PS3619.O437S57 2004
813'.6—dc22 2004004185

Set in Minion
Designed by Anne Winslow

Printed in the United States of America

PUBLISHER'S NOTE
This is a work of fiction. Names, characters, places, and incidents either are the product of the author's imagination or are used fictitiously, and any resemblance to actual persons, living or dead, business establishments, events, or locales is entirely coincidental.

For Nathaniel

Acknowledgments

I owe a debt of gratitude to those people in my life—my angels, mentors, and friends—who gave me the courage to stay on the path. To my stellar editors, Andra Olenik and Elisabeth Scharlatt, for their inspired vision and dedication to this book. To Patricia Bozza, for her keen attention to detail. To my agent, Irene Skolnick, for making this all happen. With admiration and respect to Kaylie Jones, for her unswerving faith and insight. And to Betsy Crane, for her friendship and example.

Many thanks to my constant readers and advisors: Tim McLoughlin, Renette Zimmerly, Janine Veto, Pamela Brandt Jackson, Adam Levin, Christopher Rothko, and Thane Rosenbaum. To Betsy and Richard Shuster, the truest of friends, for allowing me to bring Grace with me everywhere, even to poker night. To Michael Fleisher, for helping me see what I couldn't. To John Lippert, Jennifer Reicher, Carole Ridley, and Richard Zabel, for always being there.

And with love to my mother and father.

1
The Duro-Lites

When Grace and Laz got married, her parents gave them twelve Duro-Lite lightbulbs for their dining room fixture. "They'll last till your twenty-fifth wedding anniversary," her mother had promised, kissing her cheek. Grace shrank at these unscripted tender moments. Her father added with a wink, "I'll put my money on the bulbs." This, Grace knew, had more to do with her father's utter and complete faith in the Duro-Lites than lack thereof in their union.

November would mark their fifth anniversary. They had been one of those presumptuous couples who get married on Thanksgiving weekend, forcing all their closest friends and relatives to wear black tie after gorging the night before on chestnut stuffing and pecan pie. "Just roll me home," Laz's oldest friend, Kane, had joked as he adjusted his cummerbund, but even he got into the spirit after a few cosmopolitans. At the very least, their anniversary was easy to remember. Only three more weeks.

Laz had been gone since Halloween. It wasn't the first time he'd left with no explanation, but then only for a night, a couple of days, a week at the most.

She remembered the day he left—how intently he had been studying his cereal as if reading tea leaves. "Gracie, I'll be back in a little while." He left as if he were going to the bank or to buy the Sunday *Times* (although they had it delivered) or to walk the dog (but they had none). An ordinary good-bye.

"SEÑOR BROOKMAN IS AWAY?" Marisol, their housekeeper, had asked Grace the Friday after he left.

"Yes," Grace responded. She'd covered for him before—calling his editor, rescheduling his Tuesday squash game, turning down the invitations that seemed to come with more ferocity whenever he was gone. She once even edited one of his articles, which his editor later told him was some of his best work. Laz was always so grateful when he returned, lifting her in his arms into the bedroom and making her forget his absence. And without hesitation, Grace added, "But he'll be back on Sunday."

"So I'll make some of his favorite custard for him before I leave."

"I'm sure he'll love that," Grace said automatically. Marisol made the most perfect caramelized custard. Laz liked to eat it warm right out of the serving bowl, one heaping spoon at a time.

"I can die now," he would tell Marisol and kiss her hand.

GRACE HADN'T INTENDED for the deception to continue this long. She'd assumed he'd be back in a matter of days and everything would return to normal.

And yet Sunday arrived, and Laz did not. Grace went into the living room, carrying a ramekin of Marisol's custard and a large spoon, and played one of Laz's favorite CDs. She blasted it just as he would have done until the coffee table vibrated and the doorman called up to say the neighbors had complained. Just as if he were home. Grace's father once gave Laz a pair of headphones, thinking he'd solved the problem, but Laz never used them. He said he preferred to be surrounded by the music as if in the eye of a tornado.

It began with these small things. Monday, she left a knife with peanut butter and an empty orange juice glass by the sink. Tuesday, his unedited manuscript on the coffee table. Wednesday, a bouquet of sweet peas on the windowsill behind the baby grand, some loose change on the hall table. Thursday, a cigarette butt in a seashell from their honeymoon in Belize, his rumpled tuxedo shirt over the side of an armchair.

"It's nice to have him home again—the house is filled with joy," Marisol commented, as she swept the remains of the ashes with a soft rag.

Laz's presence began to feel tangible. It was easier than Grace had expected. Easier than telling everyone that Laz had left and she didn't know where he was or when he was coming back. It was all in the details. She began to see Laz as an accumulation of habits and idiosyncrasies, things left out, half done, out of order.

Grace put a pair of his socks and underwear in the laundry basket each night. Sometimes she'd sleep in his undershirts to give them a semblance of having been inhabited by a warm body. And each morning she'd take out one of his button-down shirts from the closet, slit open the plastic cellophane from the dry cleaner's that he said kept the shirts crease-free but which Grace thought didn't allow the fabric to breathe, apply some Old Spice to the underarms, and throw the paper collar in the garbage. One of the hardest things to do was learning to leave the toilet seat up in the second bathroom, but that, too, eventually became habitual. She found she could be quite meticulously unruly if she put her mind to it.

Laz was often out late, coming home long after the night doorman was off duty, usually leaving before José came on in the morning. Sleep was at times inconsequential to him; he was fond of saying it could never be too late or too hot, but there were those times when he'd sleep for almost two days straight and nothing could wake him. Grace now began to get up early—a practice against her nature, as she needed a lot of sleep in order to feel like herself, and then not fully until around midday—so that she could run to the deli and get José the cup of coffee that Laz always left him on the concierge desk.

She had a growing feeling of being overwhelmed by these details, but continued with a strong sense of purpose. In order to streamline her morning routine, she bought a supply of the coffee cups they used at the deli with the Greek motif *We Are Happy to Serve You*, and prepared the coffee herself. She worried that José would notice the difference, so she made inquiries after the first couple of days.

"How's the coffee?" she asked.

"Just the way I like it," he answered. "Mr. Brookman is so thoughtful."

EVERYONE LIKED LAZ. Not just in a superficial way, either—they each considered him among their closest friends. At Grace's ten-year high school reunion, at least a dozen people had come up to him, certain that he had graduated with them. When he said that he was just accompanying Grace, they looked at her as if trying to place her. *Didn't you leave after tenth grade?* or *Weren't you a grade below?* or *You used to be blond, right?* After some awkward attempts at small talk, they turned back to Laz. It may have been the way he listened, so people felt understood, or how he seemed to be sharing his soul with them, or the way he remembered minute details, or how he always made them laugh.

One rainy, waterlogged Sunday, after a week of not hearing from him, she discovered his hammered-gold wedding band—the one they'd had made in Florence—behind a rusting can of shaving cream. She had been on a rare cleaning binge that morning, having just finished polishing the silver and wiping the dust from the moldings, and thought the medicine cabinet could use a bit of reorganization. She didn't expect to find Laz's wedding band off his finger. She sat down on the edge of the bathtub. Grace remembered how Laz had haggled with the Florentine merchant until they not only reached a fair price but also were invited to his house for a lunch of bruschetta and veal shank, along with receiving three bottles of Chianti Classico and a private tour of San Gimignano the following day.

It was conceivable that the ring might have been there for months. Grace did not consider herself to be the most observant person (sometimes it took her weeks to notice that a particular store had closed on their block, having been replaced by a Pinky's nail salon or a Starbucks coffee shop). But the ring? She knew better. Laz had abandoned the ring as sure as he had abandoned her—at least for the time being. She steadied herself on the edge of the tub. Her thoughts spiraled, caught between longing for his return and the desire for its deferral. She held the ring in her palm, the light glinting off its uneven surfaces. How could something so light carry so much weight? A symbolic circle of gold now marooned beside an aerosol can.

As she placed the ring back in the medicine cabinet, she ruefully acknowledged, after wiping away a smudge on the mirror, that Laz was going to be gone longer than she had anticipated.

On his birthday, twelve days after he left, Grace had a Greenberg cake delivered and two bottles of Veuve Clicquot and cassis for kir royales as usual, and she found it not too difficult to polish off almost an entire bottle by herself. All major events for Laz seemed to occur in November—his birthday, the publication of his first book, the signing of the movie deal, their wedding day. He always called it his lucky month. They may have even met in November, although it was still up for debate. It was at a Halloween party, and Laz swore it was just minutes after midnight.

Grace set the cake on the small glass table by the window and lit the candles, letting them burn just long enough for tiny drips of blue and yellow wax to adhere to the mirrorlike dark chocolate icing. She had fielded phone calls from friends and family all afternoon. She thought that she would most certainly be discovered in her charade when his mother called with birthday wishes, but Mrs. Brookman hadn't heard from him, either, which was not that unusual, so Grace just said he'd call her soon. Grace insisted the doormen take the remains of the birthday cake. Even though she'd always said the cake was too rich for her, she'd eaten two slices, just as Laz would have done.

That night, in one of his dove-gray Calvin Klein T-shirts, she felt strangely closer to him than she ever had before.

THE DAY AFTER Laz's birthday, one of the Duro-Lites burned out. Grace wasn't sure whether to take it as a sign of fate, a dimming glimpse of the future, or the futility of a modern warranty. She stared at the bulb long and hard, and rubbed her eyes as if she might still be dreaming. Laz had seemed so close the night before—almost there. She thought of the trick candles they'd had at his thirty-seventh birthday last year—twenty friends, a pot of Grace's vegetarian chili, and the chocolate cake.

"Make a wish, Laz," Kane had prodded.

"Why? I have everything I could possibly want," he said, squeezing Grace's hand. He'd meant it, too, she was sure of that. But that night, as on numerous others, she had dismissed the signs that something was amiss. When the candles began to flicker and rekindle, Laz's expression changed. A look flashed across his face that she'd never seen before. He suddenly seemed absent or like a stranger, as if in that unguarded moment a glimmer of someone else had surfaced. Grace kissed him on the cheek, and just as quickly, he was back to his old self—everything as always.

Grace found she was holding her breath, waiting for the Duro-Lite to reignite as the candles had. Then the phone rang, and she heard her father's voice on the answering machine. Fitting. Her father had won the bet—Laz had left before the bulb had given out—but she wouldn't let her father know that. Instead, there was a big commotion and a heated discussion about whether to sue the company for selling them defective bulbs or the possibility that they had bought a case of pirated bulbs. Conspiracy theories were very popular in Grace's family. Nothing like a good plot to keep the family united.

"What does Laz think?" her father asked.

"He thinks the wiring was faulty, so he said we should call in an electrician to check it out," she said.

"He's such a levelheaded fellow, that Laz is," her mother added from the extension. Grace's mother was usually listening in on the extension, for some reason, perhaps having to do with wanting to hear what people said when she wasn't around. She pretended not to be eavesdropping, but that was pointless; as much as she tried to be unobtrusive, she couldn't help but interject.

"I think we bought bum bulbs," her father said, exhaling slowly. He sighed often, especially over the telephone. Grace could picture him in his worn leather chair, looking as if he might deflate like one of those surrealist Edvard Munch *Scream* balloons they sell at party stores. "Not even five years. I told you we should have gotten the Satcos."

"Laz said he'll take care of it. Write some sort of letter to the company," Grace added. "As soon as he gets back from London." Grace found that sending him on a trip now and then served her purposes well. It gave her a chance to refuel the energy necessary to sustain two lives and provided a break from her new reality, which was quite time-consuming. "He'll be back the day after tomorrow," she said. She suddenly felt like a character in one of Roald Dahl's dark tales, in particular the one about the landlady who stuffs her boarders so they'll never leave. Grace hadn't realized how accessible her own dark side was, and she found a degree of comfort in following the dictates of her new role as if it lay already mapped out for her.

THE FOLLOWING EVENING, the night of their weekly Scrabble-cum-potluck dinner at her parents' house, was the first true test for Grace. The week before, to her relief, the game had been called due to the imminent approach of Tropical Storm Irene, even though it had still been miles off the coast of the Carolinas.

Weather was of vital importance in her family. The telephone number for the National Weather Service was on speed-dial and was consulted each morning. It was important to get the most up-to-date weather report, so calling a few minutes after the hour was best, and only then could plans be finalized. Otherwise it was "We'll have to see."

When Grace was a child, her father used to give her "rain showers" in the bathtub. Grace, her Mary Poppins umbrella poised above her, would wait for the approaching squall as her father flashed the lights on and off to simulate lightning. In the sixth grade, she had been kept home from school for a total of eighteen days because of wind, rain, ice, snow, or bitter cold. "You never know when the picture windows from one of those skyscrapers will fly out," her father would say. Grace knew then not to question it, and even now on exceptionally windy days found herself looking up, just in case.

GRACE'S PARENTS HAD moved to an Upper East Side building from Stuyvesant Town when Grace was thirteen years old. Her parents loved the building for all its amenities, most notably the in-house dry-cleaning service, their glass-enclosed terrace, and the sleek, ultramodern kitchen. Space-age, her mother still said when referring to the now twenty-year-old interior design, which included white leather chairs and a chrome banquette.

White-brick buildings were just coming into vogue at that time, with no thought whatsoever to how emissions or other things in the air might eventually sully the pristine exterior. But her parents chose instead the only blue-brick building in existence at the time, which her father thought blended perfectly with a clear blue sky. Grace thought it more closely resembled the tube of her mother's creamy cerulean-blue eye shadow that she once mistook for a crayon when she was a child, and which her mother still wore for special occasions.

As Grace walked into her parents' building, she saw the usual cluster of elderly widows wearing their best outfits as they lounged in the lobby, and she was struck by a wave of recognition, as if they, too, were just filling the time since they'd lost their husbands. It's just that theirs were dead, and hers was simply missing. And yet there was a finality to both. As she passed by them, she felt sorry that their husbands, unlike Laz, would not soon return.

THE SUGARMANS HADN'T yet arrived, although they lived less than five blocks away. Grace's parents and the Sugarmans had been neighbors in Stuyvesant Town, and both couples had long ago decided to stay no farther than a zip-code distance from each other, whether it be in Manhattan or Delray Beach, Florida, where they had adjacent condos. It would have been easier if Grace and Laz had opted for the same proximity to her parents, but Laz preferred the West Side, and Grace's family had had to come to terms with that.

"By the way, how did he like the sweater we sent him for his birthday?" her mother asked as she set out the Scrabble board. She was petite, dressed in what she called her uniform, which consisted of a knee-length skirt, sweater set, a gold pendant, sheer stockings, and low-heeled shoes. Her hair was swept up off her forehead, accentuating what she considered to be her best features—her large, deep-brown eyes and small, straight nose. She had been a brunette, like Grace, but now her hair was golden-honey blond, from a tube of Loving Care. Other than her hair color, Grace had inherited only her mother's eyes. The rest of her features, including her height, her slightly off-center nose, and her wide smile, were from her father.

"He loves the sweater," Grace answered. Until now, she had rarely found it necessary to lie, even by omission. Her mother had always told Grace when she was growing up that when Grace wasn't being honest, a red splotch the size of a thumbprint would appear right above the bridge of her nose between her eyebrows. Grace thought she was beginning to detect a furrow line right in that same location.

Grace had forgotten to wear the special Scrabble shirt her mother had had printed. It was a black shirt with white lettering arranged in a crossword pattern: Grace's name interlocked with the first *A* in Lazarus, along with Milton and Paulette, and Bert and Francine Sugarman in connecting block letters, complete with a small registered trademark symbol at the bottom.

"Not to worry, Laz left his last time he played. Why don't you wear it?" Her mother said this so reassuringly that Grace wished, as she slipped the shirt over her head, that she could believe this would somehow make everything all right.

"Sweetie, tell Laz that they're predicting a bad storm for late tomorrow. Is he flying into Kennedy?" her father asked.

"I think so," Grace answered.

"Could be long delays. He may even have a layover. Tell him to call ahead to make sure the flight hasn't been canceled." As she listened, Grace thought the three of them made a good, if unwitting, team.

By the time the Sugarmans arrived, her father had printed out two copies of the five-day local forecast from the National Weather Service.

Francine Sugarman was a renowned cook among their circle of friends, and these Sunday Scrabble games were often more about food than etymology, although Bert always faithfully lugged his *Oxford English Dictionary* from their apartment on East Sixty-fifth Street in case of any disputes, which he clearly relished. Bert and Laz shared a love of words. For Bert, his dictionary was like a thirty-pound, two-volume security blanket, while for Laz, words were the source of some greater understanding, as if when the roots of a word were traced back to its source, there was order at last.

"Your mother tells me Laz isn't going to be joining us," Francine said to Grace in the kitchen. Francine's silvery white hair had recently been cut severely short, further accentuating her pale blue eyes and her distinctive nose, which Grace's mother suspected had been "done." "And I made my famous sweet-and-sour meatballs just for him," she added. And they *were* for Laz. Certainly not for Bert, who was diabetic and for whom the meatballs were supposedly off-limits (although he was known to sneak a few when Francine's back was turned), or for Grace, who was a vegetarian. "You know you can freeze them and then thaw them out when he gets back. I'll send you home with a container of them."

Francine's containers had her name embossed both on the lids and the bottoms, and with masking tape, their contents labeled in indelible ink. As Grace looked at the assortment of containers on the kitchen counter, she wondered when this meal had actually been prepared. In Francine's skilled hands, thawing had been elevated to an art form.

"Your microwave heats much more evenly than mine," Francine commented as she and Paulette watched a serving bowl turning inside the microwave oven.

"Paulette," Milton called from the dining room, where he was arranging the tiles upside down and in a diamond pattern, "remember what the doctor told you about your eyes."

"What?" Francine asked.

"Oh, nothing, just something about microwaves causing cataracts," Grace's mother answered, dismissing him as if she were shooing a fly. She opened the door to the microwave and gave the meatballs a stir.

"You could always try smoking marijuana," Bert chimed in from the dining room.

Grace had heard this exact exchange dozens of times, and she could predict what Francine would utter next with more accuracy than the National Weather Service could predict tomorrow's weather.

"Honey, I told you before—that's for glaucoma," Francine called back from the kitchen.

THE GAME PROCEEDED uneventfully, at least in terms of Grace and her dissembling. Her husband was mentioned throughout the game in statements such as *Laz would have gotten the triple-*

word score, or *Milt, save some meatballs for Grace to take to Laz,* or *Doesn't Laz's shirt look cute on Gracie?* Bert won the game, which he attributed to the fact that Laz was not there. In the final round, Grace had a *q, y, x, r,* blank, *m,* and *w,* but she was challenged by Bert when she put down *quim,* which would have been her highest score of the game.

"That's not a word," her mother said. "Don't you have a *t* or something?"

"It's a word all right," Bert said, with a customary downward swivel of his head, which looked more like he was trying to suppress a burp than an illegitimate word.

"What does it mean?" her father asked.

"Oh, never mind," Grace said, snatching the tiles off the board. She felt as if she had been caught by the principal kissing a boy in the stairwell at a high school dance. Laz often read aloud to Grace from obscure nineteenth-century volumes he found at the Strand bookstore downtown. Some of the books were on the racy side. *Quim* was one of their favorite words. Like *buzz* or *gargle,* it sounded as it felt. Grace wondered if Bert's dictionary contained the archaic word for G-spot as well.

"It is a word. But it's slang and therefore not permitted," Bert said officially.

"Good, honey," her mother said. Grace looked at her mother, who obviously thought she had bestowed upon her daughter the most lavish of compliments. "Next time you'll get it right."

THAT EVENING, WHEN Grace returned home, she put the container of Francine Sugarman's sweet-and-sour meatballs in the freezer. Francine said the meatballs would keep for over a year. Hopefully, that wouldn't be necessary, Grace thought, as she drifted off.

2
Jane Meets the Invisible Man

The dimness in the dining room was bothersome to Grace. So in order to compensate for the burned-out Duro-Lite, the next morning, after leaving coffee for José, she carried in a standing lamp with a pink bulb that she found especially pleasing. When she plugged it in, she discovered that the outlet was not near enough to the table, and went into the pantry to find an extension cord. Grace was absolutely certain that there was one in the utility cabinet above the broom closet. The cabinet smelled of old rubber cement and lemon oil as she pushed aside rolls of duct tape, tins of shoe polish, and old rags.

After several minutes of searching to no avail, she began to grow testy and felt a sudden craving for Saltines that she attributed to having had two cups of tea on an empty stomach, which often left her queasy. She reached farther in the cabinet, thinking the cord might have been shoved to the back. Laz referred to the cabinet as the black hole of household products, and now Grace understood why. She was trying to think of other likely places an extension cord might be when the telephone rang.

"Grace?" It was Kane. "You sound out of breath. Something wrong?"

"Hi, Kane," she answered, brushing the hair off her face. "I was just looking for an extension cord."

"Literal or figurative?"

"Kane, really." She was not in the mood for his playfulness. "I've turned the apartment upside down looking for it."

"You lost it?" he inquired.

Grace could practically hear the wheels in his head turning. "What are you implying?"

"Just that maybe it's time that you cut the cord."

"Kane, I'm talking about an extension cord."

"So am I."

"And anyway, I didn't lose it, I misplaced it," she said.

"My point exactly, but you'll never admit it. I'm just calling to let Laz know hockey's canceled this week because of the Peewees."

"I'll tell him as soon as he gets back."

After Grace hung up the phone, she returned to the cabinet, rummaging around a little, but still unable to locate the missing cord. She did find several odd items and miscellany, like a beaded evening bag with a broken strap, several remote controls with no batteries, a pumpkin carving kit, and a mismatched glove she thought she might someday make finger puppets out of.

Just as she was about to close the cabinet and step down, she caught sight of a photograph. She'd never been fond of the picture. Kane had copied it for them. It was taken seven years ago at the Halloween party at which Grace had first met Laz. They were all in costume. She was standing next to Kane, and Laz had his arm around Grace's friend Chloe. There was a layer of dust over the plastic frame, and Grace removed the picture to look at it more closely. Laz had joked that he wouldn't show up on film since he was, after all, dressed as the Invisible Man. But he was quite visible then.

Grace had met Kane before she met Laz. Technically, she and Kane had been dating, although it was laughed off as a non-event for both of them. As with all such events, it was often funnier in the retelling.

Once Laz and Grace laid eyes on each other, of course, it was a fait accompli to Grace—she knew that they would be together, despite the fact that she was dating his best friend. After the party, Laz simply took Kane aside and told him that he was going to steal his girlfriend from him, to which Kane responded, "Be my guest." It wasn't until much later that Grace even questioned the sequence of events. Mostly, her ego was a bit bruised that Kane hadn't put up more of a fight, but she wouldn't have changed a thing. She might not have married Laz otherwise.

Grace and Kane had had friends in common and were introduced to each other the summer before the party at a group house in Great Barrington. It was the Fourth of July. Kane had been playing blow pong, and in between sips of beer and Louis Armstrong–like exhalations that sent the Ping-Pong ball sailing across the table, he'd flirted with Grace. They shelled peas into a large glass bowl for dinner, decorated shortcakes in patriotic splendor with blueberries, strawberries, and whipped cream, and by the end of the weekend had formed a certain bond. Over dinner one night, Grace heard numerous references to Kane's friend Laz, his name invoked as if he were some sort of legend. Once back in the city, she and Kane went to a few movies together and kissed only once. He brought her a bouquet of yellow roses, which Grace later interpreted as a friendly, rather than amorous, gesture.

That Halloween, Kane had invited Grace to a costume party, and she'd asked if he had a friend for Chloe, her oldest friend, who was in town from Chicago. Grace dressed carefully, pulling her wavy brown hair up into a Wilma Flintstone–like hairdo and adjusting her strapless bra under the off-the-shoulder leopard outfit she had dug up in the back of her closet. She wore a pair of faux-lizard sandals even though it was raining, and she had to jump over puddles to hail a taxi. Chloe was less than enthusiastic—she hated costumes—but with a little prodding, she succumbed to wearing a peasant blouse and a white kerchief. With her tattooed ankle, spiky black hair, rhinestone cross, and blue Doc Martens, she looked like a punk rock milkmaid.

It was almost eleven-thirty by the time they arrived at 120th Street and Riverside Drive at an unlived-in mansion belonging to a friend of Kane's. The mansion was the perfect setting for a Halloween party. It was legendary for its underground tunnels and passageways that led to the river for unspecified purposes, which were the subject of much speculation during the evening. Kane had opted for an S-and-M Tarzan, complete with a leather whip and a wild black wig, to complement Grace's Jane. Halloween was not Grace's favorite holiday. While walking on the streets of Manhattan around Halloween, she often couldn't tell who was in costume and who wasn't, and it unnerved her.

The moment Grace first saw Laz standing in the darkened vestibule, something about him struck a chord in her, in spite of the fact that his face was wrapped in gauze and he was wearing a hat and mirrored sunglasses. She said hello and then proceeded to spill beer on him when she nervously tried to shake his gloved hand.

"You, I won't forget," he said with a smile as he dried his hands with a cocktail napkin. She knew that first impressions could be misleading—she had been misled before—but this was different.

When Laz asked Chloe if she'd like a tour of the mansion, Grace thought it was very gracious of him to entertain her friend, but then she remembered that Kane was her date and she turned to him.

"I know," Kane said. "Women and dogs—it's like he casts a spell on them."

It wasn't just women and dogs, though, it was everyone. People seemed drawn to him, like a long-lost friend.

Grace was amazed that by the end of the evening Laz, who had undone the gauze but kept on his sunglasses and gloves in deference to H. G. Wells, knew intimate details about everyone present. Of course, they knew of him, too, from the articles he wrote for *Esquire* and his appearances on public television, but mostly for the Amnesty International award for his book on Kosovo, from where he had just returned. His book, entitled *Waking the Ghosts,* documented the six weeks he had spent impersonating a mute Muslim prisoner in a Serbian concentration camp, which he had done in order to write firsthand about the atrocities there. The account was deemed groundbreaking and courageous, catapulting him to almost rock-star status among other journalists. The book had done remarkably well—it was a sensation, actually, and it led to a two-book deal. There was even a Pulitzer nomination. Grace had read an excerpt in *Vanity Fair*. It didn't hurt that Laz was also photogenic and well spoken, and gave the impression that none of the money or acclaim mattered to him, which only seemed to earn him that much more respect.

As Laz talked animatedly about the impact on children orphaned by war, Grace tried to listen attentively, but all she knew was that when he looked at her, which he did often, her cheeks flushed as if he could tell she was busy unwrapping the rest of him in her mind.

After the party, the four of them walked north on Riverside

Drive past Grant's Tomb to where Laz's Saab was parked. The rain had stopped, but the weather had grown colder. Laz put his jacket over Grace's shoulders and took her arm. Even their strides matched.

The Invisible Man had terrified Grace when she saw it as a child on Creature Feature. Her parents had left her with a new babysitter who made Jiffy Pop then turned out all the lights and closed the curtains in order to create the proper mood for watching the film. For months and even years afterwards, Grace had the distinct feeling that she was being followed on her way to school and that when she showered, she could feel the Invisible Man's fingers tickling her back. But with Laz, none of those old associations applied.

Laz drove them back to Grace's building to her one-bedroom apartment on the top floor of a brownstone. Grace made hot chocolate and the four of them played a game of *Trivial Pursuit*. After they all left, Grace took off her costume and picked up the gauze Laz had left on the coffee table, wrapping it loosely around her hands and up her forearms as she sat on the windowsill and finished her cup of cocoa.

GRACE SLID THE photograph back into the frame. She and Chloe had since drifted apart, but she couldn't remember why. When had they last spoken? It had very likely been nearly a year. Their lives had taken such different turns, and, in truth, Chloe and Laz had never really warmed to each other.

She considered what it would mean to see him walk through the door right now. He could, she knew, at any moment. He had done so before. There was no reason to believe he wouldn't again. Grace never questioned why he was with her. For her, the answer was plain. She had witnessed the lulls, which often turned into dark sieges, when he'd crawl into himself, sometimes not calling for days. She gave him room to breathe, always welcoming him back, no questions asked and demanding no answers. He felt safe with her. Safe to withdraw because he knew she'd always be there to fill in the gaps.

The first time he'd left like this, he was gone for two days, sending Grace into a hysterical frenzy. The night before, they'd talked until dawn and had never seemed closer. He told her about his father's abandoning him when he was three and said that he could never bear to lose her, too. When he finally fell asleep, he looked like a small child. The next day, when he didn't come home for dinner, Grace telephoned friends and family, then eventually the police and hospitals.

Francine Sugarman brought over platters to feed the dozens or so people keeping vigil in Grace's apartment. She even offered to spend the night, having arrived equipped with an overnight bag and her electric blanket, which then blew a fuse. Kane brought bagels and whitefish salad; Grace's mother, a noodle kugel and a package of generic English muffins she'd found at a two-for-one special. Relatives from New Haven, whom Grace hadn't seen for years, dropped by for a few hours, lining up on the sectional couch as if for a matinee. Bert Sugarman took one look at the assortment of people and food and joked, "Who died?"

Grace still remembered the expression on Laz's face when he walked through the door to a roomful of anxious people, all clamoring for an explanation from him, although he had hidden his displeasure well.

"Where on earth have you been?" Grace's mother demanded.

"Where were you?" Milton asked.

"We were worried sick about you," Francine said.

"You couldn't have just picked up the phone?" Bert asked.

Laz shrugged his shoulders and kissed Grace on the cheek.

"If I'd known I'd be getting such a big reception, I would have shaved," he said and laughed, but underneath his smile was an icy look that still made Grace shiver, as if she were the one who should apologize for causing such a stir.

Everyone present sat back and gave a collective sigh of relief. "Thank God you're all right."

The second time Laz disappeared, she called only Kane. "Don't worry, I'll find him," he told her. "I think I know where he might be."

Four hours later, Kane and Laz walked through the door. Laz had gotten in the car and just kept driving until he reached Kane's lake house. When Kane found him, Laz was sitting on the front porch. Grace helped him off with his shoes and put him into bed, watching him until he fell asleep.

"Next time, don't get anyone involved, Gracie," he said when he finally emerged two days later. "No one understands me like you do. Not even Kane. I'll always come back. I promise. You have to trust that."

The third time he left was longer, although she couldn't remember exactly how much longer. Grace vowed to tell no one, waiting each night for Laz to return and occupy an apartment that he apparently had decided not to live in.

The next few times after that were even less distinguishable, and it began to matter less and less to her. Grace knew that any attempts at questioning him would be fruitless. He would provide no answers for her. And while she tried in earnest to feel her way around the perimeter of his defenses for a way in, he'd already slipped out the back.

For Grace, the wedding vows would always fall short. Even if Laz had taken a vow to be physically present along with the vows to love, honor and cherish, it could not have kept him home. Laz was not a conventional missing man. He wasn't out with the boys, carousing the town, slumped over a drink in a smoke-filled, mildewy bar, or playing poker or bowling until all hours with his buddies, or even hanging out at a strip club. That would have been easier to accept. Boys will be boys, after all. But Laz wasn't acting out. He was simply unlocatable.

Eventually, Grace settled into the rhythm of his abandonment and return, the ebb and flow of the tidal shifts in his appearances. She began to prepare herself for each leaving, holding down the fort with a force equal to his withdrawal, so that by the time Laz handed her the final pink slip, she would have already filled his position.

She put the photograph into the cabinet and closed the door. With the dust and fingerprints on the plastic obscuring the image underneath, it looked as if Laz were really fading.

3
A Perfect Match

Tuesday was Marisol's day off, so Grace could get ready at a more leisurely pace, rather than rushing around in an attempt to leave evidence of two lives. Actually, editing herself was becoming more of an issue, as she was often leaving too many things out and felt that this, in and of itself, could lead to suspicions.

When she and Laz were first married, it had taken Grace some time to get used to the idea of having someone in the house doing the cleaning. Her father had always been the one to do the dishes and the vacuuming in her family. And Laz, not one to pitch in with the household chores, had found Grace too disorganized for his liking. Disorder rattled his nerves. After returning from vacations, Grace would habitually leave her suitcase on the floor for weeks until she eventually ran out of clean clothes. She was lucky if her clothes were right side out in the closet or if they were on hangers at all.

Laz was the type of person who liked the food in the cabinets lined up according to size, and his neckties hung on an automated rack, arranged in a color spectrum. Once he realized that Grace would not adopt his organized ways, he suggested that they hire someone full time. Having Marisol around had made Grace feel self-conscious at first, and she used to dust and do the dishes before Marisol arrived. But eventually she, too, came to rely on this externally imposed order, until she felt she couldn't get along any other way.

TUESDAY MORNING, AS she used a lipstick brush to scrape a small amount of her favorite lipstick out of its tube, leaving only enough for one more day, she decided it was time to restock. She'd been wearing the same color of lipstick for years—when Laz had first kissed her, when he proposed, and when they were married. She usually bought makeup in triplicate in order to avoid the scrutiny of the makeup artists at the department stores; she felt that they looked at her as if she had no idea whatsoever how to apply foundation or eyeliner, let alone mascara, poor clueless dear.

When Grace went off to college, her mother took a part-time job at the Estée Lauder counter at Bonwit's in order to fill the void in her life due to what she referred to as her empty nest, even though Grace lived at home and commuted daily to Barnard. Known to make surprise appearances in Grace's room with Q-Tips or sponges, Grace's mother reminded her of a bird of prey swooping down with a ten-pound vanity case. Her lesson: It's all in the application, a matter of having the proper tools; the art of creating another self comes with practice. Her mother hadn't spent nearly as much time trying to teach her to contemplate what she was trying to conceal, as she did trying to perfect her ability to do so.

Mid-November was almost peak season for shopping. As soon as Grace entered the bustling world of Bloomingdale's, where her mother had first espoused her most intransigent myths, she was transported back to childhood with the accompanying full range of insecurities. She rarely went to department stores, always feeling lost in the shuffle without the guidance of a weathered shopper such as her mother, who could assuredly negotiate the aisles. The first floor, with its gleaming black-and-white tiled floor, was hallowed ground for Paulette—a place for transformation and the hope of redemption in every department. Just beyond the revolving doors, where shoppers and fragrances competed for air space, anything was possible. And if need be, it could always be exchanged.

As Grace stood in front of the glossy white Clinique counter, listening to the cosmetologist—with her *chocolate* lip liner and white lab coat—explain that they no longer carried Grace's shade, she was confronted with the dismal possibility that there was no perfect lipstick, no perfect husband, except in memory, like the Bonne Belle Lip Smackers she and Chloe had mailed away for in seventh grade—*Cherry 7-Up*. Just the perfect lipstick for the moment like that Heraclitean river that you can't step into twice.

HER EXPERIENCE AT the cosmetics counter was considerably more upsetting than Grace had anticipated. As she walked up Lexington Avenue, she began to feel what she could only identify as a modicum of panic, so she decided to hail a cab and go directly home.

She turned on the television and switched the channel to CNN. Just as she was putting on the kettle for tea, she heard a headline that caught her attention and went into the living room: *Kosovo Controversy—Fact or Fiction?* The voice of the reporter droned on like an annoying buzz from a fluorescent bulb. *A journalistic account of his harrowing experience in a Muslim concentration camp has come under scrutiny, as new evidence is mounting against . . .*

Grace heard the title of Laz's book and reached again for the remote control. Laz had always said there would be people out to discredit him. But now, locked in her own mercy mission of self-preservation caused by his disappearance, she couldn't afford to become distracted by Laz's misery—self-inflicted or otherwise. She didn't want to feel sorry for him. In order to orchestrate his absence, and evaluate their marriage and her place in it, she found it necessary to maintain complete focus and a measured stance. She would tune out news reports and avoid the papers. Laz's troubles may now involve a national scandal, but in her home everything would be preserved, even Laz's reputation.

As she pointed the remote control at the television to switch the station, she thought of her mother, who had read an article in *Prevention* magazine about the dangers of infrared rays. She had seen her mother duck and weave, accusing her husband of zapping her on purpose when he was changing channels, to avoid being caught in the line of fire.

On the next channel was a holiday fluff story about a company called Heaven Scent that could re-create any fragrance. Grace rarely wore perfume and was reminded of the Little Kiddle perfumery she'd received as a hand-me-down from an older cousin. She recalled using the medicine dropper that came in the kit and working with the precision of a scientist to create the perfect balance of apple blossom, lilac, and lily of the valley. When she'd gotten it just right, she spilled it all over the kitchen floor, and her father was forced to take his dinner into his study for weeks because of his highly developed olfactory sensitivity. Once in a while, Grace would catch a whiff of that same fragrance when she was in the unlikeliest places, such as the Port Authority Bus Terminal, and feel a childlike sense of disappointment that her perfume had not been unique at all.

The television program then gave the name of a company that

could match your lipstick color to your outfit or to your poinsettia, if you so desired, by your sending in a sample of the color—even a swatch of fabric—to a cosmetic lab. Sunblock, shimmer, or flavor could be added to achieve an individual lipstick that could even bear the user's personally chosen name.

Grace scrambled for a pencil and wrote down all the information for the lipstick company along with the Web site address: www.perfectmatch.com. The fortuitousness of the sequence of events surprised her. All was not lost, as her father would say, and she went into the bathroom to get the tube of Velvet. She rolled it up, hoping there was enough left. Perhaps it was possible that everything past could be recaptured.

Grace went into the study, sat down at Laz's desk, and turned on the computer. She liked the musical tone emitted as she logged on. Laz had insisted they buy the most up-to-date model, the newest progeny loaded with the latest software, but somehow it was considerably slower in booting up than her old black-and-white PowerBook, which she rarely used and at which she was only semi-proficient. Grace much preferred pen and paper, preferably pink paper, which always lifted her mood. It reminded her of her high school days, most of which were not all that memorable, but as was Grace's tendency, she looked back at most things with a generous quantity of nostalgia.

Actually, she preferred pink to just about any color. She once inquired at her gynecologist's whether her brand of IUD came in pink instead of the generic-looking white—a pink shimmery material would have done quite nicely.

Once the computer booted up, she typed in the password. It was easy to remember—their wedding anniversary, now only eleven days away. As she waited for the modem to connect, she thought about the night before Laz had left. Grace had felt him stirring in the middle of the night and she'd put her hand on his shoulder. He had turned to her with what she had construed as desire at the time —but now saw as urgency—and had pushed himself inside her until she knew he'd come not once or twice, but at least three times in rapid-fire succession. She was used to his high level of desire, but in retrospect she wondered if he had been making up for lost time in advance.

Invalid password. Please enter the password again. Grace thought she must have typed it in too hastily. Then she noticed the problem. Instead of their own screen name, it read *GUEST*. Grace thought back to the last occasion when someone else may have used their account, but drew a blank. She must have pressed the wrong command. She switched the name to *gingko*. The first time Laz had kissed her, the gingko trees that lined the street she lived on were like a bright carpet of yellow paper fans strewn across the pavement. Only a few weeks later, the street would smell rancid from the tree's overripe seeds littering the sidewalk.

She heard the whirring off-key notes as she was connected to the Internet. She typed in the Web site address of the lipstick company and waited for the page to appear. She hadn't received a single e-mail, not even a weather update from her father, Miltonfyi@yahoo.com, who sent group e-mails and newsletters frequently; they concerned such topics as the shortage of rain in the South that might send the price of orange juice skyrocketing or the threat of global warming.

The lack of mail was disheartening, and Grace suddenly felt like running out and joining FriendsoftheFriendless.com. She was comforted by the thought that it would not be long before she would once again have her lipstick, along with an e-mail confirmation to boot.

She watched the screen as the images popped into view like paper flowers opening when dropped in water. She read the heading utterly confused by what she saw. *What do you desire in a perfect match?* A questionnaire followed, along with information on how to register, in flowing pink script. It was a dating service. Grace looked at the address, realizing she had inadvertently typed the letter *a* before *perfectmatch.* She found her mistake only mildly humorous and was about to log off when one of the questions caught her eye. *Can you describe your perfect match in three sentences? If so, then he or she is only steps away.*

Grace was curious to see if she could describe Laz with such precision. She began to type and found that rendering Laz was easier than breathing. "He would read *Oblomov* aloud in bed with champagne and many breaks." *Why get out of bed, if Oblomov doesn't?* he had said, and how could Grace argue? She remembered the breaks more clearly than she remembered any of Goncharov's words—mostly the sound of Laz's voice, the rumple of warm white sheets. She continued typing: "When he smiles, there is no hunger for anything else. And when he leaves, he always comes back."

Three sentences. Succinct and to the point. She was pleased with herself, as if the sheer act of accomplishing the task would somehow bring him back. But as she reread her words, she found herself growing uncertain. Maybe three sentences were not enough. She attempted to type another line, but stopped. Did these three sentences say it all? She rubbed her eyes. She felt the beginnings of a headache. The screen grew fuzzy. No words came.

She selected the lines she had written and pressed the delete key, when suddenly her session was interrupted. She ran to the wall jack, plugged in the phone cord, and picked up the receiver. It was Kane.

"Me, again," he said.

Grace noticed the receiver was sticky and held it away from her ear. Laz liked to eat while he was talking on the phone; this was probably honey from a peanut butter sandwich. She'd tell Marisol tomorrow.

"Hi, Kane. How are you?"

"I'm getting fed up with your husband. He hasn't answered a single one of my e-mails."

"I don't think he got any e-mails. I was just on-line. Maybe you sent them to the wrong address." She had a passing thought about the unexplained "guest" she'd found on her computer and quickly dismissed it from her mind. She was about to relay the whole story about aperfectmatch.com to Kane, partly because she knew he would get a kick out of it, but mostly as a diversion from the subject at hand, when she got another call and told Kane to hold on.

Grace pushed the talk button on the handset and heard a dial tone. She pressed the button again, and in the split second while she waited for the connection, she thought that she might have just missed Laz and cut off Kane as well, but then she heard Kane's voice singing to the radio in the background.

"In a cheery mood, Kane?"

"Always when I talk with you, sweetie."

"Careful, Laz might get jealous," she said, but even she knew how preposterous that was. Laz had never once shown even the slightest amount of jealousy. Kane became silent—a rare occurrence for him. She wished the call-waiting would beep again.

"So, are you going to go up to the lake for Christmas?" Grace asked, suddenly noticing that she was sweating even though she hadn't been warm a moment ago.

"No, my sister's having the clan over," Kane answered. "But I'll be up at the lake for New Year's."

Each year, Kane drove them up to the mountains to a Christmas tree farm near his cabin. Grace loved Christmas—she would get so caught up in the festive decorations around the city that she wished they could keep them up all year long. Her parents and the Sugarmans had always celebrated Christmas, even though they were Jewish—a nonsectarian, watered-down version, with potato pancakes just to hedge their bets—but they drew the line at having a tree, which they thought was somehow sacrilegious. But to Grace, the lights and the smell of pine were the most special parts of all.

Her first Christmas together with Laz, he'd insisted on a nine-foot Douglas fir that was too large to fit inside Kane's Jeep and that had to be tied onto the roof. It had taken a long time to cut down, and Grace's fingers had gone numb from the cold even though Laz had given her his sheepskin gloves, which were too large for her and so well-worn that they'd assumed the contours of his hands.

Kane's house was a mile away from the tree farm, and when they returned to the house, he lit a huge fire. They were ravenous, but the only thing to eat in the house was a box of stale Wheat Thins, some crisp apples, and two cans of salmon. Everything else, including a six-pack of Moosehead beer, had iced over.

"How about we all go skating?" Laz suggested, after their meager lunch. He stood up, wiped his hands on his jeans, and looked out the window.

"It hasn't been cold enough," Kane said. "It still needs a few more weeks."

"Come on. Let's test it." Laz didn't wait for an answer; he was already pulling on his boots. "Who's coming?"

Kane shook his head.

"You guys worry too much," Laz said as he walked out the door.

Grace watched from the frost-covered window, pressing her fingertips to the glass as Laz walked along the perimeter of the lake then ventured out farther onto the ice. Finally, Kane followed him out and stood by the side, calling him back. Laz stopped walking and began to stomp on the ice with the heel of his boot as if to indicate that it *was* ready. Kane walked partway onto the ice and pointed to the window at which Grace was standing. Laz turned and waved. Grace waved back, but in her head she was thinking over and over again: *please don't fall.* When Laz and Kane returned to the house, Laz wrapped his arms around her.

"See, Gracie believes in me," he said. As he lifted her into the air, Grace watched her handprint melting on the frosted windowpane.

On the ride home, Grace took off her boots and curled up under a woolen blanket that Kane kept in the backseat, and closed her eyes. Laz was in the front with Kane. Every so often, Grace felt Laz's hand rubbing the soles of her feet, which would clear away her mental image of the ice cracking beneath him. The sensation of having the soles of her feet stroked made her nose tickle—becoming one of Grace's time-tested signs of true happiness.

So we'll see you Saturday, right?" she asked Kane.

Still holding on to the hope that Laz would soon return, Grace had planned a small gathering at Sky Rink on Saturday, the week before their fifth anniversary, for thirty or so of their friends and family. Nothing fancy, just pizza and a hero from Ralph's.

"I wouldn't miss it," he answered. "Five years. Unbelievable. Tell Laz to call me when he gets in."

"I will."

"Grace?"

"Yes?"

"You know you don't even need to ask. I'll always be there for you." Grace knew there were missing links in the conversation. She had intentionally dropped them like a stitch in needlepoint, to achieve the desired pattern. She knew Kane wouldn't press her further than she was willing to go.

"Actually, I'd love it if you'd make a toast."

"Anything for you, Grace."

Her nose began to tickle as if she were about to sneeze.

4
Innocents Abroad

Grace was not in the right frame of mind to teach her class, but it was Wednesday, the night Chimera Books, a used bookstore in the west eighties, had been generous enough to allow Grace to use their back room to teach her ten-week course on bookbinding. Laz had done a reading there when his book first came out, the room filled beyond capacity, some people sitting on the windowsills or the stairs. Bookbinding was a term Grace used loosely in the course description that she placed in *The Westsider*. She believed that most of the students came for the swirling, marbleized endpapers and especially for the gold leaf, which was as magical as butterfly wings for Grace. She had learned the art of bookbinding from her father, mostly creating blank books, to be given as gifts. Occasionally, someone would bring in a flaking family heirloom to class, which would require more guidance than Grace could provide. In those cases, Milton was called in for a consultation.

The bookbinding course pleased Grace's father to no end, and this in turn pleased her. Laz called it her "little notions thing," which Grace took as sweet rather than demeaning. She knew how much he valued her insights into his own work, not to mention her editorial and proofreading skills, which usually involved her sitting on his lap, with some form of stroking or removal of items of clothing going on while she tried to work. She thought someday she might actually fill one of her little notions books with more than just notions, and maybe Laz would sit next to her while he proofread her words—as soon as she wrote anything and when he came back, of course.

GRACE'S FATHER HAD learned bookbinding from his father but never went into the family business, instead finding his calling in podiatry. There wasn't a single book in her parents' apartment that was not beautifully bound, often in embossed leather, with hand-sewn folios, a tenderly repaired spine, and sometimes even a dust jacket.

Her mother's cookbooks were wiped clean with appropriate solvents and dusted carefully so as not to cause any damage; they were covered in a clear laminate material for protection from the elements or spills. "People keep their cigars under better conditions than their books," Milton often grumbled. "I have some cigars older than you, Gracie, and they're as good as the day I bought them," he'd say as he refilled the humidor with water, even though he had given up smoking when Grace was a freshman in college. Her parents had recently installed a dehumidifier and ionizer to help keep the apartment dust-free. If her father could just control the climate outside, he'd be a happy man.

He was also a stickler for detail and was never satisfied with any job unless he'd done it himself. More than a few house painters had quit after completing only half the job, refusing to return his phone calls, frustrated by his insistence that they repaint a room one too many times because of barely detectable drips or streaks. Grace had always secretly thought her father should have gone into plastic surgery instead of podiatry, but she kept this to herself, realizing that she and her mother would then have been prey to his inexorable desire to preserve and restore.

During the first year that she and Laz dated, Laz had a bookbinding workshop set up for Grace's father in an empty storeroom in the basement of her parents' building. After befriending the super, Laz was even permitted to break through to an adjacent washroom so that Milton wouldn't have to run upstairs to wash his supplies. Her father subsequently spent much of his free time in the basement, emerging from time to time to check on the weather.

"Still snowing out?" he'd ask, surfacing for air or a light snack. Except for going to his office, which was across the street, he might never have ventured out at all. The workshop had been a gesture worthy of a lifetime of appreciation, but Laz thought it was never enough. To him, Milton was the father he'd never known.

The following spring, at Grace and Laz's engagement party with the Sugarmans over Peking duck at Shun Lee, her father gave Laz a present wrapped in brown butcher paper. As Laz opened it, Grace's father had been simply bursting with pride. Inside was Laz's two-volume first edition of Mark Twain's *The Innocents Abroad*—pristinely restored—along with two plane tickets. *For a pleasure trip,* her father had written on a note card. Grace told her parents that they shouldn't have done it, and she'd really meant it, too, because she knew that the value of the book was now quite compromised. She didn't know how her father had even gotten hold of the books.

"Didn't he do a beautiful job?" Grace's mother beamed. "He

even relettered the title in gold with a tiny hammer. And look at the new endpaper. Milton never comes out of that workshop. He's like a little cobbler."

"Blueberry or peach?" Bert asked.

"Bert!" Francine said, slapping him on the shoulder as she leaned over to admire the books.

"Surprised?" Grace's father asked.

Laz turned the books over in his hands, raising his eyebrows and opening his eyes wide in disbelief. Grace expected him to be polite as always, but when he addressed her father and said solemnly, "Mark Twain would have been honored," Grace realized that he was not just being polite, but was truly touched by her father's kindness. The books were displayed behind glass among his other first editions like precious wax flowers.

It was after her and Laz's return from six weeks abroad, loosely following Twain's peripatetic inclinations, that Laz wrote a journal article entitled *The Disintegration of Words,* and Grace's class was first conceived.

THE PAST TWO DAYS had been unusually rainy, and Grace had been vigilant about leaving two wet umbrellas in the vestibule and then removing one of them, to indicate Laz's absence. She also left a pair of Laz's tan-colored Docksiders that she had held under the faucet until they were soaked through and had turned a mucky dark brown. Marisol arrived on Wednesday with a bunch of eucalyptus cuttings arranged with purple asters, which she had brought especially for Laz, who liked the fragrance.

"Feels like a holiday," Marisol announced after she hung up her coat and went into the kitchen to fill a vase with water.

"Good morning, Marisol. Thank you for the flowers."

"My pleasure, Señora Grace." Grace was sitting at the dining room table, which was still rather dimly lit, as she had not remembered to pick up another extension cord.

She had decided after the previous day's mishap that she was better off contacting the custom lipstick company by mail. She wrote the address on an envelope and filled out the appropriate information, such as how many tubes she would like, and settled on three. There was a two-week wait after the company received the lipstick color sample, sometimes longer if it was a difficult match.

As instructed, she made a streak on a sheet of white paper and covered it with Scotch tape. Grace thought better of having them add a flavor, aware of the olfactory power that fragrances had on her. Even essence of vanilla, innocuous as it might sound, could conjure up for Grace a trail of memories that invariably led back to some unwanted locale she had hoped never to revisit. She couldn't go wrong with fragrance-free. Sunscreen seemed a sensible addition, but she decided against adding frost or glossiness. All she wanted was an exact duplication, a seemingly simple enough request. Grace sealed the envelope and got up from the table.

"Marisol, could you give the telephone receiver in the bedroom a wipe? It's a little sticky."

"Certainly, Señora Grace."

But no sooner had Grace uttered the words than she had misgivings. The thought of wiping away the stickiness, Laz's fingerprints along with it, made her feel a disproportionate sense of loss.

That evening, she arrived slightly late at the bookstore with her supplies due to her feeling preoccupied and a little bit on the sluggish side. Her students were already waiting. The bookstore had been decorated with tiny icicle lights around the windowsills as well as with red, purple, and yellow dreidel lanterns that had been strung along the shelves, as Hanukkah was early this year. Grace's family had never celebrated Hanukkah when she was growing up, which she thought nothing of until recently. Her mother had become obsessed with celebrating every Jewish holiday, usually with a roast of some sort and noodle kugel, suitable for every occasion.

"It's traditional," Paulette would insist, even on Passover, when noodles are not permitted. But then Francine Sugarman's honey-glazed pork chops with bread crumbs and Parmesan cheese violated every law of kashrut known to mankind.

The store looked so festive that Grace perked up and began to feel festive herself. She even accepted a glittery holiday crown, which all the salespeople were wearing. As she set up the materials—small-gauge needles, white PVA glue, and a ream of rice paper, she looked up quickly and noticed a young man, probably not yet of legal drinking age, watching her. He was dressed in jeans and a snowboarding sweater—the generic style typical of people in that zone somewhere between college and work. In his hands he held a volume that was clearly in need of repair. He seemed interested in the proceedings but reticent about interrupting.

As she looked at him, he glanced down at the book in his hands and flushed slightly. Grace couldn't help but stare. Everything about him—his eyes, his messy brown hair and delicate eyebrows, his almost beardless complexion, even the way he held himself, half slouching—reminded her so much of Laz it was uncanny, and she found herself drawn to him.

She started off her students with the sewing of the pages, having them first thread their needles with the nearly transparent thread, then she went over to speak to the young man. As she walked toward him, she imagined a few silver hairs sprouting at his temples, as if every step she took were measured in years, not feet, and that by the time she reached him he would be Laz.

"Can I help you?" she asked. She looked more closely at the book in his hand. The spine was cracked and warped, the binding fraying. She gestured toward it. "Are you interested in repairing that book?" He turned the book over and Grace read the title. It was Twain's *Innocents Abroad*. She was thrown by the coincidence.

"I'd like to sign up for the bookbinding course," he began, and Grace heard in his voice a confidence that was belied by the flush in his cheeks. She couldn't help but notice that he was staring at her; then she remembered the crown on her head, and she removed it.

"The next session doesn't begin until January and runs for ten weeks," Grace explained. "You can sign up at the front desk, if you like." She smiled and explained that the course was really an introduction to bookbinding, all the while trying to place his accent, which was vaguely Southern. She discounted her initial reaction as rooted purely in magical thinking.

Her mother had always said she had quite an imagination, though it had never been tested as it was now. He did remind her of Laz, but only in the most superficial ways. And the book he was holding was not in fact a first edition, but rather part of a specially bound collection of literary classics. He thanked her, and Grace figured that the chances of his actually signing up were slight, as he'd probably be back in college by then. She returned to her students, who had sewn their books backward while she was talking to the young man. Her mind was still off on its own peregrinations, not unlike Twain's, but with the added advantage of never having to physically go anywhere.

When Grace returned home that evening, she turned on the computer on the chance that Laz had sent her an e-mail. The icon indicated she had mail, and she felt instantly buoyed. Grace was utterly amazed at the number of letters she'd received since she last logged on. Suddenly, the world made sense to her again. All the letters that Laz had been sending her must have gotten jammed or lost somehow and now were miraculously retrieved. There were at least fifty unread e-mails. However, as she scrolled down, she saw that not one of the e-mail addresses was familiar. Then she saw one from aperfectmatch.com and understood immediately what had happened. In her haste the night before, she must have hit the wrong command and sent, rather than deleted, her meanderings about *Oblomov* and her description of Laz.

Click here to sign up for your one-month free trial membership. We are so sure you'll be satisfied, we have sent you a sampling of responses. Grace was stunned. Here were fifty-some-odd strangers—*odd* being the operative word—who wanted to read aloud to her in some way, shape, or form.

A kind of grotesque curiosity overcame her, and although her first instinct was to delete each and every one of the e-mails, she found herself unable to do so. Oblomov, himself, might have even contemplated leaving the safety of his bedroom, throwing off his dressing gown, and hightailing it out of there. Grace felt a morbid impulse to continue and began to read. The respondents ranged from a lawyer from Montclair, New Jersey, who listened to books on tape while commuting, to a student of Russian literature, to one man who said he liked to watch the Turner Movie Classics station in his pajamas, to a few widowers and even some who Grace suspected were e-mailing from behind prison walls.

She scrolled up and down several times, thinking she must have missed the one from Laz, then signed off. She tried to erase the image of the pajama-clad gentleman from her mind and felt fortunate that she was not single and alone in what seemed a very uninviting abyss.

5
The Magic 8-Ball

Until recently, Grace had been unaware of how simple it was to deceive. Not to *be* deceived—she'd always known that it was easy to let oneself be fooled. That was a personal choice people made. Grace was not gullible. Rather, she chose—and this was a great distinction for her—to have faith. Deception was her new hobby. What she found most disconcerting was how much she liked it.

Just as she was about to leave the house for her anniversary party at Sky Rink, José called up and said there was a UPS deliveryman who needed her signature. A few moments later, Grace opened the door to the deliveryman, who was holding a large carton with the word FRAGILE taped along the sides, and THIS WAY UP on the top. If only everything came with such clear instructions.

"What's this?" Grace asked, knowing that the question didn't even warrant a response. She signed the slip of paper and closed the door. The carton was light and filled with bubble wrap, tissue paper, and Styrofoam peanuts, and it took many minutes of unwrapping until the contents were revealed. Inside the box were six Duro-Lite bulbs, each nestled in an individual gold-colored cardboard sleeve, like a honeycomb. Grace thought her father must have written to the company and they were replacing the defective bulb, which to Grace meant that she no longer had to mourn the bulb's premature demise. She left for the party, thinking that the other bulbs had another twenty good years left in them still. Not to worry, as her father would say.

LAZ WAS AN expert skater, captain of his Wednesday night ice hockey team. Kane was the goalie, but he hadn't played since injuring his wrist four weeks ago. They played at odd times, sometimes from three to five in the morning, practicing on Sundays before dawn when the ice was free. Kane usually brought some Coronas and limes.

The first time Laz took Grace skating, he'd arranged for the ice to be empty, still shining from the Zamboni. She had felt the warmth of the peppermint schnapps radiating through her chest as he stood behind her on the ice and taught her how to shoot a hockey puck.

The temperature was unusually mild for November—almost seventy degrees. Her father mentioned something about a jet stream from the Gulf of Mexico. It was strange weather. Grace was not against the warmth, but she preferred the weather to fit the season and felt out of sorts when it didn't. She liked cool temperatures when it was supposed to be cool, warm ones when it was supposed to be warm. Just as she didn't like hot fudge on her ice cream, or, worse still, whipped cream, which had no discernible temperature at all.

The night's deception was easier than Grace had expected. She showed up as planned at eight, dressed in jeans and an ivory turtleneck and carrying her white figure skates. When Laz didn't arrive, she made a small fuss and hobbled over on her ice skates to the pay phone in a feigned attempt to reach him.

"He must have missed his train," she told Kane. "He spent the day fishing in New Hope and I haven't heard from him. Will you please make sure everyone has fun, in spite of this?"

"My pleasure, Gracie. But he's going to have to come up with a good one this time." Kane kissed her on the forehead, a not unpleasant sensation. "Tell Laz he doesn't deserve you—I'd tell him myself if I ever saw him."

Grace skated across the ice to greet some late arrivals. As she did, she closed her eyes and imagined that Laz was leading her. The feeling was close to elation, but when she opened her eyes, she found herself about to careen right into a woman she'd never seen before. Grace veered off to the side, banging into the plastic railing. The woman was dressed in a short black skirt and stockings, with a red hat on her head, her hair tucked underneath the collar of her fitted black down jacket. Grace looked down at the woman's feet and saw that she was wearing brown hockey skates, identical to Laz's, only smaller. Before Grace had a chance to say she was sorry, the woman darted off, disappearing in the crowd.

Grace had been a skater in her youth, although her mother had insisted she skate only at indoor rinks for fear of thin ice. Grace, herself, was similarly uncomfortable with depths—two dimensions were more preferable to her. Grace learned to skate at an East Side indoor rink that was enclosed in glass like a giant fish tank. It wasn't until Grace was a teenager and had been invited to her best friend's sweet-sixteen party that she even ventured to step onto the ice at Wollman Rink in Central Park.

"There's concrete underneath," she'd told her mother, trying to reassure her.

"You never know, dear," her mother answered. Grace remembered how hard she had tried to think light as she skated along with her girlfriends that day.

Grace was a reasonably good skater still, and as she twirled around on the ice, she was overcome by a feeling of optimism, a feeling she attributed partly to the 3/4-time *Skater's Waltz* and the synthesized winter chill, but mostly to the belief that Laz would soon return.

AROUND TEN THAT evening, a bouquet of two dozen sterling roses, a case of champagne, and a scaled-down replica of Grace and Laz's wedding cake—a chocolate confection embellished with colorful frosting to rival van Gogh's sunflowers—arrived along with apologies "from Laz." Grace had only remembered ordering one dozen roses, but Laz was such a good customer at the florist that they must have thrown in another for good measure. Grace had also struggled over how to word the card—how to make it sincere without effusion. She had finally decided that less was more and had written, *From your loving husband, who will make it up to you when I get home.*

Kane made a toast, which began "In absentia" and ended with "To my best friend, wherever he may be, we're not saving him any cake, and if he doesn't get here soon, I'm taking Gracie. Just kidding, Milt. Love you, Paulette, and you too, Laz." Everyone laughed and clapped. Grace could always count on Kane to fill these social gaps until Laz showed up—better late than never, he'd always say. All the guests remarked on the exquisite flowers, claiming that the cake was too beautiful to eat, but then all except Bert Sugarman proceeded to devour it and to comment about how truly blessed she and Laz were to have each other.

As she looked around at her and Laz's friends and family, Grace was aware that just the pretense of Laz was enough for them to feel they were part of his life. And people wanted to know her, his wife, because by virtue of being near her, they were close to him. But as little as they knew her, they knew Laz even less.

After the party, Kane carried the shopping bags filled with anniversary presents down the elevator and through the parking lot to his car. Most of the presents were useless gifts: an array of tacky bottle openers, which Laz collected from around the world; an electronic drum set with matching headphones; and his-and-her Lladró figurines, from the Sugarmans. It didn't matter that the presents were ludicrous, the more ludicrous the better. Laz would have loved them.

Kane opened the passenger-side door for Grace and put the bags in the back. He got in, buckled his seat belt, and reached under the seat. Grace saw that he was holding a square white box that was wrapped with a gold elastic ribbon diagonally around it.

The box looked so familiar. Grace tried to place where she might have seen it before, then she remembered boxes identical to this one that Laz used to bring home for her from the novelty store on Amsterdam Avenue, each filled with some vestige from her childhood.

"Oh, you shouldn't have," she had exclaimed one time, kissing Laz as she opened a box containing two spinning pups. When she was a child, her father used to enchant her by insisting that the miniature magnetic dogs could move by themselves. Laz had set the pups up on the dining room table and sent the black and white Scotties flying across the glossy surface, making them do figure eights around the salt shakers.

Kane stopped at a light and handed her the box.

"Open it when you get home." Grace looked at Kane and realized that even though he was smiling, his eyes looked far away, sad even. She tried to brush away the feeling that she was in part responsible for his disappointment, that he missed his friend, too, and she was deceiving him. Grace held the box on her lap, and they rode home in almost complete silence until they stopped at a light a block from her building.

"Laz missed a great party. You know he loves you, right, Gracie?"

"Of course, I do."

Upstairs, Grace pulled off the ribbon and lifted the lid from the white box. She unfurled the tissue paper and took out a shiny black globe. A Magic 8-Ball. Kane had written a note: *To Grace and Laz. For when there are no answers.* Grace wondered if Kane knew, but she remembered how he'd looked in the car, and she knew that he couldn't possibly. Then she noticed the carton of Duro-Lites by the front door. She'd forgotten to thank her father.

"Will Laz come home before another bulb burns out?" she asked, closing her eyes. She turned the 8-Ball over and waited for an answer to appear. *Ask again later.* But Grace could not wait. She shook the ball until there were bubbles in the inky blue liquid. Finally she got the answer she was waiting for. *You may rely on it.*

6
It's a Mystery

The day after the anniversary party, Grace awoke with a dull ache in her temples, which she suspected was from the champagne. She'd had a fitful night's sleep. At three in the morning, she had awakened from a dream about Laz. His voice had vibrated in her ears and she had heard the faint tinkle of pocket change. *I hope you liked the flowers, Gracie.* It had seemed so real; she'd even felt the warmth of his breath on the back of her neck as he spoke. In the morning, she found Laz's gold-knot cufflinks on the night table. A nice touch, she congratulated herself, not that she recalled having put them there. Next time she'd go easier on the champagne.

She wasn't looking forward to the Scrabble game that evening. The thought of trying to put two words together, let alone more than two letters, seemed overwhelming. She wanted to float in a tub of warm water—sprinkling in twice the recommended amount of Dead Sea salts so that the water turned a deep sky blue, which had a strongly soporific effect. Her morning cup of mint tea did little to revive her.

She contemplated returning to bed, but then remembered the carton of Duro-Lites that had been delivered the day before and decided to replace the burned-out bulb. If changing the bulb didn't serve to brighten her spirits, then at least it would brighten the room. She stood on the stepladder with a new Duro-Lite in her hand, steadied herself, and screwed the bulb in. It was too bright now, so she tried adjusting the dimmer. After several tries with no noticeable dimming, and a phosphorescent tint to everything she looked at, she decided to call the building's handyman.

Before the handyman arrived, Grace closed the bedroom door and slung Laz's favorite yellow Hermès tie over the doorknob. They had won the tie in a raffle last May at a diabetes ball chaired by Laz's mother. It had a striking pattern, but right now Grace thought its motif looked more like squiggly sperm on lily pads rather than green tomatoes.

She recalled many nights when Laz had come home late—too late, he'd said, to call—not wanting to wake her. But the truth was, he knew she would be up waiting for him. After one of those late nights, Laz would usually sleep till noon. Grace had continued the tradition, asking Marisol to forgo the vacuum so as not to wake him, and even Grace found herself trying to be extra quiet. Sometimes, with the shades drawn and the bed slightly rumpled, she could almost fool even herself.

"YOU HAVE A big problem, Mrs. Brookman," the handyman said as he removed the light plate. She caught herself before she said she knew. He was in his stockinged feet as if he, too, were trying not to disturb Laz, having left his work boots by the door, a detail that Grace found somewhat disagreeable.

Whenever anyone called her Mrs. Brookman, Grace would turn around, half expecting to see Laz's mother in a teal blue leather pants suit, waiting for the driver to take her to Zabar's and announcing to whoever was within earshot how exquisite their octopus salad was. Laz called his mother a dame. Grace didn't call her anything. Just a casual, "Oh, hi," when she called.

"I'm gonna have to take the whole thing out—the wires are crossed," the handyman said, clearly losing his patience. "But I can't do it today." Grace nodded. "I'll be back tomorrow with the right splitter. Whoever put this in did a lousy job."

Grace knew full well who had done it. She remembered how Laz had twisted the red and blue wires together, snipping them with the wire cutter. He'd tested the dimmer, artfully ignoring the few snaps and sparks that shot out from the switch, then lifted her up onto the three-leaf table.

"Keep the lights off until I come back. You could short out the whole line," the handyman said. Grace imagined the entire West Side going dark because of an accidental flip of the light switch. She gave the handyman a ten-dollar bill and closed the door after him.

WITH THANKSGIVING LESS than a week away, Grace decided it was wise to thaw out the cranberries in advance for the relish she was going to make. She found the cranberries in the freezer behind two Ziploc bags of bagels and the container of Francine Sugarman's meatballs. Grace's mother had purchased the cranberries last year, a week after Thanksgiving, when they went on sale. "Only fifty-nine cents," her mother had beamed. As Grace reached for the bag, she saw the frosted glass fishbowl she and Laz had put in there three years ago. Frozen in the ice was a key to his old apartment.

They had argued about his not giving up the apartment, eventually agreeing to put the matter on hold, at least symbolically. They would thaw the key out and deal with it later. Grace had read about this technique in an article about relationships, and it seemed to work—except that they had never thawed the key out or spoken of it again. In the top drawer of Laz's dresser, however, there was a spare key, and Laz still went to his old apartment occasionally to write or listen to his old records.

The fishbowl had once contained a goldfish and a Japanese fighting fish. On one of the previous occasions when Laz had left, Grace neglected to feed the fish or to change the water in the bowl. Every time she passed the bowl, she told herself she would feed them later. By the time Laz returned, the water had become so clouded that Grace couldn't even see the fish, who were by then floating belly-up on the water's surface.

GRACE WAS STILL holding the fishbowl in her hands when the phone rang. Her fingers had frozen to the glass. She ran the bowl under warm water, dried her hands, and put the bowl back in the freezer. The machine picked up. *Hi, Gracie, it's Dad. I didn't send the bulbs.* He paused, sighing deeply. *It's a mystery. Give a call.* Normally, Grace liked her father's expressions, such as *Give a call.* Or *Greetings!* instead of hello. But *It's a mystery* was one she'd never liked.

She had mentioned the bulbs to her mother on the phone last night. Her father had already gone to bed. Now a mystery was at hand, and the family was mobilizing like ants marching to a sugar cube. Mysteries were common in Grace's family. There had been the mystery of the disappearance of the roll of quarters, still unsolved to date.

"I don't know," her father would say. "I guess it's a mystery." And the subject would be dropped until the item was located weeks, maybe months, later in her father's sock drawer, where it had been all along.

And then there was the mystery of the gas-guzzling car, which eventually turned into a conspiracy theory about someone from the garage driving their car. Or the mystery of the Electrolux vacuum, still a sore subject in their family; it was discovered inexplicably years later in the linen closet concealed like a body inside Grace's blue nylon camp sleeping bag. The method was never questioned, or its purpose analyzed. *It's a mystery.* That catchall phrase was used by her parents as liberally as salt for all unexplainable occurrences, the equivalent of *poof* to prestidigitators.

Grace hated mysteries. She wanted an immediate answer to where the roll of quarters could have gone. She would search all over until she was exhausted and nauseated. When the item was still not located, she felt as if some supernatural power was at work. Extension cords could disappear without a trace, and things could happen without warning, like bulbs arriving with no explanation.

LAZ'S ABSENCE AT that night's Scrabble game was one mystery that everyone seemed eager to let slide, for now.

"Laz is where?" Bert asked, swallowing a stuffed grape leaf in one bite.

"Utica," Grace answered. "He's giving a lecture at Hamilton College."

"Utica? Really, there's quite a storm expected for the day after tomorrow," her father interjected. "A nor'easter," he said, as if he were a Long Island fisherman. "Could dump a foot and a half of snow."

"Tell him to pick up some sheets while he's there," her mother said.

"What are you talking about, Paulette?" Milton asked.

"You know—J.P. Stevens. The sheet company."

"He's probably too busy to pick up sheets, dear."

"Well, he might feel like browsing."

"Why didn't you go with him, Gracie?" Francine asked.

Grace's mother nudged Francine and whispered, "You know, Laz says she's becoming agoraphobic."

"Agora-what?" Bert asked.

"I'm not agoraphobic, I'm *acrophobic,*" Grace said, remembering the onset of her fear on a trip across the Continental Divide. "And this was just supposed to be a quick trip."

"Agoraphobia. Is that a fear of sweaters?" Bert asked, flipping through his *O.E.D.*

"Sweaters?" Francine asked.

"You know, like angora," Grace's father joked. "Gracie's afraid of fuzzy sweaters."

"Did you see that movie *Arachnophobia*?" Paulette asked Francine. "I go weak in the knees when I see a daddy longlegs. Gracie hates spiders, too. Right, sweetheart?"

Actually, Grace didn't mind spiders. It was moths that made her uneasy. The way they got into her drawers and ate through her sweaters, leaving tiny holes even when the drawers were closed tight, or the way they found their way into sealed garment bags. Worst of all was when she found a dead moth on the windowsill and how the moth turned to dust when she touched it, as if it had never been quite real at all. She could not tolerate the smell of mothballs, so theoretically Bert was correct—whenever she could avoid it, she did not wear wool.

"Could you just go already?" Bert snapped.

"Whose turn is it anyway?" Grace's mother asked, passing the grape leaves.

GRACE TUNED OUT the bantering and bickering. She thought about the nor'easter. It was still unseasonably warm out. The thought of snow when it was nearly sixty degrees outside seemed utterly improbable. Still, when she returned home, she turned on the Weather Channel. The swirls of clouds and jet streams captivated her.

As she watched, she began to see the dramatic tension and even a narrative drive to the gathering clouds and high-pressure systems—a testament to the underlying forces of nature. She began to see her father's obsession with weather as almost poetic, noble even. There was a dirgelike pattern and rhythm, a mournful tone. Laz might not make it back for the holiday. It was an unusual thing to wish for, but a nor'easter might just be the answer to her Thanksgiving prayers.

7
Woodstock

The snow arrived in huge drifts all along the eastern seaboard, making air travel impossible, causing long delays on Amtrak's service, but somehow bypassing the tristate metropolitan area and reconfirming Grace's faith in the National Weather Service. Laz would no doubt miss the holiday, and everyone, especially Grace, felt the loss.

THE AMARYLLIS HAD begun to bloom. Laz had brought the plant home just before he left—a wooden crate containing three bulbs covered with sphagnum moss.

This morning, Grace noticed a tight red blossom on one stalk. After she had come up from bringing José his coffee, the blossom had begun to open. Grace usually left the tending of all plants to Marisol, who fertilized them, trimmed off dry leaves, and knew exactly how moist to keep the soil. Grace either overwatered or neglected the plants altogether. When Laz gave her the amaryllis, he told her that it would bloom for six weeks (which she now took as some sort of sign), and then would need to be cut at the stem and kept in a cold, dark place for six months. His words resonated, and she wanted to tell the amaryllis that there was no need to rush.

Grace looked out the window, marveling at the sight of families gathering on both sides of the street more than two hours before the start of the Macy's Thanksgiving Day Parade, some carrying stepladders and planks of wood to contrive curbside seats. It was an unspoken assumption that Grace and Laz would host a brunch every Thanksgiving for all their friends and relatives who had small children so they could enjoy the spectacle of the parade without obstruction or exposure to the elements.

The parade was still a wonder for Grace and for Laz, the two of them bundling up each year to watch the balloons being inflated the night before. The year that the remake of *Miracle on 34th Street* was filmed, they had been able to watch the parade over and over as they drank their morning coffee, like a perpetual Thanksgiving.

Grace's family was small, or rather, there were only a handful of relatives she and her immediate family kept in touch with. Grace had been a teenager when she'd finally realized that Francine and Bert weren't her aunt and uncle.

She knew her cousins in a fleeting way; they generally came out of the woodwork just before the holidays. She didn't know all of their names, so when a group of them arrived at nine that morning to watch the parade, Grace just said a general, "Come on in," which she was afraid sounded insincere and flat. She led her guests into the living room, where they assembled themselves on the window seat like sparrows at the boccie court in Central Park.

MARISOL HAD PREPARED the batter for the Dutch Baby the previous day, which she told Grace to bake in a preheated oven for twenty minutes before serving. Grace placed a half stick of butter in the hot pan, watching it sizzle and melt. Then, as per Marisol's instructions, she poured the mixture into the center of the roasting pan. After placing it in the oven, she sat on her knees to watch the batter bubbling and rising along the sides of the pan, something she remembered having done as a child. She still found it utterly amazing that the end product would turn out so perfect—a giant popover, hollow and steaming. And it worked every time.

The doorbell rang, and as Grace stood up she felt disoriented and wondered if the daily routine of putting on an act was catching up with her. When she saw Kane standing in the doorway, holding a white box, she suddenly felt an overwhelming urge to tell him everything.

"Happy Thanksgiving, Grace."

"You, too, Kane," Grace said, taking the box from his hands. "Another Eight-Ball?" she asked, smiling.

"I think one's enough, unless it's not working."

"No, I think it's been quite accurate thus far." Kane unwrapped the knitted scarf from around his neck, and Grace could see his skin was blotchy and red as if he, too, had an aversion to wool. He followed her into the kitchen, where the Dutch Baby was rising nicely, and he opened drawers to look for a pair of scissors. He cut the string from the box and removed one of the almond croissants that Laz was so fond of. He broke it in half, handing a piece to Grace.

"We might as well," Kane prodded her. She accepted, aware that the tightness she was feeling around the waist of her skirt was due in part to her sudden affinity for all the sweet things that Laz liked to eat, which she no longer could resist in his absence. It was also due to her sudden, unexplainable urges for foods such as the quesadilla grandé *with* sour cream she'd ordered the night before, when she'd always been perfectly satisfied with a whole wheat spinach wrap.

The almond croissant was completely unsatisfying and she immediately wanted another.

"Nice Baby, Gracie," Kane commented.

"What baby?" she asked.

"The one in the oven, of course. Is there another one?" Grace felt her cheeks flush, and she laughed nervously, then began to cough from the second croissant she was still chewing. She gave Kane a playful nudge on the shoulder.

"Thank you, it's Laz's favorite," she said finally, after the coughing had subsided and before the hiccups began. Grace always got the hiccups whenever she coughed. According to her mother, Grace did nothing but hiccup in utero, like an embryonic call for help emitted in code. She went to the sink to drink a glass of water from the opposite rim, the only cure for her hiccups, which could sometimes be known to last for an entire day.

The Dutch Baby made a beautiful presentation on the buffet. Since the dining room fixture had still not been rewired, Grace lit candles instead.

"Very Martha Stewart," Kane commented, admiring the outlines of leaves that Grace had stenciled with powdered sugar over the popover. Grace ladled raspberry purée onto everyone's plates except those of the children, who preferred maple syrup, and whose sticky handprints she later found smudged along the windows. Kane took his plate and whispered into Grace's ear as he pointed to a serving dish of a creamy-white mixture.

"And that is?"

"Francine Sugarman's famous artichoke dip, of course—circa 1997, although carbon dating can be inaccurate," she whispered. "And if anyone offers you a round orange ball, don't take it. It's a sweet-potato-and-shrimp dumpling from last New Year's brunch."

"Pity Laz isn't here to enjoy this," Kane said. Grace busied herself rearranging the serving platters, consolidating and shifting food as Kane spoke. "He never missed a Thanksgiving before." Grace found herself literally unable to look at him, and she realized how odd she must appear performing these tasks.

"Grace?"

"Just a second, Kane, I think I left the oven on," she said, and quickly left the room. She found some solitude in the kitchen until she heard a commotion from the living room and came out to see what was happening. The yellow tip of Woodstock's crown, then his beak and eyes were pressed against Grace's window, peering in, his body slamming back and forth in the strong gusts of wind as the balloonists tried to right him. Grace thought the window would surely break. She felt the need to brace herself against the nearest, sturdiest object, which happened to be Bert Sugarman.

"Look, he wants to try some artichoke dip," Kane joked, luckily not within earshot of Francine. Grace let go of Bert and ran to the window to pull down the Roman shades in case the glass shattered, just as Woodstock was pulled back under control to the sound of cheers from the street below.

"Never a dull moment at the Brookmans'," Kane said.

Hoping to beat the holiday traffic, most of the guests left before Santa Claus passed by on his sleigh. Kane was one of the last to go besides Grace's mother and Francine, who were busy packing up the leftovers. Grace handed Kane his coat and scarf at the door and he kissed her on the cheek.

"I'm counting on you for tonight," he said. "We'll just have to do it without the creep this year." Grace had completely forgotten about their post-Thanksgiving tradition of going out and playing drinking games, their way to decompress after an overload of stuffing and family. The thought of Kane alone made her feel awful.

"I wouldn't miss it. We'll have just as much fun without him."

"That's the spirit, Gracie," he said, kissing her on the other cheek. "Nine o'clock. Tap A Keg."

"It's a date," Grace said. As she closed the door behind him, she could hear her mother and Francine talking in the kitchen.

"Half a Dutch Baby. Such a waste!" Francine said.

"It doesn't freeze well," Grace's mother explained. "It gets mealy."

"It's a crime," Francine sighed.

"I told her to do the waffles. You never have a problem reheating waffles."

Grace tidied up the pillows on the window seat and felt a chill from the casement windows. She pressed her palm to the glass. It felt like snow. She didn't need to watch the Weather Channel; she could feel it in her bones.

8
The Butterball

Grace chopped up two cups of walnuts on the butcher block countertop and added them to the cranberry relish. The walnuts gave the mixture a more substantial look, which was necessary because she'd neglected to buy another bag of cranberries. After the holidays, things would be much less hectic, or maybe more so, depending on whether or not Laz was home by then.

She dressed in the tan-colored leather pants Laz's mother had given her, thinking it was only polite since the elder Mrs. Brookman would be joining them for Thanksgiving. Grace had some trouble lacing up the front of the pants, sucking in her breath as she tied a bow. They were a little snug, but it was the first time she'd worn them, and she assumed that they would loosen over the course of the day.

The first time Grace's parents met Nancy Brookman, they had acted as if they were preparing for royalty. Grace's mother had her hair and makeup done by Phaedra at Frédéric Fekkai, instead of by

Renatta at her usual salon down the block, and she bought a new outfit. She even hired Marisol to help serve, tying a starched white apron around Marisol's waist. Grace's father broke out a bottle of cognac from 1917, which was served out of the Baccarat snifters they'd received for opening an account at Apple Bank. Bert affected a strange, quasi-European accent all evening, as if he'd been schooled in Bombay. The only one who had not acted impressed with Nancy Brookman was Francine, who snubbed her all evening.

"I know a girl from the 'Coops' when I see one," she told Grace's mother after Laz's mother left, not realizing that Laz was standing in the doorway behind her.

The Coops was a progressive apartment complex, built in the 1920s, north of Allerton Avenue, where Francine and Bert had met as teenagers. Grace had always wondered about Nancy Brookman's hybrid accent, which switched depending on the situation, going from upper-crust diction to practically street slang, when she spoke to the garage attendants in her building.

"She's not from the Bronx; she's from Newport," Bert corrected Francine.

"And that outfit—a knockoff of a knockoff! Who does she think she is, anyway? The Queen Mother?" Francine continued, sealing a Ziploc bag.

"No," Laz answered, sneaking up from behind and taking a bite of leftover spinach pie. "That job's already been filled."

WHEN GRACE LEFT her apartment building, snow was falling like powdered sugar being sifted over the city. It seemed to defy gravity, flurrying upwards and sideways, and Grace couldn't imagine how it managed to stick to the pavement. The first Valentine's Day she and Laz were together, snow had piled up on her windowsills overnight. Laz had rung her buzzer at six in the morning, running up the stairs while carrying two pairs of skis under his arms. It had been strangely light out; even though it was not yet dawn, the sky glowed pink through the shutters.

"Get dressed. We're going skiing," he said. He was wearing an orange stocking cap with a pom-pom on the end. He looked like a jester.

"You're nuts. It's Sunday—and just barely," she said, turning to go into the kitchen. "Come on—I'll make us breakfast."

"I got you the day off tomorrow. The car's still running," he said. "The mountain awaits us." Grace stopped and threw her arms around him. She had never so much as taken a personal day before.

Grace taught ceramics at a private school in Manhattan. She got immense pleasure from watching her students work, forgetting everything else as they transformed the clay and themselves. Once she and Laz married, she gave up the job without so much as a word of protest after Laz pointed out that it was just glorified babysitting and that she should focus on her own work. But after she resigned, sculpting became less of a priority, somehow. At the time, it hadn't occurred to her to put her job, along with the key, in the frozen fishbowl.

On the drive up to the mountain that Valentine's Day, they talked nonstop, as if they needed to get caught up after decades, and not days, of not seeing each other. Laz told her about one of the two times he'd seen his father since he left, at a diner near his prep school.

"I had a grilled cheese with tomato and a milk shake. I remember he kept taking out his pocket watch to look at it, but it wasn't even wound up. And he didn't offer me a ride back to school," Laz told her, swallowing hard and clearing his throat. "But he gave me his broken watch. He asked me if I had enough change for the bus, and then he put his hands in his pockets as if he was afraid I might ask him for something else. I only saw him once more, at my college graduation, and afterwards he disappeared into the parking lot, without even saying good-bye."

Grace and Laz arrived at Belleayre before it opened and got the first lift tickets of the day. BE MY VALENTINE was printed on the tickets. On the ski lift, Laz told her that he wanted to marry her. His lips warmed her cheek. As Grace's skis alighted on the snow, Laz blazed the trail ahead of her. This pattern had seemed so simple then, desirable even. All she'd had to do was follow.

WHEN SHE ARRIVED at her parents' apartment in the afternoon for Thanksgiving dinner, her mother had already set out a large selection of bowls and platters for Grace to choose from in which to put her contribution to the feast. There were bowls made of leaded crystal, stainless steel, porcelain, wood, even huge melamine ones in neon colors from her mother's modern period. Most of the bowls were actually for Francine Sugarman, who would empty the contents of her plastic containers into the appropriate receptacles, but only after a lengthy discussion of the serving situation—into the middle of which Grace had just entered.

"The asparagus need an oblong platter," Francine complained. "You can't serve asparagus bent like that."

"Francine, I don't think I appreciate your tone," Grace's mother said, grabbing the asparagus as though they were a bunch of weeds and dumping them onto another platter. "There, is that better?" In Paulette's haste, a few of the spears had snapped in half like twigs, still partly frozen from Francine's Sub-Zero. Francine's jaw clenched but she didn't say a word. Bert, still wearing his wool coat and galoshes, walked into the room carrying bakery boxes.

"Here are the Sacher tortes from our trip to Vienna last spring.

You're going to die when you taste them." He put the boxes down on the sideboard and surveyed the proceedings. "Everything looks beautiful, Paulette," he said, dipping his finger into the sweet-potato purée. "Needs a touch more in the microwave, though." And then, as if on cue, he added, "Where ever did you find baby asparagus this time of year?"

Francine and Paulette suddenly burst out laughing and put their arms around each other, admiring the table as if it were a piece of art.

"What?" Bert asked quizzically. "What did I do now?"

GRACE'S FATHER WAS busying himself in his study, as was his habit. He'd invariably appear just in time to perform his appointed tasks, which, for Thanksgiving dinner, involved answering the doorbell when guests arrived, serving drinks, and carving the turkey. He thought it wiser to stay clear of the combat zone until the last possible moment. If Laz were here, he'd have been in the study as well, while Grace's father proudly showed off his latest high-tech gadget, such as the paper shredder, which he used to shred everything from junk mail to newspapers.

Grace's mother and Francine went into the kitchen to check on Francine's sweet-and-sour meatballs. Grace sat down at the kitchen table and began filling the turkey-shaped salt cellars and rolling the linen napkins into the minipumpkin napkin rings. The pilgrim centerpiece she'd made in the fourth grade had only recently been relegated to the hall closet after having adorned the Thanksgiving table for two decades.

"It's times like this I wish I had a second microwave," Grace's mother sighed.

"Did I mention I'm going to Paris in two weeks?" Francine announced.

"Really? On a tour?" Grace's mother took the meatballs from the microwave and poured them into an orange melamine bowl.

"Don't waste the sauce," Francine said, using a plastic spatula to wipe around the inside of the bowl until it was so clean that it looked as if it had just come out of the dishwasher. "Too bad Laz is missing my meatballs again," Francine said. "Grace, should I pack up another container for him?" Grace looked up from the table, thinking about the other containers still in the freezer at home.

"You really don't need to go to any trouble," she answered.

"Don't be silly, it's my pleasure. Just bring back my containers this time." Even if Grace weren't a vegetarian, there was no possible way she could have consumed that many meatballs before the next Scrabble game.

"Why don't you give her the recipe, for goodness' sake?" Grace's mother asked, for what could easily have been the hundredth time. Francine bristled.

"You know *real* cooks don't follow recipes," she responded, with a quick toss of her head. "Anyway, I'm off to Le Cordon Bleu soon," Francine continued. "Two weeks with the world's most renowned chefs—what could be better?"

Bert walked into the kitchen and sat at the table, his coat off, but still wearing his galoshes.

"Those frogs won't be able to improve on these," he said, spearing a meatball with a plastic toothpick. "How much would you pay for these meatballs in a restaurant?" he asked, while making a second attempt at spearing another meatball, which was swiftly intercepted by Francine. "And I'm losing my dancing partner."

"Bert, really, I think you of all people can make some sacrifices for once," Francine said, shooing him away from the table.

"And who will take care of my butterflies?" he asked.

"Oh, right," Francine said, "The lepidopterist. A plastic butterfly garden and he thinks he's Vladimir Nabokov. All they need is a little sugar water. I think you can manage."

"You need a dancing partner, Bert?" Grace's mother asked, shooting Grace a look that made her want to crawl under the table.

"Mom, no, please."

"You can dance? How's two weeks from next Tuesday? It's Mambo Night at Hadassah," Bert said. Then he grumbled, "That is if Laz doesn't mind, although I wouldn't blame him for laying low while the press is swarming. It's been a veritable hotbed of controversy over his book. Everyone is—"

Grace's mother's mouth fell open. "Why, Grace is a fabulous dancer!" she shouted with enthusiasm in an effort to drown out Bert. "She would love to join you at the Hadassah dance."

Grace fumbled with the napkin she was holding. While part of her wanted to engage in the conversation with Bert, she allowed herself to be waltzed away by her mother's well-choreographed intentions. She thought about the dance classes at the Barclay School of Dance she'd taken as a child. Everything from the powdery insides of her white gloves to the squeak of her Mary Janes felt immediate and tangible. She'd won second prize in the dance competition—a disappointment that her mother was never able to let go of—taking home a ballpoint pen that could perform the times tables and division, instead of garnering the silver ballet slipper trophy.

"Yes, Mambo Night at Hadassah," Bert said. "You don't want to miss that."

"I'll have to let you know."

"Fine, but don't wait too long, I might be snapped up by some twinkle-toed chippie while Francine's away."

THE BUTTERBALL TURKEY was taking longer to pop than expected and was causing some concern. Even Grace's father found himself drawn unwittingly into the drama that was ensuing in the kitchen.

"It's been in since eleven. I had it on a timer so it would start while we were over at Gracie's," her mother said.

"Don't get yourself all worked up, Paulette," Grace's father said, stroking her hair with his oven-mitted hand. "I'm sure it just needs a few more minutes. It's very scientific, you know."

"I think we should try to unpop it, in case it's stuck," Francine suggested. "I just have a sense about these things. This would never happen in a microwave."

"I hate turkey," Bert said, peering into the oven. "It's so dry." As he stood up, he caught Francine's eye. "But yours is delicious!"

"Nancy will be here any minute," Paulette said, wiping her hands on an orange-and-yellow checkered dish towel. "And I'm not even dressed."

"Not to worry, dear," her husband reassured her, tying an apron around his waist. "Your turkey is in good hands."

Nancy Brookman walked into the kitchen just as the popper was unstuck with a set of pliers. It shot off like a missile, hitting the ceiling and landing in the dish drain. "I knew it was done," Milton said triumphantly.

"I let myself in," Nancy announced. Grace's father rushed over, wiping his hands on his apron.

"You look wonderful, as always," he said, taking her shorn mink coat.

"Naturally," she answered, removing her sunglasses. She handed him her gloves and her tan-and-white Prada bowling bag, which she'd picked up in Milan the previous summer, months before the waiting lists started forming at the Madison Avenue boutique. Of course, *bowling bag* was a misnomer since it probably contained little more than some tissues and a pair of leather riding gloves. "I understand my good-for-nothing son won't be *gracing* us with his presence—no pun intended," she said, but accentuating the word nonetheless.

"He sends his love," Grace said.

"We got an e-mail from him. He was so sorry to be missing the holiday," her father added.

"You got an e-mail from Laz?" Grace asked.

"From my favorite son-in-law. Just this morning."

"What did he say?"

"He said to save him some leftovers," he answered. Grace felt like running to the computer to see if he'd sent her one, too.

"Just like his father," Laz's mother said. She looked Grace up and down. "I see you're wearing the outfit I bought you. They love me at that thrift shop. I know the good stuff when I see it."

"It's secondhand?" Bert inquired, having spent so many hours waiting for Francine to emerge from the Loehmann's dressing room that he considered himself an authority on women's fashions. He felt Grace's pants. "Like butter."

"I knew Gracie would appreciate that the money went to a worthy cause. Lung cancer or juvenile diabetes, I can't remember which. It doesn't really matter. Just so she feels she's making a contribution."

Grace's father returned from the front hall and began the carving process, sharpening the electric carving knife on a flint stone before determining the exact direction of the grain, as if following a topographical map, and giving out samples as he went along. By the time they sat down, they were already fairly full.

"The stuffing is wonderful, Paulette," Francine said, spooning gravy over her plate.

"Thank you. I used matzoh meal this year instead of bread

crumbs." The stuffing and turkey, along with Grace's cranberry relish, were the only things not from one of Francine's containers.

"Makes all the difference," Francine agreed.

Grace got up from the table to refill the water pitcher.

"Looking a little thick, Grace," Bert said. "Around the middle."

"Bert!" Francine snapped at him. "I knew you shouldn't have had that second Campari. Grace is like a feather! Very willowy."

Grace returned with the pitcher and placed it on the table. The leather pants had not yet stretched out. The two helpings of stuffing she'd had, which were not technically vegetarian, along with a generous serving of sweet potatoes, had not helped the situation. She hadn't had any appetite whatsoever for the soy turkey loaf her mother had prepared for her. She excused herself, saying she needed to check her messages. What she really needed was to lie down. It wasn't so much the stress of having to pretend in front of everyone, it was that just sitting upright was cutting off her circulation.

She walked down the hall to her childhood bedroom and closed the door. Everything in the room—from the green-and-pink checkered curtains and bedspread, to the grassy-green carpet and pink ceiling—could not have been better preserved. On the walls were posters by Peter Max and Degas. Even the pink terry cloth robe on a brass hook by the door was in its proper place, as if Grace had just come home for a snack after junior varsity volleyball practice.

Grace looked at herself in the mirror. She turned sideways, inhaling and holding in her stomach. Bert was right, the pants were not all that flattering. In fact, from the right angle, there was a striking resemblance between herself and the pale underside of her mother's Butterball, trussed and laced and about to burst.

As she was standing before the mirror, she had a flash of Laz wearing the pink terry cloth robe the first time he'd met her parents. Grace and Laz had been walking across the park on their way to the Metropolitan when they were caught in a sudden downpour. Grace had suggested they dry off at her parents' apartment, which was only a few blocks from the museum.

No one was home when they arrived, and Grace and Laz dripped all over the floor by the back door as they toweled off. Grace put everything in the drier and changed into a pair of old hip-hugger jeans with heart pockets on the back and a baseball shirt that were hanging in her closet. She offered Laz the robe to wear while his clothes dried. She suppressed giggles, although he seemed to be completely comfortable, sashaying around, as if he might seduce her.

A few minutes later, they heard sounds from the front hall. Laz quickly retied the robe, Grace tucked in her shirt, and they went out to greet her parents.

"Nice to finally have the pleasure, Laz," her father said, as he shook Laz's hand, seemingly oblivious to the fact that his daughter's new boyfriend was wearing women's clothing. "It's torrential out there."

Grace's mother nudged her in the ribs and whispered, "I like him. We're not going to let this one get away. Nice legs, too," and then went off to make a pot of coffee, which they drank out on the glass-enclosed terrace as they watched the rain.

GRACE SAT DOWN on the bed. It was a white captain's bed with two deep drawers underneath. She hadn't opened the drawers in years. They contained that part of her life that she referred to as pre-Lazarus, but which she really thought of as pre-Grace. Whatever was in the drawers was now obsolete, or beside the point.

Grace unlaced her pants and rested her head on the bolster.

She'd never really liked her room, but as she gazed up at the pink ceiling, snow falling lightly outside, the sounds of plates and silverware being cleared in the dining room, she wished she could stay there forever.

"WHO WANTS SOME Muscato in honor of Laz?" Grace heard her father say as she returned to the dining room table and sat down.

"Would you like a glass?" her father inquired, offering her a fluted glass filled almost to the top.

"None for me, thanks," Grace answered.

"How about an espresso macchiato? Or a latte?" Her father had recently purchased a deluxe cappuccino maker from Zabar's. She shook her head.

"Any word from Laz?" he asked.

"He says he'll be home by midnight."

"Glad to hear it," her father said. "Tell him he was missed."

"Pie?" Grace's mother asked, displaying a pecan pie in front of her as if she were on *Let's Make a Deal.* Grace looked at the caramelized pecans and the dark syrupy center. Normally, she wouldn't have been able to resist. She glanced over at Bert who was spooning pineapple sections and melon balls onto his plate.

"I think I'll pass," she said, trying to take a deep breath. She couldn't wait to get home, check her e-mail, and change into something elastic and comfortable. And then she remembered she'd promised to meet Kane later.

"More for us," her father said. Grace looked at her watch and then at those assembled around the oval table. There was little changed or missing from previous years, except for Laz, and his absence seemed hardly to make a difference.

"I have to get going. I'm meeting Kane in an hour," Grace said after dessert was finished. Grace's mother ran to the kitchen and returned with a shopping bag filled with leftovers. Laz's mother put out her cigarette in the remains of her pie and turned to Grace.

"I'll give you a ride. The car's downstairs." Grace's mother gave Francine Sugarman a knowing look.

Even if Grace had stayed another five hours, it still wouldn't have been enough. She stood up from the table and gave her mother a quick kiss on the cheek.

"Call us when you get home to let us know you're okay," her father said.

"And don't forget about Mambo Night," Bert reminded her. "Polish up your dancing shoes."

"I won't," she said, looking at her father. "I mean, I will, Dad."

On the ride home Grace stared out the window, running her finger over the fogged-up window in squiggles. Laz's mother lit a cigarette and turned to Grace. "Word has it Kane's in a relationship," she said, taking a long drag of her cigarette. "Someone named Greg."

Grace found it astonishing how casually Laz's mother was relaying this information, as if she were telling her instead that Kane had just changed his address and not his sexual orientation.

"Greg?" Grace asked, incredulous. Kane had dated many women off and on over the course of the years, and the idea that Kane was gay was unimaginable to Grace.

"His mother told me at the conservancy luncheon last week. It sounds serious. Heaven knows how long he's been keeping this one from us," she said, blowing a stream of smoke out of her lips.

"He didn't mention anything to me," Grace said.

"Well, he's not exactly forthcoming in matters of the heart, you know."

Grace's mind raced, shuffling information around in her head and trying to piece it back together. The yellow roses and the lack of amorousness on Kane's part toward her when they were dating now made more sense, but nothing else did. Grace wondered whether Laz knew. Certainly he would have said something to her if he did. The ride through the park was suddenly making her feel queasy. The car stopped in front of Grace's building. As she was getting out, Laz's mother put her hand to her mouth and blew Grace a kiss.

"Kisses, darling. And I'm counting on you for the origami tomorrow at ten. I'll meet you at our usual spot. By the way, we need you to head up the solicitations for the auction at the Historical Society again. I told them you'd love to do it."

Laz's mother was a docent at the American Museum of Natural History, along with her other charitable duties for which she was always volunteering Grace. She had once overheard Laz's mother tell someone, "Oh, Grace will do it—she has nothing else to do." Every Christmas, Grace helped with the origami tree ornaments because she was, as Laz's mother said, *so good with paper*. Between her bookbinding class and cochairing of various committees, Grace "did nothing" for more than twenty-five hours a week.

"Much love to Lazarus," she said, tilting her head. Grace touched her hand to her mouth and watched as the darkened window closed. It might be quite some time before Laz's mother realized her son was gone.

Upstairs, as she put the container of meatballs next to the other containers of meatballs in the freezer, Grace wished she'd had that glass of Muscato after all.

9
Bottoms Up

The carpet was barely visible through the clothes that Grace had flung around the bedroom, and it looked as if a giant pressure cooker of blouses and pants and skirts had exploded on the plum-colored Einstein Moomjy. The leather pants were inside out on the floor, having put up quite a fight. Grace wondered what the statute of limitations was on returning things to a thrift shop.

She had given Marisol the following day off, which she now sorely regretted. The room was in a state of complete disarray. She'd quickly checked to see if there was an e-mail from Laz when she got home, but her mailbox was empty. Now nothing she put on felt comfortable. Even her standby outfits, like the clingy Vivian Tam midnight-blue netted dress that came to her ankles and always made her feel just right, looked as if it had hung too long on the wrong hanger, misshapen and suffering from low self-esteem because it had just awakened in a stranger's bed and didn't have the cab fare home.

Kane didn't care about how she looked, she knew that, and Tap A Keg was a dark, smoky bar even in daylight, but Grace was in a frenzy. She gathered the clothes, stuffed them into her walk-in closet, and closed the louvered doors. Then she opened Laz's closet and pulled out a pair of his most worn jeans along with a pale gray cashmere sweater.

The closet was getting dusty. Where the dust was coming from, Grace had no idea, but it was beginning to settle on the tops of the wooden hangers, the collars of Laz's fine wool suits, and his shoes. Laz was asthmatic and could not tolerate dust, an affliction that exempted him from serving jury duty, but which didn't stop him from smoking, often a pack or two a day. Sometimes Grace found herself taking labored, shallow breaths in synchrony with his.

The jeans felt good as she pulled them over her hips and fastened the button fly. They were too large for her, soft and frayed from many washings—in some places almost white.

As soon as Grace buttoned the sweater, she felt immediately calm. She could smell Laz faintly through the knitted cashmere. She brushed her hair and pulled it back, fastening it with a clip. Then grabbing Laz's favorite leather jacket, she left to meet Kane, amazed that she was nearly on time—a sign that everything was still somewhat under control. The mess in the closet was now quite out of sight, soon out of mind. Now if only she could just shove Kane back into the closet as well.

Kane was sitting at the bar, impeccably dressed as always in flat-front pants and a navy roll-neck sweater, chatting amiably with the bartender. He smiled when he saw her and put his arms around her.

"Grace," Kane said, looking her up and down, "is it Halloween? Or are you just in drag as Laz? I don't miss him *that* much." Grace felt Kane's clean-shaven cheek against hers as he kissed her, inhaling his citrusy smell and all the while gauging her reaction to him now that she had the new information about him. Her reaction was the same as it had been when they'd been quasi-dating. Nice, but no jolt. She thought she must have a sense about these things.

"The usual?" he asked. Grace nodded. Kane reached into his pocket and took out a folded cocktail napkin that he'd picked up in Nantucket at a bar where he swore they made the best cosmopolitans. On it was written exact instructions for making the drink. Kane placed the napkin on the bar for Pete, the bartender. Grace watched as the bartender went through each step ceremoniously: wetting the rim of two chilled cocktail glasses with cranberry juice, then dipping them in granulated sugar; adding ice in the shaker; pouring in the measured amounts of vodka, cranberry juice, lime, and a dash of Cointreau; then shaking it twice and straining it into the martini glasses.

The bartender placed two napkins on the bar and, with a great flourish, presented them with two sparkling-pink cocktails. He looked like a kid, wearing baggy jeans and a backwards baseball cap, the antithesis of how neatly Kane was dressed. Kane's hair was cut considerably shorter than at the anniversary party, brushed forward. It looked so shiny and soft, almost velvety, and Grace had an urge to pet him.

"What'll it be this year?" he asked. "Quarters? Whales, Tales, Prince of Wales? Flotsam and Jetsam?" Grace glanced around the room. The jukebox was playing "Monkey in Your Soul." Laz loved Steely Dan. Grace took a deep breath before answering. She did not want to get drunk. She'd play a couple of rounds and then make some excuse for going home early.

"How about I've Never?" she suggested, mostly because it was a game that involved sips, not shots.

"A lightweight, huh? We'll just see about that," Kane said, motioning to the bartender that they were ready for their second round, even though they hadn't touched their first drinks. The bartender agreed to join them, although he preferred club soda. The three of them clinked glasses and Grace did her best to drink down to the bottom. The bartender waited for the verdict. "Perfection," Kane announced. It was their ritual to start all drinking games after one preliminary drink; Grace could nurse the next one if she played well. Laz was known to be ruthless in these games, but Kane would take it easy on her. If she got drunk, she wasn't sure whether she'd be able to do the same for him.

"I'll start," Kane offered, rubbing his chin with his hand. He was pretending to be deep in thought as if the weight of the next few words he uttered could alter the universe as they knew it. "I know," he started slowly. "I've never snuck into a movie."

Grace lifted her glass to her mouth and took a sip, as did the bartender. Kane feigned a state of shock, leaving his glass on the cocktail napkin.

"Why, Gracie, I'd never have guessed," he teased, finally picking up his glass.

Usually, Grace was the only one left semisober after this game, because she was not the type to overstep bounds. Now nothing was out of bounds.

"You got lucky that time," Grace admitted. She thought for a moment, and then said, "I've never read someone else's mail." Kane laughed.

"This game's rigged," he said, taking a large gulp. "Do you have surveillance equipment set up at my mailbox?"

"I just had a feeling you were the type." Kane looked from Grace to the bartender who left his glass untouched as did Grace.

"It was only a Christmas card, for goodness' sake. And it was an accident," he muttered, pretending to be hurt. It was the bartender's turn.

"I've never told someone I loved them to get them to sleep with me," he said with a grin.

"Now we're getting somewhere." Kane seemed amused, taking another sip of his cosmopolitan. "But I thought I meant it at the time," he added.

Grace left her glass on the bar, shooting Kane what she hoped was her most penetrating and punishing glare, but the more she looked at him, the more disconcerted she began to feel. Images darted through her mind like dragonflies. It wasn't the idea of Kane with a man that was hard to accept, but rather the realization that the person to her right, whom she considered one of her closest friends, and who was now tossing mixed nuts into his mouth willy-nilly, had kept something this vital from her. He seemed like a virtual stranger. That fact was indeed harder for Grace to swallow than the triple sec. In one smooth motion, she lifted her glass, closed her eyes, and drank the contents down. Kane's jaw dropped open.

"Tell me it isn't so," he said.

"Maybe I was just thirsty," she said coyly.

"That's not in the rules," he protested. Grace felt the radiating heat in her chest from the alcohol, penetrating her mother's usually impervious stuffing.

"Okay, so I'm guilty," she said. Any images of Kane and Greg that Grace may have been entertaining in her mind were now significantly dulled. Pete refilled their glasses and topped his off as well. Grace hadn't bothered to keep tabs on whether the bartender—*Pete,* as he had to continually remind her, as she seemed to show a preference for calling him Larry—had drunk on that last round. It was of little concern to Grace. In fact, surprisingly, little at that moment went beyond the *Oh, well. Who cares?* level of importance.

They played a couple of more rounds with statements ranging from "I've never slept with my eye doctor," to "I've never cheated on anyone," and even, "I've never had sex in a department store," until Grace's glass was almost empty for the third time. She hadn't counted on the bartender being such a wild card. It was her turn again. She couldn't think of anything. Her hair clip had come undone, her hair falling across her face in the style of an Afghan hound. She tossed her head and realized for the first time that she was getting drunk. Her head bobbed like a marionette whose puppeteer was absent, and it took a while for the room to reorient itself.

Grace began to feel warm and took off Laz's jacket, hanging it on the back of the bar stool next to her. The sight of the jacket casually flung over the back of the stool in just the insouciant manner that Laz would have done gave Grace a start. She half-believed, for an instant, that he had just gone to get gumballs from the dispenser in the men's room.

"She's plastered," she heard Pete comment, the words muffled as if she had cotton in her ears. Grace stared at him through her hair.

"Yup, she's looped, all right," Kane agreed.

"Why are you talking about me in the third person?" Grace interjected. "Didn't anyone ever tell you that's very rude?" Pete and Kane exchanged glances. "Anyway," Grace continued, "she's not plastered, she's just a little bit tipsy, and she needs to go to the ladies' room."

"I stand corrected." Kane brushed her hair from her eyes, tucking the ends behind her ears. "Gracie, maybe it's time to . . ." Grace looked up at him, and for some reason, reached toward him and ran her hand over his head.

"It's so bristly," she said, making an attempt at standing up. She placed her hand on Kane's shoulder to steady herself. His sweater was so soft, the feel of his shoulder so solid and warm under her hand—she wanted to keep her hand there. "I don't think I've ever felt this material before."

Kane looked at her. "Grace, it's wool."

"Oh," she said, trying to laugh it off. Then she stood up, holding onto the bar. Her legs felt rubbery, like one of those Flatsy dolls she had so coveted as a child. She felt unable to make the journey to the bathroom right then, so she eased herself back onto the stool. She hadn't thought about Flatsies in years, and had a sudden recollection of a cold, gray day when she'd gone to visit a friend for an afternoon. Grace had once asked her mother for a Flatsy when they were in a toy store, but was steered to the paper dolls, which, in her mother's view, had more instructional value. While her friend was out of the room, Grace hid her friend's Flatsy underneath her Danskin shirt. It was a simple task because Flatsies, true to their name, were soft vinyl dolls that looked three-dimensional from the front but which practically disappeared when turned to the side.

She remembered looking at the Flatsy when she got home. The experience of sheer pleasure quickly turned to resentment because she felt too guilty to ever actually play with it but confession was out of the question. She kept the doll in her pocket for days, until her mother washed her pants without checking the pockets—the heat of the drier melting the Flatsy into an indistinguishable marshmallow mass.

As she held on to the bar stool, in a cosmopolitan cloud, Grace wondered which side of herself she'd chosen to neglect. Even under the influence, the question should have been rhetorical.

"I NEED CHANGE for the gumball machine," Grace announced, reaching into the pocket of Laz's jacket and rummaging around. She had decided not to bring a purse, placing her keys and some money in the zippered pocket. She felt the empty pocket, then searched the other one, pulling out a roll of Life Savers and a pocket organizer that Laz had been missing. She remembered how frantically he'd been looking for it.

"Here, Grace," Kane offered, handing her two quarters. Grace shook her head.

"No. My keys," she said. "They're not here."

"Are you sure you didn't put them in the pockets of your cardigan sweater? I mean, Laz's cardigan," Kane asked. Grace was beginning to feel as if she had cotton not just in her ears, but in her mouth as well. She nodded her head.

"Don't worry, Grace. We'll find them," Kane said, in a voice that was immediately soothing in a tell-me-another-story sort of way. She hadn't remembered his voice ever having had that effect on her before, and she felt as if she were in a trance. Kane removed the jacket from the stool and shook it. Grace heard a jingling sound and let out a huge sigh of relief, her shoulders relaxing. "There's a hole in the lining, Grace," Kane said. "Here are your keys and your lipstick as well. Oh, and ticket stubs to *Don Giovanni,*" he added, which he tossed into the ashtray on the bar.

Grace reached for the lipstick and then drew back her hand. The tube was unfamiliar. Though she tried to disguise her reaction, Kane obviously caught the look of confusion on her face.

"Well, I assume it's not Laz's," he teased. "It's not his shade." Grace shot him another look.

"No, it's mine," she said quickly, taking the keys and the lipstick from him. "I just didn't remember it was there. Thanks."

She looked at the silver tube, turning it over in her hands. She must have bought the lipstick and not remembered it. Or it might be one of the free samples her mother was always giving her. The more she looked at it, the more it did begin to look familiar, until she was certain that it was indeed hers. She examined the tickets. Laz didn't care for opera, and Grace was positive they'd never gone.

She looked at the date: October 14, seven-thirty P.M. She picked up the keys and the ticket stubs and put them into her back pocket. When she got home, she'd check her calendar. He'd probably mentioned it and she'd just forgotten. Francine was always claiming that blueberries could improve short-term memory. Grace made a mental note to buy some in the morning, although they were out of season and probably imported from somewhere like Chile, costing five dollars for a half pint, but she knew she'd likely forget anyway.

Grace stood up, this time more slowly, took the quarters and the lipstick, and excused herself, walking to the ladies' room with a hypersteady gait as if she had just been asked to walk a straight white line.

THE BATHROOMS WERE demarcated with etchings: the men's room with a picture of two buoys, for *boys*; the ladies' room with gulls. There was a urinal in the ladies' room for reasons unknown, always a startling sight for Grace. She recalled one post-Thanksgiving night with Kane and Laz when she had mistakenly gone into the men's room, and seeing no noticeable difference, she had been totally unaware of her error until she exited to a standing ovation from the amused patrons, Laz leading the cheer with, "Gracie thinks she's one of the buoys."

Tap A Keg had gone all out for the holiday season with garlands and pumpkin lights hung from the stalls. And in the urinal was a chocolate turkey with a huge red plaid ribbon around its neck.

The bathroom lighting was harsh. After washing her hands and splashing her face with cool water, Grace applied a light layer of lipstick. Turning the lipstick over to read the name, she tried to focus. She squinted, not allowing for the possibility that the reason she couldn't remember this tube had nothing to do with her lack of phytochemicals. Grace was just able to make out the name—Opal. Of course. How could she have forgotten?

The wind whistled at the window, disturbing a light layer of soot on the sill. The chocolate turkey peered back at her from its ice-packed perch with its off-center candy corn eyes and vacant expression, as if to say stranger things than this had happened here. She had the impulse to flush the urinal in an attempt to send the turkey to an icy end.

She took one of the quarters that Kane had given her and inserted it in the gumball machine, cranking the handle. She waited until she heard the sound of the gumball hitting the metal hatch, then opened it. Pink. She inserted another quarter into the slot—pink again. Just what she had hoped for.

Grace sat back down at the bar and held the gumballs in the air as if she'd just landed a sea bass in the gulls' room. After not getting the reaction she had wanted, she put them in the pocket of Laz's jacket. She insisted on playing a few more rounds of the drinking game, to Kane's—and even Pete's—protests.

"I've got one," Grace announced, after finishing her cosmopolitan. "But I'd like a glass of white wine for this round, please." Pete placed a glass of wine in front of her, staring at her in what Grace found to be a strange sort of way, and left the bottle uncorked. "I've never . . ." Grace began, feeling fortified with an uncommon sense of abandon. Kane was her friend, or so she thought, and she couldn't help but be angry at him for keeping something of such magnitude from her.

"I've never kept something from my best friend in order to protect him," she said, finally. It hadn't come out quite the way Grace had imagined it would, having just formulated the words perfectly in her head only seconds before, but it was adequate.

Kane's expression turned grave and he hung his head slightly as he picked up his glass and chugged. Grace felt awful. She hadn't intended for him to take this badly. She put her hand on his shoulder to let him know that all was forgiven, and then she realized that she was guilty as well. She reached for the open wine bottle, stuck one of the red-and-white striped straws from Pete's station into the neck, and began to drink. As soon as Kane realized what she was doing, he turned to her, took the bottle from her hands, and touched her lightly on the chin.

"Come on, Grace, let's get you home."

"Not yet, I'm just getting started," she said, as if possessed. Grace reached out for the bottle once more. Kane took her wrist before she could grab the wine. She braced herself up on both elbows and turned to face him. "I've never had a same-sex affair," she said, finally. Kane was silent. The words bounced back and forth like Ping-Pong balls in her head, but it wasn't entirely clear to her whether they'd actually left her lips. The only thing she knew for certain was that her head was now in Kane's lap.

"Time to go, Grace," Kane said, gently lifting her like a rag doll to an almost-standing position. "And we have to get up for the tree tomorrow." Grace thought it sweet the way Kane used the collective pronoun. It was just like him to remember that she had the origami in the morning.

On the way out the door, Grace slipped and lost her balance, landing smack on the sidewalk, leaving a well-defined imprint of her bottom in the snow. Kane helped her up, brushed her off, and hailed a taxi. They didn't speak at all on the ride home. The cold air cleared her head. It was after midnight. She turned to him, wishing she could take back everything she'd said at the bar. For the first time all evening, no words would come.

"You don't need to say anything," Kane said finally. And Grace knew everything would be all right.

• • •

Upstairs, she removed the ticket stubs from her purse and placed them in the silver tulip bowl on the dining room table. Out of habit, she turned on the light switch and watched with horror as another Duro-Lite burned out with a hiss.

As she reached her hand out to turn it off, she caught sight of her reflection in the antique mirror on the far wall. What she saw shocked her. Her lips were the color of orange sherbet—a caricature. No wonder Pete and Kane had looked at her so strangely when she had come out of the ladies' room. She looked again at the bottom of the tube. Her vision was clear now, the lettering even clearer: Coral. Fish lips. Never in her life would she have even contemplated buying that shade. It was worse than wearing frosted blue eye shadow. She wiped furiously at her mouth and lay down on the couch in the living room, as images of chocolate turkeys with orange lips drinking out of bottles with straws spun in her head.

10
The Ugly Duckling

The next morning, just before dawn, Grace found herself covered with the afghan that her grandmother had crocheted for her when she was in college. Grandma Dolly had stopped crocheting long ago, once arthritis had settled into the joints in her fingers. Now she was in a nursing home, after having suffered her third stroke. Grace rarely used the afghan anymore for fear that the whole thing would unravel in an unfathomable acrylic heap. Her toes were poking through one of the many holes that had recently begun to grow larger, no longer able to be held at bay with a strategically placed knot here or there.

The afghan was a diamond-patterned, multicolored throw made out of that type of variegated yarn that switches from one vibrant rainbow shade to the next without the knitter's having to deal with the nuisance of continually ending off. It was machine washable, although Grace's mother had sewn in a label that read DRY CLEAN ONLY. What puzzled Grace now was how she had managed to get it out of the hall closet and cover herself without a flicker of recollection—or falling over a single piece of furniture.

As she pulled her foot out of the hole in the violet-fuchsia section, and watched a loose thread disappear like a sand crab, Grace was slightly tempted to use clear packing tape to mend it. Once, in a rush to get to Laz's book party, she'd used Krazy Glue to adhere a button on a silk skirt. It had seemed sensible at the time and had actually held quite well during the party until Laz's editor came up to her and asked, "So, what do *you* do?" Just as she was about to answer, the button on her skirt popped off. Laz was by her side like a shot, grabbing her by the small of her back, a ploy to hold up her quickly descending skirt.

"We keep each other together," he said. Then he turned to Grace. "Please try to keep your skirt on," he whispered.

She had slept in Laz's clothes, and as she lay still, gazing at the smooth white ceiling, she was overcome by a sense of peace, as if she had merely dreamt the last few weeks and that Laz was actually just out picking up some scones for breakfast. She could have sworn she smelled coffee. As she began to grow more fully conscious, the reality—along with the events at the bar with Kane—came flooding into her mind, replacing the peace and calm with a dull thumping in her temples. She had definitely overindulged. She wanted to call Kane and reprimand him for neglecting to inform her that her lips had been the color of clementines.

She got up slowly and managed a slow wobble into the kitchen to put the kettle on and to start the coffee for José. For herself, she selected an Earl Grey tea bag. As she opened the paper sleeve, the tea bag tore open. The tea leaves spilled out over the countertop and tiled floor in a mess, only made worse by the application of a damp sponge. The only thing these leaves portended was a difficult morning. She opened another tea bag, thankful that it was still dark out. Even so, the thought of putting on sunglasses crossed her mind. She poured the coffee for José into the cardboard cup, added two spoons of sugar, a splash of hazelnut creamer, and pressed the lid on tightly.

The lobby was deserted when she got downstairs. A stack of newspapers on the floor was the only sign that it would soon be daylight. Grace was surprised to see a cup of coffee already on the concierge desk, along with a cinnamon cruller wrapped loosely in wax paper. Farther down the hall, she saw a man with a bicycle coming out of the bike room, dressed in plain black warm-up pants and a hooded windbreaker. He adjusted the seat of his bicycle and headed toward the door, not looking up. As he passed Grace, she noticed he was wearing shiny black dress shoes with white socks, an anomaly she chalked up to New York quirkiness. She put the cup of coffee she had made next to the other one on José's desk, grabbed her newspaper from the pile, and went back upstairs.

GRACE SAT DOWN at the dining room table and took a sip of her now tepid tea from her butterfly mug. The white tips of the *Don Giovanni* ticket stubs poked out from the silver bowl and bore an uncanny resemblance to moth wings. She tried to ignore the tickets for the time being. There was obviously some reasonable explanation, which she was convinced she would discover later when she put her mind to it or deployed her imagination in another dimension.

Suddenly she heard the sound of Laz's voice, as if in a dream, and she realized that the answering machine had clicked on without her knowing the phone had rung, and she was listening to Laz's greeting: *You have reached the Brookmans. We'll call you back later when we get a chance.* Grace ran over to the phone. She must have turned the ringer off, although, again, with no recollection of having done so. However, in the state she had been in the previous night, nothing was inconceivable.

Before she could get to the phone, the person had already hung up. Grace convinced herself that it could only have been Laz. She waited for him to call back. When the phone rang again a few seconds later, she realized that her breathing had been tight and uneven until then. She let the phone ring a second time, savoring the sensation of calm, like the first smell of lilacs, then she picked up the receiver.

"Grace. Thank God." It was her father. "We called you all night and you didn't answer. We're calling from our new cell phone. It's the latest model. Our old one's like a dinosaur. How's the reception?" Grace's parents had been the first of their friends to get a cell phone, but it was of little use as it was usually not charged up, left at home, or locked in the glove compartment by accident.

"Fine," she answered. "Loud and clear. Are you out?"

"No, we're home, just testing it out. We were starting to get worried about you. Laz get in all right?"

Grace looked at the message light. Seventeen calls. She'd forgotten to call her father to tell him she had gotten home safely. It was a ritual they still practiced, however outdated.

Laz had thought it quaint at first, but eventually found it a burden, especially during the many fruitless searches for telephones during their travels through uncharted territory. Sometimes, the search itself became the whole purpose of the trip, like their unending hunt through the Judaean hills until, out of nowhere, a telephone booth had appeared as if it were an apparition on the outskirts of a Bedouin village, right beside a Coke machine. Grace's father had given her a beeper three years ago for her thirtieth birthday, which Laz claimed must have accidentally dropped out of her unclasped backpack into the surf off Grenada during a boating expedition. His explanation put to rest Milton's suspicions of foul play.

"Dad, I'm sorry. I was rushing to meet Kane and I completely forgot. I didn't mean to worry you." Grace could hear a muffled sniffle on the other end and then a high-pitched blow, which signaled her mother's presence. "Tell Mom I'll call her later," she said.

"I will," her father assured her. "And Laz really must come over and see the new Canon copier. Fifty pages a minute—unbelievable. And it collates. He's going to get a real kick out of it."

"Milton, leave the lovebirds alone," Grace's mother blurted out. "I'm sure they have plenty to catch up on."

"Mom's right, sorry. Enjoy. Bundle up—the temperature's dropping. And don't be a stranger."

SHE HUNG UP the phone, suddenly remembering the e-mail her parents had received from Laz the night before. She ran to the computer and turned it on. Laz surely had e-mailed her, too. She clicked on the incoming mailbox. There were several from Laz's editor, one from Miltonfyi@yahoo.com, and a confirmation from the lipstick company. Then she saw one with an unfamiliar address: *Oblomov*. It was Laz! She was delighted beyond belief. Not only had Laz contacted her, but his reference hearkened back to one of their sweetest times. She opened the mail and read: *I think we should meet. How's tomorrow at eight at the Pink Tea Cup? Bring Oblomov.* It was unsigned. Tomorrow? She looked at the date. It had been sent before midnight. *Tomorrow* meant tonight.

The tone was so formal and unlike Laz. Was this Laz, or someone else? And who did she really want to show up? Maybe a stranger would be better. At least for now, while she sorted through things. In place of the marriage, there would be mystery men—the one she had married, and perhaps new ones as well.

Grace stared at the clock on the computer. Nearly an hour had passed. She must have been daydreaming, although about what she had no clue. She could go blank, almost at will, turning off her mind when convenient, such as when she had been on hold with the UPS tracker, trying to trace the mysterious bulbs to no avail, or when she was stuck in traffic or just feeling overwhelmed. Kane was one of the few people who ever inquired about her "absences."

"Grace, you can't just go blank," Kane once said, while they watched the Super Bowl at his apartment.

"Yes I can," she countered.

"You have to be thinking about something. Or trying not to. Like what are you thinking about this instant?"

"I don't know. Nothing, really."

"Come on, don't play dumb."

"I'm not playing dumb—I'm trying to tune you out."

"Okay, but I'm going to ask you every two seconds from now on."

"Just watch the game and leave me alone," Grace said.

Kane leaned over and kissed her on the cheek. "Never," he said. "That, you can count on."

GRACE TURNED OFF the computer. She dressed and then went into the bathroom to wash up. As she was putting away her toothbrush, she saw a flash of gold on the top shelf of the medicine cabinet. Reflexively, she adjusted the can of shaving cream until the ring was concealed to her satisfaction, and closed the cabinet door. Then, hoping to clear her mind, she turned on the water full blast and washed her face a little more vigorously than usual, but the doubts she had about her rendezvous at the Pink Tea Cup still remained. After drying her face, she brushed her hair and pulled it back. Before leaving the bathroom, she checked the medicine cabinet once more to make certain that Laz's ring was still out of sight.

Grace's bedside clock read nine-thirty. If she didn't hurry, she was going to be late for Laz's mother. She ran to get her coat. As soon as she opened the closet door, she knew that something was missing. Where Laz's leather jacket had hung last night was now a bare wooden hanger. One by one, she pushed aside each coat in the closet, even working her way through to the second rod in the back, until she realized that she must have left it at the bar. Tap A Keg probably didn't open until noon. She decided to go there after the museum, pledging never to have another cosmopolitan—ever—as she slipped her arms into the silk-lined sleeves of her pink cashmere princess coat, a present from Laz for her last birthday.

The Museum of Natural History was busy, even at this early hour, filling up quickly with families and tourists. Grace stood under the prow of the Native American canoe in the Great Hall and waited nearly twenty minutes for Laz's mother to arrive. As she came around the bend, Nancy was easy to spot in her winter whites, as she liked to call them, and her thigh-high lizard-skin boots. She gestured as if annoyed that Grace was late, instead of it being the other way around.

"Come on, darling, everything's already set up. No time to waste." Nancy led her through the hall of reptiles, past the Eskimo exhibit, and into a room that featured a life-size diorama of Native Americans presenting maple syrup to the pilgrims. The origami tree loomed in the background, unadorned. There were two long tables set up with stacks of colored origami paper and metal folding chairs for the volunteers.

Grace sat down and got right to work. It was easier than making chitchat with Laz's mother, especially after the little talk they'd had about Kane the night before. She preferred to concentrate on folding paper. She soon became so immersed that she practically forgot that Laz wasn't actually at home, catching up on sleep or watching football, as she'd told her mother-in-law.

Grace's hands had formed these creases so many times before, the paper seemed to fold itself. She created the usual array of animals, lanterns, and stars, choosing the iridescent sheets over the plain colors. Unfortunately, Laz's mother was not so well occupied, and as was her usual propensity, she began to gossip with anyone at the table who would listen. Grace was in the middle of making a silver swan when Nancy began talking about Kane.

"He's quite a catch for anyone, you know. We'll see if this one can hold his interest."

"He seems happy," Grace said absently as she folded the swan's tail into the center. She was about to create the wings when Laz's mother turned to her.

"You look a little puffy. Anything you're keeping from me? You better not be planning on making me a grandmother. Are you?" Grace looked at Laz's mother. She was about to speak when she realized that she had inadvertently decapitated the swan she was working on, its tiny silver head crushed between her thumb and forefinger.

"We can't be wasteful, Grace," Laz's mother chided. "Try to concentrate." Grace left the headless swan on the table and reached automatically for another piece of paper. She began folding but felt all thumbs.

She thought back to the last time she'd gotten her period. It was still second nature for her to mark the date in her calendar. It couldn't have been more than four weeks ago, four and a half at the most, but she couldn't be certain of it. Her cycles used to be so regular.

The possibility that she might be pregnant was not an unpleasant prospect. She allowed herself to entertain the idea, imagining the scene that night at the Pink Tea Cup. Laz would be seated at a small table by the window. She'd enter, her skin aglow. When he saw her, he'd get up and approach her, and without needing to utter a word, he would take her in his arms, hold his fingers to his lips, and tell her that this is what he'd wanted all along.

Grace replayed this scene in her head several times, fine-tuning the lighting, the wardrobe, and the dialogue, until the realization that the scene would go nothing like that in reality crashed down on her. Her IUD was purportedly ninety-nine percent fail-safe, and, moreover, Laz had never wanted to have children.

After making a few final folds, Grace regarded her swan for the first time. She had chosen a piece of paper in an unfortunate mustard brown. The wings were lopsided, the body on the squat side; it was not at all graceful. The head looked twice the normal size and was turned down slightly as if ashamed of itself. Grace was about to throw it in the garbage, trying to be as inconspicuous as possible, when a little girl who'd been sitting at the far end of the table ran over and snatched the swan out of Grace's hand.

"Look, Mom," she cried, as she held the mutant swan in the air for her mother and all present to see, "it's the Ugly Duckling."

SEVENTEEN SWANS LATER, Grace exited the museum and stood on the street in front of a pretzel vendor. It was just after eleven. She'd have to wait outside Tap A Keg for nearly an hour. A puff of steam emerged from an open manhole, obscuring the pretzel man's cart from sight as she started for home.

The metal stands were still up from yesterday's parade, laced with puckered frost. Her father was right; the temperature was dropping. Each breath made her head pound as if she'd eaten ice cream too quickly. Grace had always found something appealing and romantic about the bleachers, each year eventually convincing

Laz to sit on the top tier the night before the parade with a thermos of hot chocolate. But today, as she passed a couple nuzzled together on the bleachers with their hands in each others' pockets, she felt a vast sense of deprivation and wished the city would hurry up and dismantle them.

José greeted her as she walked into the lobby. "Señor Brookman always knows when I'm doing a double. He leaves two cups of coffee for me. And he knows I can't resist sweets. My wife says I'm getting fat. Tell him no more crullers, though, I need to go on a diet." Grace assured him she would.

When she got upstairs, she found a stack of mail waiting in the vestibule and picked it up, glancing quickly at the letter on top of the pile as she reached for her key. She had to read it twice. *To Our Single Friend.* Her initial reaction was that it had been delivered to her by mistake. She was not single. But as she looked again, she saw her name on the envelope. Instinctively, she touched her wedding band. Her head began to pound again. The more she tried to reconcile all the opposing thoughts, the more she felt as if she were losing hold. She wished she could go blank—blanker than blank—but instead her head was spinning with no off switch.

11
Past Due

Inside, Grace ripped the envelope addressed to *Our Single Friend* in half and was about to throw it in the garbage when she caught sight of the familiar logo and began to read: "We at A Perfect Match are thrilled to have you as a member. . . ."

This was too much. Grace felt invaded as if by some obsessive, matchmaking stalker.

She'd received other odd solicitations before in the mail and over the phone—even an offer to buy flavored condoms from an Orthodox prochoice organization, whose products came in flavors such as Cookies and Cream, Baked Apple, and Peppermint Stick. They were all glatt kosher and no-cal, just in case. Grace had politely declined, explaining that she and her husband had already purchased a supply elsewhere. She tried to suppress the image of Laz in a minty-flavored, candy-striped prophylactic, the whole episode arousing in Grace a queasy feeling akin to the time she stumbled upon a caterpillar-shaped vibrator on Francine Sugarman's nightstand.

THE BILLS WERE beginning to accumulate like leaves from some deciduous tree. Laz had always taken care of the finances, writing checks in between mouthfuls of Marisol's sweet concoctions. Grace straightened the pile, dismayed that there was still nothing from the lipstick company, and noticed one envelope with the words *Past Due* in red letters on it. Just as she was about to open it, the intercom rang. She stuffed the bill underneath the latest issue of *New York* magazine and pressed the button.

"Mr. Kane to see you," José announced.

She had no recollection of having made plans with Kane the night before, although he could be known to drop by on a whim. Moments later, the doorbell rang. When Grace opened the door, there stood Kane, looking like he'd just tumbled out of bed, which wasn't an unlikely scenario considering he owned his own software company and could work from home.

"Feeling a little bedraggled this morning, Kane?"

"Just a little. Thanks for your concern. I had an early doctor's appointment." Grace noticed that Kane's arm was no longer in a sling, but supported by an air cast made of clear plastic.

"Your arm's better?" she inquired in a sympathetic tone, but the concern was more about how to get Laz out of his Wednesday night hockey games now that Kane would soon be playing again. Maybe Laz's elbow would flare up with an acute case of tendinitis.

"The doctor says a few more weeks."

"By the way, I'm never going out with you again," she said. "Thanks for telling me my lips were bright orange."

"You looked quite fetching, actually." Kane checked his watch. "My car's double-parked. Tell Laz he better hurry if he wants to get back before dark."

Grace was at a loss. Back from where? She stared at him, trying to find some thread in the conversation that would help her understand what he was referring to. Did he and Laz have a game that Grace had forgotten about?

"Don't tell me Laz isn't up yet. I thought you said he was all excited about going upstate for the tree." Then she remembered talking with Kane at the bar about the tree.

She found herself faltering. She fumbled with the buttons on her cardigan sweater. "Laz had to go to this . . . thing," she said, finally.

"He had to go to a *thing?*" Kane asked. "What kind of thing?"

"He tried get out of it. Really. But he just couldn't," she said, trying to sound firm but appropriately apologetic.

"If I didn't know Laz better, I'd take it personally."

"It's not that, Kane, really. He just couldn't get out of this . . ." Grace paused, trying to find the right word.

"I know—that *thing,*" he said, looking down at his hiking boots. Grace noticed that they were brand new. He looked like a small boy dressed up for the first day of camp.

"I'm sorry." Grace hoped Kane didn't think that Laz had bailed out because of the Greg situation. Kane picked up *Time Out* and began flipping through the magazine distractedly. Grace looked at his unshaven face and his hair, which was somehow disheveled despite its short length. It was out of character for him to be even the least bit unkempt, but in a strange way, it made him look more masculine. She shook the thought from her mind. Laz's mother *could* be wrong. After all, Kane wouldn't keep something like this from her.

"Well, I'm up for it, if you are," he said stoically. "Why let him ruin a perfectly glorious day?" He put down the magazine. Grace thought about the tickets and the bills, about her seemingly not-forthcoming period and the jacket at Tap A Keg, and with the precision of a bug zapper on an August night, she decimated these thoughts from her consciousness. The thing she wanted most of all right then was to not think, so she agreed to go. And depending on how things went at the Pink Tea Cup, a tree would serve as either a nice homecoming or a comforting consolation prize.

"I'll just be a minute," she said as she left the room to put on a pair of old boots and to locate Laz's sheepskin gloves. When she returned, Kane was on the phone, speaking quietly.

"Around six, I think. Depending on traffic." He paused. "I know," he said, in a tone unfamiliar to Grace, "I wish you could come, too." Grace noticed a folded piece of paper on the front table that looked like it had been torn out of a magazine, and she opened it. It was part of the classifieds. On one side was the weekly horoscope and on the other side a section from the personal ads.

Grace read: *Men Seeking Men*. It was one thing for Kane to be dating someone named Greg, quite another for him to be browsing the personals! Was he looking to cheat on Greg? She'd always known him to be faithful, and this possible indiscretion upset her more than anything. When she heard Kane hang up the telephone, she folded the page quickly and pretended to be busy sorting through the mail when he walked in.

"Ready?" he asked.

"As ready as I'll ever be," she answered, trying to appear casual, but her voice was noticeably higher in pitch. "How long a trip is it again?"

"If you don't want to go—" he started.

"No, I do. I just need to be back. Laz and I have plans later. It takes about an hour, right?"

"Closer to two, but you guys always fall asleep, so it must seem shorter. It's like driving with two lumps."

"Laz doesn't always fall asleep."

"I beg to differ." Grace thought back to the ride home that first year, and the feeling of Laz rubbing her feet.

"Well, maybe he just rests," she said. She handed Kane the folded piece of paper. "Is this yours?"

"I hope you don't mind. I tore it out of one of your magazines. Just some stuff I'm interested in." Grace found his tone uncharacteristically flippant. So now they were swingers, no less! She looked at him, trying to pick up any traces of his having been found out. He seemed as regular as ever.

"Not at all," she said. "I certainly have no need for it."

THE DRIVE UP the Taconic was more scenic than Grace had remembered. She and Kane chatted as usual, the only difference was Grace's painful self-consciousness about her choice of topics.

"Where are you going with Laz tonight?" Kane inquired.

"Il Duomo," she answered. Grace had slipped up. She didn't know why she hadn't just told him she was meeting Laz at the Pink Tea Cup.

"Il Duomo?" Kane asked. "Isn't that the place Laz calls the Old-Age Home?"

Grace remembered one meal there with her parents. Laz, after scanning the room, which was filled to capacity with white-haired gentlemen and their "blond," coifed companions, had asked the waiter if he recommended the gnocchi.

"It's not one of our *zippier* dishes," the waiter replied, suggesting instead the spinach ravioli and the shrimp diavolo, both of which turned out to be bland, saltless, and utterly flavorless, leaving the blood pressure and cholesterol levels of Il Duomo's patrons uncompromised. Grace's father had salted his dish as if he were salting the city streets after an ice storm. After that, *zippier* turned into one of Laz and Grace's standard expressions.

"This is another Il Duomo," Grace covered.

"Maybe we—I mean I, could join you."

"We?" Grace asked. She couldn't help herself. "Kane, I know about Greg." A look of complete surprise came across Kane's face.

"You do?"

"Laz's mother told me yesterday at Thanksgiving." Grace tried to keep her tone light. She fiddled with the latch on the glove compartment.

He turned to her as if having figured out something vitally important. "Oh, that explains why you were acting so weird last night."

"What are you talking about? I wasn't acting weird. I'm fine with it. I just wish you had told me yourself."

"It's all so new, Grace. I'm just sort of taking it all in. But we couldn't be happier. I can't wait for you guys to meet." Grace was not overly pleased to be included under the heading *guys*. Kane began talking animatedly, as if relieved to finally be able to speak freely. "You're going to love each other," he assured her. "You're so alike."

"Really?" Just then, the glove compartment flew open and a stack of dog-eared AAA guides and a tire-pressure gauge tumbled onto Grace's lap. She attempted to push them back in, but no matter how hard she tried, the door wouldn't stay shut.

"And we understand each other so well," he continued. Grace suppressed the urge to say, *I can imagine,* taking this time to rearrange the travel guides. She slipped one unusually thick guidebook into the side pocket on the door, and with a firm shove, managed to shut the door.

"I'm happy for you," Grace said. Then, more quietly, "Laz will be, too."

"You haven't mentioned it to him?"

"I thought he'd like to hear it from you," she answered. She kept one foot planted firmly on the glove compartment door, eyeing it warily just in case it flew open again, like some unpredictable, menacing jack-in-the-box.

"I'd be glad to, if I ever get ahold of him," he said, sighing.

Kane got off the highway and turned onto a two-lane back road. They saw a sign that indicated the way to the Christmas tree farm, and proceeded up the gravel driveway. Grace was glad she'd worn boots, as the snow was starting to melt and get slushy. She followed Kane down a dirt road, slipping her hands into Laz's gloves.

As she walked behind Kane into the thickening woods, Grace was reminded of being knee-deep in snow in Central Park with Chloe. They couldn't have been more than ten at the time and had been sledding all morning. Grace had followed Chloe, pulling her sled reluctantly behind her in search of a hill that Chloe insisted was just beyond the bend. They circled around what looked like the same circuitous, snow-covered paths until they were clearly lost. Grace became panicked but, to her own amazement and relief, she somehow found the way back before Chloe's mother realized they were missing. Grace now suddenly noticed that she'd taken the lead once more—Kane behind her, walking in her deep footprints.

"How tall?" Kane asked, inspecting the branches of a moss-green Scotch pine. It was about a foot taller than Laz. Grace told him it was perfect. Kane was wearing a gray Woolrich jacket, sturdy boots, and striped hat. *Nature boy,* Laz liked to call him when he was in the wilderness. Even in the outskirts of New Jersey, he metamorphosed into a sort of well-heeled version of a scout leader, always prepared. Kane took out his Swiss army knife and sliced off a strip of bark.

"Is it fresh?" Grace asked.

"Grace, it's still growing. I just wanted to see if it was well hydrated." Kane motioned to a young guy leaning against a red pickup truck, apparently the universal signal that they'd chosen a tree and were ready to chop it down. Kane did the honors, as always, air cast notwithstanding, wielding the saw with the same unswerving focus that Grace's father used on the turkey with the carving knife.

After wrapping the tree in green plastic netting, Kane and the young guy managed to fit the tree crosswise in the Jeep, one end in the front seat and the trunk sticking out the rear window, leaving Grace to sit in the back. Kane gave her a plaid wool blanket to help her keep warm. Surrounded by branches and covered with the blanket, Grace felt as if she were in a fragrant nest. Kane pointed out sites along the way, offering bits of information in his tour-guide voice, like, "That's Twain's house—it's shaped like a hexagon," or, "Don't Pass Me By—the best banana cream pie in a hundred-mile radius."

They passed a lake on the left side. The surface was coated with frost, making it look frozen. With the unseasonably warm weather, though, it couldn't be more than just a superficial layer of ice.

It was almost dusk—that gray, undelineated time of day that Grace's father referred to as *accident time,* the time, he claimed, when overtired children had to be rushed to the emergency room for stitches, although Grace had never so much as skinned a knee. If Milton was driving at this time of day, he would pull into a roadside diner and wait for night to fall. It was usually only a twenty-minute stop, just long enough for a hot brisket sandwich with horseradish and a chocolate shake, which he consumed in religious silence.

Grace was about to suggest that she and Kane stop for a bite to eat—she was suddenly ravenous, when all day she hadn't had much of an appetite—but she wanted to leave enough time to get Laz's jacket from the bar. She thought about what she had to eat in the house—some leftover soy turkey loaf, pureed sweet potatoes, bagels, blinis, and enough frozen containers of Francine's meatballs to reach to Grace's fourth-floor window.

The fragrant smell of pine made Grace drowsy. She removed her boots and stretched her feet out over the divider in the front. Something about being driven home made her feel like a child. Kane was a good friend. She knew he always would be. Nothing had changed between them.

Grace felt herself drifting off, and in the last remaining minutes of twilight, she thought she felt Laz's hand on her foot. When she woke up, it was dark and her nose was tickling.

"Can we make a quick stop at Tap A Keg?" Grace asked, as Kane drove down Riverside Drive.

"Why? Are you up for a couple of rounds?"

"Hardly," she said. "I think I left Laz's jacket there last night. I can't find it anywhere." Kane looked at her in the rear-view mirror, his eyebrows raised.

"Well, you definitely didn't leave it at Tap A Keg. You had it on when we left."

"Are you sure?"

"I distinctly remember zipping you up outside," he said. "Right after your unfortunate fall."

Grace wrestled with this new piece of information. "Well, I'd like to check anyway," she said.

"Suit yourself."

Kane waited outside with the Christmas tree while Grace ran inside the bar. It was smoky, as usual, even though no one seemed to be smoking. The specials board listed Alaskan oysters and venison burgers, two dishes she would be suspicious of even in a four-star restaurant. Grace was relieved to see that the same bartender was behind the bar and that he recognized her.

"*I've never . . .*" he began, trying to contain his amusement, "had an affair with a bartender."

"Very funny," she said with a perfunctory smile.

"I guess that means no, huh?"

Grace scanned the room, pretending to ignore his last comment. "I think I left my husband's jacket here last night."

"Your husband's jacket?"

"Yes," she answered.

"I didn't find anything," Pete said, folding his arms across his chest. "But I'll ask the day guy when I see him tomorrow."

"I'd really appreciate that," Grace said, reaching into her bag for a pen. She wrote her telephone number on a cocktail napkin and asked him to call her if he found the jacket. Then she started for the door.

"Wait, I have something for you," he said, holding out a closed hand. Grace watched as he opened his hand to reveal two pink gumballs.

"How did you know?" she asked, taking the two gumballs from him.

"Just a hunch," he said. The gumballs had stained his hands pink, which he wiped on his white half-apron. Grace smiled and walked to the door.

"Don't be a stranger," he called after her. Grace was struck by the familiarity of the phrase. It was one her father used, and like most of his expressions, she was not used to hearing them in common parlance, at least not by anyone even remotely close to her age, and it engendered in her a feeling of kinship between herself and the bartender.

"I won't," she assured him.

KANE HAD TAKEN his time setting up the tree, puttering with the stand and turning the tree to get just the right angle. Now he was lying on the floor, adding a spoon of sugar to the water in the base, which he said was to help the tree stay hydrated, but which Grace took as a ploy to prolong his stay. She couldn't blame him —

he was probably hoping Laz would come home—but it was beginning to get on Grace's nerves.

"I'm meeting Laz in twenty minutes," she blurted out, finally. He stood up and wiped his hands on his jeans.

"I guess I better be shoving off. Unless you've changed your mind and you want to join us."

"Let's do it another time. Laz said he'd like to make it an early night. Say hi to Greg, though," she said, as she watched him get into the elevator.

Grace plopped down on the sectional couch in the living room and looked at the tree. Any other year she would have made mulled cider, and she and Laz would have been halfway finished with the decorations by now. Laz liked to throw the tinsel all over the room, creating an icicle wonderland. Even weeks after the tree had been taken down, the vacuum cleaner having inhaled more than its fair share of tinsel, Grace would find strands of it clinging to her clothing and hair.

She got up to change her clothes. As she walked out of the room, she became fixated with the indentation she'd made in the couch. Her body had left a noticeable depression in the down-filled cushion, which seemed somehow deeper than usual.

Grace looked at the calendar, turning it back to October. There was a pumpkin sticker on October 31. She tried to find the date of her last period, but no days were circled. None in September, either. Ever since fifth-grade sex education, she'd been religious about keeping track of her period. She remembered the way that the nurse had fastened a pink-stained sanitary napkin onto a stuffed Snoopy, emphasizing the need to keep strict records of their still-latent reproductive cycles. Grace took the message to heart, but the demonstration also had the effect of anthropomorphizing her stuffed animals in a way she had never imagined.

She flipped through the calendar once more. And then she remembered that she had started using Laz's date book in the fall to avoid scheduling conflicts. She went to his desk and turned the pages back. Opposite a picture of Monet's *Water Lilies*, there was a red circle on the fourteenth of October, making her period approximately two weeks late, but still well within her "usual" range. Coincidentally, that was the same date as the ticket stubs that had been in the pocket of Laz's jacket. Underneath the date, written in Laz's scrawl, Grace read: *Championship Game. Seven o'clock.*

The details came back to her with such precision that it was uncanny. Laz had wanted to cancel his plans that night because she hadn't been feeling well, but Grace had insisted he go. Before he left, he brought her a hot water bottle for the cramps and a cup of chamomile tea. He had been so solicitous, even calling her around ten to tell her the game had gone into overtime. When he came home that night, he set the trophy on the bedside table and covered her with the afghan.

"You missed a great game, Gracie," he'd said, stroking her hair. "I thought about you all night."

Any feelings of doubt about that night flew out of her head. The memory was warm in her mind. Grace got the ticket stubs from the silver bowl. Laz had wanted to stay home, she reminded herself over and over again—as she tore the tickets into tiny pieces and watched as they fluttered into the garbage can.

12
The Pink Tea Cup

The Pink Tea Cup was crowded when Grace arrived holding a tattered copy of *Oblomov*. Several sheets of yellow paper were tucked between the pages. Laz sometimes marked his spot in a book with a torn tissue or movie stub, never dog-earing the page, something Grace's father also abhorred. One Christmas, Grace had given Laz a silver bookmark adorned with a biblical scene that had yet to be identified, which he'd never used. It was still in the top drawer of his dresser, along with the gold pocket watch from his father and the key to his old apartment. Before she left the house, Grace had taken the key as casually as she might an old umbrella, just in case, and had put it in her purse—either a lucky charm or her last resort.

A loose approximation of a line had begun to form by the door, and the windows were fogged up, making it difficult to see in. She made her way to the front and down the steps. Once inside, she saw that all the tables were occupied. A tall young woman wearing black jeans and a camisole approached her.

"Can I help you?" she asked.

"I'm meeting my husband," Grace answered. The hostess nodded and walked away.

"That's a bit presumptuous, don't you think?" a voice said. She spun around to find a man with flyaway hair and a big toothy smile.

"Excuse me?" Grace said, moving slightly to the side. The man was uncomfortably close and smelled faintly of rubber cement. She had her answer. She knew full well that this man in front of her was one of the lunatics from A Perfect Match, but she made the choice to keep up the charade.

"I mean we've barely met," he said, chortling. He was dressed in a red turtleneck sweater and chinos, very unexceptional, except for his highly polished black wing tips. Underneath his cuffed pants, Grace saw a flash of white socks.

"I'm expecting someone," she lied, glancing toward the door.

"I know," he responded, giving Grace what he must have thought was a knowing look. She wasn't certain, but she thought she may have even detected a wink. She looked at her watch and tried to appear occupied, hoping he would move on. She was about to turn her back to him when he made a gesture with his hands like a magician and presented her with a single long-stemmed rose.

"Please," she said, trying her best to sound firm, but found herself feeling surprisingly touched. "I told you I'm meeting someone," she said again, this time more softly. Grace noticed he was holding a copy of *Oblomov*. The man hung his head and shuffled his feet.

"I understand. It happens all the time," he said as he backed away. "I just thought—since we had so much in common."

"I'm sorry," she started to say, looking down. But before she could continue, he was gone, leaving the book and the rose on a nearby table. She picked up his copy of *Oblomov* along with the rose and then left.

SHE STOOD OUTSIDE the door to Laz's old apartment quietly, as if waiting for an invitation, holding the key in her hand. The door had been sanded so many times that it looked like driftwood, the fine carved woodwork nearly washed away. Voices could be heard echoing down the wide hallway, and the sound of footsteps overhead was a distant aria. All sensation began to drain out of Grace, her breath sucked away. She mistook the rumble of the elevator for her racing heartbeat; the reactions of her body, for feelings. She was the trespasser here, all the while holding the key, but unable to enter what was once a home, but which was now a forbidden place.

Outside, gargoyles loomed above to protect the inhabitants from evil spirits. But what if those spirits had already slipped through, let in by the gatekeepers? She swayed a bit. She had come this far, but found she could go no farther. All she could do was stand at the threshold. She turned to go, dropping the long-stemmed rose and the key to the floor.

THE CHRISTMAS TREE looked ghostly in the dark living room without the adornment of lights or ornaments. It had only been two hours since Kane had left, but the apartment seemed completely abandoned.

She turned on the sconces above the mantelpiece as well as the table lamps, but it made little difference. Even the color of the walls seemed to drain the room of light.

The fiasco at the Pink Tea Cup had left her feeling dejected, though it hadn't been entirely her fault. Stuck between the pages of the man's copy of *Oblomov* she found a business card: Adrian

Dubrovsky—Private Investigator. On the same page, a passage was marked with a yellow highlighter: *Life is poetry, if people don't distort it.* In the margins, scrawled throughout the book, were notes written in ink in an unfamiliar language, which Grace took to be Russian.

Laz would have found the incongruity of this situation amusing, but for Grace, the evening's occurrences coupled with her feeling that she'd just been stood up by Laz left her with an emptiness she was unable to shake. Thankfully, Marisol would be in on Monday to string the lights and make the apartment hum again, but at the moment, it was as if Grace were in a black hole, deeper even than the utility closet.

She went into the kitchen, aware that all she had eaten since the morning were some stale sourdough pretzels that Kane had in his car and the two gumballs. She felt herself drawn to the utility closet, where she took out the picture from Halloween. Removing it from its frame, she studied it, trying to decipher Laz's body language. She couldn't tell if his arm was actually around Chloe, or just behind her.

Without thinking, Grace tore the photograph into small, centimeter-size pieces, which she regretted immediately. She sat down on the floor to try to fit the pieces back together, but no matter how she configured them, there was no repair.

Finally, she swept the torn pieces of the photograph into her hand, placing them in a plastic bag for safekeeping.

LAZ'S GLASSES LAY on the bedside table, as if he had just removed them to wash up for dinner. Grace lifted them from the nightstand and, holding them by the rims, inspected them in the light. She was careful not to disturb the traces of his smudged fingerprints, so as not to tamper with the "evidence."

She put them on. She didn't need glasses, and Laz's prescription was strong, but as her eyes strained to decipher the blurry images before her, Grace imagined what he might have seen if he'd been there. She looked in the mirror. Her features were undelineated. Laz might have walked right by her if he saw what she was seeing now. She tried to reach out to pick up a glass of water she had brought in, but with no depth perception found herself grasping at air. She closed her eyes, resting the tiny muscles and nerves that create sight. Suddenly, she remembered something that had occurred the day before with unnerving clarity. A headline she had seen in a newspaper at the corner newsstand flashed before her: BOSNIAN PRISON STORY UNCOVERED. She'd walked by quickly.

Her head was now swimming—the words appearing in her mind more like fragmented pixels than symbols. She opened her eyes and removed the glasses, her vision taking a while to readjust to normal. Then she placed the glasses back on the nightstand.

Grace spotted the Magic 8-Ball on the floor underneath the desk, back in its white box. She hadn't consulted it since the night of the anniversary party, having filed it away as a cute but useless item. Now, for some reason, she felt herself drawn to it. She picked it up as if holding something precious, gave it a good shake, and asked in a half whisper, "Am I pregnant?" The answer appeared: *Ask again later.* Very sound advice, she thought, although *later* was open to interpretation.

THE NEXT MORNING, Grace decided to tackle the bills. She had begun to avoid the dining room, which seemed uninviting without the Duro-Lites, and now the living room was haunted by the sight of the unadorned, seven-foot Scotch pine that resembled a Trappist monk. When Grace was alone at night, the only rooms in which she didn't feel like she was floundering were the bedroom and kitchen. She wondered if, after a while, the apartment, like her marriage, would begin to shrink from atrophy.

She went to the hall closet and looked for the Rolling Stones CD *Beggar's Banquet,* which Laz always played while he did the bills. Background music was a must for him no matter what was in front of him, and now Grace, too, thought that this was the only way bills were done. The CDs were neatly lined up and alphabetized on the shelf, but the one Grace was looking for was nowhere to be found. She even searched the piano bench, before deciding to choose a record from her old album collection.

After Grace met Laz, he had eventually replaced most of her records with CDs. Those albums that remained were stored in a carton on the floor of the closet. She opened the box and saw her soundtrack to *Fiddler on the Roof* and *My Fair Lady,* along with her Bangles and Carly Simon albums, none of which suited her mood. She settled for the Pretenders, *Learning to Crawl,* wiping the cover with her sleeve. It was an album that Chloe had given to her in college. She'd forgotten she still had it.

Chloe had written on the album cover: *To your New Wave. Don't go back to being a pretender.* Grace and Chloe had shared a dorm room during the fall of their junior year, while Chloe's roommate was on exchange in France. It was the one semester that Grace lived on campus, and it was now a distant memory for her. That semester, she and Chloe, wearing thrift-store clothes, studied until eleven each night and then went out to readings, parties, or to hear music in obscure basement clubs. Grace switched her major from Classics to Fine Arts and spent most of her time in the art studio sculpting.

When Grace returned to her parents' apartment at the end of the semester, her mother took one look at her hands, which were dry and cracked from working with clay, and said, "Get your coat!

We're going for a paraffin manicure." Grace's hands were dipped into a vat of hot wax and wrapped in Saran Wrap. After the wax hardened, it was peeled off, revealing Grace's smooth, exfoliated hands.

"Are you getting married?" someone next to her asked, as her nails were drying.

Grace hesitated. She didn't even have a boyfriend at the time. Her mother answered for her. "Yes, she is," she said. "We just don't know when."

THE LID TO THE record player was covered with dust, and Grace's fingers made long streaks across the smoky gray plastic. She had the distinct feeling of being watched, though she knew she was all alone. She put the record on the turntable, switched it on, closed the lid, and went into the kitchen.

The stack of bills seemed to have expanded like an accordion, the roll of stamps unfurling in front of Grace on the table. This may have been the first time she had ever done bills. When she lived alone, her father had set up a system so that all her bills were paid electronically. She'd never even balanced a checkbook. She was an accountant's nightmare. Not that she didn't keep records—she kept everything—she just didn't know where.

She shuffled the envelopes. Then she remembered about the bill underneath the *New York* magazine and ran to get it. She'd received letters with the words *Urgent* or *Past Due* on them before, but they were usually form letters from her congressman or credit card applications. Once, she accidentally tore up an envelope, thinking it was junk mail, only to discover that it had contained tickets to game six of the World Series. She was shocked to see that the letter under the magazine was an actual notice of eviction unless payment was received within two business days.

At first she assumed it was in reference to the mortgage payments on their co-op, but then when she read further, she saw that it was for back rent on Laz's old apartment. The letter was dated the day before Thanksgiving. She wrote out a check for it and decided it would be better to deliver it by hand as soon as possible. Grace could never fully understand why Laz needed to hold on to the apartment. She would have relinquished any part of her past if he'd asked her to.

She thought about the key frozen in the fishbowl. She tried to focus on the remaining bills, but the numbers swirled like confetti in her head. Finally, she got up from the table and walked over to the refrigerator.

As she opened the freezer door, her vision fogged from the burst of cold air. Behind the ever-increasing stacks of containers of meatballs and the box of frozen blinis from her father's sixtieth birthday Beluga Bash two years ago, she located the fishbowl. She removed it, holding it with both hands and gazing into its depths as if it were a crystal ball. She knew what Laz would say if he were to walk in on this scene: "Why spoil things?"

The ice had a bluish cast, completely unmarred by cracks. Grace thought about the lake at Kane's house. Each winter, the lake was covered by a dark layer of ice, forbidding and unfathomably deep; but in the summer, the water was so clear that the bottom looked magnified. She remembered how she and Laz had once sneaked out to skinny dip while Kane was making breakfast. As she held on to Laz's shoulders, gliding across the lake on his back, it was as if she were skimming air, not water. Grace always found it unimaginable during the winter that it was the same body of water that had seemed so inviting only months before.

The frozen key was just a faint glimmer within the sphere of ice. The bowl held approximately one gallon of water. She remembered the clerk in the pet store explaining the ratio of water to fish: for every inch of water, you could have one fish. He hadn't mentioned any such limit on keys or other unresolved marital issues.

Grace guessed that the ice could take several days to thaw. She considered putting the bowl in the microwave, but then remembered Francine's admonition about sparks from metal. And the glass might crack if she submerged it in a bath of warm water. She placed the bowl on the kitchen counter, moving it away from any heat that might be emanating from the counter's fluorescent light fixture, and wiped her hands on a dish towel. If she had a thermostat, she probably would have considered turning it down. She wasn't even certain if she was prepared to use the key this time. If the ice wasn't melted by Monday, she would have her answer. Time would tell, she decided, glad that the decision was out of her hands.

GRACE SPENT THE rest of the afternoon coordinating Laz's "comings and goings," so as to avoid any more conflicts like the one with Kane the previous day. She plotted Laz's life out in minute detail, using her pink pen to fill in his daily planner a month in advance, even down to such mundane activities as appointments with the dental hygienist and trips to the hardware store or to the Russian baths on Tenth Street.

She consulted her father's latest e-mail update for the extended weather forecasts and other family events. She'd have to check the date for Kane and Laz's annual ice fishing trip at the lake, but for now she penciled in an acute case of the stomach flu as well as a list of some ready-made excuses to have at her fingertips.

Most of the time, other people supplied her with the alibis: *Laz working as usual? Away, again? Off on some humanitarian mission?* She marked the days he would be "out of town" to coincide with family events, such as Grace's parents' annual Hanukkah potluck dinner or the Sugarmans' New Year's Day dim sum brunch. The pink pen she was using began to run out; she shook it and pushed on the tip, but it was dry. She switched to a blue pen and a legal pad, which was not nearly as pleasing, but considering the complexity and organizational demands of her mission, she felt she needed to adopt more serious tools.

Grace noticed that Laz had written *Contact, eight P.M.* on New Year's Eve in his calendar, and she figured he had ordered tickets for the play at Lincoln Center. He had obviously felt confident that he'd be back by then, sitting beside her to ring in the new millennium. When she got to her own birthday, she stopped. There was a red circle around the date. Underneath, Laz had written in almost illegible handwriting: *Grange, nine P.M.* Or did it say Grace? Grange Hall had never been one of her favorite restaurants, but she supposed it was the thought that counted.

Her birthday was only two weeks away. As a child, her parents used to take her to the Hawaii Kai for her birthday, which they pronounced as if it rhymed. She always felt like a princess as she drank out of a coconut and sat in a high-backed wicker chair, wearing several flower leis around her neck. Now she left the space as it was, wondering whether she'd be spending this birthday alone.

Once she finished organizing the next few weeks, she felt unusually celebratory, buoyed by a feeling of great accomplishment. She decided to treat herself to dinner, so she made a reservation at her and Laz's favorite restaurant. As she was getting dressed, the telephone rang.

"Just wanted to check and see what you were up to tonight," Kane said. Grace glanced at the date book to make sure she wasn't forgetting anything and then answered with confidence.

"Nothing much. Just a quiet dinner at des Artistes."

Kane was silent. He started to say something and stopped. "Sounds nice," he said, finally.

While cradling the phone under her chin, Grace attempted to fasten the clasp of her pink sapphire choker—a present from Laz last Valentine's Day. She had never been able to do it herself, sometimes even going downstairs and asking José for assistance. Laz had given it to her while she was in the shower. The three smaller jets had been on full force until the bathroom had steamed up and water dripped from the ceilings and walls, but even through the mist, the sapphires had glinted like stars as Laz had fastened it around her neck.

"About Monday," Kane said. "Greg wants to know if we can go to a place that has spelt pizza." Monday was Pizza Night. Every other Monday they went to Ralph's for deep-fried zucchini sticks and a large pie. Kane had cancelled the last two.

"Spelt pizza?" Grace asked. She put the necklace down, unable to clasp it. It wound around itself slowly like a jeweled serpent.

"Yeah, Greg has me off wheat. Something about the gluten."

"What else does Greg have you off?"

"Well, dairy, too," he admitted sheepishly.

"So we're having Spelt Night," she said. "Sounds appetizing."

"I'm not laughing," Kane said, not quite his snappy self. "If you guys can't make it, we'll understand." He seemed to be giving her a too-convenient out, which somehow took away the challenge for Grace. She had already penciled in a family emergency to get out of Pizza Night, but it was a last-minute excuse and she couldn't use it until Monday afternoon. Even though she'd never planned to go, she found herself irritated that Greg was trying to alter their plans.

"Count us in," she said adamantly, as if trying to protect her turf.

"You really won't be able to tell the difference. Except you have to drink a lot of water," he added.

Café des Artistes was crowded when Grace arrived. The restaurant had a timeless quality. Everything, from the lacquered bar to the murals of nymphs on the walls, made Grace feel as if she'd stepped into another era. She indulged in the five-course tasting menu, including a cheese course, which featured unpasteurized delicacies smuggled in from France. No wine, just to be prudent. Her waiter was a handsome and ubiquitous young man, who stood nearby at the ready to refill her water glass, replenish the minibaguettes, or offer seconds on the beggar's purses.

As she was taking a bite of her pear sorbet, the waiter brought over two glasses of Muscato and set them down in front of her. Grace looked at him questioningly, as if to say he must have made a mistake.

"From a Mr. Kane," he said. Grace looked frantically around the dining room, trying to think how she would explain Laz's absence. Noticing her futile search, the waiter added, "He called and said to send his best." Grace tried to laugh it off, but even as she brought one of the glasses to her lips, she felt her heart pounding in her ears. Laz had once told her that *Muscato* meant "tiny flies" in Italian, and as she took one perfunctory sip, she imagined the carbonation like the flutter of wings.

Grace asked the waiter for the check, passing on the candied orange rinds and the madeleines. She waited for her coat by the entrance, protected from the wind by a glass storm door. Still slightly preoccupied by the near miss with the Muscato, she didn't notice a couple as they entered the restaurant. There was a sudden stir among the patrons as a celebrity entered the restaurant. The staff began flurrying about, and Grace felt herself pushed rather forcibly from behind as another couple passed by. Grace turned, and as if in slow motion, she took in fleeting details.

"A quiet table in the back, please," she heard the woman say, as the maître d' led the couple to a secluded booth.

The woman was striking, with wavy, shoulder-length auburn hair, probably only a few years older than Grace. She looked familiar, perhaps being an actress who played character roles. Grace glanced at the man accompanying the woman. From the side, he reminded her of Laz, and she dropped her coat as it was handed to her. She composed herself, blaming the sip of Muscato, and looked more carefully. There was a definite similarity, but he was much younger than Laz. In fact, he looked a lot like Laz had in his Dartmouth College yearbook.

As Grace turned to go, she caught another flash of the young man's face and couldn't shake the feeling that she had seen him somewhere before. Only later, on the walk home in the bitingly cold air, as she thought about the ice melting in the fishbowl, did it register: He was the young man at the bookstore.

THAT NIGHT, GRACE dreamt that she and Laz were lying in a hammock, their legs entwined. Laz murmured, "Baby, baby, baby," until the hammock began to sag and stretch from their weight, the diamond-shaped holes growing larger and larger, no longer able to sustain them. In the dream, Chloe was mending the hammock with variegated yarn spun from a giant spool. Grace awoke in a cold sweat, her T-shirt drenched, but the answer to her birthday dilemma was suddenly apparent—she would visit Chloe in Chicago.

13
The Painted Lady

It was tradition on the Sunday after Thanksgiving that the Sugarmans would host the weekly Scrabble game. What was not usual was the fact that Bert was doing the cooking, or that it was hibachi night. Bert had gone to great lengths to prepare the spectacular evening. He had even purchased a traditional Japanese charcoal grill. Earlier in the day, Francine called Grace expressly to tell her to dress in loose, comfortable clothing suitable for sitting on the floor. Grace was happy to oblige, as anything other than stretchy, oversize articles of clothing made her feel like lying down, especially after last night's five-course gustatory binge.

Grace showered, dried off, and surveyed her face in the bathroom mirror. She looked pale. She felt as if her mother's hand was guiding hers as she applied her makeup before heading over to the Sugarmans'.

• • •

Grace arrived at Bert and Francine's penthouse apartment to a flurry of activity. Grace had brought a bouquet of white daisies and thistle, which she knew Francine liked. This, in turn, set off the obligatory commotion of a ten-minute appraisal of all the vases in the house and caused a lamentation about the Lalique that Bert had knocked off the mantelpiece ten years ago, which would have been simply perfect for Grace's bouquet. It was decided that the stems were too long and needed to be cut in order to look right in the Orrefors vase.

Bert was dressed in a white bib apron and chef hat. He sharpened his knives on a carving stone in the kitchen as Francine hovered about silently, clucking her tongue. The hibachi grill was set up on a low, square coffee table in what Francine referred to as the Bali room. The room was a small token to appease Bert's lifelong yearning to live in Indonesia. A microcosmic replica straight from the pages of *Travel*, it was complete with low leather stools, embroidered throw pillows embedded with tiny mirrors, beaded curtains, and potted palms. Early on during Grace and Laz's courtship, Laz had given Bert a rare artifact he'd picked up on a trip to Borneo. It was now displayed on a pedestal by the window. That token, along with their shared affinity for etymology, served to ingrain Laz forever in Bert's heart. With floor-to-ceiling windows on all sides, in the summer months, the Bali room was like a hothouse. But on sunny winter days, it was usually quite pleasant. This afternoon, however, it seemed unmitigatingly gray.

Grace's father, seated on the floor and wearing a wool cardigan he had borrowed from Bert, was reading aloud the directions for the hibachi grill.

"It says here," he began, adjusting his reading glasses, which still had the drugstore price tag on the earpiece, "the grill should be ignited twenty minutes prior to cooking. And never used indoors."

"I have this all under control, Milt," Bert said, waving him off and proceeding to light the grill with a sparker. Grace saw a flash out of the corner of her eye and turned to see a huge flame shooting into the air. Bert quickly covered the grill, cautiously looking up to see if Francine had witnessed the pyrotechnics. Assured that she hadn't, he turned up the flame. "It heats up better this way," he explained. Then he turned his attention to the preparation of the mushrooms, slicing them an eighth of an inch thick with utmost precision. "Boy, Laz must really be tied up to miss this."

When everyone was seated, Bert bowed ceremoniously. Francine poured low-sodium soy sauce into small triangular dishes and passed out chopsticks and wasabi. Bert uncovered the grill and brushed the surface with oil. Shrimp, onions, and mushrooms sizzled as Bert tossed them high into the air with his spatula to a round of applause led by Milton. The smell of the shrimp was beginning to make Grace's stomach turn. Bert added the steak and, with a flourish, threw his spatula in the air. The white plastic spatula twirled like a drum majorette's baton. Everyone watched as it missed Bert's outstretched hand and landed instead on the grill, melting like wax onto the caramelized onions. Grace's mother gasped. Francine almost choked on a pickled carrot. Bert reacted quickly, dousing the grill with what he thought was soy sauce, but which turned out to be sherry. Flames soared and the guests ran from the scorching heat.

"My best spatula," Francine grumbled, as she got up from the floor, smoothed her skirt, and left the room.

Francine quickly returned calm and collected, carrying a fire extinguisher, and sprayed the grill with what looked like whipped cream. "No problem," Francine reassured everyone. "Chicken Kiev in three minutes and thirty seconds."

• • •

The Scrabble board was set up after dinner. They played several rounds while sipping steaming green tea and eating tender litchi nuts. Bert had planned to serve pineapple flambé, but everyone insisted it be eaten uncooked. Grace declined because of the brandy.

"First a vegetarian, now a teetotaler?" Bert asked.

"Whose turn is it?" Grace's mother interrupted.

"I think it's Paulette's," Francine answered.

"No, it's Grace's turn," Bert corrected her.

"It's my turn actually," Grace's father said in an unusually firm voice as he placed the letter *x* on the board to form *ox.*

"You opened up a triple-word score, Milton. Don't you have anything better? Laz would never have left that open."

"I'm planning ahead, dear," he said, picking up another tile. "Using a bit of strategy." Grace tried to focus on the board. The letters looked blurry, as if they were underwater. The thought that she might not be pregnant but have a brain tumor instead crossed her mind, and it almost seemed to make more sense. Laz would undoubtedly be there for her for cancer, but not necessarily for childbirth. Before they were married, he had been adamant about not having any children. They took up too much time and he said he didn't have the patience. His decision had seemed so overly intellectualized that Grace had thought he would eventually warm to the idea. It might even keep him home.

She rearranged her letters almost unconsciously and placed them on the board. She felt as if her very participation at these weekly gatherings was programmed into her.

"Flumm? What kind of word is that?" Bert asked. Francine shushed him. Grace moved the tiles across the board, attaching them to her father's *ox.*

"Flummox," Grace announced.

"Never heard of it," Bert said.

"Look it up in your *O.E.D.*," Grace's father suggested.

"Go ahead," Francine quipped.

"I'm sure it won't be in there," Bert said, getting up from the table and going over to the dictionary. He opened the volume and sighed. "I knew I should have gotten the abridged edition," Bert grumbled under his breath.

"Bravo, Grace," her mother said. Then, with a self-satisfied smile, she proceeded to add *ed* to *flummox,* her own score nearly tripling that of Grace's.

"Oh, by the way, how was your anniversary last night? We would have called, but we didn't want to bother you."

Anniversary. The word hit her like a burst of frigid air. She could not believe she'd forgotten. She tried to console herself with the idea that she had, indeed, celebrated at their favorite restaurant. The anniversary must have registered on some level, no matter how unconsciously so.

"We went to des Artistes," she answered, finally, growing queasier and queasier.

"You went to dinner?" her father asked, furrowing his brow.

"Lovely," her mother chimed.

Grace wobbled as she stood up from the table. Bert raised an eyebrow.

"Too much celebrating last night, it looks like," he said.

"Can I use your telephone?" she asked Francine.

"Certainly. You need to call Laz?"

Grace nodded. She feared if she tried to speak that she would not have been able to keep her food down.

"Use the one in the bedroom—it'll be more private," Francine offered.

• • •

GRACE WALKED DOWN the hall toward Francine and Bert's bedroom. Just as she was turning the corner, she saw her father standing in the shadows.

"Honey, I need to talk to you," he said softly, touching her arm.

"Sure, Dad," Grace said. As her eyes adjusted to the darkness she could see that his expression was grave. "Are you all right?" she asked.

"Oh, yes, I'm fine. Never felt better," he said, lightly patting his stomach. "Now that your mother has me doing laps around the reservoir." His expression changed quickly and he stammered to find the right words. "It's . . . about Laz," he said, finally.

"What about Laz?" Grace asked, trying to appear unfazed.

"Grace, I saw Laz on *Bookspan* last night talking to that guy who's been trying to discredit him. Something about an eyewitness in Kosovo who—" He paused. "I just thought you might need to talk, that's all." Grace's thoughts careened, trying to find the right response.

"He's been on that show several times," she explained. Grace's father looked at her with concern.

"It was live, Grace. From Washington. I turned it off before your mother came in the room. I didn't want to upset her. Are you and Laz having some kind of marital problems? Because when Bert and Francine went through their little rough patch a few years back . . ."

Grace remembered when Francine had gone to stay with Grace's parents for five days after a disagreement with Bert. She had slept in Grace's room and moped around the house in curlers, until Bert came over with a bouquet of roses and took her home. Grace felt herself beginning to lose her resolve as she took in the full measure of her father's concern, but the pretense was as much for him as for herself.

"Laz and I were out to dinner last night," she began. "That was just a rebroadcast of a show he did weeks ago. You know, because of the holiday. Don't worry, Dad, things couldn't be better between us." Grace tried to rein herself in. She knew she was beginning to sound manic. She took a deep breath. "Everything's fine. We had a wonderful anniversary."

"Oh, I'm so glad, sweetie. I knew there was a good explanation," he said, kissing her on the cheek. As he did, a small black comb fell out of his shirt pocket. He bent down, fumbling as he picked it up. "Now go call Laz and tell him he was missed. And let him know that I'll have the edition of Melville finished by next Friday, if I can swing it."

"I will," she assured him, watching as he disappeared down the hall.

GRACE SLIPPED THROUGH the half-open door to Francine and Bert's bedroom. Her feet sank into the soft-pile carpeting as she closed the door quietly behind her. The flowers she had brought were on Francine's ornately mirrored vanity by the window. She couldn't stop thinking about her encounter with her father in the hallway. The worst part for her was that rather than feeling regret for having lied to her father, she wished he'd taped the show so she could play it over and over again to look for some clue as to why Laz had left her.

For a second, Grace thought she saw something moving among the flowers. Unnerved, she went over to the bed and turned on a small lamp on the nightstand. She knew she was on Francine's side of the bed because the base of the lamp was a porcelain lady wearing a frilly petticoat. The mate was on Bert's side.

Small figurines were posed on every flat surface in the room like a display in a store window. She thought about Laz's wedding band behind the rusting can of shaving cream. It seemed so out of character for her to have forgotten her own anniversary when she'd kept track of everything else so well.

She looked out the window but all she saw in the glass was her own overly made-up reflection. Still feeling a bit queasy, she considered lying down but abstained, not one to take liberties in someone else's home. Instead, she sat on the edge of the bed, relieved to be alone. She felt an odd sense of calm among the frozen figurines. She picked up a small porcelain figurine next to the lamp. It was cold and smooth in her hand—a mother and child holding onto the brims of their watery-blue sun hats, perhaps walking on the beach.

She thought again about Laz and their first Valentine's Day together. The BE MY VALENTINE lift ticket was still on her ski jacket. The memory was clear in her mind. She could conjure every detail—the touch of Laz's lips on hers, the sting of the wind on her cheeks. She wondered if he remembered it, too.

And then another detail of that day, which she'd almost forgotten, began to surface. It had been late afternoon. Grace remembered the deep-blue color of the sky just before their last run. While they were on line for the lift, Grace noticed a young girl wearing a pale blue jacket who had fallen off the rope pull and was crying quietly. Grace knelt down to help her up. Laz stood blocking the sun behind her. *She's old enough to take care of herself. We're going to miss the last run,* he said, steering Grace toward the lift before it closed. Laz pulled the metal bar over Grace's legs, and she looked back once more as they left the ground and ascended into the clear blue sky.

GRACE WAS ABOUT to leave Francine and Bert's room when she became peripherally aware of a shadowy fluttering in the lamp shade. She immediately felt the familiar palpitating in her chest as she recognized the dull thump of a moth against the lightbulb. She rolled up Francine's *Redbook* magazine and prepared herself.

The moth fluttered against the shade, coming in and out of focus through the fabric, looming surreally larger as it pressed its wings against the shade. It reminded Grace of the giant Woodstock balloon that had almost crashed through her window. She struck the shade with the magazine, and the moth fell to the nightstand and lay motionless. She struck at it again, and then once more just to be sure, surprising herself with her spirit for retaliation.

The room suddenly grew bright, and Grace saw Francine and Bert in the doorway. Francine's mouth fell open as she digested the scene.

"Bert's Painted Lady!" she cried. "Grace, you just killed Bert's prized butterfly!"

GRACE'S GUILT OVER killing Bert's butterfly was offset by her elation at now having an excuse to leave the Sugarmans' early. The mood had changed after the incident, as if an ominous high-pressure system had descended upon them. Grace assured Bert that she would make reparations, although she had no idea where to find a replacement caterpillar. She'd seen cardboard butterfly kits sold at the Museum of Natural History, but she was doubtful they'd suffice.

Grace said her good-byes, and after a needless discussion about the best way to get back across town, she left, laden with two Food Emporium bags brimming with leftovers.

14
The Doppelganger

When she arrived home, the first thing Grace did was to go into the kitchen and check on the fishbowl. The ice had melted substantially, and the key was now encapsulated within a smaller ball of ice, the size of a grapefruit. Like a fortune-teller, she held the fishbowl in her hands and gazed into the water. The ice would be melted soon, but the fishbowl did not contain the answers Grace was looking for.

Inspired, she went in search of other methods of prognostication. The Magic 8-Ball was still under the desk in the bedroom, and Grace decided there was no harm in giving it another try. Suitably skeptical, she gave the ball a gentle shake, not wanting to jostle it unnecessarily, and asked again if she was pregnant. She read the answer: *Yes, definitely*. At first she was incredulous, so she proceeded to ask again, watching with amazement as *Yes, definitely* appeared in the tiny window three more times in a row.

Grace hastily put on a pair of sweats and ran down to the corner drugstore to buy a pregnancy test. She asked the salesperson for a double bag in order to conceal her purchase, but from whom she wasn't certain. Once home, she immediately performed the test and waited, her hands shaking, until the three minutes were up. She scanned the results and sighed with relief as she saw that only one pink line had appeared in the test window, putting to rest any fears—along with any stray hopes and dreams—about having a baby.

Grace wrapped the pregnancy test in tissues, stashed it in the garbage can, and then went into the bedroom. She picked up the 8-Ball, embarrassed that she had given it so much credence, especially since the pregnancy test was ninety-nine percent accurate and there was no toll-free number on the back of the 8-Ball. She let the ball drop to the floor and gave it a good kick, watching as it rolled under the bed. It was just a silly plastic toy filled with colored water. And yet, as hard as she tried to ignore it, she couldn't help hoping it knew something that the pregnancy test did not. She lifted up the dust ruffle and rescued the 8-Ball from a field of dust bunnies. Leaning over the side of the bed, she turned the ball over to reveal the answer: *Yes, definitely.*

Grace awakened the next morning filled with optimism. She had slept soundly. Marisol would arrive shortly and order would once again be restored. The lights would be strung on the tree, caramel custard would simmer on the stove, and the dust bunnies would be swept clean.

After bringing down José's coffee, Grace called Chloe and left a message that she and Laz would be in Chicago for her birthday. Then she began to straighten up, or, rather, to arrange the room so as to give the impression that the apartment had been inhabited by Laz. The amaryllis was almost in full bloom, with another flower about to burst open like a brilliant ruby flame.

She hummed as she displayed items around the house that she and Laz might have used over the holiday weekend—a pair of gloves, boots, two crystal flutes for their anniversary celebration, a half-eaten currant scone dripping with jam, *Oblomov* still marked with a folded scrap of yellow paper on the desk, a cashmere sweater on the coat rack. She even left drawers and cabinets half-open—one of Laz's habits, which used to drive her crazy but which now seemed endearing—as well as chairs pulled out from the table. It was the part of the day she derived the most pleasure from—setting the scene.

As she was leaving the evidence of Laz having eaten a peanut butter sandwich by scattering a few crumbs on the counter and leaving a knife in the dish drain, she glanced at the fishbowl and noticed that the ice had melted completely and that the key was lying at the bottom. She plunged her hand into the still-icy water and, feeling very much like a nursery rhyme character, pulled out the key. Even this she took in stride, secure in the knowledge that she was prepared to handle whatever she would confront in Laz's apartment.

The phone rang. It was Marisol's niece with the news that Marisol had eaten contaminated jambalaya and would not be in until Wednesday at the earliest. Grace spent the next few minutes walking aimlessly around the apartment, like a dandelion in search of a swift breeze.

Now that all her efforts that morning had been wasted, she needed something to occupy herself. Her grandmother's afghan, draped over the side of a chair, looking tattered and forlorn, provided her with the solution. She decided at once to take it to the yarn store on Broadway to see if they could repair it. It was as though she'd found her mission. With a few deft strokes, all would be right again, even if only with the afghan. And on the way home, she'd stop by the managing agent to pay the back rent on Laz's old apartment. After consulting the combination thermometer/barometer her father had installed outside the kitchen window, and with afghan, checkbook, and key in hand, Grace left the apartment.

On the front table in the vestibule, she noticed a white postcard from her gynecologist, reminding her of her appointment for her yearly exam. She took this, as opposed to all other signs, as proof that the planets were aligned and cooperating fully.

It was a beautiful, clear day and everything, including the sidewalks, sparkled. Grace felt enlivened, better than she had in weeks. She walked up the steep flight of carpeted stairs to the yarn store, which had been on Broadway for as long as she could remember, and pressed the buzzer. She heard the click and opened the door. She didn't see anyone at first as she walked inside. The walls were lined with skeins of yarn in every shade, balls of wool piled high in wicker baskets. Sweater samples hung on wooden dowels above the large windows, and in the middle of the room was a long wooden table with ornate legs and clawed feet. On it were half-finished pieces in an array of textures and patterns, unidentifiable swatches of knitting left in progress.

From behind the counter a woman appeared. She was lifting a large box from the floor, which she set down on the table. Her hair, the color of raspberries, was piled high on her head, and she wore an overly formfitting dress in a floral pattern, with a lavender shawl over her shoulders. Grace waited. Finally, the woman looked up and asked, "Can I help you with something?"

Grace opened her bag. "I was hoping someone could repair this."

"We don't do repairs," the woman answered curtly. "We instruct, make patterns, troubleshoot, sell the materials. But we won't do it for you."

"Oh," Grace said. "I don't know how to crochet."

"How bad is the damage?" the woman asked, softening a little. She put on a pair of tortoiseshell glasses and reached into the shopping bag, spreading the afghan out onto the counter, as if about to perform a complete medical exam. She ran her milky-white hands along the frayed edging, shaking her head as she assessed the situation.

"You're better off starting over," she said finally. "There's less here than is missing." Grace felt like snatching the afghan away from this woman, who bore a strong resemblance to a Little Kiddle doll.

"I couldn't do that."

"Start fresh. It's too *ungepatchket,* anyway," the woman said, without a trace of sentiment. Grace had heard her mother use that word to describe Francine Sugarman's taste in decorating. Actually, anything pre-1960s was *ungepatchket* in her mother's mind.

"I need to try at least," Grace said quietly. "I've had it for so long."

"Suit yourself."

"Do you sell this kind of rainbow yarn?" Grace asked.

"You mean ombré?"

"I guess so," Grace replied.

"We don't carry any acrylics. And Woolworths has been closed for years."

Grace's eyes inexplicably filled with tears as she folded up the afghan and put it carefully back into the bag. She turned to leave. Just as she was reaching for the doorknob, the woman approached her and put her hand on Grace's shoulder.

"I could teach you a few simple stitches. It might take your mind off of things."

Grace sat down on a small stool as the woman dug through a basket until she found a skein of ombré yarn in soft muted shades of purple, sage, and teal. The woman made a simple slipknot, looped it over the crochet hook, and within a matter of minutes was showing Grace how to make a granny square. Grace's hands moved slowly and awkwardly at first, until she began to get the hang of it. By the time she finished her square, she felt serene. She looked at the four-by-four-inch square in her hands and could not believe she'd made it.

"One by one," the woman assured her. "That's all it takes."

"I had no idea it was so simple," Grace said.

"What's your name?" the woman asked, snipping the end of the yarn with a pair of tiny gold scissors that were shaped like a stork.

"Grace," she answered.

"I'm Penelope. Grace, most things are simple—it's people who complicate things." She put five skeins of wool and a crochet hook in a plastic bag. Grace offered to pay, but Penelope refused. "I'll just put it on your tab," she said. "Come back when you've done a few, and I'll show you how to put them together. And leave the afghan. I'll see what I can do with it."

THE LOBBY OF LAZ'S old building had been recently refurbished, restored to an extroverted facsimile of its former Beaux Arts splendor, with a cobbled carriage entrance, gilt paneling, and crystal chandeliers. The limestone exterior of the building was being repointed, and the entire southern side was sheathed in black netting. It looked like a giant veil had been suspended from the cupolas. For all the improvements, though, the building still had the same stale smell that had always permeated the hallways and stairwell—a sort of olfactory melange of burnt toast, papaya, and mothballs.

The Barclay School of Dance that Grace had attended during all of her preteen years had occupied a grand studio on the mezzanine level in the same building, with floor-to-ceiling mirrors and double-height windows. Grace's mother used to sit on the faded chintz couches in the lobby, waiting for Grace to emerge, lollipop in white-gloved hands, usually a hole in the knee of her white tights from where she'd skidded in her Mary Janes across the polished floor. Laz thought the image was funny and had called Grace his little debutante, one night waltzing her down the marble hallway toward the elevator bank..

She and Laz had lived in his old apartment together for less than six months, until Grace could no longer tolerate the confined space and the noisy, whip-crazed neighbors, whom Laz had once threatened in the middle of the night by knocking on their door, wearing little more than his sheepskin slippers. The next night, the neighbors, Alexander and Julian, were invited over for brandied pear canapés and white wine sangria. Later, Laz laughed about the lively neighbors next door. He had a selective memory, as did she, but he only seemed to remember the good times in that apartment, most of which predated Grace entirely.

Grace recognized the concierge as she passed by on her way to the elevators. He waved as if he thought she still lived there. Grace took the elevator to the sixteenth floor, where the office of the managing agent was. She opened the door and approached the receptionist, who was tapping her long, turquoise nails against the desk.

"I'd like to pay this bill. It's two weeks late." She felt the words catch in her throat, feeling as if she had just told the receptionist that her period was late and not the rent. The receptionist took the bill from Grace's hands and studied it. Then she looked at the check Grace had written.

"You need to get this check certified," she said flatly. "And we need to schedule a date for the asbestos abatement."

"That shouldn't be a problem. I'll arrange it with my husband."

The woman gave Grace the once-over, her eyes eventually resting on the ring on Grace's left hand.

"That's some ring," she said, finally. Grace had grown accustomed to people staring at her engagement ring. It was quite a ring—a two-carat, emerald-cut diamond with sapphire trillions. When Laz gave the ring to her, Grace had at first been embarrassed by it. Laz had originally planned on giving her his grandmother's engagement ring, a more modest diamond in a basket setting, but a week before he was going to propose, his mother told him that the ring had been stolen. She had collected a huge sum of money from the insurance agent, enough not only for a replacement ring but also for her to remodel her kitchen. The ring was eventually discovered in her safety deposit box along with her stallion's certificate of genealogy, but by that point, Grace and Laz were already off to Belize.

"I should mention," said the receptionist, "there have been a few complaints about noise from your apartment." Grace tried not to appear startled by this information. After all, Laz had been known to sublet the apartment from time to time. He usually mentioned it to her, though.

"I'll take care of that," she assured the receptionist.

GRACE TOOK THE elevator down to the fourth floor and stood in front of the door to Laz's old apartment. The key and rose she'd dropped on her previous visit were gone. Even though she had the key from the goldfish bowl, she felt obliged to ring the bell. After waiting for an appropriate length of time, Grace put the key in the lock and opened the door. If anyone was living here, there were no visible signs of occupation—no food, recent newspapers, or disarray—nothing to suggest that the apartment was currently inhabited.

Laz's college desk and cinder-block bookshelves looked as if they hadn't been touched in years. Even the television that could access only the local stations, and then with plenty of interference, still had the tinfoil rabbit ears attached to the antenna. Grace noticed how dusty everything appeared, the surfaces covered not with ordinary soot and dust but with particles that had a shiny, almost opalescent sheen.

Grace continued to look around the room as if she were at an exhibit of pre-Columbian art. From the fluorescent light fixtures to the makeshift, faux–wood grain kitchenette, the apartment was no-frills. Laz had liked it that way, the antithesis to his mother's Bauhaus duplex on Park Avenue. The only remnants of this apartment's former glory were the sealed-off dumbwaiter, which had once brought up dinners to the hotel guests, and the gas fireplace. Laz's mother referred to the apartment as "the tenement." On Laz's thirty-second birthday, one of the few times his mother ever deigned to visit, Grace had prepared a dinner of rack of lamb and scalloped potatoes. The meal was eaten at a card table surrounded by metal folding chairs, and they spent a good part of the evening fanning the overly sensitive smoke alarm, which went off even when Laz blew out the candles on the Greenberg chocolate cake.

Grace was surprised to see the spinning pups on the coffee table, merrily skating across its dust-covered surface. And then she saw an extension cord, tangled with plugs, leading in all directions to various electronic appliances. It looked uncannily like the one she'd been missing. Where before she might have considered the mystery of the extension cord solved, now she had only more questions. She knew that these were not just simple coincidences; she began to wonder if she and Laz were engaged in an unwitting game of cat and mouse. Still married, but not together—it was as if they were playing chess, just not on the same board.

Grace sat down on the edge of the couch. It was an emerald green velvet pullout that Laz had slept on in college, with a concave foam-rubber mattress that was missing several springs. Laz used to replace them with twist ties, which Grace would later find underneath the couch when she dry-mopped. She recalled how much effort it used to take to fold the mattress and close the couch. Sometimes, she would have to physically jump on it. Grace ran her hand over the fabric. The velvet was worn to a pale green on the arms and seat cushions, which they used to flip regularly.

She remembered the morning not long after they'd moved in together, when she found a black-and-white photograph of a woman inside one of the zippered seat cushions. Laz had said that it had probably been forgotten by the previous owners of the couch. It was such a sensible explanation that she felt ashamed for even bringing it up. The next evening, he blindfolded her and led her down twisting corridors, up a spiral staircase, and outside. When he removed the bandana from her eyes, Grace was looking out over the skyline.

"I thought the roof was closed," she said.

"It is," he answered. "I paid off Jorge." Grace smiled, and then she noticed a hammock in the most northern corner, under a thatched covering, and a book on top of a stack of black roofing tiles.

"Look," Laz said, walking over to where the hammock was fastened, "someone's reading *Oblomov*." He and Grace had been reading it aloud nightly for weeks. He picked up the book and opened it, the spine cracking. They had bought their copy at the Strand bookstore, and it still had the price written in pencil on the inside cover and the ex libris bookplate from the previous owner.

Grace leaned against the metal railing, taking in the unobstructed view all the way up Broadway past Columbia University almost imagining that she could see the outline of the mansion where they'd first met. That night, as they lay in the hammock, Grace felt secure that these memories would always be there for her, grounding her and Laz, especially during the times when they were apart.

SHE COULDN'T REMEMBER now if they'd actually ever finished reading *Oblomov*. But it had never been about getting to the end. They had a way of stopping and picking up again without missing a beat. A wave of exhaustion came over her, so she put down the shopping bag and rested her head on a tasseled pillow. As she drifted off, she wondered how *Oblomov* ended.

The next thing she was aware of was a loud knocking on the door. It had grown dark outside. She heard the sound of rain on the air conditioner. As she tried to reorient herself, she recalled a fragment of a dream that hovered above her in her half-waking state. Laz was standing on the other side of a doorway, which was covered by a huge cobweb. As he walked through it toward her, not a trace of the web adhered to him.

She stood up from the couch to open the door and caught sight of a brown leather jacket that looked identical to Laz's hanging from a hook. Stunned, and afraid that she might still be dreaming, she reached out to touch it. She pulled the jacket off the hook, causing a windbreaker and a baseball cap to tumble to the floor. She pushed her arms through the sleeves and plunged her hands into the pockets. As soon as she did, her heart sank. The jacket she was wearing, although almost identical to Laz's, had no hole in the lining. As she took it off, she noticed two frayed army patches on the sleeves. It was not the missing jacket she was looking for, but it had clearly belonged at one time to the missing man.

• • •

AS SHE WAS RIDING down in the elevator, Grace realized that she'd been so distracted by the leather jacket that she'd completely forgotten all about the person knocking at the door. Probably a maintenance man to schedule the abatement, she told herself.

When she descended to the lobby, another concierge was on duty. She glanced at a brass clock above the desk and saw that it was a quarter to six. She'd slept for over three hours! She hadn't yet canceled spelt night, and Kane and Greg would be expecting her and Laz at seven.

"You just missed Mr. Brookman," the concierge called to her, as she passed his desk. Grace stopped and turned around.

"Excuse me?"

"Mr. Brookman," he repeated. "You just missed him." The shopping bag with the crochet hook and wool fell out of her hands, and Grace watched as a ball of ombré yarn rolled away, leaving a rainbow trail in its wake.

"Laz was here?" she managed to say. The concierge shook his head and smiled.

"No," he corrected her. "The *young* Mr. Brookman. He just came by to drop something off."

15
Spelt Night

Back at her own apartment, Grace called Kane to cancel, but there was no answer. Then she reconsidered. She was so hungry that spelt pizza with tofu mozzarella was beginning to sound appealing. Just as she was about to leave, the telephone rang. It was her father.

"Been out?" he asked, not bothering with pleasantries.

"Yes, actually. I just got in. Why?"

"Mother's friend Mrs. Kreiger called and said she saw you in Laz's old building."

Grace was used to this level of surveillance. Still, it was shocking how quickly the information had been conveyed, as if it had been done by means of a global satellite scanner. There was a decided method to her father's interrogation, an occupation he relished, and no matter how mundane her crime, she knew she'd have to endure his inquisition. It was a nuisance at times, but she also knew how much he enjoyed it—a sort of holdover from his *Perry*

Mason–watching days, so she played along, answering his questions as if on the witness stand. While she was talking, she busied herself by unknotting the yarn that had spilled out of her bag. She heard a muffled cough on the extension, an indication that her father's very own sidekick was listening.

"Doing errands?" her father asked.

"I was just coming from the yarn store. The afghan Grandma Dolly made me needs some repair," she answered, yanking on a particularly tight knot. Grace's grandmother had once told her a story about how prospective brides in the shtetlach of Europe were given a knotted-up ball of yarn, and if they had enough patience to undo all the knots, they were deemed to be a worthy match. Over cups of tepid tea with lots of milk and sugar, Grandma Dolly had made Grace practice on shoelaces or delicate gold chains. Luckily for Grace, for whom a pair of sharp scissors seemed now the only solution to such knots, those customs had long been abandoned. She still had several knotted skeins remaining, the shtetl's judgment of an old maid.

"But the yarn store is blocks from there."

"When it started raining, I ducked into the lobby to avoid getting wet," Grace answered. Laz's building had two entrances. She could actually walk a stretch of almost ten blocks virtually untouched by the elements by wending her way through various buildings, hotel lobbies, subway stations, garages, and covered courtyards, a route that her father had mapped out for her.

"Ah! Good thinking. Did you use the Hotel Mirabela's side entrance?" he asked.

"Of course," Grace answered, stretching the truth still further like a piece of warm taffy. "And the Apple Bank."

"I tried to show your mother once, but you know her—she could get lost in a phone booth." Grace heard the sound of "someone" clearing her throat. "Well, anyway, your mother got this silly idea that you were up to some sort of covert activity," he said, taking pride in his deductive skills.

"Well, you can reassure her I was not smuggling wool," she said. There was rustling on the extension and Grace could almost hear her mother bursting from the effort of trying to remain unobtrusive.

"I hope it's not real wool," her mother finally said. "Wool pills."

"Oh, and if you're going out," her father warned, "make sure you and Laz take mass transportation. It's going to be treacherous tonight once the temperature drops. Like a sheet of ice."

THE RAIN HAD ended, the temperature had dropped, and the streets were indeed treacherous. The taxi ride downtown to meet Kane was a more adventurous journey than Grace would have liked. She had no idea that cars could move sideways.

The restaurant was minimalist in style: long maple tables, chrome chairs, and a silent, rippleless waterfall cascading down a granite wall. Kane was sitting by himself at a table near the window. From his expression and the empty bottle of organic beer in front of him, Grace guessed that something was troubling him. She wondered if he and Greg had had an argument, and she felt relieved—though also a little guilty—that Laz's absence would now be eclipsed by Kane's greater need for comfort.

"Are we dining alone?" Grace asked. Kane got up from the table and kissed her on the cheek.

"Greg got caught up at the studio. You know how those things are."

"Yes, I do," Grace commiserated.

"Laz couldn't break away either?" he asked, taking a sip of his hops-free lager.

"Unfortunately not. And he was really looking forward to meeting Greg."

"Another time, I guess," he said.

"Definitely. We'll do it soon. The four of us." The conversation continued in this vein for another few minutes until Grace could no longer stand the forced civility and tried to concentrate on the menu. She reached for a spelt breadstick, which, she was loath to admit, was actually quite tasty.

The waiter, who, in Grace's mind, was paying an inordinate amount of attention to Kane, came over to take their order. Grace noticed the eye contact and the nuanced gestures of the waiter toward her old friend, and she felt suddenly proprietary toward Kane, who seemed completely oblivious to the waiter's overtures. They ordered a large spelt pizza with mushrooms, two organic fennel salads, and two soy milk shakes with wheat grass juice.

"That's my favorite," the waiter beamed, still hovering around their table.

"Hey, you know," Grace said, trying to ignore the waiter's unctuous glances, "I was looking at that picture of the four of us at Halloween. Remember—when Laz was the Invisible Man?"

"Yes, of course. I was there, remember? Me Tarzan, you Wilma."

"By any chance, do you happen to have another copy of that picture?"

"Why?"

"I thought I'd send one to Chloe," she answered, not mentioning that her copy was now torn to pieces.

"Are you sure Chloe would want a reminder of that night?" The question surprised her.

"What do you mean?"

"It was sort of weird, don't you think?" Kane looked down, smoothing out the tablecloth with his hands. "At least for me it was." Grace didn't know how to respond.

"Well, if you can find it," she said, finally.

"I'm sure I have it somewhere," he said. "Unless it pulled a vanishing act, like your husband. He's even more invisible than usual."

She had assumed that what Kane had been alluding to was Laz's very conspicuous absence over the last few weeks, but then it occurred to her that she must have been doing such a good job of simulating his presence that he was not even missed. Or maybe they didn't really miss him after all. And maybe neither did Grace.

"Oh," she said. "I see what you mean. Kind of like how my father covers every book in the house with plastic laminate." Kane broke into a smile.

"Exactly. Like the time he gave you a *Zagat* guide with a dust jacket?" he joked. Grace felt relief at their having finally begun to find their usual rhythm, the kind of easy conversation that she didn't have with anyone else, not even Laz.

"Yeah. He calls them prophylactic covers. Just in case anything spills on them. He even coats them with a special solvent to repel dust mites."

"Sort of like *safe texts?*" he asked. Grace gave Kane a disdainful look. The waiter returned with two salads and what appeared to be a soggy disk laden with mushrooms that was sprinkled with bits of unmelted shredded tofu.

"You always take things one step too far," she said. Grace took a bite of fennel salad, which tasted a little too close to Black Jack gum for her liking, a predilection she'd had for a while during her grammar school years. As she lifted the soggy slice of pizza to her lips, the mushrooms slid off onto her lap. "It's not too late to make a break for it," she conspired. "Ralph's is only two blocks from here. I promise I won't tell Greg."

"Speaking of Greg," Kane began, "We're thinking about moving in together." Grace almost spit out the water that Kane had advised her to drink in order to wash down the spelt, which had already begun to coagulate in her mouth.

"What? Isn't that a little premature?" she asked in a tone that sounded more accusatory than she'd intended.

"Premature? Do you think I would make this decision lightly?" he asked.

"No," Grace answered tentatively, trying to regain her composure. "I just mean you haven't known each other very long."

"Long enough to know we're compatible," he countered, spearing a cherry tomato with his fork.

"Haven't you considered that this might just be a passing fancy?"

"A passing fancy? Look, let's not talk about Greg right now."

"I just mean," she said, formulating her words slowly, realizing that she was in touchy territory, "that these things eventually tend to lose their appeal."

"Really?" Kane reached for his glass of water and leaned back in his chair as he took a long drink.

Grace knew she was walking a precarious line. She cringed at her words, but it was too late to take them back, and for some reason, she was unable to stop from adding more. "Once you get over the novelty of it, that is," she said.

"The *novelty?* I'm not quite following," Kane said, staring at her. "Maybe I'm just not ready to talk about Greg."

"Don't you want to at least see what Laz thinks about this?" she asked. Even before she said it, she knew she'd gone too far.

"Well, far be it from me to make any sort of informed decision without first clearing it with Laz. I thought you of all people would be happy for me." Just then, an attractive woman passed by their table. Grace was perplexed while watching Kane's head turn.

"You don't have to pretend with me," she blurted out. She wondered if the soy milk shake was spiked.

"Pretend? Grace, what are you talking about?" With that, he picked up his fork and focused on eating, looking up only once to motion for the check. Suddenly, Grace felt a hard lump forming in her throat. If she tried to utter a word—any word—she knew she would dissolve into tears.

Kane paid the bill, glancing repeatedly at his wristwatch, and they sat in silence as they waited for the change. The waiter had insisted on wrapping up what remained of the spelt pizza and fennel salad, which he handed to Kane.

"You take it home. For Laz," Kane said, passing it to Grace.

As Kane held the door of a taxi open for her, he barely met her eyes. Until just then, she had been so busy perfecting her performance, she hadn't realized she was lonely. As the taxi pulled away, Grace looked out the rear window, trying to catch a glimpse of Kane, but all she could see was the glare from passing cars. She had just offended one of the people closest to her. She searched in vain for an explanation for her erratic behavior. If it weren't simply a case of premenstrual hormones gone awry, and if she continued with this trend, then by the time Laz did finally come back, she might just have managed to alienate everyone within her proximity.

THAT NIGHT, SHE dreamt that Kane was driving her home in a car filled with sterling roses, but instead of stoplights, there were Magic 8-Balls at each corner. The 8-Balls glowed green like neon halos, but when she and Kane approached them, the 8-Balls turned red. At each corner, the same message was displayed: *You may deny it.*

16
Watson and Crick

There were seven messages on the answering machine when Grace got upstairs. It was only nine o'clock, but it felt like midnight. She wagered a guess before playing the messages that at least five of them were from her father, hopefully one from Kane. That would leave one remaining message. It was the last one that Grace held out for with white-knuckled tenacity, like a child clinging to a helium balloon.

The first one was from her father. *Hi, Gracie, it's Dad.* She skipped ahead to the next message, which was from Laz's mother, reminding her about an auction solicitations meeting on Wednesday. Then another one from her father. *Dad again. Just calling to see if you got home safely.* She assumed the next message would be her father again, but it was from Chloe.

Hi. It's me. It's been a long time. I guess you haven't heard. My mother died in September. I was in briefly to sort through some things, but not really in the Thanksgiving mood. Call me. I'd love to talk to you.

Grace replayed the message. She hadn't realized that she and Chloe had drifted so much that Chloe wouldn't have even called to tell her about her mother. She remembered when they used to talk every day.

She played the next message. *Grace, it's your father. Give a call when you get in.* She hit the delete button. The next message was garbled. She heard a woman's voice mumbling in Spanish. Grace recognized some of the words. *No está en casa.* Finally, after some confusion and shuffling sounds, she was able to discern Marisol's voice: *Señora Grace? My niece will be in tomorrow. The doctor says I cannot work until Thursday. Gracias.*

Grace played the final message. Just a long dial tone. She rewound it and played it again, turning up the volume in the hopes of hearing something that might indicate that the call had been from Laz, and not simply a wrong number. She was about to replay it for the third time when the telephone rang and she hit the delete button by accident. She picked up the phone and had already said, "Hi, Dad," when she heard an unfamiliar voice on the other end.

"Hello. Is Lazarus Brookman there, please?" a woman inquired. She had the kind of voice Grace recalled from poetry workshops she'd taken in college—self-assured and polished.

"Hello?" the woman said again.

Grace had a flash of recognition, like the sighting of a lightning bug, but each time she thought she'd caught hold of it she came up empty-handed. Grace was about to answer when the woman began speaking to someone in the background. "Let me handle it," the woman said, her voice slightly muffled.

"He just stepped out," Grace told her. "Can I take a message?"

"No, thank you. I'll call back," she said, hanging up before Grace could get her name.

Grace went to the closet to hang up her coat, and to her amazement, there on the same wooden hanger where it had always hung was Laz's leather jacket.

She touched the jacket and had a strange impulse to embrace it, instead zipping it up and adjusting it on the hanger, as if it were a disheveled child just home from school. In the morning, she'd take it to the tailor to get the pocket lining mended.

As soon as she closed the closet door, she was suddenly overcome with exhaustion, when only a moment ago she'd felt elated. The jacket had returned, but with it, only more questions. The Magic 8-Ball wasn't wired to deal with conflicted emotions, and neither was Grace. She proceeded to go into her default mode, blanking out all self-doubt and worry—even the sound of the woman's voice now escaped her—until the only thing she thought she needed was a good night's sleep.

WHEN SHE WOKE UP, she had no recollection of having fallen asleep, just the awareness that she'd had no dreams, a span of time with no thoughts—a feeling close to bliss, as if her memory, along with the dream about Kane, had been erased. It was still dark out. She thought it must be nearly dawn, but when she looked at the clock she saw that it was only four in the morning.

As a child, when she couldn't sleep, she'd think about her father's beige argyle sweater. Most of what he wore was either beige or some other neutral tone. Her father, a creature of habit, ate the same breakfast—cornflakes, half a toasted English muffin with currant jelly, and a cup of Postum with nondairy creamer—without fail each day. Grace found this predictability soothing, as regular and soporific as the pattern on his argyle sweater. She tried to close her eyes now, but she was strangely alert. She decided she might as well get up and string the Christmas lights.

The lights were in the utility closet inside two large plastic bags, next to some unopened cans of paint and tile grout that Laz had purchased during one of his home-repair phases, which had never come to fruition. The lights were a tangled mess of wires and bulbs, as Grace never had the patience to wind them back neatly. She preferred the stuff-them-in-a-bag-and-forget-about-them method of taking down the tree; she didn't mind the necessity then the following year of having to run out to the hardware store to buy new lights.

She set about trying to separate the strands that had twirled together like some genetic experiment gone haywire. There were equal numbers of white and colored strands, and many of each. Grace liked every inch of the tree to be lit up so that it blazed. Last year when they'd decorated the tree, Laz had said that if they strung the lights end to end, they would span the length of the George Washington Bridge.

As Grace untangled the lights, she thought of the meteor shower that she and Laz had seen on Block Island the first summer they were together. On a clear August night, they had been huddled by the dunes. Laz had pointed to the sky, which was streaked with sprays of light, and told her that for him it was what was in between the stars that intrigued him. Grace told him she preferred the stars themselves.

"Tell me what you can't do," he asked, pulling her closer. "I love you as much for what you aren't, as much as for what you are. Maybe more."

"I can't do a cartwheel," she said. "Or be alone." At the time, Grace had found the request strange, like trying to define something by its negative image, but now it made perfect sense. However, she still preferred the lights.

• • •

THE MOST DIFFICULT part of untangling the Christmas lights was having the restraint not to tug too hard, so as not to unwind the double wires that made up each individual strand. Grace found this particularly trying, as her initial inclination was to wrench them apart with brute force. Her second thought was to get a pair of scissors and cut them. She succumbed to neither strategy, forcing herself to remain in a state of calm and balance that was utterly unfamiliar to her. She had once read that the smell of lavender was supposed to have a relaxing effect on the mind, and she would have lit an aromatherapy candle now if she'd had one. Instead, she settled for trying to conjure a mental facsimile of the smell.

After several minutes, managing only a vague olfactory approximation of essence of apple, she gave up. Although unsuccessful, the distraction had served its purpose. In the meantime, she'd been able to disengage several strands from the chaotic jumble. She marveled at her work, then inspected each strand to make sure that no bulbs were missing or broken.

The tree had settled in over the last few days, spreading out like a houseguest with a lot of luggage. It looked significantly larger than when Kane had first set it up. Grace moved the furniture to give the branches more space and hoped that the tree would not continue to expand.

Once Grace began stringing them, the lights went up easily. She fastened the strands together, following the natural flow of the branches, and before she knew it, she was ready to plug the cord into the outlet. The tree lit up in a sparkle of white and jewel colors. Grace stood back to admire it. The lights soon began to blink in a perfectly timed sequence that, for Grace, mimicked and in some way even surpassed the randomness of stars.

She was tired when she finished, the first hint of morning a pale glow above the park. She prepared José's coffee, took it downstairs, and, exhausted, went back to bed.

Grace had forgotten that Marisol's niece was coming that morning, so she was surprised when she was awakened by the sound of the vacuum. She looked at the clock. It was nearly eleven. Grace jumped out of bed, realizing that she'd neglected to leave any further evidence of Laz around the apartment. Laz's side of the bed appeared eerily unslept on, the pillows neatly stacked, the comforter uncreased. She pulled down the comforter, rumpled the sheet, and twisted it into a tornado-like formation. Laz was a fitful sleeper, often sprawling diagonally across the bed, the pillows ending up tossed on the floor. Grace, on the other hand, could sleep in one position all night. In the morning, all that was needed for her side was a light smoothing of the bedspread and fluffing of the pillows; otherwise, it was hard to tell that anyone had even slept there.

After a few final touches—Laz's razor blade and a tube of toothpaste in the garbage can; an unopened tin of Altoids on the dresser; his tattered black Dartmouth sweatshirt, now faded to a grayish green, slung over the back of the chair—the scene was set. It was more for Grace's own benefit, she acknowledged, than for Marisol's niece, on whom the fine attention to detail would be lost since she was not well acquainted with Laz's habits.

Grace bent down to retrieve Laz's sheepskin slippers out from under the bed and had the sudden impulse to try them on. They were far too large for her, of course. She could feel the indentations that his toes had made in the thick fleece. Instantly, her feet began to overheat in them. Laz wore them all the time, complaining that his feet were always cold, but still preferring the aesthetic of bare floors or area rugs to wall-to-wall carpeting. If pressed, though, it was the carpet's seeming permanence that scared him.

Except for the kitchen, every square inch of Grace's parents' apartment, including the closets and the bathrooms, was covered with a thick, wool Berber. To Grace, it felt homey. Her mother had put her foot down, however, when Grace's father had suggested using the scraps to line the kitchen cabinets. Her father had even invested in an industrial-strength rug shampooer, which he lugged out religiously every month.

Once, on a trip to Morocco, Grace and Laz had visited a local rug shop. An array of brilliant carpets hung from the rafters, others were piled high on the floor. Laz had remarked to the owner of the shop that he liked the fact that the carpets could be rolled up and taken with them if they ever moved.

Sipping a glass of mint tea, Laz pointed to a small flat-weave rug. The owner shook it out and let it fall gently to the floor. "This one I could slip into a backpack," Laz joked, making the merchant smile. When Laz saw the expression on Grace's face, he put his arm around her and pulled her close. "Don't worry, Grace, I'd slip you in there, too—if there was room," he said, laughing. "You never know, you might wind up leaving me. But you'd need a six-piece set of luggage, and that's not even counting the passage for your family. And you can't forget the Sugarmans. Travel light—that's my motto. If I teach you one thing, that should be it."

GRACE REMOVED THE slippers from her feet and arranged them to look as if Laz had just kicked them off. She bent down to smooth the dust ruffle. As she stood up, she felt a sharp twinge in her lower right side. She took three deep breaths until the pain subsided.

She looked around the room and admired her work, deciding she might have missed her calling as a stage manager, or at the very least, a competent window dresser. The room looked like a life-size diorama. As if the curator of a museum, she formulated the caption in her head: *Portrait of a Marriage, circa 1999*. She angled the door for the best possible view, stopping just short of cordoning off the room with a velvet rope.

Marisol's niece Dolores was polishing the silver when Grace walked into the kitchen. Grace was dressed in a black sweater and a pair of gray pants that had just come back from the dry cleaners and were a bit on the tight side. "*Buenos dias,* Señora Brookman," Dolores said, smiling.

"Good morning. Beautiful day, isn't it?" Grace said.

Dolores nodded. "*Sí,* but it's *mucho frío,*" she answered. Grace noticed that Dolores was still wearing her blue down jacket.

"Please call me Grace."

"Certainly, Señora Grace," she responded, as she carried the silver bowl into the dining room and placed it in the center of the table. Before Grace could warn her, Dolores flipped on the light switch. With a quick flash, the dining room fixture and the lights in the entire apartment blew.

When Grace called down for the handyman, the superintendent told her he'd send someone up right away—one of the many perks of being generous tippers at Christmastime.

The handyman arrived within minutes, once again removing his shoes, although Grace would have much preferred footprints to the sight of his canary yellow socks. It was only a matter of minutes before the apartment once again blazed with the light from the Duro-Lites and the Christmas tree sparkled in the living room.

"Remember to turn off the circuit breaker the next time if you need to replace the dimmer," the handyman advised her, as he bent down to put his shoes back on. She noticed that they were not his usual work boots, but a pair of shiny tap shoes, which, paired with his baggy blue carpenter's pants, gave him a Chaplinesque appearance. He stood up, lingering a bit until Grace pressed a twenty-dollar bill in his hand and bid him good-bye.

After he left, Grace went into the dining room to test the dimmer. She lifted it up and down and felt a sense of complete satisfaction as the Duro-Lites dimmed to a quiet, calming orange and then brightened. Out of the corner of her eye, she noticed a strange flickering from the living room, like the flashes from a silent summer lightning storm. To her dismay, she realized that the Christmas tree lights as well as the sconces above the mantelpiece and the Arts and Crafts lamps on the end tables were all dimming and brightening in unison with the Duro-Lites.

When Grace turned the light off, the lights in the living room went off as well. She flipped the switch back on quickly, hoping she could somehow fool the circuits. Once again, the Christmas tree and all the other lights went on. She jiggled the switch, thinking the wires were just stuck together and that she could somehow unstick them, but it didn't help. Her first inclination was to call the super again, but instead she decided to adjust the lights so that the Christmas tree and the Duro-Lites were all at a tolerable level of brightness.

Then she went to the closet to get Laz's jacket to take it to the tailor's, along with a pair of his pants that needed hemming. When she got back, she would call Chloe.

The tailor at Aphrodite Cleaners was busy sewing buttons onto a thick shearling coat when Grace walked in. He nodded for her to sit down on a folding chair, then he ended off, cutting the thread with his teeth, and walked over to her.

"These pants need hemming," she told the tailor, "and there's a tear in the pocket lining of the jacket." The tailor unfolded the pants and examined them.

"How long?" he asked. Grace hadn't remembered to measure the length of Laz's inseam, although she was certain she could come pretty close to the measurement if she tried the pants on.

"Is there someplace I can change into them?" she asked.

"Right in there," he said, indicating a small half-curtain to the left of his sewing table.

The tailor didn't question whether the pants were hers or not. She went behind the curtain into a space no larger than a telephone booth and put the pants on. They were not as large as she'd anticipated. Clearly, the sugar binge she'd been on over the last few weeks was beginning to take its toll. The waistband skimmed her pelvic bone. As she adjusted the pants low on her hips, she pictured how Laz's body fit into hers, the way his hands could practically circle her waist when he stood behind her.

"The hem should just graze the floor," she told the tailor when she emerged. She stepped up on a small stool and stood in front of the mirror as he knelt down and marked the pants with a white wax crayon. She was amazed by how much she resembled Laz, at least from the waist down, except for her shoes, which were high-heeled boots. She felt like a picture in one of those children's flipbooks that mixes and matches different heads and bodies—a strange hybrid creature. A Chimera. As Grace stood in front of the mirror, she wasn't sure where the line of demarcation was, where one began and the other one ended. And who was inhabiting whom now?

"Which one needs repair?" the tailor asked, picking up Laz's jacket and turning it inside out.

"Excuse me?" Grace asked.

"Which pocket has the hole?"

"Oh, the right one," she answered.

"Do me a favor and check to make sure there's nothing in the pockets. You wouldn't believe the things people leave."

She slid her hands into the pockets. These pockets that had once held Laz's keys and change, into which his hands had slid so many times to keep warm, were now empty. Not only was his PalmPilot gone, but so were the Life Savers. Grace felt as if she'd been fleeced by a phantom pickpocket. She wondered if the vanished items might lead her to her vanished husband, a trail she knew she wasn't yet prepared to follow. For now, it would remain another mystery.

DOLORES WAS STANDING in the doorway, waiting for Grace when she arrived home. She hung up her coat, ready to write the name of some cleaning product on a shopping list, assuming that Dolores had run out of Brillo Pads or Murphy's Oil Soap, which Marisol used liberally on all surfaces and that soaked through even the Sunday *Times,* leaving the pages nearly translucent.

"Excuse, me," Dolores began. "Marisol says Señor Brookman forgot to leave her pay." Grace was baffled. She'd been so diligent about writing checks to pay the bills, but then it dawned on her that Laz must have always paid Marisol in cash.

"How much do we owe her?" Grace asked.

"*Cinco* weeks," Dolores answered. Something about hearing the number, even in Spanish, made Grace's head spin. To her, it felt as if Laz had been gone no longer than a matter of days, despite all evidence to the contrary—such as the fact that the supply of deli cups, which had come in a pack of fifty, was more than half depleted. Grace had stopped counting the days sometime after Laz's birthday. November might as well have been frozen in one of Francine's containers.

"*Cinco?*" Grace repeated. She opened her wallet and gave Dolores all the cash she had on hand. "I'll go to the bank right away for the rest. Please tell Marisol I'm very sorry."

The telephone rang. She picked it up, half expecting it to be a bill collector.

"Grace? It's Chloe."

"Chloe," she said. "It's so good to hear your voice. I'm so sorry about your mother. I wish you had called to tell me."

"You know how it is." She paused, sniffling a bit. "It's been rough." There was another pause. Then Chloe said, "So you're coming to Chicago?"

"For my birthday," Grace answered, although she was already having misgivings about the plan.

"Laz, too?" Chloe inquired.

"Yes, he'll be tied up with some conference, but I thought you and I could spend some time together if you want."

"It's been a long time."

"I know. I'm really sorry I've been out of touch," Grace said.

"Me, too. Let's make sure to change that."

Grace hung up and dialed the toll-free number of the discount travel agent whom her father had once told her about, and she booked a flight to Chicago for the day before her birthday, using frequent-flier miles accrued by Laz on his many transatlantic flights. Out of force of habit, she asked for two bulkhead seats—Laz liked a lot of legroom. By the time Grace had realized her mistake, the agent had already put the order through, so Grace decided to keep it. She told herself it was in order to avoid wasting more time, but what she was really feeling was trepidation about traveling alone, which was somehow alleviated by the thought of Laz's disembodied presence. He was like her new imaginary friend—if only he didn't demand so much attention.

Later that evening, Grace was straightening up after Dolores. It seemed that Dolores had a similar propensity as Grace did of shoving things in incongruous places wherever they fit, and Grace noticed her bag of ombré yarn stuffed into the umbrella stand.

She opened the bag and pulled out the crochet hook and a skein of yarn. Removing the paper sleeve, she located the end and proceeded to begin a chain stitch. At first it was slow and laborious, but soon the yarn began to slip easily through her fingers, the stitches forming as if automatically. When the chain was a good length, Grace began to crochet, pulling the yarn under and through and wrapping it around the hook until she came to the end of the first row. The edges curled up and it didn't look like anything, but after several more rows, Grace began to detect the beginnings of a pattern.

For an indeterminate span of time, no thoughts entered her mind. The yarn alternated in a pleasingly unpredictable way, varying in tone and thickness, with intermittent flashes of fuchsia. The rhythmic pattern was spellbinding. She wondered if crocheting could become addictive, as she considered the merits of a twenty-four-hour yarn store and tied the ends of one skein to the next.

After crocheting some more, she started to tire of repeating the same stitches and decided to make variations in the pattern by adding a stitch here or there, inserting the hook into the same stitch twice or dropping a loop, which created a clustered, starlike effect. She liked not having to follow a pattern; however, she did have to pull several rows when she tried to get too fancy.

Before she knew it, the bag of yarn was empty. Only after she'd ended off the last stitch did she realize that it was well after midnight and that she'd crocheted something—what, she wasn't sure, a sort of continuous flow of color and texture that spanned the entire length of her living room.

17
A Grimm Tale

Kane did not call the following day or the next. It wasn't noticeable at first. His calls were not all that regular—varying from once or twice a day to once a week, or even less frequently. It wasn't that he wasn't calling, it was the *way* in which he wasn't calling that Grace knew was somehow different.

She'd already left two messages for him. The first was to provide an excuse as to why Laz couldn't make hockey that night—a fundraiser his mother had roped him into—and the other was to try to make amends for the other night. Both calls went unanswered.

Another stack of mail had materialized on the front hall table. Grace likened the pile of mail that had begun to overrun her life to the suburban phenomenon of trying to maintain a manicured lawn, the bills like stubborn dandelions and the junk mail like fallen leaves. She wished taking care of the bills were as simple as upgrading to a more powerful leaf blower or a more potent weed killer.

Among the bills, she saw a letter from A Perfect Match. Ordinarily, she would have just ripped it in half, but after the meeting with the strange Mr. Dubrovsky, her curiosity was piqued. When she opened it, she saw that she'd been mistaken. The letter was from the lipstick company, informing her that they needed an additional five dollars and ninety-five cents per tube and another sample of the lipstick, if possible, which would have to be sent to the laboratory in Minnesota for further analysis.

Grace was disappointed. She was almost certain she didn't have anymore Velvet, but she went into the bathroom and dug into her vinyl makeup bag on the off chance that she had missed it. She stored the bag on the windowsill above the broken radiator because her mother once told her that the shelf life of makeup is shortened if it's exposed to heat or humidity, advising her to keep her extra lipsticks in the freezer. If Grace followed all of her parents' advice on proper storage, her freezer would be filled to capacity with film, batteries, stockings, and makeup, probably even Duro-Lites.

The bag overflowed with tester-sized tubes of moisturizers, eye shadows, perfume samples, lip and cheek stains, shimmery face powder, white lip gloss, metallic eyeliner, and an array of age-defying lotions that her mother had given her, none of which Grace ever used. Francine gave leftovers; her mother gave beauty products. Grace always felt a pang of guilt when she even entertained the idea of tossing the entire makeup bag in the garbage, just as she would have felt if the did the same with Francine's meatballs.

She was about to give up her search when she noticed an orange pump bottle containing a hydrating body mist called Happy. She read the directions on the back of the bottle: *Spray it. Be Happy.* Enticed by the promise it made, she opened the top and sprayed it over her neck and forearms. It couldn't hurt, her mother would say. The citrusy smell was pleasant enough, but Grace didn't notice any other effects. If only it could be that simple, she thought as she tossed it back into the transparent makeup bag and went to get dressed.

She chose what she considered to be one of her more pulled-together outfits—a cream-colored cashmere turtleneck and her new purple suede skirt—for her visit to her grandmother at the nursing home.

Grace was an unseasoned shopper and left most sartorial decisions to other people. Elliot, one of the salespeople at Barneys, called whenever something came in that they thought suited her, like a pair of must-have black pants, a puckered pink shell, or the beaded silk sarong that Grace had later found for a fraction of the price on a foray with her mother to the Woodbury Commons Outlet. Yesterday, Elliot had left a message telling Grace that he was holding a Katayone Adeli suede skirt for her, but when she went in to try it on, he made the gentle suggestion, not able to fully conceal his raised eyebrow, that they go up another size. Decorum stopped him from suggesting they go up still further. "It *will* stretch," he assured her.

Grace recalled numerous Saturday shopping expeditions with her mother over the years, the two of them often coming home with matching outfits, such as the satin blouses with bell sleeves and macramé vests, or the bright floral minidresses with white peace sign belts. Shopping was her mother's forte as well as her form of therapy—a cure-all for whatever ailed you. They'd spend hours scouring the racks and then, shopping bags in hand, find the nearest Burger Heaven for what her mother referred to as a little *lift*, which consisted of half a cantaloupe, a medium-rare burger on half a bun, and a large Coke. But at the end of the day, Grace would feel anything but uplifted. While clothes were her mother's means to attain her desired image of herself and that of her daughter, for Grace clothes would never be more than another ill-fitting costume.

WHEN GRACE WAS FIFTEEN, she broke up with her first boyfriend. Her mother wasted no time questioning her about the particulars of the breakup, bringing a box of Fiddle Faddle and some tissues to Grace's bedroom as though having prepared all her life for this mother-daughter bonding moment. Grace was too numb to cry.

"I hear you broke up with that sweet Jamie. What happened?" her mother asked. Grace pulled her feet underneath her and tried to find the right words.

"I didn't feel like me anymore," she said quietly. Her mother looked at her quizzically.

"You're still you. Jamie liked you just the way you are."

"It wasn't him. It was me. It was as if I had found the perfect outfit and wore it everyday and never wanted to change it—you know, like that polka-dotted dress I wore until it didn't fit anymore?"

"I know exactly what you mean," her mother said, nodding. "Variety is the spice of life. But that dress was adorable on you."

"Only the more I wore the dress, the less I liked myself in it. I didn't know who I was supposed to be or what I was supposed to wear. It was like I'd run out of outfits."

Her mother put her arm around her, and passed her the box of caramel corn and a handful of tissues.

"Honey, not to worry," she said. "Lord and Taylor is open until nine, and there's a sale in the junior department. We'll have you back to yourself in no time."

GRACE ZIPPED UP her skirt and pulled her hair back with a clip. There had never been any question in her mind that her mother was not capable of more. Grace had always tried to accept her mother's good intentions, even if they came in the form of frilly skirts and turquoise belts, but in Grace's mind she was still in some metaphorical dressing room, trying on clothes chosen by someone else.

Going into the kitchen for a quick cup of tea, Grace opened the cabinet, and there, next to a canister of peppermint tea, she saw the familiar silver tube of Velvet, shining like a beacon in the darkness. It did strike her as a rather odd place for the lipstick, but it was just like her to have absentmindedly put it in there. She felt the sense of elation she usually felt on Christmas morning.

Grace thought about the rhinestone lipstick holder that Laz's mother had coveted at last year's Historical Society auction. Even though the auction was for charity, and Laz's mother would have received a tax deduction for the purchase, she'd refused to go above the estimated value and had lost out to Francine Sugarman, who had instructed Bert to outbid anyone while she was at home with a case of the flu. Bert had waved his paddle as if he were a table tennis champion, once even bidding against himself as Laz's mother lowered her paddle to her lap.

Laz's mother still eyed the lipstick holder with a sneer every time she saw Francine pull it out of her purse—which Francine did often and with obvious pleasure—because she, Nancy Brookman, would never pay full price. Grace thought she might bid on it herself at this year's auction so that she would have a special place to hold her custom-blended lipstick, when it finally arrived. She regretted having not renamed the lipstick—"Velvet" seemed somewhat generic now.

She wrote a check for the required extra amount, placed the lipstick sample in an envelope, and sealed it. She felt as if she were participating in some cloning experiment and wondered if she sent them the smudged fingerprints from Laz's eyeglasses, would they be able to come up with a reasonable replica of him as well?

Taking the envelope, along with the bag containing her crocheting in case she had time to stop in for more yarn on her way to class, she went to visit her grandmother.

• • •

Grace rode the bus up Riverside Drive just past Columbia Presbyterian Hospital to the nursing home. Grace's grandmother had lived in Washington Heights in a redbrick apartment house on the cliffs of the Hudson, overlooking the river for nearly forty years.

When Grace was a teenager, Dolly used to take her aside and tell her that when she died, the apartment would belong to Grace. "I know you'll take care of it—it's my museum. You understand." Grace had always thought she would move there, keeping it intact, as her grandmother had wished, but Laz wanted something "in the city." To him, Washington Heights was like another country, even though it was within the city limits. When Dolly had moved into the nursing home six years ago, the apartment had been given up, her possessions appraised and then sold.

After Dolly's first stroke, Grace had brought Laz to the hospital to meet her. Dolly had squinted her eyes and pointed at him. "I know you," she said, with seeming certainty.

Dolly had come to the United States from Lithuania with her older brother when she was nineteen. The rest of her family perished during the war a few years after that, at which point Dolly had begun collecting. While her children and husband were off at school and work, Dolly went scavenging in antique shops. "Junk shops," she called them. She would return with heavy pendulum clocks, porcelain teacups, carved wooden chairs, hiding her treasures in the closet until one day they'd suddenly appear, blending in among the other household items, as if always having been there.

The bus continued up Riverside Drive, past Grant's Tomb and the mansion where she and Laz had met. It was now abandoned, the property surrounded by a barbed-wire fence. The windows had been replaced with plywood, the doors boarded up. Grace looked back, hoping to glimpse some signs of restoration, until the bus turned and the mansion was no longer in sight.

GRACE GOT OFF the bus and walked up the stone steps of the nursing home, where she found Dolly propped up in bed, gazing out over the Hudson River.

"Grace," she said, slurring slightly. "When will this plane land?" Dolly's room was bare, except for an embroidered bedspread with silk tassels and an antique porcelain clock—one of dozens that she'd collected—that ticked loudly.

When Grace was in college, she had visited her grandmother weekly. Grace remembered the details of one particular visit as if it were yesterday. Dolly had come to the door wearing an ankle-length peasant skirt and a purple shawl around her shoulders. On her head she wore a flowered kerchief, her white hair braided and twisted into a tight bun, which was held in place with a tortoiseshell comb.

"Grace, you're here! I have spinach pie all ready for you. Come have a little something."

"Dolly, I told you I would bring lunch this time."

"What? You'd rather eat from a store?" she asked, putting her arm around Grace's waist.

"I have that cake you like."

"Well, with Zabar's, I can't compete. Come, let's sit."

Grace followed Dolly into her living room. The room was large but so crammed full of furniture that it was difficult to walk through without bumping into something. The door to the terrace was open and there was a breeze. Grace sat in the courtship chair. It had two worn mahogany seats, which faced in opposite directions. The carved center arms were linked together, as if in an embrace. Dolly took in the scene, smiling and nodding her head.

"You look perfect there. Just perfect."

Then Grace noticed a broken spinning wheel next to the fireplace. She'd never seen it before and went to touch it. "Is this new, Dolly?" she asked.

"Oh, no, Grace. It's been here all along."

GRACE NOW LOOKED at the outline of her grandmother's small frame under the bedspread, and at the bare, uncluttered room.

"Will this plane land soon?" Dolly asked again. Grace wondered which way her grandmother thought she was traveling—to America, or back to the girlhood home in Lithuania she'd spent her life trying to recapture.

"Soon, Dolly," Grace said. "I promise."

THE YARN STORE was crowded, and at first Grace didn't see Penelope. Then from out of a basement storeroom, Penelope emerged, huffing and puffing from the climb. She was carrying an armful of yarn, which she set down, and she nodded to Grace. One of the balls of yarn rolled off the counter and disappeared behind a basket like a frightened mouse. Grace bent to pick it up.

"Thanks," Penelope said. "It's Grace, right?"

"Yes," Grace answered. Another customer, a petite woman in a shearling coat and a black beret, was waiting to be rung up. Grace felt she was in good company. If only she'd discovered the meditative qualities of crocheting sooner.

"So, how's it going. Are you hooked yet?" Penelope asked, deadpan. She had clearly used the pun before and had no reason to punctuate it with a laugh. Grace smiled.

Grace placed her yarn bag on the counter and reached inside. "I'd like to buy more yarn."

"You're finished already?" Penelope asked, her eyes widening as Grace pulled out the seemingly never-ending stretch of crochet from the bag. Even Grace was surprised at its proportions, which seemed, like a yeast dough, to have more than doubled in size since the previous night.

"Once I started, it was hard to stop," Grace answered.

"I like the pattern. What book did you use?"

"I didn't," she admitted. "I sort of improvised as I went along."

By this time, a small group had gathered around the counter, hands outstretched to examine the length of Grace's crochet.

A tall woman wearing a long black coat that was covered with cat hair came over to the counter. "Interesting pattern," she said discerningly, as she inspected the edging. "But what are you making?"

"I'm not sure," Grace said. The idea that this would eventually have an end didn't appeal to her. Part of her believed she could just keep crocheting ad infinitum.

"It's a process," Penelope said with authority.

"Nice bobbles," another woman commented. Grace thanked her, even though she didn't have any idea what bobbles were, and in any other context she might have been duly insulted. A heavyset man, not more than thirty, with shiny brown hair approached the counter. Grace noticed that he was wearing a hand-knit sweater of a bright blue wool tucked into a pair of too-tight jeans.

"My grandmother taught me how to crochet when I was eight," he told Grace with a faraway look in his eyes. "Whenever anything was bothering me, we'd sit down to crochet, and it would all just go away. And that was before they knew about serotonin levels." Grace couldn't help but nod. "My name's Scott," he said, extending his hand. "I started a men's group called Crocheting Through. We meet in the basement of the Presbyterian Church every Thursday night. In homage to my grandmother." He sighed. Grace was afraid that he might start crying. "I really miss her a lot." She'd had no idea that people could bond over a few simple stitches.

"You've got the knack," Penelope said. "If I didn't know any better, I'd say you've been crocheting all your life. I started repairing that afghan you brought in, but I think you can handle it from here. Don't be afraid to rip. You have to be ruthless, otherwise you're wasting your time. If you don't do it right, it'll just fall apart in other places," she explained. Grace felt her cheeks grow warm. Somehow, after seeing Dolly in her bare room, the holes seemed preferable to the idea of undoing her grandmother's stitches.

"If you don't mind, I'd rather you did it," she said. Grace walked over to a basket and pulled out a ball of soft yarn.

"Those are nice if you're going to make a throw," Penelope told her. Grace liked the sound of that. It seemed less daunting than making a sweater or something else that required precise dimensions. A throw. Casual and homey.

"How many will I need?" she asked.

"It depends on how big you want it to be. One skein will work up to be about a ten-by-ten-inch square."

"Well, I guess I'll need about twenty, then," she decided.

"I should just give you some straw and see what you come up with," Penelope said with a laugh. Grace smiled but didn't get it. Noticing Grace's perplexed expression, she added, "You know, like Rumpelstiltskin."

"Oh, of course," Grace said.

Penelope put the yarn in a bag. "By the way, I've been looking for someone to work part-time. I don't know if you'd be interested."

"My days are pretty full," Grace answered. "Can I think about it?"

"Of course. Take your time." Grace was struck by the camaraderie and support among the patrons in the tiny, cramped shop. She pictured them all gathered around the long oak table, comparing stitches and giving advice on projects. If ever there were an actual Friends of the Friendless, this place was it.

CHIMERA BOOKS WAS moderately crowded for a Wednesday evening. Grace walked to the back of the bookstore, greeting the salespeople with a newfound openness. It was as though she were seeing the place for the first time, embracing every idiosyncratic detail of the store—from the worn wooden Escheresque steps to the warped bookshelves and the smell of cloves from the holiday wreaths. One of the clerks had brought in a bûche de Noël, and Grace decided she would not pass on a slice. She took out her supplies, placing the hand drills and metal burnishers on the long worktable alongside the three-inch-square sheets of gold leaf she'd bought at Lee's Art Shop.

The room didn't have adequate lighting—the antique brass billiard lamp that hung from the ceiling gave off barely enough light to read by. Yet the dimness didn't deter Grace's students in the least as they fashioned folios out of rag paper. Grace had brought in a few hurricane candles, which were useful not just for the added light they provided but also the added warmth, needed because of the draftiness from the large, warped windows. Some of her students actually preferred the dim lights, saying that it hearkened back to a simpler time. Grace agreed. In the low lighting, the gold leaf fluttered like butterfly wings. With a little ingenuity and a light dusting of gold, Grace thought she might even be able to fool Bert with a paper rendition of his beloved Painted Lady.

She heard laughter and the popping of corks from the front of the store, so she finished up her class preparations and decided to join the festivities. As she walked through the stacks, passing people as they browsed, she noticed an edition of Kafka's *Metamorphosis* and pulled it from the shelf to see if it was a first edition.

Her father had taught her how to identify rare books, and she was about to turn to the title page when she felt a hand on her shoulder. She turned around to see the young man from the other day, who was not only standing before her but wearing the leather jacket that she'd seen in Laz's apartment. The next thing she was aware of was a sharp pain in her lower abdomen and then the hard *thud* as she fell to the floor.

Grace had never fainted before, and even though she was lying down, she wasn't really sure what had happened. The concerned faces above her were a clear indication that something was wrong, so she immediately tried to get up. As she braced herself on a low shelf, she saw a book entitled *Your Natural Childbirth,* with a graphic photograph of a baby still attached to the placenta on the cover. Grace immediately felt herself growing woozy again. Maybe she should have put more faith in the 8-Ball and not the pregnancy test. She closed her eyes, then felt herself being lifted to her feet by a strong set of arms, which led her to the front of the store and eased her into a large leather club chair by a window. When she was seated, she looked up at the young man standing in front of her.

"Sorry I startled you. You were really out over there," he said, sounding a little impressed. "I'm Griffin."

"I just got a little dizzy, that's all," she told him. "I'll be fine, thanks. I have a class to teach."

Someone brought a glass of water, which Grace sipped slowly. Griffin pulled a chair beside her and sat down. Grace looked at his jacket. She knew there were things he could explain, but something held her back from asking. She pulled her hair into a ponytail and looked at him. He was sweet looking, and, close up at least, his resemblance to Laz was less noticeable. The jacket, however, was another story.

"Your jacket—" she started to say, and then stopped.

"Oh, yeah. It was my dad's."

"Your father gave it to you?" she asked. "When?" Once she started asking questions, she knew she'd be unable to stop.

"Well, he didn't exactly give it to me," he said. "I mean, I've never actually met him. My mom kept it for me. He wore it in college. It's not very warm, though, or maybe I'm just not used to the cold." It occurred to her that Griffin might be Laz's son. All the crocheting in the world would not make this go away.

"Why? Where are you from?" she asked.

"From Atlanta. But I go to college in Maryland. I'm a sophomore at Johns Hopkins. Premed."

As he spoke, all the strange occurrences of the last few weeks began to fit together like a puzzle—from the edition of Twain to the couple at the restaurant and the concierge's reference to the *young* Mr. Brookman. It had been Griffin all along.

"How did you know where to find me?" she asked.

"From an article my mother saw in a magazine. She wrote a letter to my father. Didn't you get it?" Grace shook her head, and then vaguely remembered the folded piece of paper stuck in the pages of *Oblomov*.

"So you came looking for him?" she asked. Griffin looked at his fingernails, which were chewed down to the cuticles, and then shoved his hands into his pockets. Laz bit his nails, too.

"I'm sorry I wasn't honest with you," he said, his voice melting into a more Southern tone. "I wasn't all that sure how I'd be received." His cheeks flushed all the way behind his ears. Grace could see he'd cut himself shaving.

"So," Grace started to say tentatively, "am I a stepmom?" It was a totally alien concept, especially considering that Laz couldn't have been more than Griffin's age when the boy was conceived. He smiled.

"I was hoping you could help me get in contact with my father, but I know this may be a bad time with the controversy and all."

Even if she did know where Laz was, she couldn't imagine that this would be a happy reunion. "He gave you the keys to his apartment, didn't he?" Grace asked, trying to change the subject.

"He left them for me with the concierge, but he never showed up. My mother says that's typical." He paused. "She didn't want me to get my hopes up, but I told her that I had nothing to lose." Grace nodded, but she knew he was wrong. Either way, he had something to lose. And more so if he ever met Laz.

"He's away now," Grace told him, trying not to meet his eyes. "At a conference."

"When will he be back?"

"He wasn't sure," she answered. "Sometime next week. I think." Grace felt perspiration trickling down her back. The store suddenly felt stiflingly hot, and Grace knew that she had to get outside.

"You're looking pale again," Griffin said. "Can I get you something?"

"Is it hot in here?" she asked. Not waiting for a response, she bolted for the door.

Once outside, Grace braced herself against a mailbox. It had begun to snow and big wet flakes stuck to her suede skirt. Griffin followed behind.

"Are you okay?" he asked, putting his jacket over her shoulders.

"I'm sorry. I just needed some air," she explained.

"I know the feeling," he said, reaching into his army-green knapsack. He rummaged through a zippered compartment and took out a box of Altoids, opened it, and held it out to her. Laz always had a box of Altoids in his pocket, too. Grace took one, marveling that a father and son who never knew each other could have the same small things in common. Maybe the gene for a predilection for peppermint was passed down like eye color or left-handedness. There was no need for genetic testing.

"My mother says peppermint lifts your spirits," he told her. It would have been preferable had Griffin appeared out of thin air. Having a mother implied a relationship with the father, and that was something Grace was not prepared to confront. "And ginger is good for motion sickness." He pulled out a bag of crystallized ginger. "You should try some for your stomach."

"My stomach?" Grace asked, perplexed.

"You're holding it. I thought it might be bothering you." Grace hadn't been conscious that she was clutching her stomach. She put her hands to her side, suddenly aware of a nagging pain. She wondered if it might be some kind of psychosomatic wishful thinking for a baby. Maybe Griffin's appearance triggered something, shining a light on possibilities she'd never allowed herself to dream of. Surprisingly, the mint did revive her.

"Thanks," she said. "I feel much better." She looked at Griffin and found herself trying to dissect his features, deciding which ones to embrace, which to disown—the squared-off angle of his chin, his long fingers, and even the way his hair fell over his forehead were all clearly from Laz. But his sad yet still trusting eyes, she knew, had to have come from someone else.

She looked at her watch. "I need to get back inside now." Griffin looked expectantly at her. She knew he was waiting for her to take some initiative, to invite him for dinner or suggest they meet sometime. "Will you be in town long?" she asked, finally.

"Until after the New Year," he said. "Then the next semester starts."

She hesitated. It wasn't enough that Laz had left her. His leaving now took on greater nonmarital dimensions—it was parental, as well. And, worst of all, he'd left her to clean up messes related to his leaving someone other than her.

He'd clearly been unable to confront his wife *and* his son. Laz's departure was perhaps beginning to make sense. After all, the deshrouding of his book and the return of his paternity-seeking son was a bit much for someone already predisposed as a marital flight risk.

She looked at Griffin standing in front of her with a look of hopefulness and expectancy. "You can call if you need anything," she said. She knew as she handed him a slip of paper with their phone number that what she was offering was inadequate, that anything less than making Laz materialize at this very instant would invariably fall short.

"Thanks," he said. Grace gave him back the jacket. She watched him zip it up, restraining that part of her that wanted to turn up his collar. He kissed her on the cheek, a gesture that took her completely by surprise, and turned to leave.

"Take care," she called after him as she watched him walk down the street, swinging his arms like Laz did. She felt a strong tug toward him as he turned the corner and disappeared from sight. Then she went back into the bookstore to teach her class.

18
Bringing Up Baby

On Friday morning, the day of her gynecologist appointment, Grace noticed some light spotting. She chided herself for having even entertained the idea that she was pregnant, an idea that now evaporated from her consciousness. It figured—just like how her hair always looked its best on the day on which she was scheduled to have it cut, or how something missing turned up immediately after she'd either replaced it or forgotten about it altogether.

Dr. Sarah Gaylin's office was just off Fifth Avenue, on the ground floor of a town house. This was only the third appointment that she'd had with Dr. Gaylin. Her last gynecologist had had a lecherous manner, along with hair plugs that made him look like one of those pomanders stuck with cloves that Grace's mother made during the holiday season and that Grace dutifully hung in her closet until the orange shriveled and it was safe to dispose of.

Grace took the crosstown bus through the park. She spent a few minutes writing her to-do list in her Filofax—*pick up dry cleaning; order Fruit of the Month for Laz's editor; order champagne for his agent; send thank-you notes for anniversary presents*—feeling satisfied by how orderly she'd made her life.

The decor in the doctor's waiting room was Old World, with leather club chairs and heavy drapes, reminding Grace of the Oak Room at the Plaza Hotel, where Laz's mother had a standing Thursday night reservation. Grace half-expected to be offered a drink by a waiter in a dusty black jacket, except here the customers were an assortment of women in various stages of pregnancy, reading parenting magazines and eating dried fruit.

After twenty minutes, Grace was ushered into a small dressing room by a nurse in a pink uniform. She knew there was a reason she liked this place. Even the gowns were a soft rose color.

Soon after, Dr. Gaylin knocked on the door and walked in, greeting Grace with a warm smile. She was tall—probably close to six feet—and under her white coat, she was dressed in a tailored skirt, sheer stockings, leather pumps, and a long strand of pearls. Her head had a perpetual tilt to the side that gave her an approachable, friendly appearance, and her hair was an indeterminate hue that changed from gold to strawberry blond, depending on the light. She possessed a certain regal, angelic quality that Grace was drawn to.

"How have you been, Grace?" she asked, looking at the chart and then sitting down on a stool to begin the exam.

"Everything's fine. I've been a little tired, but who isn't? Oh, and my period was a little late this month."

"How late?" she inquired.

"About two weeks. Almost three, I think." Grace gazed at the pale, striped wallpaper.

"Was your period normal?"

"Well, today is the first day, and it's still very light. Probably just stress from the holidays," she said.

"Any pain? Cramping?"

"I did notice a sharp pain a few times," Grace said.

"On which side?"

"The right, I think," she answered. "Why? Is there something wrong?"

"Grace, I'm going to do some tests. It's really just a routine precaution that I like to take with my patients who have IUDs. When a period is late, I like to make sure that everything is normal by checking blood levels and doing a sonogram."

Grace swallowed hard.

"What are you checking for?"

"To rule out the possibility that you're pregnant."

"I couldn't be pregnant," she insisted. "I did a test."

"In very rare instances, those tests can yield false negatives. I'd just like to make sure."

"What kind of instances?" Grace asked. She was about to explain that her husband had not so much as touched her in the last five weeks, but stopped herself as she did some mental calculations and thought back to the night Laz left.

"Nothing to worry about. As I said, it's just a precaution," Dr. Gaylin reassured her, buzzing for the nurse.

"Let's check the beta hCG levels," the doctor told the nurse when she walked in. After drawing blood, the nurse prepared for the sonogram. Dr. Gaylin explained each step as she went along, but as the procedure progressed, all Grace was aware of was the halolike glow of Dr. Gaylin's golden hair and the faint humming of the machine.

Grace listened as Dr. Gaylin explained about hCG levels and how in ectopic pregnancies that they don't double every forty-eight hours as they do in normal pregnancies. Although it was rare, the hormones had apparently been too low to register with a standard urine test. The information took time to sink in. Laz had never wanted children and Grace thought she'd accepted that. But as images of spinning musical mobiles, swaddling blankets, and her and Laz pushing a stroller along Riverside Drive flashed through her mind, she realized she had yearnings of her own. From one minute to the next, she bounced back and forth between feeling desolate and ebullient. And although she'd just been confronted with Laz's offspring, Griffin was not hers. Now she would have a child of her own.

"When will I be due?" she asked Dr. Gaylin.

"I don't think you understand. The embryo has embedded in the fallopian tubes. It's not a normal pregnancy."

"What chance is there that it will just get unstuck?" Grace asked. "And wind up in the right place?"

"I'm afraid that's not possible," Dr. Gaylin answered. "I'm going to have to administer a shot of methotrexate, which will in essence make the embryo disintegrate in the fallopian tube over the next several days." Grace found this information impossible to comprehend. How was it possible to lose something that five minutes ago she hadn't even known she'd had? The high beam from the halogen light turned Dr. Gaylin's hair a garishly unnatural cotton-candy pink.

Suddenly, Grace found the color repellent. "Will it be painful?" she asked.

"It shouldn't be. You can go about your daily activities, and then we'll check the hCG levels again in four days. We can call your husband to take you home, if that would make you feel more comfortable."

As Dr. Gaylin spoke, Grace felt a swelling in her chest. She was unable to breathe in deeply enough, as if it were a feeling she couldn't reach. Uncertain what she was about to do—cry or scream, or both—she waited until the urge subsided before she answered.

"He's out of town," she said softly.

THE WINDOWS OF the bus were covered with frost. Thoughts of Griffin surfaced again. She had an urge to crochet a scarf for him—a long, warm, tightly woven scarf, not as a consolation prize, or an affectionate gesture, or even to keep out the winter chill. Now she was deprived of both a husband and a child. She needed Laz home *now*. But not for her usual reasons—in order for Griffin to strangle his AWOL father with the scarf she would make him, Laz would have to be physically present.

She thought of the strange man she'd met at the Pink Tea Cup. Mr. Dubrovsky, she recalled, with the fluffy hair. She remembered the bold print on the card he had slipped in his copy of *Oblomov:* Private Investigator. He could help her track Laz down.

WHEN SHE GOT HOME, Grace turned on the dining room light and dimmed it (along with the Christmas tree and all the other fixtures in the living room). Everything seemed too bright. She noticed the amaryllis was still blooming.

As she searched for Mr. Dubrovsky's copy of *Oblomov,* she decided she'd treated him poorly at the restaurant and now regretted it. Hiring him to help her to find Laz might rectify the situation, but finding his *Oblomov* was an entirely different matter.

Marisol's niece had turned out to be a demon of a housekeeper, cleaning so well that Grace couldn't find anything. That morning, when she was looking for a washcloth in the linen closet, she discovered a stack of neatly folded shopping bags stuck between a stack of bath towels, and she found her moisturizer next to some Spanish olive oil in the pantry. The apartment was unquestionably spotless—the brass doorknobs buffed to a blinding sheen, the books dusted and replaced. However, now they were arranged by size, rather than alphabetical order. It was lucky that Laz wasn't there to witness the reorganization. It would have been too much for him. Plus, Dolores's caramel custard was tasteless and flat.

So it came as no large surprise to Grace to find both Mr. Dubrovsky's copy of *Oblomov* and her own in the kitchen, next to a cookbook of the exact size and color. She pulled the two books off the shelf, noticing the lemony smell of Murphy's Oil Soap emanating from their damp spines. As she held the books in her hands, Mr. Dubrovsky's business card fell onto the counter along with the two sheets of crinkled yellow paper from her copy. The yellow pages appeared to be a letter, and the writing was clearly a woman's handwriting. Grace wondered how long it would take for the ink to get bleached by the sun until not a trace would remain if she left the pages in direct sunlight.

She unfolded the letter and began to read:

> Brookman, It's been over nineteen years since we last saw each other. You can't keep denying that Griffin is your son. He's exactly like you, at least who you were then. He needs you now, and you must take responsibility. He's adamant about contacting you, even though you refuse to answer my calls. I can't stop him from going. Please have the decency to meet him. What happened between us is not the issue. Yours, Merrin.

Grace felt her head begin to pound and her eyes sting. Laz had never mentioned the name, not even in passing. Kane would probably know of her, although, maybe not the whole story. But even if they were speaking to each other, she still wouldn't have been able to ask. She folded the pages and placed them back in the book.

She left Mr. Dubrovsky's book on the front hall table, glancing at it one last time, as if she were checking to make sure an iron were unplugged so the counter wouldn't get scorched. Then she picked up Mr. Dubrovsky's card, and with a strong sense of purpose, walked down the hall to the bedroom.

The door was closed. She'd flung Laz's yellow Hermès tie over the doorknob and rumpled the bedcovers that morning. As she held the brass handle, letting the silk tie slip through her hand to the floor, she became aware of a slight humming sensation in the tips of her fingers, some incoherent impulses bumping around in her consciousness. She had almost been able to fool herself before. But now, as she stood in front of the bedroom door, she wished Laz really were in there. Not so she could greet him and welcome him home, but for the express purpose of doing him some sort of bodily harm. And then Grace had another incongruous thought, one in a series of non sequiturs: *And he can pick up his own damn dry cleaning, too!*

She went to the phone and dialed the number on Mr. Dubrovsky's card, but his voicemail picked up. After the beep, she began to explain: "Mr. Dubrovsky, this is Grace Brookman. You might not remember me. We met at the Pink Tea Cup. I apologize for the misunderstanding that night. I'm calling because I'm trying to locate someone. I can fill you in on the details when we speak. Also, I have your copy of *Oblomov*." She left her number and thanked him before she was disconnected.

Impulsively, she dialed the number of Flik's Video 2 Go store and asked them to deliver every Katharine Hepburn movie they had in stock as soon as possible, stressing her affinity for *The Philadelphia Story* and *Bringing Up Baby*. If that couldn't take her mind off the methotrexate coursing through her body and the letter she'd found in *Oblomov,* then nothing could.

Later that afternoon, the videos arrived, and suddenly life was refined, elegant, and romantic. Grace's mind wandered, conjuring scenarios. She imagined a reunion between Griffin and Laz: Laz would be overjoyed and beside himself with emotion, lifting Grace up and spinning her around, then embracing his son for the first time. Grace would prepare a light supper of penne with shiitake mushrooms and pan-seared tuna with a lentil salad. For dessert, a warm tarte Tatin with crème fraîche and espresso served out of the demitasse cups they'd bought in Portugal. They would eat in the kitchen because it was cozier. After dinner, Laz and Griffin would disappear down the hall to Laz's study to talk, and Grace would curl up with a cup of tea, admiring the snow falling outside and basking in their newfound familial bliss.

Grace wanted to jump up immediately and call Griffin with the good news, and then felt ridiculous when she realized that not only had she spent an inordinate amount of time planning an imaginary menu, but that there was, in fact, no news to tell.

Her thoughts turned to Kane. On their first quasi-official date, Kane had taken Grace to the Regency Theater for a Katharine Hepburn marathon film festival. He had brought along a wicker basket containing a loaf of raisin bread, Muenster cheese, Martinelli's apple juice, and Thin Mints, all of which they shared as they watched movie after movie until well after midnight. As Grace thought about how much she missed Kane, she wanted to scream out to Katharine Hepburn in *The Philadelphia Story,* "Don't lose him! He's your only true friend."

When her mother called, it was a welcome distraction. "Sweetie, you're home for once."

"Hi, Mom, how's everything?"

"Fine. Except for Francine. She's beside herself." Grace half-watched the film and half-listened, finding it was a perfect balance between reality and fantasy.

"Why, what's wrong?" Grace could hear her father saying something in the background.

"Milton, I'm talking to Grace. And it's my business what I tell my own daughter, thank you," she said. "Sorry, honey, your father says to send his love. Anyway, it's Bert, who else?"

"What about Bert, Mother?"

"Don't call me *Mother,* Grace. You know how that irritates me."

"Sorry, Mom. What's wrong with Bert?"

"He's been acting strangely lately. Francine doesn't know what's gotten into him."

"In what way?" Grace asked.

"You know—wearing turtlenecks, Kenneth Cole loafers, after-shave. And he's parting his hair on the other side. Poor Francine. She even found a copy of *GQ* in his briefcase."

For as long as Grace could remember, Bert had dressed in the exact same way: pressed polyester trousers, a collared shirt in a pale check or stripe, and white tennis shoes. Perhaps he was just compensating for his own insecurities about Francine leaving for two weeks. Grace didn't divulge this theory to her mother, afraid of the conclusions that her mother would invariably jump to, but did congratulate herself on her sleuthing abilities. Clearly, she could find Laz herself if she ever were to put her mind to it.

"I'm sure it's nothing," Grace said. "Remember when Dad brought home that Huk-A-Poo shirt from that business trip?" Her mother was silent. "Whatever happened to that? It's probably a collectible by now."

"I threw it out," her mother answered. "It was a woman's shirt."

"Oh." Grace realized that she'd taken the wrong path. She knew full well that if left to his own devices, her father would either violate every fashion dictum, or just stay in his pajamas for most of the day. Since the Huk-A-Poo incident, he was not permitted to pick out any of his own clothes. "Well, I'm sure it's nothing," she continued. "It's probably just a stage he's going through."

"Well, you can see for yourself tomorrow."

"Why tomorrow?"

"Grace, don't tell me you've forgotten about Francine's good-bye party? We're going gallery hopping and to Chanterelle for dinner. Honey, I left a message with that new Dolores of yours. Didn't she tell you?"

"I guess not." Grace tried to think of a way out. The thought of going anywhere while the methotrexate was taking effect, let alone an entire Saturday with the Sugarmans, was daunting to say the least.

"It'll be an adventure," her mother said. Grace had heard *that* expression one too many times. On one such "adventure," Grace's father had to be helicoptered out of Mesa Verde after he had become wedged in a crevice. "We'll pick you and Laz up at one. Francine and I are off to Loehmann's today to try and take her mind off things. I'll keep an eye out for something cute for you to wear for Mambo Night."

Before Grace could tell her mother that Laz wouldn't be able to make it—she couldn't remember if she had told them that he was in Yugoslavia or some other extinct locale—her mother had already hung up.

THAT NIGHT, GRACE dreamt she was in *Mary Poppins,* but instead of Julie Andrews and Dick Van Dyke, it was Grace and Kane floating above the tables in the Pink Tea Cup with Bert Sugarman and Griffin. They were all laughing and drinking tea out of oversize pink floral cups, and Grace kept spilling her tea. Every time she would try to right her cup, she would begin to descend slowly to the floor, and Kane would take her by the wrist and pull her back up. "We need to keep telling jokes," he said, but whenever Grace tried to tell one, she forgot the punch line.

Grace didn't like to dwell on her dreams, but the next morning, this one stuck with her in all its Technicolor details. As a child, she'd had a crush on Dick Van Dyke, his inclusion being the only element of the dream that made sense to her. Bert Sugarman's cameo in the dream would remain, for the time being, a walk-on without meaning.

19
The Installation

It was raining the following day, the kind of drenching rain that never lets up. Grace went into the kitchen to make tea, still holding out some hope that the outing with her parents and the Sugarmans would be postponed. Dr. Gaylin was right. There was no pain to speak of.

Just as the kettle was coming to a boil, Grace noticed that the amaryllis on the dining room table had begun to wilt. She propped up the stalks against the side of the bark trellis that encircled the crate, but the stalks just bent in the opposite direction like overcooked asparagus. She remembered the instructions to cut the plant down a few inches above the base of the bulb, but now, as she sipped her tea, she opted for neglect, deciding that it could wait until Monday.

Francine, swathed in a full-length silver trench coat, vinyl boots, and her signature plaid Burberry umbrella (large enough for a golf foursome), was not in the least deterred by the rain. Even Bert, whose new shoes were not waterproof, trudged on like a trooper. His appearance was indeed significantly altered. He sported a black fedora, and Grace could detect the beginnings of a goatee.

"Mother went on quite a spree," Grace's father said as they crossed Ninth Avenue. "Did she tell you?"

"Don't exaggerate, Milton. I just bought a few things, that's all."

"So, Francine," he continued, "you're off to Paris on Monday. It's going to be some trip, huh?"

"Of course, it will be. Even more, in retrospect," Francine answered. "Grace, tell Laz I'll whip him up some culinary delight when I get back from Le Cordon Bleu," she added, shooting Bert a punishing look as they walked down the street to begin their gallery-hopping adventure.

The galleries were on a side street, in renovated garages that bore no resemblance to their former incarnation, although Grace's mother kept insisting that she smelled gasoline. Bert held the door open for Grace and then sloshed his way through to the entrance of a photography exhibit. Grace felt as if she were sleepwalking as she followed her parents and the Sugarmans in and out of gallery after gallery. She was unable to absorb anything she saw, as though her mind was covered in some impervious, repellent material.

Their last stop on the tour was a huge installation by Damien Hirst. Grace could hear Bert's shoes squeaking across the floor as they all wandered about the gallery in their rain gear like a family of longshoremen. Grace walked in the opposite direction.

The exhibits were diverting enough—a blend of art, technological finesse, and arresting imagery—and Grace soon found herself mesmerized by the sight of a large white ball suspended by a current of air. In the next room, there was a huge glass tank filled with green water. Swimming around inside the tank were dozens of large black, orange, and silver fish. It was like the aquarium except for the life-size gynecologist's table complete with stirrups also inside the tank. The only thing missing was Dr. Gaylin in a wet suit.

The fish began to swim fervently about in what looked like a feeding frenzy, but there was no food, only large air bubbles coming out of a tube. Also in the tank, on a small table, was a rusting computer, a broken watch, and a white mug next to the computer keyboard. Grace walked around to the other side of the tank, and as she did, she saw that the mug had letters on it. She looked closer. They spelled out the name *Bert*. She read the title of the piece: *Love Lost.*

At first, she thought she must still be asleep, and that the whole day, including Bert in his hat and this strangely apt installation, was just a dream. But this was far too clever even for her, so she knew she was certainly awake. Her *Mary Poppins* dream now seemed patently obvious—Bert is the name of Dick Van Dyke's character in the movie. Grace was surprised that it had taken her so long to unravel the connection.

These images not only penetrated Grace's psyche, they had hooked her, and she felt as if she were about to be devoured by the fish. She walked over to a bench in the center of the room and sat down. She considered contacting Damien Hirst and asking him how on earth he'd managed to distill her life and encapsulate it into a seven-by-seven-foot tank.

Grace saw her father walking toward her. "Francine's getting antsy," he said. "Some exhibit, isn't it?" Grace took one of those deep breaths she'd learned in yoga but that she had never mastered, because holding her breath for any length of time, even for only seven seconds, terrified her. The breath, at least now, did serve to calm her somewhat.

"Yes, it's really something," she agreed, not sure what she was agreeing to. She heard someone approaching from behind. Bert sat down, holding his hat in his hand. A more dejected sight Grace had never seen, and she surmised that the new look had not served the purpose he'd hoped for.

"You have any Mylanta, Milt?" he asked.

"How many you need?"

"Two will do it, thanks," he said. Grace's father reached into his pants pocket and pulled out two tablets still in the plastic sleeve. Bert proceeded to pop them into his mouth and chew them, the white powder adhering to the corners of his mouth.

"Who's ready to eat?" Grace's father asked.

"Ready as I'll ever be," Bert said. Then he turned to Francine, who had joined them. "Time to shove off, honey." He reached for her arm, but she quickly pulled it away.

Grace stood up from the bench, but as she did, she felt the room grow dark.

"Grace, what's the matter?" her father asked. "You look peaked." He put his hand to her forehead. "And you're burning up."

There was a pounding in her ears and the room began to spin. As she fell back on the bench, an image of dozens of tiny, dazzling butterflies circled around her. When she opened her eyes, her parents and the Sugarmans were standing above her. She sat up slowly. Something flat and disklike was beneath her. She grabbed hold of it, and discovered Bert's now-flattened fedora, which she handed to him.

"For heaven's sake, Grace needs a doctor," Bert said in a panic. "Who has a cell phone? Someone should call Laz. Where the hell is he anyway? He should be here. Especially at a time like this. It would be easier to get Henry Kissinger on the phone!"

"Calm down, Bert, you're acting hysterical," Francine said.

"You're frightening Grace. She needs calm, rational people around her now. Why don't you take half a tranquilizer? It'll do you good. Grace doesn't need a doctor. Everything's fine. Look, the color's coming back into her face. Go make yourself useful and get some wet paper towels."

Bert scurried away and returned with a handful of soaking wet paper towels, a trail of water behind him. Grace pressed the towels to her forehead. She was beginning to feel better when she noticed bloodstains on her khaki pants.

"Honey, are you having pain?" her mother said quietly, sitting down on the bench beside her.

"Not really. It's just a very heavy period, that's all," she told her. "I got a little light-headed, don't worry."

Her mother, quickly assessing the situation, reached into her oversize tote bag and rummaged around. "Everything is under control. No need to get excited," she said and miraculously pulled out a pair of black satin cargo pants and a rhinestone belt with the Loehmann's tags still attached.

"Paulette to the rescue," Grace's father beamed.

"And here—you might need this," she said, stealthily handing Grace a blue-wrapped sanitary napkin as if it were a bag of hashish. "Why don't you go to the ladies' room and change? And here's a couple of Aleve. First thing Monday, we'll make you an appointment with this new doctor I found. Then we can have lunch at the Whitney. Doesn't that sound nice?" Grace hadn't really heard a single word. Her mother handed her the pants along with two white pills. Then, wrapping her raincoat around Grace's waist, she escorted her to the ladies' room and then waited for her outside.

Grace looked at herself in the mirror. Her complexion was the same pale yellow color as the letter from Griffin's mother. It would have been so much easier to go blank, but she couldn't. For once she agreed with Bert. Laz should have been here—just as he should have been at other times these past five weeks. She was afraid, and she wasn't supposed to be bleeding.

When she emerged from the ladies' room, still walking a bit unsteadily, she was met with nods of approval from Francine and her mother as if she were about to venture out for her prom night. Her father and Bert stood off to the side, Bert holding his misshapen hat in his hands.

"I knew they'd be perfect on her," her mother said. "See how they skim her hips and elongate her torso?"

"You do have an eye for these things," Francine agreed.

"They're one size fits most. No iron. Those pants, a crisp white shirt, a red cashmere sweater, a good pair of shoes, and you're ready for a week in Europe," she told Francine. "All set, everyone?"

Grace touched her mother on the shoulder. "I think I'm just going to head home," she said.

"Honey, are you sure? It might make you feel better to be with people."

"No, really," Grace said. "I'll talk to you later. Have fun." Grace kissed her parents good-bye and wished Francine a good trip. She watched as the four of them left the gallery. As soon as they were out of sight, Grace called Kane.

20
Little Odessa

Kane picked Grace up right in front of the gallery. Miraculously, on the ride to Brooklyn, just as they were crossing the Manhattan Bridge, the rain ended, Grace's bleeding stopped, and the sky turned a deep, clear blue, with bright stars and light, puffy clouds.

They were on their way to Little Odessa, where a surprise birthday celebration for Greg was planned at a Georgian restaurant. Grace would have preferred the quiet of just Kane's company, but it was better than being alone while things were invisibly disintegrating inside her.

"I'm glad you called," Kane said, turning off his windshield wipers.

"I hated the way we left things the other night," Grace said.

"I know. Me, too."

"I didn't think you'd ever want to speak to me after all the awful things I said to you."

"You and Laz are two of my closest friends. I don't want there ever to be tension between us."

"I still don't know what came over me," Grace said.

"Too much wheat grass, I guess," Kane said.

"I don't know. Whatever it was, I'm sorry. We really are so happy for you."

Kane reached his hand out and touched Grace's arm. "It's all forgotten. I can't believe you're finally going to meet Greg."

Grace looked out the window at the passing neighborhoods—attached brick row houses delineated by only slight stylistic variations, and then stretches where there were only stores. Kane pulled off Kings Highway and drove through the center of Brighton Beach, although the idea that they were anywhere near the ocean seemed unbelievable to Grace. It looked like any outer borough of the city, except that the lettering on the storefronts—even the Duane Reade and the Barnes & Noble—was written in both English and Russian.

They parked and walked several blocks down the main thoroughfare, then turned left onto what looked like a deserted street. Kane's cell phone rang.

While Kane was on the phone, Grace saw his shoulders slump. "How long will you be?" she could hear him say. After a few minutes, he ended the conversation and put his phone away. "Looks like Greg won't be able to make it until dessert," he told her. "Some emergency at a photo shoot." Grace felt a sense of empathy toward Kane. Their relationships had more in common than he knew.

They walked in silence until, out of nowhere, a restaurant appeared, its lights blazing and its interior festooned with brightly colored streamers and red-and-green garlands. Even though it was only five-thirty, every seat, except for those at a long table reserved for Greg's party, was taken. A silver disco ball spun from the dropped ceiling, sending flashes of prismlike lights around the mirrored room.

In the back, on a raised platform, a man wearing a white jacket and tight spandex pants was playing a synthesizer, and Grace recognized the melody of "Surfin' U.S.A." Everyone at the restaurant was swaying and singing along, although the words were in Russian. She scanned the faces in the room as she followed Kane to their table, which, unfortunately, was right next to the speakers. Kane made apologies for Greg's absence, and just like at the anniversary party, things went on in spite of the missing man of the hour.

"Are you okay?" she shouted to Kane over the music as they sat down.

"Oh, yeah. Comes with the territory."

"I know what you mean. But at least we have each other," she said, linking her arm in his.

"Always will."

They didn't have to look at menus; Kane had ordered in advance. The food arrived on huge platters and bowls that were filled with Russian delicacies—grilled eggplant, spinach purée, smoked fish with pickled beets, spicy minced string beans, cheese-filled pie, and a basket of warm airy bread that the waitress placed on a high silver stand. Everyone took a spoonful of each dish and passed it along. Grace noticed that she'd worked up quite an appetite.

The man next to Grace turned to her and extended his hand. "I'm Carmine. Greg's old man."

"I'm Grace. A friend of Kane's."

"Gotta love that guy! Grace, you have any idea what this is?" Carmine asked, as he examined an unrecognizable dish.

"I think it's some kind of meat," Grace said.

"It's cabbage," the waitress said curtly, as she walked by.

"Tastes like my mama's meatballs, may she rest in peace," Carmine said. "Only without the meat, obviously."

Kane flagged down the waitress for another glass of wine. As Grace watched the spinning disco ball and listened to the warped sounds from the synthesizer, she found herself growing hypnotized. Even the Russian lyrics to the Beach Boys' song were beginning to sound comprehensible. She took a long swig of Kane's wine and looked at the people assembled for Greg's party. Friends and family. One of Greg's cousins got up to do the chicken dance, which Grace had once seen at a wedding. The setting and the cast of characters had changed, but not much else. With only a few minor differences, this was the Italian version of her parents and the Sugarmans. Even Grace's role was the same.

"Miss, this is the best wedding I've ever been to," Carmine said. The waitress gave a perfunctory smile.

"He thinks he's a comedian," his wife, Sophia, said, taking a bite of food and turning her back to him.

"What? I was just being friendly," Carmine said. "Grace, would you care to dance?" As Grace listened to the music, which now sounded a bit like a synthesized version of Elvis Costello's "Watching the Detectives," she thought about Adrian Dubrovsky—or was the elusive Russian detective watching her?

"Thanks, but I'm going to have to take a rain check," she said. Someone passed Grace a dish of something surrounded by a mass of clear jelly. Another mystery vegetable, perhaps. She looked at the pale, oval slices on the platter and decided to try one. She had just taken a small bite when she noticed the knuckles on the underside. They jiggled slightly. She set down her fork as she realized that she may have just ingested the toe of a pig. She felt nauseous and turned to Kane, unable to speak.

"Grace, what's wrong? You're breaking into a sweat."

"Nothing," she managed to say, feeling herself begin to gag. "I think I'm going to go."

"But Greg will be here any minute. Can't you stay just a little longer?"

"I really can't. I want to leave before I get up and start doing the chicken dance. Tell Greg I'm sorry."

"I wish I could drive you home," he said.

"It's Greg's birthday. You should be here."

"Why? Greg's not."

The DJ, who also happened to be the maître d', called a car for Grace. It arrived in less time than it took her to put on her coat.

Kane walked her outside and hugged her. "I'm really glad you came," he said. "I couldn't have gotten through this evening without you."

"If you only knew," she said, giving him a hug.

GRACE GOT INTO the back of the black sedan and gave her address to the driver, then dozed off despite the bumpy ride home. She awoke with a jolt to see someone other than José holding the car door open for her. As soon as she stepped out of the car onto the cobblestone driveway, she realized at once that she'd given the driver the wrong address. She was standing in front of Laz's old building. Perhaps some delusional side effect of the methotrexate had catapulted Grace five years back in time, so that when she turned the brass doorknob of the apartment, Laz would be inside waiting. She turned back to the car, but the driver had already sped off, without collecting his fare.

"Good evening," the doorman said. "Mrs. Brookman, right? I'm really enjoying the book Mr. Brookman gave me." She stared blankly at him.

"A travel book," he continued. "He left it for me yesterday." And then Grace understood. She knew what book without having to ask.

"*The Innocents Abroad*," he beamed. "A hand-bound, leather edition. I can't wait to read it."

"I'll tell him."

"He's such a nice young man," he said. She wondered why Griffin would have given away a book that had been a gift from Laz, but perhaps he felt that the books were poor substitutes and that he'd rather have nothing.

Grace walked into the building and down the marble corridor to the side entrance, where she could get a taxi heading in the right direction. The chandeliers gave off an eerie yellow light. Reflected in the Baroque mirrors that lined the hallway, Grace saw the fuzzy outlines of what looked like Mr. Dubrovsky sitting on a velvet chair. His legs were crossed, he wore black wing tip shoes, and on his lap he held a hat. She spun around to see if he was indeed really there, but the chair where she'd thought she'd seen him was now empty. No sign of Mr. Dubrovsky or his reflection.

Grace thought that she must have experienced some kind of Manhattan mirage, the consequence of too many blinis after having grown faint earlier. Then checking her own reflection in the mirror, she walked outside to find a taxi home.

"THERE'S A PACKAGE for you," José said, as she walked into the lobby. Grace was afraid that it was another dozen Duro-Lites. Her second thought was that her mother had dropped by with more spoils from her Loehmann's spree.

José went over to the concierge desk and lifted up a small, unmarked carton, which he brought over to Grace. "It was delivered by messenger," he told her. She cautiously took it from him. It was almost weightless. She turned it around to read the return address. There, in bold pink lettering, she read the words A Perfect Match.

Upstairs, Grace opened her front door to the sound of the telephone. It had been several hours since she'd left her parents at the gallery with the Sugarmans. They were likely to be checking up on her. Grace placed the box next to the stack of Katharine Hepburn movies on the hall table and picked up the phone.

"Grace—it's Griffin." His voice was muffled, as if he was talking to her from another planet.

"Griffin," she repeated. "I can barely hear you."

"I hope it's not a bad time."

"No, I just walked in. Is everything all right?" she asked, shrugging off her coat and walking into the living room. The satin pants her mother had given her at the gallery were slippery and made a distracting swishing sound as she walked. She sat down on the Victorian love seat that she'd just had reupholstered in a lilac chintz, and she had to hold on to the armrest to keep herself from sliding off.

"Well, I just thought you should know that they're going to start the abatement Monday morning."

"The abatement?" Grace asked.

"For the asbestos," Griffin answered. "They said it should take about a week or so. They've already covered everything in plastic."

"How can you sleep there?" Grace asked.

"I sort of made a slit in the plastic large enough for me to slide through. It'll be fine," he assured her. He paused. Grace could hear what sounded like hail falling on an air conditioner in the background. "Except for the falling plaster, that is."

"What plaster?" Grace asked, beginning to grow alarmed.

"They're working on a pipe upstairs."

"Griffin, it's not safe for you to stay there." She thought about the dismal black netting on the windows and imagined Griffin covered head to toe in white dust. She scolded herself for not having checked on him when she was there.

She was about to tell him that he should look for a room in one of the residence halls on Broadway when, without thinking, she told him he should come stay with her. There was plenty of room. It made perfect sense. There were two extra bedrooms, which were unoccupied. The more she thought about it, the more the idea of having somebody around began to appeal to her. It would only be for a week, and she was going to Chicago on Friday anyway.

"Are you sure that would be a good idea?" Griffin asked. Grace knew he was referring to Laz's lack of responsiveness. In a way, she thought his staying at their place would mollify the situation somewhat.

"Please consider it. I'd like to get to know you better."

Griffin hesitated. "You really don't need to do this," he said, finally.

"I know. I want to." Grace began to feel animated, more so than she had in weeks. She wanted to ask him all sorts of questions, like what kind of cereal he ate in the mornings, how he took his coffee, what section of the paper he read first. Toast or English muffins? Or she could make waffles. He was a bit on the thin side, after all, she could hear her mother saying.

She harbored a secret hope that he would eat Grape-Nuts cereal with two-percent milk, take his coffee black with two sugars, and read the Op-Eds followed by the sports section while holding a slice of lightly toasted raisin bread in his hand—just like Laz. Then with a start, she corrected herself. It wasn't Laz who liked raisin bread, it was Kane. How could she forget? Laz liked a currant scone covered with crème fraîche and a spoonful of raspberry jam, which inevitably dripped onto the newspaper.

It was agreed, after another few rounds of demurring and insisting, that he would come first thing in the morning. Grace sat in the darkness, holding the phone in her hand and enjoying the quiet with the knowledge that the end of solitude was in sight. She was also half-waiting for her father's postdinner, just-checking-up call, which, surprisingly, never came.

It was almost ten o'clock when she went into the kitchen to get a knife and proceeded to open the carton from A Perfect Match. Underneath several crumpled sheets of packing paper, she found a small, rectangular box sealed in bubble wrap. She undid the tape and let the wrapping fall away.

Inside were three pristine silver tubes. She cradled the lipsticks in her hand, reluctant to open them. How the lipsticks had arrived so speedily, she did not know, but she didn't question it.

She chose one, carefully pulled off the top, and twisted the bottom of the tube to reveal a perfectly angled tip, which she touched to the back of her hand. The consistency was smooth and cool, like the skin of an apple. She applied the lipstick without a mirror, following the contours of her mouth, and pressed her lips together. She could reorder to her heart's content and never run out. She walked over to the mirror.

Since Laz had left, except for hibachi night, she'd become accustomed to just a light coating of gloss. Velvet, the lipstick that she'd put on every morning for years, the color that had become second nature to her, now looked unfamiliar. She turned the dining room light on high and stared into the mirror. Her lips looked almost fake, not like hers at all. This was not the person she remembered. The Christmas tree began to blink as if objecting, too. Grace ran to the bathroom and wiped off the lipstick with a tissue and threw the tubes in the wastebasket. They landed with three hollow thumps on the bottom.

21
Down the Hatch

A little before eleven o'clock, the telephone rang. Grace let the machine pick up. She wanted nothing more than to rest and forget this strange day, and she was in no mood to hear the details of Francine's farewell dinner. She heard the sound of her mother's voice as she walked down the hall to the bedroom.

Darling, it's Mom. We had a lovely evening with the Sugarmans. A shame you weren't feeling quite yourself. Dad wants to know if you'll tape his show for him. He felt a little twinge, so we took him to Lenox Hill for a thallium stress test. We're just waiting for the . . . Grace ran to the kitchen and grabbed the phone so quickly that it almost flew out of her hand.

"Mom?" she said, out of breath.

"Grace. I was in the middle of leaving a message," she said, sounding slightly irritated that she'd been interrupted. "I didn't wake you, did I?" she added as an afterthought.

"No. I'm up. I heard the message. Why didn't you call me earlier? How's Dad?"

"We didn't want to worry you. It's probably nothing. They're just being very thorough."

"Do you want me to come over?" she asked, trying to hear through the static in her ears even though the line was clear.

"That's sweet of you, but Bert and Francine are here. Bert bumped into one of his old college friends in the waiting room. The man's wife has gallstones. Anyway, it shouldn't be too long. Don't worry. We'll call you first thing. You need to get some rest, dear. Give our love to Laz when you speak to him," she said and then hung up.

Feeling helpless, Grace went into the living room, sank down onto the couch, and stared at the blinking Christmas tree lights. Beside her was the bag of yarn still untouched from the other day, the perfect over-the-counter antidote to her racing mind. She took out some yarn and began a chain stitch, mindlessly crocheting as she allowed her thoughts to unravel. She could no more stop the obliterating effects of the drug in her system than influence the outcome of her father's tests, or telepathically summon Laz back to her side. However, she could create something out of, or in spite of, the chaos, something that had order, symmetry, and purpose—whatever that might be.

She continued crocheting well into the night and must have dozed off for a while when the telephone rang. The sky was pink—not a predawn pink, but the kind of pink that might signal snow. It could have been three in the morning or sometime past eight; it was impossible to tell. She'd tucked the phone underneath her legs, and she could feel the warmth emanating from the battery pack.

The results of her crocheting efforts covered her lap—a rectangle approximately two feet by four. It confounded Grace how the intervening hours had slipped by unnoticed, but the proof was in her hands. The dimensions were unremarkable. The stitches were plain, but pleasingly regular. It was too small for a throw and too large for a scarf for Griffin.

As she folded it back to retrieve the phone, tiny sparks of electricity sent a tingling sensation down her arms as she realized that what she had unwittingly crocheted was a baby blanket. She held the blanket in her arms, but it only accentuated the weight of an unfillable absence. She knew there was no way to mourn an unacknowledged loss, although her hands had so deftly tried to orchestrate a symbolic remedy. For the briefest of moments, she allowed herself access to the knowledge that she felt pain.

The phone continued to ring. As she pushed the button on the handset, she expected to hear her mother's voice telling her that everything was fine, but she was startled by an unfamiliar man's voice.

"Mrs. Brookman. Adrian Dubrovsky here." Grace bolted upright. "Mrs. Brookman?" he said again.

Grace could hear the quiet tapping of computer keys on the other end. Her father often fiddled with some gadget, too, while he spoke to her on the phone. She walked into the kitchen to check the time. The clock on the microwave read six-fifteen. "Do you realize what time it is?" she asked, slowly gathering her wits.

"I apologize for disturbing you so early, but my schedule is quite erratic and I felt that we must speak." His accent was difficult to place. "I got your message. When I met you at the Pink Tea Cup, it was not as it seemed," he said. "That is all I can say at this time."

"I'm not sure what you mean," Grace said.

"I was there under false pretenses," he continued. "My situation has changed, and although I cannot go into the details, I'm afraid that my working for you would be a conflict of interest. But I would like to arrange to pick up my book. I was concerned that it might have gotten into the wrong hands." Just then, another call came in and Grace asked Mr. Dubrovsky to hold on. She pressed the call-waiting button.

"Up and *Adam*," her father said in his chipper, early morning voice. He'd been saying the expression wrong for as long as Grace could remember, but she would never think of correcting him. He was usually up well before five in the morning, reading; and by six, he was ready to socialize.

"How are you feeling?" Grace asked.

"Fit as a fiddle. I got a clean bill of health. Just some acid reflux. The doctor said I just have to lay off the spicy food, that's all."

"I'm so relieved," Grace said. Then she remembered that Mr. Dubrovsky was on the other line. "Dad, I'm going to have to call you right back."

"We have to go to Wal-Mart for supplies. Call us around ten." Grace knew how much her father disliked shopping. He had devised a schedule that required them to shop only once every month, except for perishables, which they had delivered from the Food Emporium.

"Supplies? For what?" Grace asked.

"The blizzard. Could be two feet by tomorrow night. The worst in fifty years."

"Dad, I'm glad you're okay. You had me worried. Oh, and thank Mom for the pants," she said, looking down at the satin pants she was still wearing.

Just before she pressed the button to get back to Mr. Dubrovsky, she heard her mother call out from the extension, "Don't mention it."

There was a dial tone on the other end. Mr. Dubrovsky had hung up. An odd bird, she concluded, picturing him in his striped pajamas listening to *The Brothers Karamazov* on tape. Clearly, A Perfect Match needed to better screen their members—she, like Groucho Marx, not wanting to count herself among them.

Trying to put the whole conversation out of her mind, she walked into the kitchen to prepare José's coffee. On the way, she noticed Mr. Dubrovsky's copy of *Oblomov* next to the stack of Katharine Hepburn movies on the front hall table and picked it up.

The book had obviously been well read, some pages stained and rippled from water damage. She sat on the couch and flipped through the book, trying to find the place where she and Laz had last left off. A line, marked in pencil, caught her eye: *You had really parted before your separation and were faithful not to love but to the phantom of it, which you had yourself invented—that's the whole secret.*

The line was impossibly apt. It seemed almost as if Oblomov were addressing Grace directly and not his beloved, Olga. Could this be just a random coincidence, or was it a flicker of prophesy from the nineteenth century? Or did Mr. Dubrovsky know more than even Grace had supposed? She turned the page and read more. *The man before you is not the one you have been expecting and dreaming of. Wait, he will appear and then you will come to yourself.*

The passage took her breath away. They were the same lines that Laz had read to her, but never before had they reverberated as they did now. She found herself unable to concentrate on Goncharov's words and wanted to banish them, along with her feelings, to a place even less hospitable than a Siberian gulag. They were *too* close, as if resonating from inside her almost.

Just as she was about to close the book, she thought she recognized two words written in the margins in smudged blue ink. She held the book closer and examined the letters. The words were written in some language that resembled neither Anglo-Saxon nor Cyrillic, appearing more like a strange hieroglyphic code. She could have sworn she read the words as *Brookman Redux.* She looked again more closely, but the words swam on the page like a deep-sea Scrabble game with no rule book.

She gazed out the window at the pink sky. This was turning out to be an unsettling morning. She tried to focus on Griffin's arrival, but there were too many loose ends that nagged at her, and she thought it might help her clear her head to get some fresh air. If there was going to be a blizzard, it would be a good idea to do some shopping just in case they were snowed in as Milton had predicted. She would go to the Food Emporium, which was open twenty-four hours a day; on the way back, she'd return the videos.

Laz never returned anything on time. Every library book and video he had ever rented was kept well past its due date. Once, he was fined over two hundred dollars for losing *After Hours*. They'd never even gotten to the end of the movie. Grace had found it years later, stuffed in a box containing an old orange clock radio, some letters, and other miscellany that he'd no doubt neglected to return along the way. For Laz, like the movies he rented and the books he borrowed, this was a marriage in which he was willing to incur late fees, rather than to submit to a lifetime commitment. Grace was beginning to become aware that hers might be a marriage on loan, and not for keeps.

She poured José's coffee into the cup and pressed the lid on tightly. Then she grabbed her coat, along with the stack of videos, and went downstairs.

Grace placed the coffee cup on the mahogany concierge desk. As soon as she removed her hand, she imagined the gold letters that encircled the cardboard cup rearranging like air-popped popcorn until finally settling on another phrase, one more in keeping with her mood that morning: *We Are Happy to Preserve You.*

THE BLAZING LIGHTS at the Food Emporium gave it a surreal, timeless quality. The aisles were virtually empty, except for several stock boys who were sitting on boxes, reshelving items that seemed in plentiful supply. She thought of her parents at Wal-Mart, pushing their supersized carts down the wide aisles, buying gargantuan quantities of food. Her parents had shopping down to a science, each taking a list and a cart and heading in opposite directions, somehow always meeting in the frozen foods section simultaneously.

Grace began to fill her cart with food. The predictability of the store was reassuring as she went up and down each aisle, pulling items off the shelf that she thought Griffin might like—pretzels, blue corn chips, a six-pack of Coke, Mint Milanos. It had been a while since she'd been shopping. Filling the cart felt so satisfying. For herself, Grace stocked up on Boca Burgers, fresh vegetables and fruit, soy nuts, and bread. Gone were her cravings for pastries and sweets. She decided to prepare a spinach lasagna for dinner, so she went in search of part-skim ricotta cheese.

She went down the next aisle and stopped short. She found herself surrounded by neatly stocked rows of small jars of pureed vegetables, infant formula, tiny spoons, teething rings, sippy cups, shelves of diapers, and wipes. She had the urge to empty the shelves into her cart, as if by doing so, the rest would follow.

From a distance, she saw a woman wearing a familiar-looking silver trench coat reaching to pull down a box of Kleenex from a high shelf. The woman's back was turned, but as Grace drew nearer, she saw that it was Francine and walked over to help her.

"Francine, let me get that for you," she said, reaching up to get the box of tissues. Startled, Francine spun around, toppling over a tower of paper towels in the process.

"Grace," she said, with a tight smile. "So nice to run into you. Glad Dad's feeling better." Grace was about to respond when Francine thrust the box of Kleenex into her cart and said, "Sorry, but I've got to dash."

Francine's eyes were rimmed with streaks of black mascara,

which Grace had the urge to wipe away with a moistened Q-Tip, as her mother surely would have done. Francine was wearing the same outfit she had on the day before, but then Grace looked down and realized so was she.

"Is everything all right?" Grace inquired. Francine began to busily rearrange things in her cart and then, grabbing two double packages of napkins, placed them on top, as if in an effort to conceal what was inside.

"Oh, yes. Everything's fine. Good to see you," she said quickly, and then with a quick wave, and in a blur of silver, she was off. As Francine rounded the corner, her cart practically tilting on two wheels, Grace caught a glimpse of its contents. There were dozens of bottles of chili sauce and at least twice the number of jars of Welch's grape jelly, along with several bags of minimarshmallows —strange things to stock up on, stranger still since Bert was diabetic.

Grace finished shopping and made her way to the checkout line. She unloaded her cart and realized that she hadn't purchased so much as a package of Altoids for Laz, as though, if only in pretense, she was letting him fend for himself and go hungry, too. She presented the super-bonus-savings card that her father had given her to the cashier and glanced at the headlines of the nearby magazines. On the cover of one was a photograph of an emaciated man who was dressed in loose white clothing and standing next to a McDonald's restaurant in a bombed-out village. *Bosnian Prisoner Paid for Story*. Grace turned the magazine over and quickly scribbled her address on the delivery slips.

Outside, the sky was obscured by a dense layer of clouds, and there was the feeling of snow in the air. At the corner of Verdi Square, she could just make out the outline of the cupolas of Laz's old building through the black construction netting. From the exterior, the netting looked impervious and forbidding, as if no light could get through. Griffin was probably still asleep under his plastic-wrapped bed. Grace knew that "first thing in the morning" to a person his age might extend well past noon.

The storefront of Flik's Video 2 Go was covered with a corrugated metal gate. To the side was a graffiti arrow in red, white, and blue spray paint as well as a sign indicating a drop-off slot. Without the arrow, she could have easily missed it. Opening the slot while holding the stack of videos proved awkward, so she devised a system of dropping them in a few at a time while holding the door open with her hip—until several got jammed at once and she had to put them in one at a time. The videos hit the floor with a crash. She pictured them strewn across the linoleum in disarray. She placed the last one in the slot, and as it descended, she watched with utter dismay as Mr. Dubrovsky's copy of *Oblomov,* instead of a video, flew down the chute into the heap of Katharine Hepburn videos.

Grace tried to fish the book out, but the slot had obviously been engineered much like a mailbox, allowing things only to go in. Despite the queer looks that she received from a few people passing by with dogs, she tried to look inconspicuous as she shoved her arm into the chute all the way up to her shoulder blade, persevering for several minutes. Finally, forced to admit defeat, she headed home to wait for Griffin.

22
The Abatement

Just as Grace was cleaning up the kitchen, the intercom rang. She closed the pantry door and pressed the button.

"Your guest is here," José announced.

"Thank you," Grace said. "Send him up, please."

The Christmas tree sparkled in the living room and the spinach lasagna was covered with tinfoil on the counter, ready to be popped into the oven. Grace smoothed her hair and, feeling very Florence Henderson–like, went to the door. She'd rehearsed her greeting several times in the mirror and had decided upon a welcoming but casual hello, as if she were in the middle of something and hadn't in fact been waiting for hours for his arrival. She flung the door open, surprised by the sight of Kane standing in the doorway with two white-and-orange bags from Citarella's.

"Kane?" she said, flustered.

"Glad to see me, I guess." He remained outside until Grace regained her composure and asked him in.

"It's just that I wasn't expecting you." Kane's cheeks were flushed from the cold.

"I can see. I ran into your mother buying whitefish this morning. She mentioned that you weren't feeling well. I brought you some barley soup. Why didn't you say anything last night?"

"You know how my mother is, always exaggerating," Grace said, taking the container of soup from Kane. "Thanks. But I'm fine. Was my father with her?"

"He was double-parked outside. I said hello to him on my way out."

"Did he seem all right?"

"Yes, except he kept mumbling something about battening down the hatches."

"Yeah. He's worried about the blizzard."

It was difficult to pretend with Kane. She fought the urge to tell him about the methotrexate, the Damien Hirst exhibit, the Duro-Lites, Griffin, and the strange Mr. Dubrovsky. And, of course, Laz. Kane was the only one who would understand.

"Is something wrong?" he asked.

"No, nothing's wrong," she answered, looking away. She felt like a bottle of soda that had been shaken but left unopened. Kane put his bags by the door and walked into the living room. Grace tried to look at her watch without him noticing. An accidental meeting between Kane and Griffin in her living room was more than Grace could safely negotiate.

Kane went over to the Christmas tree and touched a branch. The tinsel glistened.

"The tree looks nice."

"Thanks." He was about to sit on the couch when Grace steered him toward the window before he knew what was happening, and she took a quick peek to see if Griffin was walking toward the building.

"Greg and I are having a brunch this afternoon. We'd love it if you could make it. Just a few people." She avoided his stare.

"Thanks, but I have tons to do," she said, trying to think fast. "We're going to Chicago on Friday and I haven't done a thing."

"To see Chloe?" he asked.

"Yes. Her mother just died," she said.

"I'm sorry to hear that."

"And Laz has a conference," Grace added.

"Isn't your birthday on Saturday?" Kane always remembered.

"Yes." She began to grow excited at the prospect of a birthday celebration. Then, like all the other times she'd felt buoyed and optimistic during the past five weeks, Grace realized she had once again fallen into one of her own, well-fashioned traps. Kane reached into his jacket pocket and pulled out a canary yellow envelope and handed it to her.

"In case I don't see you."

"That's so sweet of you," she said, taking the card from him. She took his arm and escorted him into the dining room with the intention of getting him to the front door in what would seem like a natural and unchoreographed progression. As they walked through the kitchen, she hoped Kane wouldn't notice the tinfoil-covered lasagna.

"Having company?"

"Scrabble night," she said, her reflexes oiled like a finely tuned machine. In truth, she'd forgotten all about it, but that was the least of her worries. Getting out of Scrabble night was child's play.

"That's funny, I thought your mother said Scrabble was canceled because Francine needs to get ready for her trip."

"I wish someone had told me," she covered. "Well, you must have lots to do. Thanks for stopping by." She waited to see if he would take the cue and be on his way.

"Sorry you can't make it to brunch. Greg really wants to meet you."

"When we get back from Chicago. That is, if there really is a Greg. We'll make a date," Grace promised. Kane put his hands in his pockets.

"Grace?" he said.

"What?"

"Oh, nothing. Have a nice trip. Call me if you need anything."

"I will."

"And I mean anything," he said again, bending down and picking up his bags.

"Even to change a lightbulb?" she joked, but to her it wasn't really a joke, considering the unpredictability of the Duro-Lites.

"That happens to be one of my specialties," he told her.

"You know you'd be the first person I'd call if I needed anything," she said, although she knew she probably wouldn't call anyone.

As SOON AS SHE closed the door behind him, Grace went into the living room and collapsed onto the couch. Her heart was racing. She was still holding the yellow envelope, and unable to wait until Saturday, she tore it open. Out flew dozens of small strips of paper, newspaper clippings, and several fortunes from Chinese take-out.

She picked up a strip of paper to read: *Sagittarius. The planets are in line, making this the time to get what you have always wanted. Try it. Close your eyes. Make a wish. Open your eyes. Did it come true?* She turned it over. On the reverse side was the personal ad from *Time Out* magazine that Kane had cut out the day they went up to get the tree. She felt relieved and foolish to have jumped to the conclusion that Kane was out cruising. He'd always still be Kane—reliable and consistent. She read one of the fortunes: *The difficulties of life have been removed.* If Kane only knew how ironic that was, and would he agree that Laz was one of them?

After an hour, Grace decided she needed something to occupy herself, so she decided to confirm her flight. She dialed the number for the airline and waited for an operator to pick up. Chloe had recommended the airline, a small, Midwestern carrier that had good rates.

"Thank you for calling Highland Air. How may I help you this morning?" It never ceased to surprise Grace that people could be so pleasant and friendly. She was often told that she didn't seem like a New Yorker, but whenever she encountered someone outside of the tristate area, she felt as if she needed a crash course in manners. No matter how she tried, she couldn't match the effortless civility on the other end of the telephone.

"I'm calling to confirm my flight."

"If you give me your confirmation number, I'll be glad to help you." Grace gave the operator the information and waited on hold as Vivaldi's *Four Seasons* played.

"Sorry to keep you waiting. Yes, your flight has been confirmed. That's two first-class tickets to Chicago on Friday at ten A.M." It took a second for the mistake to register.

"I think that's two coach tickets," Grace said.

"You've been upgraded."

"I have?" Grace asked, confused.

"Ma'am, I'm showing two first-class tickets to O'Hare, with a return flight on Sunday at one P.M. You requested the vegetarian luncheon special with steamed edamame and miso soup, and you have a choice of grilled tempeh or a garden burger." Grace, who despised being called ma'am, once mistook a slice of tempeh for a scouring pad, but what concerned her was how this operator knew that she was a vegetarian.

"Garden burger, please," she answered.

"Will you be needing ground transportation once you arrive at

O'Hare? We offer complimentary limo service to your destination." Grace began to feel lulled into a sort of sheeplike compliance.

"Yes, thanks." She was bewildered when she hung up the phone. But after a few moments to reflect, the only explanation she could come up with was that the upgrade must be an early birthday present from Chloe.

It was nearly one o'clock and still no sign of Griffin. Grace considered sitting down and crocheting the time away, but then remembered that she'd neglected to cut down the amaryllis. She'd once left an iris bulb in the soil too long, and the next year, the plant yielded no flowers, just thin, grasslike leaves that eventually turned brown.

Grace got the shears out of the utility closet and went into the dining room. The plant had definitely seen better days—its leaves unfurled and wilted. She cut the stems two inches from the base and placed the crate in a deep shopping bag, folding down the top, which she secured with masking tape.

The coolest and darkest spot she knew of was in the butler's pantry by the back door. The window faced an alley and received no direct light. Sometimes, through the air shaft, she could hear singing from a neighboring kitchen. Grace stored onions, potatoes, and garlic in metal stacking baskets on the floor. The pantry radiator hadn't worked since they moved in, and there was a draft from the lopsided, frosted window. She tucked the shopping bag under the sill and, with a sense of having accomplished something, again went to wait for Griffin, busying herself by tidying up and putting the apartment back in order after Dolores's reorganization.

Finally, around four-thirty, the buzzer rang and Grace ran to answer it. Unable to restrain herself, she waited by the door until she heard the elevator arrive at her floor. The doorbell rang, and Grace took a breath before flinging the door wide open. Griffin stood in the vestibule wearing a gray-and-white wool hat, a black ski jacket, and jeans. He carried a small duffel bag over his shoulder.

"I was beginning to wonder about you," Grace said. All her preparations for a low-key welcome slipped away from her and she felt like a stereotypical overanxious parent.

"I guess I lost track of the time," he said, taking off his hat and running his hand through his hair. His tan canvas duffel bag was almost identical to one that Grace had had in high school. While hers had been covered with autographs, peace signs, and flowers drawn in magic marker, this one was covered with Pearl Jam and New Order stickers. Dangling from the frayed strap was a miniature snowboard key chain. Grace noticed an ironed-on patch of an airplane with an arrow pointing to a red heart. She wondered if it was a symbol of his trip to New York to find his father.

"Come in," she said to Griffin. "Let me show you where you can put your stuff."

Griffin slowly followed as Grace led the way down the hall to Laz's study. He seemed as if he wanted to take in every detail, stopping every so often to look closely at a photograph or print on the wall. When they reached Laz's study, Griffin put his bag down. Inside it, Grace could see a pair of brown hockey skates just like the ones the woman had been wearing at Sky Rink. As Griffin walked over to the walnut desk by the window, Grace realized that she had come face to face with his mother now on two occasions. Griffin sat down in Laz's leather swivel chair. The weight of his body compressed the air in the seat cushion, making a sound much like one of her father's long sighs, as if the chair, too, was relieved to have a body finally occupying it again.

The room faced north, overlooking the tops of neighboring brownstones. Grace was so used to the sight of Laz staring out the window while he was working that more than once she had mistaken the sight of the sheer curtains blowing in the wind for his silhouette. For however brief a time, those phantom images dulled the sting of his absence. Griffin seemed perfectly at home in the room. He folded his arms across his chest and leaned back, then smiled at her.

"Would you mind showing me some photographs? I only have this one picture of my parents," he said, taking a photograph out of his duffel bag. "It must be twenty years old, at least." Grace looked at the picture. If she didn't know better, she'd have thought she was looking at Griffin. "My mother doesn't have any recent pictures of my father."

The full meaning of the words took time to penetrate. Recent photographs. As if looking at them would mean that Laz was nearer to her somehow—but he was no more accessible in the photographs she had than in the one that Griffin was holding. The truth was, Laz was beginning to feel further and further away. Each day, even as she conjured him in her life with the finesse of a sorcerer, she was banishing him as well, sending him into an exile that was comparable to his own abandonment.

Grace pulled out a cloth-covered album with a tea-rose pattern from their honeymoon and sat down on the floor. Griffin sat next to her. She watched as he turned the pages—Laz waist-deep in the blue water; Laz on the porch in front of their thatched hut; Grace and Laz waving as they hiked up a dusty mountain trail before the monkeys chased them halfway down—images so burned in Grace's memory, she barely had to look at the photographs.

He closed the album and held it on his lap. "It looks like you two are really happy together," he said.

"We are," she said, unable to ignore the impact of her choice of tense. The truth fluttered around her like dust motes. *We are. We were. We will be, again.* But when? Griffin got up from the floor and placed the album back on the shelf. He picked up an ornate oval-shaped brass doorknob that had been painted silver, which was from Laz's old apartment. Laz had removed it from the front door and replaced it with a reproduction he had found at the flea market.

When Grace had been packing up to move in with Laz, he had come over to her place with a set of screwdrivers and had removed one of the original faceted crystal doorknobs. He'd done it as if it were an ordinary and usual custom, and with the same casual air that Grace's mother had when she dumped a basket of onion rolls or a plate of biscotti into her purse at a restaurant, or when she took a hotel ashtray as a souvenir. It had seemed odd at the time, but now, as Griffin touched the contours of the floral motif on the handle and measured the weight in his hand, Grace understood why Laz had taken it. There were several other doorknobs on the shelf that he'd collected from various apartments he'd lived in over the years, and she looked at them as if for the first time, wondering what other hands had turned them, what doors they had opened, and if perhaps one of them had come from an off-campus apartment Laz might have shared with Griffin's mother.

Griffin set the doorknob back on the shelf and grazed the spines of the books with his fingertips as if he were reading Braille. Grace had seen Laz do the same thing many times in secondhand bookstores, almost as if he thought he could glean something of the person who'd previously possessed the book. Griffin opened a book of poems and began reading the notes Laz had made in the margins. Then he put the book back on the shelf and went around the room, picking up objects—a silver-plated cigarette lighter embossed with an image from mythology, a small wooden puzzle box, an ashtray from a hotel in Prague, an ivory-handled letter opener.

Everything Griffin touched seemed suddenly brought to life and imbued with new meaning. The desire to discover was infectious, and Grace felt the urge to show him everything. She went to the closet and turned on the light. The closet smelled of cinnamon from a candle that had once been in there. Grace pushed some unpacked boxes out of the way until she located a metal container that was stuffed with letters. She held it to her chest as she carried it to the desk.

"He used to love to write letters," Grace told Griffin. In the top drawer of her dresser she had a stack of letters tied with silk ribbon that Laz had sent to her even though they were living together at the time. She read them often, especially when he began to feel remote to her. She sometimes even saved messages from him on the answering machine to play when he was away on a trip.

Inside the metal container were letters he'd sent home from camp and boarding school and college, as well as letters he'd written to his father over the years that had come back unopened. Laz's mother had once been on a cleaning binge and had come across the tin. When she had asked him what she should do with it, he'd told her to throw it out, but Grace had salvaged it from the discard pile and brought it home without telling him. Neither Grace nor Griffin spoke as they emptied the contents of the tin. Blue, green, and orange envelopes fluttered across the desk.

Griffin picked up one of the unopened letters and pressed the envelope between his palms. Each letter was thick, comprised of several folded pages. Laz's handwriting was visible through the envelope. Without having to say anything to each other, Griffin and Grace gathered the letters together and placed them back in the tin. There would be plenty of time to open them, if they ever felt the need.

Griffin shoved his hands in his pockets. Grace went to the closet, pushing aside a shopping bag, and placed the tin back on the shelf. Just as she was about to close the door, she saw a sealed plastic bag containing a block of clay. It had probably been in there for years. She knelt down and lifted it up, setting it on the floor. Amazingly, the clay still felt cold and moist.

"I had completely forgotten about it," she said. She could easily imagine the feeling of working the clay with her hands to get the air out, and the way that the dry, silky dust would remain on her fingertips for days afterward.

She glanced at the clock. It was nearly seven. She realized that she'd been so engrossed in their explorations that she hadn't even offered Griffin anything to eat or drink.

"Are you hungry?" she asked.

"Starving." She was about to mention the spinach lasagna with tofu filling that she had waiting in the kitchen when he said, "I've been really craving meat. It's been nothing but gerbil food since I got here." Feeling very Francinesque, she decided to freeze the lasagna for another time.

The only meat she had in the house were the two dozen or so containers of sweet-and-sour meatballs. She made a mental note to call the butcher, then went into the kitchen, thankfully able to stop herself before she uttered the words, "Dinner will be ready in ten minutes and thirty seconds."

Francine was right—the meatballs seemed to be as fresh as the day they were prepared, whenever that was. Grace set the kitchen table with two woven place mats, cloth napkins, and the William Morris dishes that she and Laz had bought at the Victoria and Albert Museum in London. The image of Francine at the Food Emporium was still vivid her mind. It had been a strange encounter, almost as uncomfortable as when she was a teenager and had bumped into her parents in the East Village, wearing their matching dungaree leisure suits. Her father still spoke about those leisure suits with great nostalgia, yearning for a bygone time. Francine had been quite ill at ease, as if she had been caught in a compromising position.

As Grace stirred the meatballs, she realized that she'd forgotten all about Mr. Dubrovsky's book, which was probably still on the floor of Flik's Video, when the telephone rang. The machine picked up and she heard Mr. Dubrovsky's voice. *Mrs. Brookman, it is vital that I speak to you . . .*

Just then, Griffin walked into the kitchen, and Grace rushed over to turn down the volume. Mr. Dubrovsky's voice trailed off. Grace wiped her hands on a paper towel and motioned for Griffin to sit down, placing the steaming bowl of meatballs on a trivet. He spooned almost half the contents of the bowl onto his plate. By the time Grace had taken a second bite of her grilled vegetable/soy burger, Griffin had all but cleaned his plate.

"These are amazing. What's in them?" he asked. Again, she couldn't tell him even if she'd wanted to. Francine never would have divulged her culinary secrets, however fond she was of Griffin's father.

"I'll try to get the recipe for you," she lied. "I actually didn't make them myself."

"Well, they're really good," he said again, reaching for the bowl. "Aren't you going to have any?" Grace shook her head, so he proceeded to spoon out the remaining meatballs.

"What would you like to do tomorrow?" Grace asked. "I could show you around the city a bit, if you like."

Griffin reached for a slice of peasant bread. "That sounds great, but I'm going up to Vermont for a couple of days to go skiing."

Grace watched as he spread a thick layer of butter over the bread, salted it, and took a huge bite.

"Alone?"

"No. Some girl I met invited me. She goes to the acting school in the building. A group of them are driving up in the morning, and they asked if I wanted to go with them." Grace had seen the acting students in Laz's building. They were always dressed in black and carried huge bags slung over their shoulders.

"When will you be back?" she asked, not wanting to sound intrusive but suddenly aware of a Stepford-like feeling of protection over him.

"Thursday late afternoon, I think."

"We're going to Chicago on Friday," she told him. Griffin put down his bread and looked up. Grace knew what he was thinking. She took a deep breath before she spoke. "But Laz is flying directly to O'Hare."

As soon as she'd uttered the words, she paused and tried to think of anyone over the course of the last six weeks to whom she had not lied, and realized that with the exception perhaps of Pete, the bartender at Tap A Keg, there was no one.

Grace brought a plate of cookies and a pot of chamomile tea into the living room. Griffin turned the Christmas tree on and off from the dining room light switch with glee, like a small child let loose at the planetarium.

"Cool light show," he said. Grace sat on the couch with her legs folded beneath her, sipping her tea.

"Glad you like it," she said.

Early the next morning, Grace went to prepare Griffin breakfast and found a note on the kitchen table. He hadn't wanted to wake her. The radiator hissed and clanked like someone knocking. Grace walked through the apartment and into the den, looking for remnants of Griffin's presence, some proof that he'd really been there. The least he could have done was to have left some traces—a half-empty glass of water on the nightstand, a paperback book, even a wet towel on the doorknob. Griffin, in this regard, was nothing like his father after all, who left evidence of himself whether he was in the apartment or not. Griffin had seemed to all but vanish. The bed was made, as if no one had inhabited it. Even the rug she and Laz had brought back from Morocco, which was constantly inching toward the window, was in its place, undisturbed.

She noticed that the light in the bathroom was on. She went to turn it off and saw Griffin's Dopp kit on the sink. It was wide open like a fish about to swallow a hook, and Grace looked at the contents: a tube of toothpaste, a double-edged razor, deodorant, dental floss, a nail clipper, and shampoo. Luckily, all the items inside were easily replaceable, although, with a blizzard about to hit, replacing them might prove difficult. She was about to zip the bag up when she noticed a familiar-looking white business card sticking out of the top. She reached for it, and as soon as she read Mr. Dubrovsky's name, she stuffed it back inside, turned off the light as if that would obliterate the knowledge, and fled the room.

Later that morning, she telephoned Flik's Video, but—as if they were Grace's willing accomplices—they claimed that they had found no evidence of *Oblomov* among the videos.

23
Frequent Flyer

The snow arrived late Monday evening and continued through Wednesday morning. It was indeed a blizzard of immense proportions, some snowdrifts reaching as high as the parlor-floor windows of brownstones. With all the snow, which was considerably more than Milton had predicted, Grace imagined Laz couldn't have gotten home even if he'd wanted to.

The snow presented Grace with an early holiday gift of excuses to abstain from almost all daily activities, including teaching her class and attending any family functions during the week. She was thus exempt from the biweekly "ancient Chinese" facials on Mott Street that her mother swore by, which incorporated ground-up pearl powder and shark cartilage exfoliant, and which left Grace's skin sensitive and prone to breakouts, lunch at Ratner's, and the requisite quick peek in at S and W's discount clothing store in the garment district, as well as a charity meeting with Laz's mother. Nancy Brookman, not heeding the advice of her riding instructor, had gone out riding and fallen when the horse lost its footing on a patch of ice, spraining Nancy's ankle in the process.

The one appointment that Grace could not get out of was with Dr. Gaylin, and so she set out midafternoon on Wednesday, traversing the snow-covered park on foot. The sun shimmered off the unmarred white hills, a short reprieve as more snow was forecast. The park was silent, all but unpopulated, with no wind. Grace trudged through the surreal stillness.

As Grace neared the East Side, the park suddenly became animated—cross-country skiers threaded their way between benches and trees, then disappeared through covered overpasses; dogs trotted through huge drifts, in search of squirrels, occasionally chasing children whizzing by on Flexible Flyers and plastic saucers.

Almost without thinking, Grace walked along the twists and turns of the paths, as the synthesized activities continued around her. Fifth Avenue loomed ahead, the impressive limestone facades in deep shadow. Grace gazed back one last time at the idyllic snow-covered scene before crossing the street and heading toward Dr. Gaylin's office.

Once inside, Grace sat down on a leather club chair and opened a magazine. There were several women in the waiting area. One, who looked at least eight months pregnant, smiled at Grace, who smiled back politely.

"You don't recognize me, do you?" the woman said. She was wearing a black headband, and her auburn hair fell just to the nape of her neck. Her scarf, folded in a triangle and tied off to the side, was imprinted with horses and riding scenes. "I'm Patsy. Laura's daughter. Nancy and my mom ride together. I met you at last year's Historical Society auction."

"Oh, of course," Grace said. "I'm sorry. I was just a little preoccupied."

"Me, too," she said, patting her stomach. "How are you?"

"Fine, thanks. When are you due?" In the background, the radio was tuned to WQXR. A female journalist was discussing hoaxes in the media. *I've been a journalist for twenty-five years, and never before have I come across a case of such blatant fabrication as with the case of the Kosovo prison impersonation . . .*

"Hey, isn't that your husband's—"

"Shh," Grace said, raising her finger to her lips. The woman must have thought the gesture indicated Grace's desire to listen to the broadcast. Just then, the nurse came in to escort Grace into the examining room. The voice of the female journalist trailed off as Grace followed behind the nurse.

The results of the hCG test confirmed that the blood levels had returned to normal, as if nothing at all had ever inhabited Grace's uterus. After spending a few moments with Dr. Gaylin, Grace headed for home.

Her mood and the weather had changed dramatically. The sun was obscured by thick, gray clouds and the park was virtually deserted, as if all the activity of just an hour ago had been a figment of her imagination. She shivered in her red parka. It felt like dusk. As she approached the park exit nearest her street, Grace thought about her empty apartment and then continued north on the park drive toward the yarn store.

She rang the buzzer and waited. Just as she was about to leave, she heard the door click and went in. Penelope was not dressed in one of her usual floral outfits, but was wearing a formfitting, blue pinstriped pants suit with exaggerated shoulders and a peplum waist. Her pants were tucked into white, fur-lined boots.

"Grace!" she said, walking toward her, arms extended. "We haven't seen you around lately."

"I know. I got caught up with family stuff," she said. This was not a lie. She had lost a child, found a child, and her father had been hospitalized all in less than a week, not to mention her husband's ongoing unexplained absence.

The sight of the shelves newly stocked with yarn was reassuring. Grace touched the soft skeins. Each one contained the possibility of a new creation. Some were more suited to one type of form than another, and there was the variable of the person working the yarn, but still, the basic characteristics were innate, as if the light gossamer weave of a fine angora had only one option. Grace was drawn to a pale lilac yarn with flecks of white. She pulled a skein off the shelf.

"That's a very fine yarn," Penelope commented. Grace squeezed it. It felt almost like nothing in her hand.

"It's wonderful," Grace said. For the first time since she began crocheting, she felt the need to have a pattern. "What should I make out of it?" she asked.

Penelope's eyes widened. "You never had to know before. Why now? Take the risk, let go of the result," she answered. Just then, the young man with the crocheting workshop stopped by to pick up a package of labels to sew into his creations that read *Made expressly by Scott*. He was wearing a nubby yellow sweater he'd obviously knitted himself, tucked into a pair of tight, black ski pants. He looked like a bumblebee.

"Hello, hello," he said, greeting Grace like an old friend. She sat down at the long oak table and set to work. She hadn't discussed the offer for the part-time job that Penelope had made her, but it seemed as if no answer was required besides just showing up.

Grace assisted three customers with choosing yarn, and she demonstrated a scallop stitch to another. By the time she was ready to leave, it was dark out. As Grace put on her coat and packed up ten skeins of the lilac yarn, Penelope brought over a large plastic bag and set it in front of her on the table.

"It's your grandmother's afghan. I did a few repairs. Not like new, but it will hold up. I hope you like it." Grace had not forgotten about it. In fact, quite the opposite. It was like Laz's leather jacket, which was still at the tailor's—she simply had no use for it now. She reached into the bag and pulled out the afghan. There were no more gaping holes or frayed ends. The afghan was whole and intact, as perfect as the edition of Twain that her father had re-bound for Laz, and inasmuch, utterly unfamiliar to her. This was not the same afghan that had kept her warm the nights Laz went to his hockey games. The holes were gone and with them the memories—the proof of being well loved and well used—the tenacity of fibers holding tight in spite of weaknesses.

"Penelope, thank you so much," she said, trying to hide her disappointment.

"My pleasure. But I told you you'd be better off starting over. It can never be the same. I'm closing up early today. I'm meeting someone," she said, batting her eyes. "A blind date." She lowered her voice. "Actually, I met him on the Internet. He's a linguist. We really hit it off. Who knows? He may be the one." Grace wished her well and closed the door behind her on the way out.

It was snowing heavily when Grace walked out onto the street. At least another three inches of fresh snow now covered the parked cars. She pulled her hood over her head and steadied herself against the wind. The lights from the cars blended into one glaring stream as she crossed the street to find a taxi heading downtown. There were several people searching for taxis ahead of her, arms laden with packages.

Out of the corner of her eye, she saw a man in a black parka leaning against a mailbox, his head buried in a newspaper. It wouldn't have seemed out of the ordinary, except that people don't usually read newspapers or wear business shoes during blizzards. She knew those shoes. They were the same sort of wing tips that Mr. Dubrovsky wore. As she approached the man, she saw him turn his head away quickly, as if he didn't want to be identified. Instead of waiting for a taxi, she began walking, quickly. She looked behind to make certain he wasn't following her, but in the bracing wind and with the glaring headlights, she could no longer even make out the mailbox where he'd been standing.

Grace quickened her pace, rushing around the corner, then stopped briefly to catch her breath. All for a book. It seemed so ludicrous. Then she remembered the card in Griffin's bag, thinking that everything was somehow related, but she couldn't connect the dots at the moment. She ducked under the awning of the synagogue that her family went to on the high holy days, just off West End Avenue. Brushing the snow off her coat, she went in.

Her father had once led her through the synagogue on a rainy day. They had gone into the sanctuary and down a flight of stairs and through a neighboring church, miraculously emerging several blocks south, right in front of the crosstown bus stop—without getting wet. She wondered if she could reconstruct the route. She proceeded toward the sanctuary while trying to keep an eye out for Mr. Dubrovsky. Could he actually be following her?

An archway that was covered in small, brilliantly colored tiles led into the sanctuary, two large doors flanking it on either side. Each door was emblazoned with a seven-pronged gilt menorah and a colorful, fanning mosaic pattern, along with other symbols of Judaism with which Grace was not familiar. She pulled at the ornate brass handle of one of the doors, but it was locked. She tried the other. After a heavy tug, it opened. She glanced over her shoulder and thought she saw a hooded figure enter the synagogue just as she slipped through the door.

She descended a flight of unlit stairs until she reached a musty-smelling basement. An eerie orange glow emanated from the single bare lightbulb hanging from the ceiling. The bulb, covered with a thick layer of black soot, looked as if it hadn't been changed in forty years, clearly surpassing the Duro-Lite record for longevity.

Looking ahead and seeing only murky shadows before her, Grace had the urge to turn back. Harnessing her courage, she forged ahead down the maze of dark corridors. She traveled for what seemed to be several blocks, then she finally entered a brightly lit boiler room with an assemblage of pipes and gears, beyond which was a door with a lit red exit sign above it. She pushed the door open to find another flight of stairs. At the top of the landing, she came to a fire door, which she opened slowly, careful not to set off any alarms, and found herself standing in the church entryway.

The building smelled faintly of incense, and she saw the requisite bulletin board covered with church announcements. A notice for a lecture that evening caught her eye: *It's never too late to become who you could have been.* She recognized the quote from George Eliot. The lecture had probably been canceled because of the snow. She zipped up her jacket and was about to leave when she heard voices coming from inside the church. Wondering if the lecture was in progress, she opened the door a crack and peered inside. The pews were sparsely filled, and at the front of the sanctuary stood a man in his thirties wearing a jade-green fleece pullover, jeans, a backwards baseball cap, and hiking boots. His hair was long and shaggy, and he had a few days' growth on his face. He looked familiar. Laz occasionally didn't shave on the weekends, and by Monday morning, his face would be completely covered by a full beard. Once, when he had left the building after not having shaved, the doorman hadn't even recognized him.

Grace opened the door wider and tried to slip in unnoticed. The man at the front caught her eye and nodded. She sat down in the last row and listened.

"Try to think back to a time as a child when you were so occupied in something that you were completely unaware of the passing of time," the man said. "You were lost in your true selves. You haven't lost that, you've just forgotten."

At first the things he was saying were the kind of typical pop psychology that was promoted on daytime talk shows. It wasn't as if Grace even thought she needed to discover her authentic self. She was simply curious what these people thought they lacked.

"We all know," the man continued. "We either forget who we were, discount it, or never seek it because it didn't fit into the scheme of our family's, lovers', friends', employers', husbands', wives', or children's expectations. Remember: It's never too late. Who could you have been?"

He stopped, left the lectern, and walked down the aisle in Grace's direction. She glanced behind her, assuming he was headed toward the back of the church. But he wasn't. She felt like someone about to become an unwilling magician's subject. As he approached, Grace suddenly realized who he was and tried to reach for her bag in an attempt to escape before he recognized her. Too late. He stood in front of her.

"*I've never* . . . ," he said, addressing Grace, with a wink. "You fill in the blank." He stared at her, waiting for a response. She stared back at him. Her heart began to pound. This meeting in the church was no drinking game. And whatever it was, Grace no longer wanted to play. Without the bar between them, she felt completely vulnerable.

"I'm sorry," she mustered. "But I really have to go." And she ran out of the sanctuary. On the street, she oriented herself and realized that she was directly across the street from Laz's old building. The snow was falling heavily and the streets were empty. The yarn and afghan in her bag were dusted with snow. She looked both ways. Thankfully, Mr. Dubrovsky was nowhere in sight. She decided to cut through the lobby of Laz's building. Her father had turned her into an urban groundhog, capable of giving a potentially dangerous stalker—as well as an intrusive moonlighting bartender—the slip. She hurried through the revolving door into the lobby of Laz's building and then into the elevator and up to the fourth floor.

When she opened the door, she saw that the apartment was covered entirely with sheets of plastic and a layer of fine white dust. By the window, under a single sheet of plastic, was an orchid. She went over to uncover the plant, which from a distance had looked too perfect to be real. There was no white dust on the leaves and, strangely, the soil was moist.

If Laz had been there, he had left no tracks. For now, the two of them, like the magnetic spinning pups, had reversed their polarity. It seemed that they could only push each other away. Snow swirled in the courtyard outside and Grace imagined a flurry of white business cards fluttering to the ground.

She was in no hurry to go home, now that Griffin was out of town. Here, in this unoccupied apartment, where no one else could possibly leave her, she felt safe. Still wearing her red parka, she lay down on the plastic-covered couch. Her eyes felt heavy. What was it about this apartment that always made her so sleepy? she wondered, her last thought as she drifted off. She awoke to the sound of the asbestos workers entering the apartment the next morning. She left quickly, taking the orchid with her, her hair and clothing now covered in white dust.

Griffin was due back that night. By nine o'clock, still not having heard from him, Grace decided to go to bed. She'd spent the evening packing—both her suitcase and a bag for Laz. With just a few well-chosen items, she was able to evoke the semblance of a whole life. At this point, Grace had it down to a science. The black satin pants that her mother had bought for her, when folded, took up no more room than one of Laz's pocket handkerchiefs. If she packed for Chicago according to her mother's principles, she would require a bag no larger than a manila envelope. She could mail her clothes to Chicago.

She pulled down a small duffel bag from the closet, filling it with Laz's clothes, shoes, an extra-warm sweater, as well as several talisman-like items, such as his eyeglasses and the gold pocket watch from his father. Ostensibly it was for Chloe's benefit—if she came to the hotel, there would have to be signs of Laz around the room, but it was really just as much for Grace's own peace of mind.

She opened the top drawer of Laz's dresser. Inside, there were belts from every trip Laz had ever taken—a white belt with blue embroidery from Morocco, a cowboy belt from Durango, a camel hair belt from Egypt. Grace could practically construct a map of the world by laying out the belts in longitudinal lines. Next to his passport, she placed the key to his old apartment. There was no need for her to ever go there again. Then she closed the drawer.

Her parents telephoned later that evening, wishing her a safe flight and a happy birthday in unison. *Call as soon as you land. What's the flight number again? You know it's going to be bitter cold in Chicago. Maybe you should go in the spring instead.*

When Grace finally heard the front door open around midnight, she remained in bed, as if physically weighted down. She couldn't face another leave-taking, not even one from this near stranger. She heard music coming from his room. Grace recognized the melody and the sound of Aimee Mann's voice—*One is the loneliest number that you'll ever do. Two can be as bad as one. It's the loneliest number since the number one.* Laz had played that song, too, sometimes over and over again.

She stared at the ceiling and thought about the fragment of the dream she'd had in Laz's apartment on her post-Thanksgiving visit. Laz had walked through the web with nothing sticking to him. She wondered why it hadn't occurred to her to try walking through the doorway herself.

The next morning, she left for the airport two hours early, long before Griffin would be up.

Grace settled herself into the plush first-class seat. The seat next to hers was reclined, the buckle fastened as if a body were actually occupying it. Grace returned the seat to its upright position and opened her book.

She thought back to her first solo plane ride, when she was eleven. She had been going to Iowa for Christmas to visit Chloe, where Chloe's father lived. Grace's parents had driven her to the airport, but at the gate, Grace panicked and refused to get on the plane. Her father gave her half a Miltown tranquilizer that he had in his breast pocket. About fifteen minutes later, she was sitting limply strapped into the orange airplane seat on her way to Iowa City, even less present than Laz was now.

About forty minutes after the plane's takeoff, Grace found herself growing anxious. For the first time since Laz had left, she was traveling out of her comfort zone. Living in the city had lately become almost as provincial as a small town for Grace. Her life for the past six weeks had been mostly contained within the very circumscribed twenty-block area of the Upper West Side. But now she was taking "her act" on the road and suddenly, after this many weeks of performing, it was as if she couldn't remember her lines. Her mouth was dry. She asked for a glass of water.

Grace unwrapped a skein of the lavender angora yarn that she had bought the other day, her lifeline to familiar ground. As she began to crochet, the feeling of dread began to lessen, until gradually it was a mere wisp like the cirrus clouds that skimmed the blue sky. It wasn't like a pill that she had popped or like a muscle relaxer to soothe the mind during periods of turbulence. By creating something new out of whole cloth, her fingers were trying to show her she could lead the way.

A pattern began to emerge, and it was clear that this project was going to require more than the seven skeins she'd brought along with her. The yarn was so light that it took almost half a skein to crochet just five inches. She tried to ration herself, but as much as she willed herself to slow down, she couldn't. Before they had been airborne even an hour, the bag was nearly empty. Only one skein remained.

The flight attendant gushed over Grace's work as she passed by on her way to get the drink cart. Grace envisioned the finished crochet weightlessly skimming the top of the dining-room table.

She put down her crocheting and pressed her forehead against the window, peering out at the horizon. An image began to encroach like a storm cloud over her mind. She saw herself with Laz on the ski slope on their first Valentine's Day. From the vantage point of thirty thousand feet up in the air, she saw Laz's face as he had taken her hand and led her to the lift. *You're too sensitive,* he'd told her. *Who would ever want kids? They just tie you down.* He had proposed that afternoon on the last run of the day. The ski lift had taken off as the words left his lips. *Marry me.* She remembered how once they returned to the city, he didn't call for three days.

Despite all their premonitions and warnings about the weather, her parents never counseled their daughter on the fault lines and sinkholes of real life. They scoured the skies for forces of nature, but they didn't see that human beings and bad marriages have their own high-pressure systems. They misguidedly thought that Laz would elevate their daughter, but they confused his breeding and background with his worth. They hadn't been able to foretell that he would only elevate Grace to the status of a single wife.

Suddenly, she felt a tug on the yarn, as if she'd caught a fish. Before fully registering what was happening, Grace watched in horror as, row by row and down the aisle, her crocheting began to unravel, caught in the efficient wheels of the drink cart. The more she tried to save it, the faster it unwound. Grace's attempt to recover the unraveling yarn sent several opened cartons of milk and cups of coffee toppling over (and the flight attendant to lose her footing), until the entire length of the plane, from first class to coach, looked as if a soggy, purple spider's web had descended upon it.

24
Soul Kitchen

The woman at the reception desk at the Four Seasons hotel very kindly informed Grace that they would require a different credit card.

"Has it expired?" Grace asked.

"No, actually," the woman answered with a sympathetic tilt of her head, "it's been frozen."

"That's impossible," Grace said. "I just used it." But as she uttered the words, she didn't remember exactly when the last time was that she'd used it. In fact, she couldn't recall having received her last monthly statement. Due to some recessive gene passed on through her mother, she was in the habit of paying with cash. What she hadn't inherited was her mother's penchant for haggling. Her mother would have asked the hotel concierge if she could do a little better on the rate.

"Let me call them," Grace said.

A lengthy conversation with the credit card company, a few

choked back tears, and a dose of reality later, Grace returned to the reception desk. The card had indeed been frozen, but by whom, Grace wasn't sure. She had just enough cash on her to pay for the deposit and a day's worth of expenses. She picked up her bags, noting how light Laz's duffel bag felt in her hand in comparison to hers and went upstairs.

THE ROOM SHE'D booked was spacious and tastefully decorated, if slightly generic. There was a vase of purple freesia and a fruit basket by the window, a floral down comforter and king-size pillows on the bed, cherry-wood dressers with matching nightstands. The room was orderly and utterly free of any residual history, which held a certain guilty allure for Grace. She felt as if she'd entered the Platonic ideal of a stage-set life.

Through the sheer curtains, from the forty-first floor window, Grace could see the shores of Lake Michigan. Noticing that the phone's red message light was blinking, Grace pressed the button and listened to Chloe's voice, welcoming her to Chicago. Grace called back, and they arranged to meet for an early dinner at a restaurant near Chloe's apartment in Wicker Park. Grace made the usual excuses for Laz, saying that he had a reception he had to attend.

Grace spent the day shivering as she wandered around downtown Chicago in her pink coat, visiting the tourist sights. Then she took a short walk along the shore. She returned to the room just after five o'clock and put on a thick pair of thermals and several sweaters over an ankle-length knit skirt. She removed the present she'd brought for Chloe from her suitcase—a blank book that she had made. On the cover, she'd mounted a packet of seeds for Chloe to plant in the spring on her porch. Underneath the packet, Grace had glued one of the fortunes that Kane had given her. The fortune had seemed more appropriate for Chloe, who was working on a novel: *You are a lover of fiction.* Grace had made the pages from shredded newsprint with flecks of wild flowers, spraying the pages with essence of bergamot, Chloe's favorite perfume. Grace thought that she might have overdone the perfume, as now the entire contents of her suitcase smelled like a very strong cup of Earl Grey tea.

Before she left the room, Grace gazed at Laz's unopened duffel bag on the wooden rack. Usually it made her feel less alone to display Laz's things, but in her present frame of mind, the last thing she wanted was his clutter to mar this wonderfully unblemished scene.

SOUL KITCHEN WAS nearly full, even though it was still early. The crowd was unusual, too—very young, tattooed, and imaginatively pierced. Chloe was seated at a round table in the center of the room. Her hair was no longer cropped short or dyed black, but fell past her shoulders in blond waves. She was wearing ripped jeans and a vintage cardigan covered with intricately beaded flowers over a pale blue T-shirt with the words *All About Me* embroidered across the front. Every once in a while, the light reflected off the beads on her sweater in a certain way, sending a sparkling shower of colors around the room.

"They're hipsters," Chloe said, referring to the other patrons. "It just comes naturally. We were never that cool."

Grace tried to take off one of her sweaters, but it got caught on her necklace and Chloe had to help her pull it off. The waiter, dressed in red jeans and a light-green shirt with depictions of major historical events on it, smirked as he filled her glass with ice water.

"Great shirt," Chloe told him. "Did you get it at Village Thrift?"

"No, at Una Mae's."

"I have to take you there, Grace," Chloe said. "You'll love it." The waiter and Chloe continued talking about their favorite vintage stores, and Grace thought at one point that he was going to join them at the table.

"Where are you from?" he asked, turning to Grace for the first time during the whole conversation.

"New York," she answered. Grace watched as the lines in his brow began to furrow.

"Like where? Upstate?"

"No, the city," she said.

He glanced at Chloe as if for verification. "Cool," he said, then went off—rather quickly in Grace's opinion—to get them menus.

Grace could barely finish half of the sweet potato ravioli and grilled spinach with dandelion greens. The waiter wrapped it up for them, and as they were getting their coats, he asked Chloe for her telephone number.

"I guess you like it here," Grace said, as they walked outside onto Milwaukee Avenue. They passed a small group of people who stood in line, waiting to get into a club next door. On the corner, Grace noticed a cluster of teenagers in hooded jackets, congregating in front of a small deli.

"A lot. I never felt like I could be myself in New York. I know you love it, but I just couldn't take looking out my window at a brick wall. Now that Mom's gone, there's not much left for me there."

"I can imagine."

"I'm still sort of waiting for her to come back." They walked around the corner toward the elevated train. Chloe stopped and turned to Grace. "If you have time, you should come over and see my apartment. Too bad it's not spring. We could sit on my porch."

"I'd really like to, but I think Laz will be finishing up with his conference soon, and I told him I'd meet him back at the hotel." She was thankful it was dark out.

"Grace—" Chloe began but then stopped. She put on a hat that looked like she'd sewn it together from some old sweaters scraps. "That's all right. Another time, then." She rummaged through her red vinyl purse for her keys. A cab pulled up in front of them. "Thanks again for the journal. Call me tomorrow and let me know what your plans are. I have a birthday present for you." As they hugged, Grace thought of the empty hotel room that awaited her. Chloe began to walk away.

"Chloe . . ." Grace called, waving the cab off. Chloe turned around.

"Did you forget something?"

"I think I have time to stop by your apartment. Let me call Laz and tell him I'm going to be late."

Chloe's apartment was a half mile from the restaurant in Bucktown. They took the long way home, walking along streets named after famous authors—Shakespeare and Dickens Avenues—that were lined with Victorian row houses and unadorned, low brick buildings with high fences surrounding them, which Chloe told her had been built before the area had become a designated landmark.

On the way, they made a stop at Myopic, a tiny independent bookstore with aisles barely wide enough for two people to stand without touching. The floor was covered with pencil shavings. Unvarnished raw wood shelves were crammed with titles that Grace had never heard of. Plaster statuettes peeked out from tiny nooks. A black cat nudged Grace's ankles and followed her around the store as she browsed. In the back, there was a garden with a round table and three chrome chairs. Chloe went upstairs to find a book about the subject of loss. Grace could hear the creaking of the floorboards above her, and she imagined the entire inventory of *A* through *F* crashing down on her.

She walked over to the register to wait and glanced at the

assortment of notices, mostly ads for sublets or part-time jobs, that had been stuck up with pushpins. Grace was about to go in search of Chloe when a yellow flyer caught her eye. It was a listing for an open pottery class. The bottom of the sheet was cut into a fringe on which there was a drawing of a tiny potter's wheel and a telephone number, written in calligraphy. It had been such a long time since she'd thrown a pot—the wheel spinning as she centered the clay, lifting the clay upward, and hollowing it until it seemed almost too thin to hold. The black cat played at her feet, scampering after a fallen pushpin, then Grace saw Chloe coming down the stairs. Before she knew it, Grace found herself tearing off one of the slips of paper and stuffing it into her pocket.

CHLOE UNLOCKED THE door to her second-floor apartment, turning the dead bolt and fastening the chain once they got inside.

"I never used to lock my door until after Mom died. I don't want anything else to be taken away."

"I know the feeling," Grace said as she walked into Chloe's kitchen. The floor was an old-fashioned, peach-colored linoleum tile with gold flecks that matched the countertops. The walls were painted a sunny yellow, and every available wall or surface was covered with artwork or knickknacks.

Grace thought of her grandmother as she looked around at the assortment of clocks, each with a different time. Antique dolls were displayed on top of the refrigerator, as were pieces of miniature furniture that could have fit in quite naturally with the Damien Hirst exhibit. Magnets and black-and-white photo strips covered the front of the refrigerator door. Grace saw a photo of her and Chloe from their senior trip to Rye Playland. The photograph was curled at the edges. In it, Grace was wearing a frayed jean jacket with a bandanna tied around her neck. Grace barely recognized herself. Even her smile seemed alien to her.

She thought of the drawer under her bed, where she suspected most of her high school paraphernalia still lay undisturbed. It would never have occurred to her to try to incorporate one part of her life into another. When one stage ended, she'd been taught to pack things away like old clothes into a camp trunk and move on to the next. Whatever didn't fit was left behind or sent to Goodwill.

When Grace first began dating Laz, her mother had taken her shopping and to get a new hairstyle. For the first time, they paid full price, trying on clothes with the solemnity usually reserved for a rite of passage. It was the culmination of all those years spent at places such as the Barclay School in preparation for this very moment. Like a shtetl bride who'd been shipped off with a goat and the family linens, Grace had a modern-day trousseau—hers from Bergdorf's, which secured her access into Laz's sphere. It wasn't what was included that had made the ultimate difference, it was what had been left out. With the aid of her mother's skilled hand, Grace had been delivered to the threshold of a marriage with one important thing missing. As she looked around Chloe's kitchen, she knew what it was. Here—in the clutter and the accumulation—was an uncensored life.

"Would you like a cup of chamomile tea?" Chloe asked. The question broke Grace's reverie and she found herself back in the false world that she'd been inhabiting all too easily over the past six weeks.

"Can I use your phone to call Laz?"

Chloe gave Grace the same look that she'd given her outside of Soul Kitchen, but this time she was shaking her head.

"Grace . . ."

"What?"

"Do you think I'm stupid?"

"Of course not. I just wanted to let Laz know I'll be late."

"Give me a break. I know what's going on. Maybe you think you can pull this off with everyone else. But Grace, please, with me? I've known you forever."

Suddenly, after a day of shivering, Grace was sweating. She wasn't sure what or how much to say.

"What do you mean?"

"Grace, Laz was in Chicago last week at a symposium on human rights, but he spent most of his time trying to defend his book, if you can even call it that. I think he even believes his story that he was in that concentration camp. It was in all the papers. He still claims he spent six weeks impersonating a prisoner. Paying one off is more like it. I even went to see him at the symposium."

"You saw him? Did he say anything about me?"

"Yes. But it was all a bunch of crap. And between the two of you, I don't know who's got the bigger problem. He had no idea that you were coming to Chicago. He wanted all the flight information. Like I'd ever give it to him. He hasn't changed one bit. I knew it from the first time I met him. I'm sorry, but I've never been a big fan of the guy." So Laz must have been the one responsible for the upgrade.

"I never meant to lie to you," Grace said, sinking into a chair.

"Why don't I make some tea and you can tell me what's been going on?" Chloe went to the cabinet and took out two unmatched mugs with floral patterns and set them down on the table, shoving aside a thick, marked-up manuscript and several back issues of *The New York Review of Books*.

Grace sighed. "I wouldn't even know where to begin."

"Wherever you want. We can edit later."

• • •

THAT NIGHT, LYING on the futon mattress in Chloe's second bedroom, Grace was unable to sleep. The talk with Chloe had been like a summer storm on a hot August evening that does nothing to unburden the night. The room was filled with sewing things. Chloe's mother had taught her how to sew and knit and embroider. A pair of gingham curtains hung from brass rods on the window and a hand-quilted blanket covered the bed. On a wooden table, an old Singer sewing machine that had belonged to Chloe's mother was set up with bobbin and thread, as if poised to begin whirring away. Next to it was a clear, plastic sorter stocked with buttons, hooks, thimbles, and metal spools.

Grace had a childhood memory of writing her name on the sides of her white saddle shoes while she was in grammar school. When her mother picked her up from school that day, she was beside herself. "Your brand-new shoes!" she'd cried. It hadn't been the first time Grace had written her name on things. She'd inscribe entire pages in her notebook with her name, etch it into her desk at school, scratch it on the upright piano in the living room. Her teacher had taken her mother aside and in a low voice suggested they set up a meeting. Grace caught the words *identity crisis,* and although she hadn't understood the meaning, from the way her mother reacted, she knew it was worse than the time she had to go to the speech therapist.

"She knows *exactly* who she is, and if she doesn't, I'll be the one to tell her, thank you," Grace's mother said in a high-pitched voice, zipping up Grace's coat and leading her down the limestone steps. When they got home, her mother handed Grace a brush dipped in peroxide and detergent. Grace's fingers turned white as she applied three thick coats of Kiwi shoe polish, setting the shoes to dry overnight on sheets of newspaper.

Tomorrow was her birthday. She would be celebrating without

Laz. Suddenly, like a homesick child at camp, she felt a longing—but not for her father's beige argyle sweater, climate-controlled rain showers, or her mother's elixirs, not even for Laz. It was a longing for something she could not yet name. When she returned to New York, she decided, she would tell her parents everything.

25
Grace's Intervention

Chloe was already up and working on her laptop at the kitchen table, wearing jeans and a purple sweater and slippers, when Grace walked in. There was a pot of coffee on the counter and the kettle was on.

"Hey. How did you sleep? Did the gunshots wake you?" Chloe asked.

"Gunshots?" Grace sat down at the table.

"It happens all the time. I'm so used to it now that I barely notice it; but the first time I heard them, I dropped to the floor and rolled like I was on *Miami Vice* or something."

"I guess I was out cold," Grace said, though she had no sense of having slept at all.

"Well, that's good." The kettle whistled. Chloe turned off the burner on the old gas stove and picked up a yellow watering can, then went over to water a flowering plant that was in a hanging basket by the window. She reached in to pick off what she thought was a dead leaf. "Damn it," she said, wiping her hands on a dish towel.

"What's wrong?" Grace asked.

"There are moths in my petunias!" Chloe unhooked the hanging basket and carefully held it out the door to the porch, giving it a vigorous shake, which caused at least a dozen gray moths to fly out and flutter away. "We've been having a real moth problem lately," Chloe said. "I'll spray later. I love my petunia, even though according to my grandmother, they're low-class flowers."

Chloe poured herself a cup of coffee. She brought over a tea strainer and some fresh mint and poured boiling water into Grace's cup.

"I want to take you to the Bongo Room for breakfast. For your birthday," she said, sitting down at the table. "They make the best eggs. A few of my friends will be there who I think you'll like. Then we could hit the vintage stores."

THE RESTAURANT WAS packed when they arrived. At first, Chloe didn't see any of her friends. The hostess, who wore a tight black turtleneck and low-waisted chinos, told them that the wait would be at least an hour.

"I don't mind waiting, if you don't mind," Grace said. But before Chloe could answer, three people at a big booth in the back waved them over.

"Oh, look. They're over here." Chloe pulled Grace by the wrist to the back of the restaurant and introduced her. "Guys, this is Grace, my friend from New York I'm always telling you about."

"Nice to meet you," Grace said, as she squeezed in between two girls named Kym and Sela, who were wearing matching llama-wool sweaters. Chloe sat down next to a guy with diamond studs in his ears and wearing a red velvet jacket over a worn blue T-shirt.

"Jeff, you wore your Kris Kringle jacket," Chloe said.

"Just trying to spread a little holiday cheer," he answered. Another friend of Chloe's arrived late, brought over a chair, and sat down at the head of the table.

"Hey, Ian," Chloe said. "This is Grace." Ian nodded to her. He kept on his navy blue pea coat and scarf, undoing only the top button. He drummed his fingers on the table, his hair filled with static electricity, almost as frenetic as his temperament. After they all ordered, Grace noticed that Ian was staring at her. She tried not to look back, but every so often she would check to see if he was still looking.

"So, have you been to Chicago before?" Jeff asked, picking a piece of lint off his crimson jacket.

"No, it's my first time," Grace answered.

"Chloe says you're a sculptor."

"No, I used to teach art, but I'm not a sculptor," she said, thinking about the notice for the pottery class and the block of clay in her closet. Besides modeling some Christmas ornaments out of plasticine, she hadn't sculpted anything in years.

"She is, too—she just doesn't remember," Chloe interjected.

"You know, I heard someone once say at a meeting," Jeff began, "'Leap and the net will appear.' It helped me get over my fear of auditioning." When he finished speaking, he had an expression on his face as if he'd just uttered a statement of profundity.

Grace had no idea what meeting he was referring to, or why he was addressing her as if she'd solicited his opinion. Anyway, the thought of leaping was unappealing enough, but the idea of doing so without the assurance of a sturdy net, harness, and a well-thought-out contingency plan was unfathomable to her. She began to feel slightly claustrophobic and took a deep breath to keep herself from scrambling over the two sweater girls to seek refuge in the ladies' room.

"Jeff, Grace doesn't know about Near West," Chloe said. Everyone at the table nodded gravely in a manner that made Grace feel slightly paranoid. "It's an AA meeting I've been going to since I moved here."

"Alcoholics Anonymous?" Grace asked. "You're not an alcoholic."

"I've been there, too," she heard someone say. Grace suddenly felt as if she'd stumbled into some lodge meeting and she didn't know the secret handshake.

"Grace, I've been sober for almost five years. And I think you knew." Grace couldn't recall the last time Chloe had gotten drunk. Of course, there'd been more than one occasion in college that she'd thought Chloe had overdone it with the melon ball shots.

"Why didn't you tell me?" Grace asked.

"I tried to on several occasions. You wouldn't hear it."

"Ain't just a river in Egypt," Jeff said.

"What does that mean?" Grace asked.

"*Denial.*"

"When did you start speaking in slogans?" Chloe asked Jeff, taking a sip of her orange juice.

"Trace it; face it; erase it," he continued.

"Replace it," Kym added.

"Enough," Chloe said, trying to stifle a laugh. "See what I have to put up with here? Maybe I'll just move back to New York and leave you loonies to fend for yourselves."

"*Grace* it," Jeff said.

"I actually like that one," Chloe said.

The omelets they'd ordered arrived on oval plates that were the size of Grace's mother's platters. Her omelet was so large, Grace guessed that it must have contained at least ten eggs, and with its side of hash browns and caramelized onions, she thought she'd never be able to finish it. Laz usually ate whatever was left on Grace's plate. She'd become so used to it that sometimes she wasn't sure if she was actually finished or just in the habit of leaving something for Laz.

Grace remembered a dinner she'd had with Laz at a bistro in Paris. Thick gold curtains had hung from the doorway to keep out the cold. She and Laz had been ravenous, having spent the day walking to Montmartre and the Jeu de Pommes. As always, Grace had left a bite of steak au poivre, a bit of pureed turnips, and a few *frites,* which Laz ate, dipping his bread in the peppered cream sauce on her plate. During dessert, she'd watched as he took the last spoonful of her crème caramel, now wondering whether he'd even considered that she might not have been finished yet.

"Your friend's a good eater," Jeff said to Chloe. Grace looked down at her plate and saw that she'd finished every last bite, while the rest of the group had barely started theirs.

"I didn't realize I was that hungry," she said.

"Take what you need and leave the rest," Jeff said. Chloe rolled her eyes. Again, Grace wasn't sure if he was talking about something other than eggs.

As Grace listened to the conversation, she began to feel a sense of belonging. Her shoulders relaxed and her breathing came easier. She found in this circle of Chloe's friends at the Bongo Room a place not to find answers—because, like Kane said, sometimes there aren't any—but to ask questions. They tumbled out fast, one after another, like somersaults. *If she gave up the illusion, who or what would be there to break her fall? And why did she need it in the first place?* Grace looked up to see Ian staring at her again. He unwrapped his scarf and finally took off his coat, throwing it over the back of his chair.

"Grace, I don't know you," he said, leaning across the table. "And if you were here longer, I'd probably ask you out. But slogans won't help you—you just need to take some steps." Even though his words seemed harsh, Grace was relieved that someone was speaking plainly.

She looked Ian directly in the eye for the first time. His eyes were pale blue, which from a certain angle looked almost silver. "You're right. I do. And that's just what I'm doing."

"Oh, thank God!" Chloe said, obviously pleased. "Everyone—meet my friend Grace."

AFTER BREAKFAST, GRACE and Chloe made the rounds at the vintage stores in the neighborhood. In one store, which was as large as one of the Price Clubs that Grace's parents frequented, Chloe pulled item after item from the tightly packed racks. She placed them in a metal shopping cart and proceeded down the narrow aisles toward the western wear department, which was next to the flannel section at the end of the aisle, just before the flowered muumuus.

Grace was struck by the vastness of the store, but what was even more amazing to her was that everything in the store had once belonged to someone else and that no two things were exactly alike. There was clearly more to this process than just finding something in the right size. She wondered what made one thing right for one person and not another. And did the clothes change the person, or the other way around?

When Grace and Chloe came to a rack of faux-leopard coats, Chloe stopped as if she'd just struck gold and looked at Grace.

"I don't think that's me," Grace said.

"Don't say that until you try it," Chloe responded, choosing one with a straight cut and checking to see if all the buttons were on. Then she grabbed a set of matching earmuffs and a pair of black motorcycle boots.

"It's lucky we got here early," Chloe said, examining the beadwork on a pearl-white cardigan. "You should see the line just to get in after twelve. And then all the good stuff's gone."

Chloe pushed the shopping cart to the dressing room and motioned for Grace to get in line. The woman ahead of her had so much in her cart that it looked like she was buying inventory to open her own vintage store. When it was Grace's turn, the attendant handing out the numbers didn't flinch at the abundance of clothes she was taking into what they called the dressing room—far too loose a term for the sheer lack of space or privacy it offered. Basically, it was a circular area surrounded by a shower curtain. Grace hung her clothes on hooks that were originally hot-and-cold water faucets and looked down to make sure she wasn't stepping on a drain. Chloe stood outside, handing her clothes from the cart.

"Put this camisole on under the cardigan, and then try on the gray pinstripes. I want to see them on you, so come out," she instructed. "And don't forget the motorcycle boots."

When Grace emerged, she was not wearing a single item of clothing she had come in with, except her black gold-toe socks, which were Laz's, and her underwear. Chloe clapped her hands when she saw Grace, and immediately directed her to a full-length mirror that was leaning against the wall. She stood behind Grace and adjusted the collar on the leopard coat.

For the first time in years, Grace recognized herself. She liked what she saw—from the slouchy pants to the sturdy boots, and even the worn-in leopard coat. She felt awake, her eyes bright and her face glowing, without a stitch of makeup.

"You're back," Chloe said.

"I didn't know I'd been gone."

"Not gone—just in hiding," Chloe answered. "Come on, let's pay and then go get your stuff from the hotel."

"What about my clothes, the ones I came in with?" Grace asked, looking at her pink princess coat draped over a plastic chair.

"Leave them. They belong to someone else anyway."

26
MAMBO NIGHT

Grace listened as the pilot informed the passengers that because of dense fog and heavy traffic flying into La Guardia they would be delayed for at least another hour. She was dressed head to toe in her new vestments, her leopard coat occupying the seat next to her like a wild animal escaped from captivity. The plane circled the airport in a nauseating figure eight. The irony was not lost on Grace, for whom another hour in a holding pattern would hardly make a difference.

When she finally arrived at home, she found a note from Griffin taped to the side of the orchid that she'd rescued from Laz's apartment. She read the letter, noting how similar Griffin's handwriting was to Laz's.

> I will always remember how you let me in and made me feel welcome. My father's lucky to have you. I've decided to go back to Maryland. I can't wait forever for something

> that might never happen. It's time to get back to my life. Thank you for all your kindness. Griffin.

She stopped and took a deep breath, then folded the letter. She hadn't been honest with him and felt she deserved no thanks. She wasn't even sure if she had a life to get back to, and this kid knew that his was still waiting for him to return.

The only other sign that Griffin had been there was a stack of plastic containers that had been rinsed out and placed in the kitchen sink. Grace filled the sink with warm soapy water, knowing that Francine expected her containers to be returned in the exact condition that they'd been given, and she suspected the sauce might take some time to dissolve.

She opened the freezer to find that Griffin had defrosted and consumed more than a year's worth of sweet-and-sour meatballs and a dozen bagels in a mere two-day span. The freezer was now empty, except for the spinach lasagna, the birthday blinis, a box of Arm & Hammer baking soda, and two ice trays that Grace didn't even remember having bought.

There were two messages from her parents on the answering machine, confirming Scrabble night. *Best wishes to the birthday girl. And bring the blinis, if you still have them. We're doing a vodka tasting.* With Francine in Paris and Grace having missed celebrating her birthday with her parents, Grace felt obliged to go. She called to report the state of the blinis and to let her parents know that she had something she needed to discuss with them. She feared that if she didn't tell them immediately, she might lose her resolve.

She called the credit card company and was relieved to find that her charge card was no longer frozen, although the limit on her account had been readjusted. She left her suitcase to unpack later, stuffing Laz's filled duffel bag into the back of the hall closet. Then, still wearing her new outfit from Chicago, she grabbed her purse and the blinis and went downstairs to get a taxi.

When Grace arrived at her parents' building, she saw that it was draped with the same black construction netting that covered Laz's old building. Huge Dumpsters blocked the driveway, and she was directed to the service entrance by the doorman.

Milton and Bert were sitting at the kitchen table when Grace walked in. Bert had brought over an assortment of frozen delicacies —pierogi, caviar, as well as a bottle of Ketel One vodka. He'd already poured himself a glass. Grace opened the box of frozen blinis and put them on the kitchen table. Encrusted with a thick layer of ice, they looked more like sand-covered jellyfish than something edible. Grace's father rose and, standing on tiptoe, kissed her on the top of her head.

"Trip okay?" he asked.

"It was fine," she answered, unbuttoning her leopard coat.

"Laz working?" he asked, as if they'd rehearsed this exchange.

"Yes. He sends his best."

"You've got a good one, there. Don't let him go." She knew the next line by heart, but just couldn't manage to get the words out this time.

Her mother entered the kitchen and stood staring at Grace, dumbfounded. "What on earth are you wearing?" she said finally. Grace's father looked up.

"Just my usual," he answered.

"Not you, Milton. *Grace.*"

"She looks the same to me. Maybe a little taller," her father said, still under the misguided impression that he stood five feet ten and a half.

"It must be the boots, Dad," Grace said, feeling herself slouching slightly. She touched the beadwork on her cardigan sweater.

"Chloe picked out some new things for me while I was in Chicago." Her mother approached her, touching the leopard coat with trepidation.

"Secondhand," she determined. "And more than gently used. Well, it's lucky I didn't send that box of odds and ends to Goodwill yet. Oh, and I picked up a pashmina for you on sale at Filenes's to wear to Mambo Night."

"Thanks, Mom, but I already have something to wear," Grace said, shrugging off her coat as well as her mother's comments. "I noticed they're doing some work on the building," she said, hoping to change the subject.

"Keep your voice down," her mother said in a hushed tone. She pulled Grace aside and looked to make sure Milton was sufficiently occupied. "They're refacing the building," her mother whispered, "replacing the blue bricks. Daddy will be beside himself when he finds out—he thinks they're just sandblasting."

Grace knew not to push any further. It was an unspoken rule in her family that keeping people in the dark for as long as possible was a gesture of love and devotion, not deceit. Her mother would no doubt keep this from Milton until the last blue brick had been removed. But, short of giving him a pair of blue-tinted sunglasses, she could not keep him in this state of innocence forever. In a few months' time, he would begin to notice that, brick by brick, his beloved blue building was being transformed into something more subdued and in keeping with the upscale neighborhood in which they lived. If he couldn't take this, how could Grace expect him to take the news of Laz's disappearance? The urge to protect him was strong.

"What's all the whispering?" Bert asked, coming up behind them with a mouthful of caviar.

"Nothing," Grace covered. "Did Francine get off all right?"

"Oh, yes, fine, fine. Except she took enough luggage for an around-the-world tour—almost threw my hip out again. She said her meatballs made quite a hit. So, what were you two girls talking about?"

"I was just telling Grace that we're going to see *Miss Julie* on Friday night."

Bert looked blankly from Grace to her mother. Grace was impressed. Maybe it was from her mother that Grace had inherited her skills at deception.

"Miss who?" Bert asked.

"We have season tickets," Milton chimed in.

"Strindberg," her mother added.

"He's Swedish," Grace's father said, in explanation. Her father always did research before attending a cultural event, reading the scores before attending operas or looking up artists on the Internet before seeing an exhibit. "A disciple of Schopenhauer and a notorious misogynist."

"A misogynist, really?" Bert piped up, as if elated that he was finally able to make a contribution to the conversation. "What kind? Deep tissue or craniosacral?"

Paulette gave Bert a quizzical look. Bert let out a deep sigh when his comment was dismissed and took a sip of his drink. Grace felt a genuine tenderness toward Bert, on whom Francine's absence was clearly taking its toll.

"What was it you wanted to talk to us about, dear?" her mother asked, popping the blinis into the microwave. Grace looked at her father, who was occupied so contentedly at the table with a new gadget that she felt her newfound resolve swiftly fading. Maybe in a day or two, when he'd come to terms with the fate of his beloved blue building. Surely it could wait.

"I was just thinking," Grace said, noticing a few scuff marks that her motorcycle boots had left on her mother's vinyl flooring, "it's been a long time since you've been over. Why don't you and Dad come for dinner Tuesday? I can make a pot of chili."

"You mean the vegetarian one from *The Moosewood Cookbook*?" her mother asked.

"Yes. The one I made for Laz's birthday last year."

"That sounds lovely. I'll bring the entrée."

"That is the entrée," Grace said.

"But you know how much Laz loves my veal roast with the wild rice stuffing."

"Laz won't be there. He has to give a talk in Pittsburgh."

"He can eat it when he gets home. He'll need some protein." Grace noticed that she was beginning to resent her mother's unending doting on Laz. The last thing she wanted was to start filling up the freezer again with things she couldn't eat, now that it had been emptied.

"Tuesday's out," Bert said. "Remember? It's Mambo Night. Must have just slipped your mind, I guess."

"We could make it a late supper," Grace suggested, hoping to allay his fears, but in truth, she'd blocked it out altogether. "After Mambo Night." Nothing short of an act of God could get her out of the Hadassah dance at this point.

"Well, how about we pop over for a quick cannoli from Café La Fortuna?" Grace's father suggested.

"Milton, you know the doctor told you to cut down on saturated fats."

"I can have a taste," he said. "Just a bite. I'll eat the part with the air."

"How's ten?" Grace asked, looking at Bert for approval. She didn't want him to feel slighted. He nodded, closing his eyes and shaking his head resignedly, as if having just given in to a tough all-night negotiation.

"We wouldn't miss it," her mother said.

GRACE THOUGHT OF nothing else over the next two days but how to break the news about Laz to her parents. She didn't know which would be harder—telling them or watching their reaction. If only she didn't have to actually be there. It could go two possible ways.

In the first scenario, after they recovered from the initial shock, her parents would assume total responsibility. In some convoluted way, they would recast the events until the entire thing was their fault. Her father, unable to take another bite of his cannoli, would then walk toward the window, thrust his hands deep into his pockets as if they might contain the solution and not just a crumpled shopping list and a few quarters, and gaze out over the park, at a loss for words. Grace's mother, growing flushed and increasingly frenetic, would spend several minutes deliberating over whether to wrap up the leftovers or do the dishes first. Her father would then notice the state of the Duro-Lites and proceed to disengage the dimmer switch and rewire the circuit that connected to the Christmas tree, after a great fuss about the possibility of being electrocuted. Then, they would all collapse into the sectional couch and put on *The Charlie Rose Show*.

The other, more likely scenario involved her parents coming over for cannolis, and Grace not saying a single word.

PERHAPS IT WAS the salty beluga caviar that her parents had picked up at Costco and Grace had indulgently eaten that caused her hands to retain water. Even two days later, Grace's fingers were swollen and her engagement ring and wedding band were uncomfortably tight. Edema, her father always called it, pumping his fingers and waving his hands in the air after he'd been to a Chinese restaurant, even though he had specified no MSG. Grace removed her rings and dropped them into a small jar, which she filled with sudsing ammonia and water. She gave the jar a shake and watched the glint of diamonds, sapphires, and bubbles swirling around. She turned it upside down. The rings made a hollow tinny sound as they hit the lid.

She found Laz's wedding band right where he'd left it, behind the can of shaving cream in the medicine cabinet. Strangely, the can felt almost empty, even though no one had used it recently, as if in the intervening weeks its contents had just dematerialized. Grace slipped his ring on her finger, imagining the configuration of Laz's knuckles, the indentations and bends in his fingers. She took it off and held it up to the light. The ring all but disappeared as she squinted through it, just a thin circle that from a certain angle was barely detectable.

The more she looked at it, the more she began to see the ring as nothing more than a piece of soldered metal badly in need of cleaning. She tried to rekindle her faith in its powers, but instead, the longer she held it, the more diminished it became. She dropped it into the jar of ammonia with her ring and gave the jar another quick shake, hoping to renew some of its former luster. A marital snow globe. The rings settled in the jar with distance between them, like two caged animals.

It was getting late. Grace rummaged through her closet, looking for something to wear to the Hadassah dance. She found a low-cut red dress and a pair of strappy sandals she'd bought before she met Laz. The one time she wore the outfit, Laz told her she looked like a contestant in the Miss America pageant. She hadn't known how to take the comment at the time, so she had relegated the dress to the back of the closet in case she needed it for a costume party. This seemed an appropriate occasion.

In a last-ditch effort to distract herself from the inevitable pain of telling her parents the truth, she prepared and fussed over a plate of brandied figs on rice crackers. It was amazing how long it took to get the figs to look just right—a task that could have expanded indefinitely, if only she'd actually had the luxury of time. She knew Bert would not appreciate her being late. She covered the plate with plastic wrap, even though the platter was still sorely lacking in aesthetic value. She was about to head out the door when the phone rang.

"Grace? Bert, here." He didn't sound quite like himself.

"Is everything all right?" Grace asked.

"I'm sorry to have to disappoint you, but I threw my hip out, and I'm just in no shape for Mambo Night. You should have seen the cortisone shot they gave me. Francine could skewer a horse with the needle they used." Grace tried to conceal her delight at this turn of events.

"Well, there's always next year," she assured him.

"I know how much you were looking forward to it."

"Don't give it another thought. I'll find something to do. Just take care of that hip."

Grace hung up the phone and was on her way into the bedroom to change when she caught sight of her reflection in the full-length mirror. She walked toward the mirror, lifting the scalloped hem of the skirt a bit, revealing her black fishnet stockings. She had a vague memory of learning to samba at the Barclay School, where she had snapped a pair of castanets in her hands and stamped her feet on the polished floor.

She hadn't danced in ages, but now, all dressed up with nowhere to go, she suddenly felt the urge. She found a Latin music compilation CD that she and Laz had won as a door prize at some charity event, and put it on.

The music was loud and the beat was infectious. Before Grace knew it, she was not only mamboing around the room, she was twirling and shimmying like a Brazilian showgirl. She didn't know what had come over her. All along, she'd been dreading the evening, and here she was having a private Mambo Night by herself. She kicked her leg high in the air, nearly knocking over a standing lamp and almost losing her balance, but it didn't stop her. She felt flushed and unencumbered—she could have danced for hours—until reality once again descended upon her. Her parents were due in less than an hour.

She sat down on the window seat, clutching her knees to her chest, and pictured her parents at home getting ready—her mother telling her father to wear his ecru pullover with the burgundy tie, her father calling down for the car to pick up the cannolis he wasn't even permitted to eat. Grace felt herself faltering. She closed her eyes and thought about the horoscope that Kane had given her for her birthday: *Make a wish. Open your eyes. Did it come true?*

As she tried to formulate her wish, she found her mind wandering off as if in an enchanted forest. The more she tried to bring herself back, the more her mind went around another bend. She found herself wishing for things that made no sense—the taste of pure dark chocolate, a wisp of lilac, untrodden snow, a lump of soft clay, a stretch of silence without fear—all things with no definite beginning or end. Strange wishes. There were none about Laz coming home and their life picking up where it had left off.

She made one last attempt to pinpoint and crystallize her wish. She concentrated. *Did it come true?* She opened her eyes. Kane was standing before her. She got up and turned off the music.

"What are you doing here?" she asked.

"I let myself in," he said. "The doorman buzzed, but no one was picking up. Grace —"

She looked at him and realized from his expression that something was terribly wrong.

"What is it?" she asked.

"Your mother called me from the hospital," Kane said. "She tried calling here, but there was no answer. It's your father. He's had a heart attack."

The room began to spin. Kane put his arms around her, and then they went downstairs to get a taxi to Lenox Hill Hospital.

27
Visiting Hours

Grace was in the backseat of the cab with Kane, her faux-leopard coat over her shoulders. Even with the heat on, she was shivering.

At the hospital, they rode up in the elevator to the seventh floor, where they found Grace's mother in the waiting room sitting on a nubby, purple armchair. Everything in the room was a different shade of either purple or green, even the huge abstract painting on one wall.

As Grace and Kane approached, Grace was struck by her mother's complete lack of makeup and her unkempt hair. She was dressed in a flannel shirt that belonged to Grace's father, and underneath she had on only sheer stockings and a pair of black snow boots. To Grace, her mother's appearance was a clear indication that the situation was far more serious than she feared. Her mother rushed over as soon as she saw them, dissolving into Kane's arms like a small child.

"He's still in the emergency room," she sobbed.

"Can we see him?" Grace asked.

Her mother shook her head. "Not yet."

"Will he need surgery?"

"They're not sure. They need to see the results from the angiogram first," she said. Kane gave Grace's mother a squeeze. Her eyes began to fill with tears. "My Milton."

"Can I get you anything?" Kane asked.

"Maybe a cup of hot tea, that's all," she answered. "Earl Grey, if they have it. If not, a bottle of seltzer."

Grace walked with Kane down the tiled hallway to the elevator. "I wish Laz were here," she said, half to herself. "If only he were back from his trip."

Kane didn't respond. They stepped into the elevator, which stopped on each floor, although no one got on or off. They walked to the cafeteria in silence. Grace watched as orderlies pushed patients on gurneys down the corridor. The cafeteria was empty, except for one table at which a man and woman were bent over a turkey sandwich that was still wrapped in plastic.

Kane filled a Styrofoam cup with boiling water and picked up a foil-wrapped Earl Grey tea bag. He paid for the tea and handed the cup to Grace.

"I should go. Your family needs you," he said.

"Kane—" she began, then fell silent.

"Don't worry, everything will be all right. I'll call you later," he said, hugging her. Grace watched as he walked down the hall and into an awaiting elevator.

"Thanks for everything," she called after him. He didn't respond, and she wasn't certain whether he'd heard her or not. She stood watching until the elevator door closed, and then she went back upstairs to the waiting room.

Grace's mother was by the window. Two women in full-length fur coats sat holding hands on a small green couch. Bert had arrived and was in the process of trying to unwrap a bar of Toblerone without making any noise, when he saw Grace approaching and pretended he was just reading the ingredients.

"White chocolate has much more saturated fat than dark chocolate, did you know that?" he asked, placing the bar back on the table.

"How's your hip?" Grace asked, although she didn't see even the slightest evidence of a limp.

"Much better, thanks. Cortisone is a miracle drug," Bert said, giving his hip a pat. He paused and took a deep breath. "Actually, my hip's fine," he said, fumbling with the top button of his overcoat. "It's just that I couldn't bear to go without Francine." Grace put her hand on his shoulder.

"You don't need to explain," she said. Grace could tell he seemed relieved not to have to say more.

"Kane brought you to the hospital?" he said, after a while.

"Yes."

"He's a decent guy," Bert said. Grace nodded in agreement. Then they both sat down to await news about Grace's father.

It was just after two o'clock in the morning when the doctor finally came to give them a report, leading them down to the recovery room. "We'd like to keep an eye on him for a few days, just to make sure." As Grace and her mother walked down the hall, the emergency room nurses looked at Grace strangely.

"Only members of the immediate family are allowed in the recovery room," one of the nurses told her.

"I'm his daughter," she said. Grace's mother whispered something to one of the nurses, who nodded and let them go in.

"What did you tell them?" Grace asked.

"I said you had just come from a costume party. What else?"

"It wasn't a costume party," she said, sounding embarrassingly like a nine-year-old after an all-night sleepover party. She couldn't help thinking that if the music hadn't been so loud, she would have heard her mother's call.

"Anyway, that coat is frightening. Now, which room did they say he was in?" Grace's mother stuck her head behind several curtains before locating her husband, who was lying on his back, eyes closed, sucking on a green lollipop.

"He's still a little groggy," a stocky nurse said as she made some notations on a chart with a chewed pencil. Grace sat on the edge of the bed, her mother on the only chair in the room. Her father began to stir. He opened his eyes and smiled weakly.

"Gracie," he said faintly, still sucking on the lollipop. He tried to raise his arms to embrace her, but with the tubes, he could only make a feeble attempt. "Would you like anything to eat or drink? There's ice water and some tea biscuits," he said, pointing to the nightstand. "They said later I can have some chicken broth."

Grace was almost brought to tears by her father's display of hospitality, as if he were hosting a party. Grace's mother got up to examine the ingredients on the package of tea biscuits. She took out her reading glasses from her purse and went over to the light.

"These are fine," she determined, opening the plastic wrapper and offering one to Grace, who shook her head.

"You look good, Dad," she said, although his body looked small and frail in the thin cotton hospital gown.

"Sorry we couldn't make it tonight," he said. "You wanted to tell us something?"

"Another time," she said, rubbing her hands together, even though she wasn't cold anymore. "When you're feeling better. You should rest now." He closed his eyes again. He was wearing a pair of blue paper slippers on his feet. A plastic balloonlike instrument was wrapped around his calves, automatically filling with air every few seconds and then deflating, to prevent blood clots. Grace's mother motioned for her to come near.

"You really should go home and get some rest, Grace. No need for all of us to stay. Bert's here if I need him. Come back in the morning when your father's feeling more himself. Visiting hours start at nine."

"If you're sure you'll be okay. I can go by the apartment if you need anything."

"Well, only if it's not out of the way. Maybe a pair of slippers and a robe, for your father. And my makeup kit."

THE FIRST THING that struck Grace when she walked into her parents' apartment just before four in the morning was how dark and empty it was. The television was tuned to the Weather Channel, but the sound was muted. She'd become so used to conjuring Laz's presence; but now, as she walked through the empty apartment closing doors and turning on lights, she realized that her actions weren't done in order to conjure a life, they were to ease the pain.

Her parents had clearly left in a hurry. All the signs of panic were there: an overturned container of buttermilk on the countertop, pulled-out chairs, the refrigerator door left open.

She pictured her mother running to her father's aid in the bedroom, where drawers were flung open and an empty bottle of medicine was on the nightstand. In the adjoining bathroom, she found cotton balls tumbling out of the medicine cabinet, a wet washcloth on the floor, and her father's black comb with a few white hairs on it. Grace began to clean up. She stuffed the cotton balls back into the now-bulging box, threw the washcloth in the hamper, and went back to the kitchen. But even when everything was put back in order, Grace could do nothing to obliterate the emptiness that remained.

She found a small, black WQXR tote bag still wrapped in plastic underneath the coat tree, like a forgotten present on Christmas morning. Her father's maroon bathrobe was hanging in his closet next to his beige and pale gray button-down shirts. With its pointed shoulders and slouched back, the robe looked only slightly less inhabited than her father had in his hospital gown. She folded it neatly and placed it into the tote bag along with his corduroy slippers. Her mother's supersize, clear-plastic makeup bag was too large to fit, so she put it with a pleated skirt, a pair of shoes, and sweater set into a plastic grocery bag.

Walking aimlessly around the apartment, Grace found herself pausing in front of her old bedroom. She went in and knelt down on the soft green carpeting. In the fifth grade, Grace had brought home two gerbils, which in a matter of weeks had multiplied to twenty-eight. The plastic cage, filled with cedar shavings, had toppled over one afternoon, sending the gerbils scampering across the kitchen floor, running behind the refrigerator and stove, never to be seen again. As Grace opened the drawers underneath her bed, she half-expected to find a scene straight out of *Miss Bianca*—her long-lost gerbils sitting on silver swings and having a tea party in a white pagoda.

Inside the deep double drawers were her possessions, although none of them were even vaguely familiar to her as she inspected them. She waited for the memories to kick in, as if somewhere encoded in the fibers of the clothes or the books there was preserved a strand of her former self.

As she rummaged through the drawers, Grace felt as if she were invading someone's privacy. The things she was looking for were no longer there and never had been. They were the things she'd lost along the way—the twenty-eight gerbils, the calculator pen, the holes in her grandmother's afghan, Laz, and herself. The things unrecoverable. The unopened drawers had once held out the possibility of recovery, and now that was lost, too. She thought about her father offering her tea biscuits from his hospital bed. She couldn't bear to lose him also. She closed the drawers and lay down on the carpet. Then finally, the tears came, silent and streaming down her face.

THE CLOCK ON the blue nightstand read six-fifteen when she awoke. Still nearly three hours until she could go back to the hospital. She went into the guest bathroom and splashed cold water on her face. On the marble pedestal sink, there were candles and beauty products arranged in neat white baskets. There were even products *pour hommes,* in case a male guest needed a bit of freshening up.

She applied some alpha-hydroxy moisturizer with aloe to her face and dabbed chamomile gel on her noticeably puffy eyelids, convincing herself that she could see changes occurring right before her eyes. The urge to improve herself was hard to resist. Suddenly, her mother's makeup kit held out a kind of promise. She got the bag and unzipped it, looking at the array of products with confusion. What looked like mascara turned out to be a mauve eye stick, the tube of what she thought was lipstick was actually cream blusher.

After she was finished, she looked like a character in a black-and-white movie that had been improperly colorized. She washed the makeup off her face and zipped up her mother's makeup kit. It would always be a bag of tricks that required a proper magician.

The clock on the nightstand in her bedroom still read six-fifteen. She went into the kitchen and stared at the clock on the wall in disbelief. It was nearly ten-thirty. She pulled on an old pair of Levi's she'd found in her closet, a light blue turtleneck sweater (slightly moth-eaten) from the top drawer of her dresser, and headed back to the hospital.

When Grace entered her father's hospital room, it was as if her mother had aged ten years from the night before. Her hair was pulled back in a short ponytail and she had raccoon eyes from lack of sleep combined with crying. Her father appeared to be asleep, but as soon as Grace walked in, he began speaking.

"Is that you, Grace?"

"Yes," she answered, bending down to give him a kiss.

"So good of you to come." His voice sounded weak.

"How are you feeling?" she asked.

"Just fine. I should be home by tomorrow. Friday by the latest."

"I brought you your slippers and a robe." He reached his hand out to touch her on the arm. His eyelids began to flutter.

"I don't know what I would do without you and Laz. And mother," he added. "It was so nice of Laz to come this morning."

"This morning?" Grace turned to her mother for verification. Her mother was leafing through the current issue of *The New York Review of Books*. She looked back at her father and saw that he'd drifted off again. Grace had expected that he would be groggy, but delusional was another thing altogether.

"Did you say something, honey?" her mother asked.

"Dad says Laz was here."

"Oh, yes. I guess I just missed him. I went down to the cafeteria for a cup of tea. I tried to make a manicure appointment at Pinky's, but they weren't open yet."

"What time?" Grace asked.

"Around six-fifteen," her mother answered. "They really should have all-night manicurists." Grace's heart froze in concert with all the clocks.

"I thought visiting hours didn't start until nine," she said. For all she knew, Laz might have been there—but just as easily not. Grace understood that this was a time when her father would have needed Laz. At his most fragile, he needed to summon his family to his bedside. Her father could tolerate Laz's absence at Scrabble games, just not when it came to heart attacks.

"The nurses must have let him sneak in," her mother said matter-of-factly. "You know how he charms people." Her father began to stir.

"He read me a chapter of that *Oblomov* book you two like so much," he said, not missing a beat. He was able to drift seamlessly in and out of conversations—even consciousness—while listening to a particularly soporific Debussy piece at Avery Fisher Hall, during one of Grace's mother's lengthy and detailed accounts of her shopping expeditions, or at a lecture at the Ninety-second Street Y, and yet still remain completely engaged. It was a talent that now seemed that much more precious to Grace as he lay recuperating in a hospital bed. "He says I'll be back on my feet way before that Oblomov guy gets out of his robe."

Grace looked around. There was no book in sight, only a tattered issue of *Reader's Digest* on the nightstand. She guessed that the drugs must still be in his system, but whether Laz had been there or not was not important. He was there now just as much as he had ever been.

Bert walked in the room carrying a huge basket of what Laz liked to call *bon voyages* fruit—apples, pears, and mangoes fit for Gulliver. On his head, Bert sported a dapper fedora, around his neck a silk scarf. He looked well rested and in good spirits, better than Grace had seen him since Francine's departure. He placed the basket of fruit on a table by the window and waited for some sort of acknowledgment, which when received, he quickly brushed off.

"It's the least I could do," he said, reaching into his breast pocket and taking out a travel-size Scrabble board. Grace was convinced that in some other pocket he had a miniature twin edition of the *Oxford English Dictionary.* "Anyone up for a friendly game?" he asked, assuming it was a rhetorical question and proceeding to set up the board.

Grace walked over to the window and stared out over the tops of low buildings that were all the same generic tan or white brick. Soon her parents' building would blend in among the rest of them, distinguishable only by slight design variations and the street address marked on the awning.

"Can we entice you to join us?" Grace's mother asked. The game was already in progress. Her father had a tile rack and was shuffling his letters, but Grace could detect the faraway look in his eyes. She recognized the tendency in herself, too, her mind evaporating into utter blankness. She, however, had not perfected the ability to remain engaged while also being elsewhere.

"I'm sorry, what did you ask me?" Grace said.

"Do you want to join us?" her mother asked again.

"I think I need to get some air," Grace said.

GRACE WALKED AROUND the corner to Le Pain Quotidien, a restaurant with long, rough-hewn tables and French country decor. Almost all the patrons in the restaurant wore large hats, their faces hidden behind newspapers. She pulled up her sleeves and leaned on the table. When her pot of Earl Grey tea arrived, the bergamot smell reminded her of Chloe. She poured a cup. Some loose tea leaves swirled to the bottom. She looked for some sign in the pattern, but none appeared.

In Chicago, everything had seemed so simple. She recalled the sight of herself in the mirror at the thrift shop. For some reason, she pictured herself unpacking a car filled with her belongings in front of a Victorian row house on a snowy street in Wicker Park. It all seemed so real—everything from the lime-green Volkswagon bug to the fuzzy purple hat on her head, until she remembered her father in the dreary hospital bed. She felt she'd never have the courage to leave.

Owning up to the truth, which in Chicago had come to her surprisingly easily, now seemed impossible. But the idea that her own father had succumbed to the power of self-deception was a far more unsettling prospect. It was like leaving her father snared in a web while she held a pair of scissors in her hand. She understood the impulse to believe in the status quo. They all wanted Laz to be there. Even in his absence, he still existed for them, as if it were as simple as slipping into one of his dove-gray T-shirts and waiting for sleep. Her father would be expecting Laz to visit again. More than anything, she didn't want him to be disappointed. Even if Laz had been there, it didn't mean he would come again. She couldn't protect her father forever. The best she could do was cushion the blow.

Just as she had poured her second cup of tea and was about to reach for a packet of raw sugar, she sensed she was being watched. She glanced up quickly. Across the wide table she saw a man, the brim of his hat pulled down over his brow. He was leafing through the peach-colored pages of *The Observer*. She noticed the headline: PULITZER PRIZE RESCINDED FOR KOSOVO CAMP ACCOUNT. The man nodded to her. A complete stranger. She gave a sigh of relief that it hadn't been Mr. Dubrovsky, but part of her was disappointed. For all the uneasiness the idea that she was being followed caused her, in some way it gave her a small amount of comfort. Someone, for whatever reason, would have been watching over her. She nodded back to the gentleman as the sugar crystals dissolved into her steaming cup of tea.

GRACE STOPPED IN the hospital gift shop for a pack of gum before going up to her father's room. As she was on line to pay, she noticed a stack of Hadassah cookbooks. Grace leafed through one, turning the pages and looking absently at the familiar, tried-and-true recipes. She was nearing the end of the book, having just passed a kugel recipe made with pineapple and maraschino cherries, when she saw a recipe for Trudie's Famous Sweet-and-Sour Meatballs. She read through the list of ingredients: two parts chili sauce to one part Welch's grape jelly. A bag of minimarshmallows were needed to sprinkle on top for a glaze.

Grace was about to close the book when she recalled the incident with Francine in the Food Emporium, Francine's cart precariously loaded with enough jelly and chili sauce to drown several cows, and it all began to make perfect sense: everything from Francine's adamant refusal to give away her secret recipe to her quick exit at the supermarket, and finally her excess baggage. She had obviously smuggled the ingredients in her suitcase for a recipe even the French would not be able to duplicate. All these years of subterfuge, and here was the recipe in bold type for the bargain price of ten dollars.

Although the vehemence with which Francine had guarded this secret was out of proportion to the reason, the idea that a secret—even one so seemingly insignificant—had grown to such consuming magnitude was as familiar to Grace as her favorite pillow. She had an overwhelming feeling of compassion for Francine. She understood the impulse to maintain the illusion. Indeed, there was safety in it, but at the same time it invariably kept everyone at arm's length. Grace and Francine were in the same self-made predicament. The deception wasn't just for them. The result of going this far and with such success was that everyone around them became invested in it. Francine may have known this, protecting her illusions like a mother lion her cubs. Taking it away seemed wrong, although Grace knew she must. The dilemma now was about finding the right time for it to be undone.

Grace's father was asleep when she entered the room. She recalled a phrase she had heard her mother once use when his mother died. *It took the starch right out of him.* She imagined her father hanging limply on a clothesline, as if all that was required to resurrect him now was the simple addition of the right solvent to the rinse cycle.

Bert and her mother were nowhere in sight, the Scrabble match abandoned midgame. Grace read the words on the board: *frigid, agog, genus, kin, null.* The usual assortment of esoteric words. She wondered how many words Bert had challenged. She glanced at her father's letters. In front of his tile holder, next to the plastic pitcher of water on the wood-grained Formica swinging table, he had spelled out the word *grace.*

Even Grace, a novice in the world of etymology, could see that there was no place on the board where it could possibly fit.

Grace sat at her father's bedside and waited. She hoped the words would come when she needed them. She looked at her left hand, and saw that she had forgotten to put her rings back on. Strangely, there was still a deep indentation in her skin where the rings had been. Her father began to stir. Then he opened his eyes.

"Grace," he said. "How long was I sleeping?"

"Not long."

"You should have woken me."

"Dad?" she said, quietly. "I need to talk to you about something. Is this an okay time?"

"It's always a fine time to talk to my daughter." The room began to grow dark. Grace looked out the window. She could see menacing storm clouds gathering in the distance. She thought about the rain showers her father used to give her.

"Do you still have that Mary Poppins umbrella?" she asked. He smiled, closed his eyes again.

"I think it's in the front hall closet. Why?"

"Just asking."

"What's it like out today?"

"It looks like it's about to storm."

"Did you wear boots?"

"Yes," she said. Grace touched her father's hand.

"What is it, Grace? Something wrong?"

"It's just that I miss you."

"I'm right here, sweetie."

"This is hard," she said. "It's about Laz."

"Laz?" he repeated, slowly.

"He's not coming tomorrow."

"Hmm," he said.

"He's not coming tomorrow or the next day. He didn't come today. He doesn't even know you're in the hospital. He's been gone. Since Halloween. I know this won't make any sense to you right now, but I did all this to protect you and Mom. I thought he was coming back. I'm sorry I didn't tell you. If I could change things, I would. Please forgive me." Grace stopped. The words seemed disembodied, even though she knew they had come out of her mouth. Tears ran down her cheeks. She looked at her father's face. His expression was calm and placid. He touched her arm.

"What's that, honey?"

"Laz is gone," she said, reaching for a tissue and blowing her nose.

"That's nice, dear. Send him our best." Grace wiped her eyes and watched the rain pelting the windowpane.

"I will," she answered. "As soon as I see him."

28
The Uninvited Guest

The next morning, when Grace arrived at the hospital, a resident was talking to her mother in that disturbing hushed tone that doctors use when something's wrong.

"His enzymes are high. We think there may still be a blockage in one of the arteries."

Grace walked closer. Her heart began to palpitate, and she considered asking for her own thallium stress test. Her first thought was that the conversation she'd had with her father the day before had registered on some corrosively subliminal level, and that it was now wreaking havoc on his system. She wished there were a version of the M.R.I. to determine whether her words had penetrated his consciousness. She feared that the truth might have done more damage to him than withholding it. Maybe the truth was vastly overrated. Maybe lies were the glue that bound people together like connective tissue, maintaining the fibers of interpersonal relationships, allowing for freedom of movement without pain. Maybe some truths are not meant to be known. Grace couldn't forgive herself. She should have let him be.

She stood next to her mother and listened to the prognosis. Then, as they wheeled her father down the hall for his second procedure in two days, Grace ran downstairs and onto the street, heading to Kane's. She would tell him everything.

SHE RODE THE elevator to the ninth floor and rang the bell. She rang again. She was about to leave when she heard sounds from within. The door opened. Before her stood a woman with long, tousled dark hair, wearing only a large blue hockey jersey. Grace checked to make sure she had rung the right bell.

"Can I help you?" the woman asked.

"Is Kane here?" She hesitated, then said, "It's Grace." The woman smiled and motioned for her to come in.

"Hold on, I'll get him." She turned to walk into the other room, and as she did, Grace saw white lettering on the back of the shirt. It spelled out the name *Gregg*. Grace's mind tried to assimilate the barrage of information that was whizzing by her. Slowly, it began to make sense. This person in front of her was Kane's Greg, only *this* Gregg was a long-legged, half-naked woman who spelled her name with two *g*s. Grace heard Kane from the bedroom. She wanted to bolt for the elevator, but he appeared before she could make her getaway.

"Grace," he said when he came out, wearing only a pair of boxers. Between the two of them, they had one complete outfit. "Is something wrong?"

"I just wanted to let you know that my father's going into surgery again. There's another blockage." Grace thought about her father undergoing surgery, entering that state of twilight sleep where there is no pain.

"Come on in. Let's talk."

"No, I really should get back," she said, glancing at her watch. She couldn't stay. Not now, with Gregg here. She knew she had no right to feel jealous, but still, with all her might, she wished this long-legged interloper would disappear. Kane was supposed to be hers—gay, straight, or otherwise.

"Stay for a little while. Are you hungry? Gregg's making blueberry pancakes." Grace imagined the wheat-free, gluten-free, egg-free, dairy-free, fat-free concoction and shook her head, knowing that she was being offered a breakfast without ingredients.

"I'd really like to, but I need to get back to the hospital," she said again. What she really needed at that time was, as her father would say, a mystery to her.

"We'll be thinking about you," Kane said, giving her a hug. "Let me know how it goes."

"Nice to finally meet you, Grace," Gregg said, slipping her arm around Kane's waist. "Kane never stops talking about you."

"You, too," Grace said, and then quickly walked to the elevator.

THE SURGERY WENT WELL—Grace's father was back in the recovery room sucking on another lollipop, Bert was in the hallway in yet another hat, and Grace's mother was giving makeup tips to a woman about to undergo radiation treatment. Although Grace had no proof that her confession had actually penetrated deeper than the surface of her father's tympanic membrane, it was a beginning, and her faith in the curative power of truth was once again restored.

"Makeup is for life," she heard her mother say. "It makes all the difference. For you and everyone around you. That, and a great outfit, of course." Grace had visions of an infomercial hosted by her mother, and she avoided looking at her for fear of being doused with some hypoallergenic beauty product or accosted with an implement supposed to endow her with perfection. Grace stayed until visiting hours were over, kissed her still groggy father on the cheek, and told him she'd see him in the morning. Then she rode back to her apartment through the park.

José held the door open for her when she stepped out of the taxi. He looked her up and down as her mother had done numerous times since her return from Chicago, and Grace prepared herself for whatever comment awaited her.

"Nice coat," he said, after appraising it. "I like your new look."

She smiled. As she passed him and walked toward the elevator, she said, "It's not new, actually. Just something I'd forgotten I had."

When the elevator doors opened and Grace stepped out into the hall vestibule, she saw dry cleaning hanging from her front door. Through the plastic, she could see Laz's leather jacket and pants, returned like homing pigeons. On the small table next to the door there was a package tied with kite string. It was about the size of one of her father's old cigar boxes, and written on the front in black marker was Grace's name and apartment number. There was no return address. She wasn't in the mood for any more surprises.

She brought the dry cleaning and the mysterious package inside, hanging Laz's jacket back in the closet. She looked down at her polyester-blend, faux-leopard coat and grazed the soft pile with her hand. She wondered if it, too, wasn't just another kind of wrapping.

But then she realized the difference—she had chosen it not to fit in or to transform herself in some way, but because for once it fit her, instead of the other way around. Maybe another day she would feel like wearing pink polka dots, or white tulle with sequins, or nothing special at all. The only thing that mattered was that it would be *her* choice.

She went into the bedroom to unwrap the package, and just as she was cutting the string, the telephone rang.

"Grace," her mother said, cheerfully. "Thank you for the raisin biscotti. Daddy loved them." While her mother was talking, Grace went into the bathroom, cradling the phone under her chin, and reached under the sink for the jar of ammonia. She fished her wedding and engagement rings out with a pencil, dried them, and slipped them on her finger—but they wouldn't go farther than her second knuckle. Her mother had always told her never to take off her wedding ring. Now she understood why.

"Cholesterol-free, and no one would ever know it," her mother continued. "If you dip them in coffee, they're just perfect." Grace was about to say that she had no idea what her mother was talking about when she realized what was in the package that was lying on her bed. She lifted it up and weighed it in her hands.

She could visualize the words, the lines, even the spaces between the words—the silent, blank patterns that emerged like breaths separating the lines. Her mouth moved as she recited a phrase from memory: *Life is poetry, if people don't distort it.* Her life was more like Silly Putty, stretched and contorted, rendered silly beyond recognition. Her life, far from poetic, was collecting dust.

She slid her finger underneath the butcher paper and let the book fall into her hands. It was Mr. Dubrovsky's beaten up, scrawled-upon copy of *Oblomov*. She had no idea how it had gotten there and even less how to return it to him. The definitive edition of *Oblomov Uninvited.* She tossed it on the comforter. Oblomov was back in bed once more.

Unless, like the raisin biscotti, it had delivered itself, Grace preferred not knowing who had sent it.

"I'm glad he liked them," she said to her mother.

29
Spring Cleaning

A week after her father's first surgery, and three days before Christmas Eve, Grace decided it was time to tell her parents the truth.

"To what do we owe this pleasure?" her father asked, when he answered the door. He was wearing a button-down shirt and pajama bottoms.

"Why didn't you call first?" her mother asked, rushing down the hall and untying her apron. "We might have been out."

"We're not out, Paulette. You haven't let me out in a week, except to go to the doctor's."

"How are you feeling, Dad?"

"Fine. The doctor says I'll be back to my old self in no time. Better than new."

"Can we sit?" Grace asked. "There's something I have to tell you."

"Sure, honey," her mother said. "I'm making some turkey broth for your father. You'll stay for lunch."

Grace and her parents walked into the living room and sat down on the couch. The shades were drawn to block out the afternoon sun. She began to tell them the story of the past three months, this time unabridged. While he listened, Milton sighed deeply and grasped for his wife's hand, which she pulled away, running it through her hair.

"There's no point in saying I'm sorry." Grace paused, then ended by saying, "It won't make this easier or take away the pain. But I am. And I love you both very much." After she was finished, the three of them sat in silence.

Finally, her mother spoke. "He'll be back—he wouldn't leave us. And we'll just act like nothing happened."

"I can't do that anymore," Grace said quietly. Her father began to sob, covering his face with his hands.

"What, Dad?" Grace asked, moving closer to him and putting her arm around his shoulder.

"I can't help you," he said, through his tears.

"That's okay. I don't need help now." Grace held out the box of tissues. He took one.

"How are we going to tell Bert and Francine?" he asked, blowing his nose.

"Why involve them yet? Nothing's definite," her mother said. Grace looked at her parents. She knew that they weren't ready to see the finality of the situation, and that this was all they could do. For now. But she also knew she had to do more.

THE ONLY DIFFERENCE preconfession and postconfession was that where before every conversation had been peppered with references to Laz, now his name simply never came up. With Grace's parents or the Sugarmans, his name was not only avoided, it was verboten, but not for the reasons that might be commonly expected. It wasn't to spare Grace's feelings or to protect her from what they feared might turn out to be a harsh reality; it was as if the mere utterance of Laz's name might in some way actually awaken the dead. It was a *shonda*—a word that almost defies translation. So, instead, they went through the motions and kept things hushed, in the hopes of not jinxing what they secretly wished would turn out to be a happy reunion.

For Grace, though, it was significantly worse than before. Now she was truly alone. While in some ways her parents' denial looked like a rather comfy choice, it was an option no longer available to her. Denial was not a gift certificate in a self-addressed, stamped envelope, redeemable at any time. It had run its course in Grace's case. She'd invented this story of a stable, stationary husband in order to keep things in place, a bracket around the relationship, a scaffolding to hold things up while she contemplated an entirely new marital strategy. But there was nothing left to hold up. The bricks were coming down.

ON CHRISTMAS EVE, Laz's mother hosted an annual evening of caroling at her building on Park Avenue and Ninety-second Street. Grace arrived early to tell her about Laz. Nancy Brookman was the only one who wasn't at all fazed by her son's departure. In fact, she had anticipated it all along. "Like father, like son," she said. It wasn't a matter of *if* he would leave, but *when.*

Nancy had hired a choir of Juilliard students to lead the carols throughout the building, with the party eventually winding up upstairs at her penthouse duplex for crepes and Irish coffee by a roaring fire. The carolers stopped in each of the four stairwells, singing several traditional arrangements as the sound echoed up the marble vestibules. The stairs were lit with votive candles, the air perfumed with frankincense. The caroling culminated with *Silent Night* around the brilliantly lit twenty-foot Douglas fir in the center of the courtyard.

Grace sang out as if she'd gone to parochial school instead of a progressive independent school on the Upper West Side. After the final refrain of *Silent Night*, her mother-in-law approached her.

"I hope you're not going to waste your time pining away for that husband of yours. You can't expect a Brookman to make good, you know. Hopeless dilettantes, all of them. At least his father had the sense to leave before he scandalized the rest of the family," she said, stopping to adjust the velvet collar on her jet black suit. "Thank God, I had the presence of mind to readjust Lazarus's credit card before it was too late." She followed the carolers up the stairs from the courtyard into the building, teetering on her slender heels. "He may be my son, but it's my family's money he's been squandering. And I hope you don't expect me to support you, either."

Grace felt emotions swelling inside her as they had that day in Dr. Gaylin's office, but this time the right words came. "I can't believe you would think that about me," she said. "But if that had been my intention, I would have been entitled to the money."

"That's what Merrin said, too, and look where it got her."

"Merrin?"

"She can write all the letters she wants, but Griffin is not my grandson, no matter what she says." Laz's mother stood in the doorway as if blocking Grace's entrance. Grace thought about the child she might have had with Laz, and that this selfish woman would have been its grandmother.

"Excuse me," she said, gathering her courage, "Nancy." The name stuck in her throat as she uttered it for the first and last time. "I've met him. He definitely is Laz's son. And you don't deserve him."

"You've never spoken to me like this before," Nancy replied, raising her eyebrows.

"I'm just sorry it wasn't sooner," Grace said as she turned to leave.

After hearing the news of Laz's departure, Marisol, in what could almost be described as post-traumatic stress syndrome, became obsessed with cleaning out Laz's closet. It was not in an effort to purge the apartment of his presence, rather it was with the express purpose of preparing for what she believed would be his inevitable return.

"Señor Lazarus will be with us soon. I know he will. *Mi lindo, lindo,*" Marisol would mumble periodically to herself throughout the day.

Grace allowed the proceedings to continue, partly out of sympathy for Marisol and partly because the closet had become so overrun with dust, plastic wrapping, and wire hangers from the dry cleaners that it had become impossible to find anything inside. Not that she really needed anything from it. Other than stationery supplies and tax returns, there was little of use at all to Grace and apparently to Laz, as well.

Everything in the closet was covered with opalescent white dust, as if the asbestos that had been removed from Laz's old apartment had migrated through the pipes and underneath the floorboards. Laz's shoes looked like they'd just returned from a walk in the snow. Marisol carefully took each pair out of the closet as if she were holding Cinderella's precious glass slippers, and lined them up on newspapers in the pantry, where she waxed and buffed them to a high-glossed sheen.

Marisol hand-washed each of Laz's Brooks Brothers shirts, painstakingly pressing them, replacing cracked buttons, and blowing into the sleeves to prevent creases, which made them eerily appear to be inhabited by an invisible body. Then she hung them on wooden hangers that had been covered with tissue paper. The shirts looked like new. Although Grace kept the thought from Marisol, the thrift store wouldn't know what had hit them when they eventually received the donation. Grace gathered up the pile she had made of plastic wrap, compressed it, and brought it to the back door, where she stuffed it into the garbage can. It took up less room than a bag of daily trash—all air and no substance.

The reorganizing and cleaning took several days to complete. Nothing was left undone, unturned, or unpolished. Once the closet was all finished, Grace had trouble closing the door. As hard as she tried to get the door to stay shut, it kept springing back open. The hinges had just given out. Laz's possessions were now on twenty-four-hour display. Each time Grace passed the closet, she was brought to tears. To her, it was akin to looking at an open casket. It bothered her so much that she put a large stack of books in front of the door, but after a while, the books were pushed out and the door would once again open. After several days, as with most unpleasant things, she learned to live with it.

Marisol and Grace continued for days as if possessed, until the entire apartment was not only organized, it was also alphabetized. Even the piano bench and utility closet were now showcases of organization, and Grace had found the missing extension cord inside an empty thermal bag, where it had been all along. Nothing was out of place or missing—except for Laz. And although his presence had shrunk considerably (now measurable in cubic feet), Grace still wasn't ready to fill the space with anything else.

One thing that Grace made sure that she salvaged was the block of clay she had found with Griffin, which Marisol had put out by the back elevator along with the trash. Marisol, having recently seen an episode of *Martha Stewart Living* concerning the proper way to fold towels, was busy attacking the linen closet, as Grace smuggled the clay back inside.

LATE THAT NIGHT, Grace sat at the dining room table with the block of clay in front of her. She unwrapped it, touching the cool surface. Its blankness beckoned to her. She looked at her hands, her only tool, and began to work the clay.

Her fingers felt clumsy at first, and she wasn't sure what she wanted to make. She pounded the clay with the heel of her hand. The more she tried to force it into a shape, though, the more resistant the clay became. She added some water with a sponge. After a while, she simply allowed the clay to move in her hands, rolling and pressing it, following its contours. As she did, she found it became more malleable, until she began to see an emerging form. In a flash, she could envision what it would be.

The sheer texture and possibility of the clay became intoxicating. Like her first crochet stitches, this piece began to take on a life of its own. She looked at the form before her. It was rough, but its dimensions, curves, and lines were clear. It was a woman sitting in a chair, her back straight, her chin lifted. But the more Grace looked at it, the more ambiguous it appeared. She couldn't tell if the woman was in the process of sitting down or getting up, as if the figure were caught midway between the two. Grace rested her hands on the table, then wrapped the sculpture in wet towels. There was plenty of time to decide.

TWO DAYS BEFORE New Year's Eve, Kane called to see if Grace wanted to take a quick ride up to his lake house. The pipes had frozen and burst, and he needed to oversee the plumber. Gregg was off on a photo shoot in Europe.

"It will be good for you to get away," he told her. "You can't stay in that apartment forever."

"Why not?" she asked, only half-joking. Truthfully, Grace had had enough of watching Marisol organize the closets. "But only if you promise not to talk about anything of substance."

"No problem. I won't say a word. We won't even look at each other if that makes you feel better."

"It does."

"Great. I'll bring the sandwiches. You bring your skates." Kane had already hung up before Grace could protest.

During the two-hour drive up to the cabin, Kane, true to his word, did not initiate any conversation other than innocuous subjects, such as rising gas prices or random icicle sightings. They arrived at the house around two. Kane carried Grace's skates as he walked up the slate steps and held the door open for her. The house smelled of pine and wet wool, just as she had remembered. She couldn't recall whether the last time she had been there it had been winter or summer, if they'd skinny-dipped or if Laz had ventured out onto the ice. It was as if a crucial file had been erased.

Kane dropped off the bag of sandwiches in the kitchen and headed out the back door, beckoning for Grace to follow him. They walked down the narrow wooden dock to the lake and Kane sat on a makeshift bench at the end of it. He put on his hockey skates and laced them up. Looking out at the lake, which was covered with a thick layer of ice, he handed Grace her skate bag and waited. She stood motionless, pondering how to get out of doing this. She gazed out over the tundralike vista, then sat down on the bench next to Kane and unzipped her bag. Once on, her skates were tight. Her ankles wobbled as she walked back down the dock and stepped carefully onto the edge of the frozen lake.

"I think I'll just watch for a while," she said. "You go on."

"Suit yourself," he said, pushing off onto the ice and skating away as if chasing a puck in a championship game. He looked so untethered. Grace tried to talk herself through her fear. What was there to fear, after all, besides falling into the depths of an icy black abyss?

She scuttled to the side and was about to get off the ice when she remembered what Chloe's friend Jeff had said over those huge omelets: *Leap and the net will appear.* She certainly hadn't been doing any leaping as of late. That would require actually leaving the apartment.

She admired the expanse of white before her, pure and unadulterated like the untouched clay. She imagined her feet making interlocking loops, a pattern she could not only follow, but could direct. She closed her eyes, pushed off, and found herself gliding out across the ice. She did a figure eight and an arabesque. When she opened her eyes, she saw Kane skating toward her.

"Can I talk now?" Kane asked.

"Will it do any good if I say no?"

"Probably not," he said, skating backward. "That was great. I just wanted to tell you that I knew you could do it. And your skating's improved, too."

"Thanks. I didn't." She felt herself inhaling deeply as if for the first time.

"Kane?"

"Yes, Grace?"

"How long did you know about Laz?"

"The day we went to get the Christmas tree," he answered. Grace remembered how he'd lingered at the apartment when he was setting up the tree. "I didn't know whether I should shake you or the tree. Maybe I should have tried harder, but I was feeling the loss, too. Laz is my best friend, and you and I have this weird relationship. Before Gregg, it was like we were this threesome. Now I have no idea where any of this is going."

"Come on," Grace said. Then she took his hand, and together they skated off to the far side of the lake.

30
Lights Out

The Scrabble-game-cum-Mexican Fiesta Night at the Sugarmans on New Year's Eve was less than festive. Even though the Bali room had been transformed into a millennium Mayan temple, complete with ceremonial statues and traditional painted bark decorations hanging from the windows, the evening was noticeably muted. While the whole city was divided between gearing up for a no-holds-barred last night of the century or stocking up on bottled water, videos, and Y2K restoration kits, Grace's parents and the Sugarmans were just laying low, hoping not to cause any more unnecessary rifts.

The Mayan temple theme, Grace thought, was quite apt—a bulwark against encroaching enemies and evil spirits. She just wondered who would be offered up as the sacrifice.

It was cold in the Bali room, so Grace's father and Bert had hooked up a space heater, which glowed orange like the mouth of a volcano. The combination of the heater and Bunsen burner for the blue corn quesadillas made the glassed-in room fog up. With the mirrors covered by swaths of fabric, it was as if, in a way, they were all sitting shiva for the dead in a Mayan temple.

Francine was dressed in a long, white authentic Mexican wedding dress, which she'd bought for twelve dollars on a cruise that she and Bert had taken to Acapulco last March. She was still very much on a high from her culinary excursion, the evidence of which was laid out in Aztec crockery and woven baskets, a veritable feast of authentic delicacies. Grace's father looked tired, but he didn't complain, participating with his usual gracious enthusiasm.

"Francine, you've outdone yourself," Bert said, taking a bite of grilled octopus with mole sauce. "You always cease to amaze me."

Francine rolled her eyes. "I think you have that backward," she said.

"You mean *I* always cease to amaze *you*?" he asked. "Why, thank you."

"Something like that," Francine answered, kissing him on the cheek.

"Looks like the honeymoon isn't over yet after all," Bert said, winking at Francine.

"Don't press your luck," she said, before walking briskly into the kitchen to attend to the black-bean soufflé.

AFTER DINNER, THE Scrabble board was set up. Between bites of warm sopaipillas dripping with honey, the game proceeded as usual, except with an eerie lack of spirit. Bert, uncharacteristically, did not challenge a single word. He brought out his *O.E.D.*, but only for inspection by Grace's father's trained eye.

"Could definitely use a new binding," Milton pronounced. "I guess you dropped it one too many times. I'll take it home with me and have it back to you good as new in a jiffy."

"Much appreciated," Bert said. "I owe you one."

"I can cover it with an antimold laminate cover, if you like."

"Only if it's not too much trouble."

"Not at all," Milton replied, more animated than Grace had seen him in weeks. "Glad to do it."

Words slipped by like minnows through a net—slang, proper names, egregious misspellings. At one point, even Grace found herself moved to challenge, but as she watched her father add up her mother's triple-letter score on the word *twizzler*, she could not bring herself to go through with it.

"Well done, my dear," her father said, bursting with pride. "This is quite a contentious match. Hats off to you all."

A little before eleven, Grace began to prepare her parents and the Sugarmans for her ensuing departure, which she knew might be a lengthy affair. Because of the fear of some millennium bug striking at midnight, the elevators in her building were going to be shut off for an hour. She thought it was a good excuse to leave early.

"You can't ring in the New Year alone. It's unheard of," Francine objected.

"Have a quick glass of eggnog with us. I made it with Egg Beaters for your father," her mother said.

"And I have my usual to-die-for chocolate mousse," Francine added.

"You don't know what you're missing," Bert said. "And I'm not even allowed to eat it."

"Bert will drive you home right after," Francine offered, as if that would entice her to stay.

"Thanks, but I really can't," Grace answered. "I have some things to do in the morning."

"You'll be here for dim sum tomorrow, won't you?" Francine inquired.

"I wouldn't miss it," she answered.

On her way to get her coat, Grace saw Bert's plastic butterfly garden on a small drop-leaf table in the front hall. Hanging from the top circular window were three grayish chrysalises, each one engaged in its own process. Their outer wrappings were beginning to take on the formation of wings. It would not be long before they molted. Grace buttoned her coat and felt a chill run up her spine as thoughts went unregistered. Her coat seemed tighter under the arms than it had before.

She walked home through the park. If she walked quickly, she would make it home before eleven-forty-five. It was a windless, cloudless night—a night when weather prediction would have been superfluous. The park was populated with midnight runners, couples carrying bottles of champagne arm-in-arm on their way to the Great Lawn to watch the fireworks, many likely to become engaged in a few minutes. A man wearing a glittery top hat ran by. Someone dressed as Baby New Year rode by on a bicycle. It was beginning to feel a little too much like Halloween.

As Grace continued along Park Drive, she felt as if she were wearing someone else's shoes that were both too large and too heavy for her. The motorcycle boots felt like a burden and her ankles ached. Each step was overly labored, and she walked with a self-consciousness she was unused to, as if she had to think about where to place each foot. She felt like a newly hatched duckling.

In the distance, she saw a crowd of runners beginning to congregate near Tavern on the Green. Just as she was about to head out of the park, she was startled by a hand on her shoulder. In the glare of the streetlight behind her, Grace had trouble making out anything more than silhouettes and obscured features.

A couple stood before her. The woman was sausaged into a shiny pink warm-up suit, matching rabbit-fur headband, and running shoes. She had reflector stripes on her jacket. The man wore a nondescript, black running outfit and ski hat. The only thing that registered about the man was his blindingly white socks. Grace couldn't process anything familiar about them until she heard the woman's voice and realized that it was, of all people, Penelope.

"Grace, what a wonderful coincidence," Penelope said, wrapping her fuchsia arms around her. "We were just talking about you."

"You were?" Grace supposed that this was the man that Penelope had met online. The man, still in the glare of the streetlight, seemed about to step forward.

"We're on our way to do the Midnight Run and then to celebrate our engagement. Adrian has just popped the question. It's a real *shiddach*." Penelope took the man's arm and brought him out of the glaring light. "You must join us."

The man's features came into view, and Grace saw the same fly-away hair underneath the black hat that she'd first glimpsed at the Pink Tea Cup, and she knew without a doubt that the person arm-in-arm with Penelope was none other than Mr. Dubrovsky, Private Investigator. Grace wasn't sure whether it was wiser to act nonchalant, wish them a Happy New Year, and make a quick exit, or to warn her friend that this guy was a nutcase. She was mulling over her options when Mr. Dubrovsky reached out his hand. Grace flinched reflexively.

"Ms. Brookman," he said, bowing slightly from the hip. "I will be forever indebted to you." As he spoke, Grace detected a hint of Maurice Chevalier in his voice, a whiff of aftershave in the bracing air. Penelope all but swooned. Grace felt herself immediately disarmed and became even more defensive. She took Penelope aside.

"Do you know who this is?" Grace whispered.

"Of course, I do. He told me the whole story."

"Penelope, allow me," Mr. Dubrovsky said, patting her lightly on the arm. "May I call you Grace?" he asked. Grace didn't respond. The whole situation was ludicrous, even by the reality-lax standards of her life, but she remained, in the hopes that it might somehow begin to make sense. He continued. "I must apologize for having deceived you. When Griffin's mother, Merrin, called and asked me to locate Mr. Brookman, I had no idea how entangled this situation would become. If I have caused you any injury, I am sorry and I would like to try to make amends. But my involvement with you has indeed changed my life. If not for you, I would never have found my Penelope."

"Oh, Adrian," Penelope said, nuzzling his neck. Grace felt herself about to sneeze, that nose-tickling sensation when things seemed right. Grace pictured the three of them strolling around the reservoir, admiring the cherry blossoms the following spring. Even Griffin and Kane along with Chloe and Pete popped into view like a Japanese paper fan opening to its full peacocklike splendor.

"I have your book," she told him.

"I have no need for it now," he answered, linking Grace's arm in his, as they continued down the path.

WHEN GRACE ENTERED her building, she knew something was amiss. José was directing people to the stairwells, and the fire doors were propped open. Instead of the usual overhead lights, there were lanterns placed along the corridor.

"Happy New Year, Mrs. Brookman," José said as she walked into the lobby.

"Thank you, José. Happy New Year to you, too. Why is it so dark in here?"

"When they shut down the elevators, the whole building blacked out. The generator is on a timer. Should come on about twelve-thirty, one o'clock. What a night! And the people in 10J were having a karaoke party."

Grace walked up the stairs to her apartment. A lantern had been placed at the top of each landing, and she noticed her shadow growing longer and longer with each step.

She opened her door, then walked into the kitchen. On the table, in front of Laz's place, was a folded napkin and knife, a half-filled glass of water was on the counter. She must have placed it there absently. Old habits, she realized, were hard to break. She could have kept up the pretense in her sleep. Opening the utility closet, she took out a flashlight, a perfunctory gesture since due to Marisol's reorganization, there was really no need for light. She could find anything, even with her eyes closed.

In the distance, she heard fireworks. She went to the window and watched the muffled pyrotechnics display. Everyone was ringing in the New Year—Penelope and Adrian were no doubt toasting at the finish line; her parents and the Sugarmans would be squabbling about how much they would pay for Francine's chocolate mousse, all over a cup of low-cholesterol eggnog; and somewhere, Laz, too, was celebrating, even if by proxy. Tonight she and Laz were supposed to have been at Lincoln Center. Laz had written *Contact* in his date book. Grace had always wanted to see that play.

Although it was not late, she was exhausted. She threw off her coat and left her clothes on the bedroom floor. Then she collapsed into bed.

She was awakened by a dream so vivid that she felt every muscle in her body vibrating. It was as if Laz were inside her mind and body. He spoke to her through synapses that she thought had been sealed off: *I'll never leave you again.* She heard the words like a distant melody. They were the very words she'd imagined in her head day after day, the words she would have had him say if she could have orchestrated his homecoming as precisely as she had perfected his presence.

I'm here, Gracie. I'm home for good. I'm never going to leave you again. The words reverberated in her head.

So hard had she wished to hear those words, and for so long, yet something about them rang false. She was sweating. She felt a weight on her chest. Suddenly, the bedside light went on as if José, himself, had switched it on from some central circuit breaker. She opened her eyes and realized she was neither dreaming nor hallucinating—Laz was lying next to her. It was not a phantom of him, airbrushed and absent of anything as unseemly as a stray hair follicle, body odor, rough hands, a too-studied look, or a masking smile, but Laz in the flesh. He was almost unrecognizable. A stranger was in her bed.

Laz lifted her hair off the nape of her neck and kissed her the way he had on the ski lift. She shut her eyes, and it was as if no time had passed and her feet were once again off the ground. She opened her eyes and saw herself reflected in his pupils.

"Happy New Year, sweetness. I love you," he said, rolling onto his back. His voice was low and slightly hoarse. "I'm so sorry. I put you through hell. But you know how I am—it was just too much for me. I couldn't take it. But none of that matters anymore. Not even the Pulitzer. What matters is that we're back together. And we always will be. This is only the beginning. I promise. I need you now more than ever." He closed his eyes. Grace pictured his side of the bed in the morning—a rumpled, twisted frenzy—unsure that he could produce evidence of himself as finely wrought as she had. "I missed you so much. I promise things will be different. You're the only one I've ever loved."

He kissed her again and wrapped his arms around her. She was about to tell him it was as if he'd never left, when he fell asleep.

The flash from the lights going on had distorted Grace's vision, making everything she looked at glow green, like a modern-day, urban Emerald City. But she hadn't been torn away from home in the wake of Laz's tornado. She was already home, no more or less now than ever.

She put her head on the pillow, staring at the ceiling. The man before her was not the one she had been expecting. She had finally come to herself. The dream was what she had thought she had wanted all along, and now that it had arrived, she was free to let it go.

At dawn, Grace slipped out of bed to make a cup of tea and to get José's coffee. It had become her ritual, but today she prepared it in an earthenware mug that Marisol had found in the music cabinet. The mug had been filled with pencil stubs and rubber bands. Grace knew she was supposed to feel unencumbered by her uncluttered apartment—no more secrets hiding in crevices, no mysteries, no surprises under the bed, nothing lost along the way, no treasures undiscovered. Everything in its place. She should have experienced something of a catharsis, but instead, she felt an absence. It had been her clutter, her circuitous route, detours and all. She just hadn't realized it until now.

The living room was ablaze as the Christmas tree and the Duro-Lites blinked in unison. She left them on and went into the bedroom to put on her motorcycle boots, taking care not to wake Laz. He was a sound sleeper. The room smelled different to her, as if she'd forgotten their particular alchemy of pheromones. She opened the window a crack and then went to stand by the door. He was home. His legs dangled off the side of the bed, the sheet twisted underneath him. His watch was on the nightstand, his shoes and pants in a corner by the ottoman. Generic details, totally lacking imagination and flourish. If she hadn't heard the sound of his breathing, she would barely have known he was there.

She ripped a page out of one of her blank books. *Glad you're back, but I'm sorry, I can't stay. I don't live here anymore. Grace.*

She placed the note, her engagement ring, and wedding band next to the orchid on the dining room table, and left her clay sculpture of the woman rising from the chair alongside, directly in the spotlight of the Duro-Lites. Then she took her grandmother's afghan, along with Mr. Dubrovsky's copy of *Oblomov*—which she would finish this time—and went downstairs to bring José his coffee before venturing out into a driving rain, as prepared as she ever needed to be.

About the Author

Photo by Nina Subin

Nina Solomon received her MA from Columbia University. She lives in Manhattan with her son. *Single Wife* is her first novel.

READERS GUIDE

Single Wife

NINA SOLOMON

A CONVERSATION WITH NINA SOLOMON

Q: Where did the idea for the novel come from?

A: The idea for *Single Wife* came from a conversation I had at Thanksgiving dinner with my family, two years after my husband and I had separated. One of my parents' best friends turned to me and casually asked me if my husband had to work over the holiday. I looked at my parents, who were sitting at the other end of the table, and realized that they had not yet told anyone about my separation. As I struggled over how to answer, I thought how simple it would be to maintain the illusion of a marriage—a few crumbs on the table, a shirt in the hamper, along with a few well-placed excuses, and a husband is conjured. The idea seized my imagination and I decided to see how it would play out in fiction. But on a deeper level it spoke to that part of myself that hadn't yet fully processed the magnitude of the separation and the human tendency to want to deny or delay dealing with painful feelings. I think writing the book was in some ways cathartic. It helped me laugh and move on faster than perhaps I would have otherwise.

Q: Are there any similarities between you and your main character?

A: Besides our affinity for tea and Katharine Hepburn movies, and an obsession with finding the perfect lipstick, Grace's story is her own. Certainly, on an emotional level, I can relate to her. And I've learned a few things from her. It's about Grace letting go of a fantasy and finding herself, while I am still a work very much still in progress. I discovered the feeling of liberation when you finally let go of a dream or a hope that's been keeping you from living your life. Like Grace, I do tend to try to protect those I love. But she's a much better dresser than I am.

Q: The novel is set in New York and has a decidedly New York feel. Does the setting influence how the characters act?

A: I was born and raised in New York and have lived here all my life. I can't imagine living or setting the novel anywhere else. That said, I think it is an interesting question. Clearly Grace's actions are influenced by her surroundings. She has a doorman and housekeeper who become her unwitting accomplices in keeping up the charade. In some ways living in a city like New York makes it easier for Grace. People lead such buys lives—you often don't run into your next-door neighbor for weeks—and so much is taken for granted, that no one even questions Laz's long, unexplained absences. They see a wet umbrella and a pair of shoes by the door and they assume there is a husband inside to go with them.

Q: What is your writing process?

A: I write at home at a small desk in the bedroom. I find that writing in the morning is best for many reasons, one of which is that lunch is a reward, although I have been known to crave a turkey sandwich at 10 AM. Discipline is very important for me. I am not only easily distracted, but also somewhat fearful of the process—it often feels very mysterious to me—and just knowing that I have an idea I want to get on the page or a passage that needs editing can be enough to get over the initial trepidation. I went through several years of writer's block, and it wasn't until the birth of my son twelve years ago that I was able to come to write again. But it was like starting over. I joined a writer's group and slowly relearned the process. They guided, supported, and inspired me and continue to do so to this day. *Single Wife* took a little under two years to write, I went through many drafts, and I loved every minute and every aspect of it. Now I couldn't imagine not writing. I am currently working on two novels, something I've never done before. The novels began as one story, but then one of the characters began to demand too much "screen" time, so I cut her out and gave her her own novel.

Q: When did you know you wanted to be a writer?

A: I knew before I could even write, when my father would type up the stories I told to him on his IBM typewriter. I had an inclination toward magical stories and poetry.

Q: What books have you loved? What authors have influenced or inspired you?

A: I could rattle off so many names of other writers who have influenced me, from Laura Ingalls Wilder to Jane Austen, the writers who conjured worlds for me. Books can be like best friends or great loves. I loved Bridget Jones because she made me feel less alone and incompetent. And it felt as if I had a whirlwind affair after I read Paul Auster's *Book of Illusions*. But the writers who create sentences as prefect as you could imagine—like Blake and Shakespeare and James Joyce, and right now I add Michel Faber to that list—the ones who make me want to throw my computer out the window and give up, are also the ones who inspire me to keep trying.

Q: There's a lot of food in the novel. What does food tell us about a character?

A: Food is such a fundamental part of all our lives: it nurtures and bonds us, gives us comfort, it is a way to show love but it can also be a means of control or restriction. In the novel, food has many meanings. Grace begins to eat foods that Laz used to eat as if she is becoming him. Then, as she begins to move away on an emotional level, she even forgets what he used to eat for breakfast. One character in the novel gets her self-esteem through cooking and vigilantly guards her recipes so that no one can ever replicate them or replace her. And of course Grace is a vegetarian, which opens up a whole other container of meatbealls in her very meat-oriented family.

Q: What did you hope to achieve in writing Single Wife? *Do you think you succeeded?*

A: It was only after I wrote the novel that I realized people would actually be *reading* it. I hope (like all writers, I think) that the novel entertains and inspires, that readers can relate to or at least root for the characters, and that at times the language brings newness to the familiar. I don't know if I succeeded, but I am certainly grateful to have had the opportunity to try.

QUESTIONS FOR DISCUSSION

1. How does Grace's deception alter her perspective on her marriage and her place in it?

2. Even though the charade began ostensibly to protect those close to her, in what ways does Grace's husband's phantom presence serve a function for Grace?

3. How did the chapter titles inform or influence your reading?

4. What advice would you have given Grace? Are there things you wish she had handled differently? Is she someone you could be friends with?

5. Do you think all relationships/marriages are based on or incorporate a degree of deception or misperception?

6. There is a haunting quality to much of the story, particularly the way that Laz seems to appear and disappear throughout the book. Do you think Laz's character is intended to be read on a literal or a metaphorical level?

7. At what point do you think Grace begins to get in touch with her emotions?

8. Does Grace's character grow throughout the course of the novel? If so, in what ways? Do you think she will continue to change after the novel ends?